Shepherd's Warning

· THE ELDERS BOOK ONE ·

Cailyn Lloyd

Shepherd's Warning

© 2019, 2022 Land of Oz LLC

Third Edition

ISBN: 978-0-578-66497-2

Cover Art by Rose Miller

For Jennie, who insisted
I finish this.

And for Mike.

One

A flash of light, reflected sunlight perhaps, disturbed his idle reverie.

Sitting astride a grumbling Case tractor, Tom Wolff gazed over his property, a hundred acres of rough and tumble farmland that rose from the shore of Lost Arrow Lake. The circular lake sat like a cobalt-blue gem in a sea of green trees. His ramshackle farm, a white two-story American Foursquare and a weathered-grey barn, sat up the hill, sheltered by tall pines and great oaks. The view was beautiful, tranquil.

Tom searched for the source of the light. Saw nothing and shrugged. He adjusted a dirty Purina Feeds cap on his head, shifted into gear, and plodded across the field, dragging a hay rake in the hot Wisconsin sun. The smell of freshly cut hay filled the air, fragrant, like clean linen.

Another flash, quick and vivid like a laser beam, startled him.

About sixty yards over, glass shards sparkled in the sunlight as they fell behind the old MacKenzie place. The house belonged to his neighbors, Alan and Elizabeth MacKenzie. They had been friends forever until Alan died and Elizabeth moved away with her two young

1

boys. Sadly, the vacant house had become the target of vandals and thrill-seeking teens.

Spotting a broken window on the top floor—a jagged black hole in the shiny pane—Tom downshifted with an irritated thrust and grumbled, "Little bastards."

He shut the tractor down and vaulted to the ground. Reached up and grabbed the pitchfork—an antiquated but effective weapon mounted on the tractor frame. A little insurance.

Tom charged across the fence line to the back of the house in a huff.

The building, built on a slope, stood three stories tall in the rear. The exposed foundation was an imposing stone wall supporting the timbered framing and stucco finished walls. A fine example of Tudor architecture someone once told him—whatever that meant. He spotted broken glass on the ground. Around the corner, the thick oak door to the basement stood ajar, confirming his suspicions.

Tom eased it open, catching a faint whiff of mold and decay in the air. Condensation covered the stone walls. The house was silent. Perhaps the little jerks had seen him coming. Were they hiding? Or had they run out the front door?

He crept warily up the plank stairs to the first floor. Last fall, he had driven over after seeing flickering lights in the house. A fork-wielding druggie, ranting about voices and slamming doors, attacked and stabbed him in the arm. After dropping the guy with a roundhouse punch, Tom had called the sheriff and earned a dozen stitches at the ER. Hence the pitchfork.

That incident landed atop a growing pile of stories about the MacKenzie place that included apparitions, strange noises, accidents, and odd deaths in or near the house. People from town insisted something evil roamed the property. Couldn't drag any of them within a mile of the place—except for the teenagers drawn there by the haunting rumors.

Tom believed none of it himself, but understood how the stories had taken root. A creepy old house, a couple of accidents, and the natural tendency of small-town people to gossip and embellish the truth? *Yep*, the place must be haunted. Over time, the stories had evolved into frightening tales.

That guy killed by the tree was weird, though.

A few years back on a clear day, a large oak branch had fallen on a hunter walking the property and flattened the poor bastard. Tom had seen the crushed and impaled body afterward.

Ugh.

Not ghostly but certainly spooky.

The only spirit that haunted him was the ghost of Elizabeth herself. She had left a year ago, but Tom still loved her, a one-sided affair that began as a childhood crush and lingered after she married his best friend, Alan MacKenzie. Elizabeth was the only reason he looked after the house. She'd never put it on the market, keeping alive a glimmer of hope that she might someday return.

What if she did? He stood no chance with her. Never had. He could still picture her though—dark haired with deep blue eyes—and felt a resonant longing whenever he thought of her.

A spasm of guilt twisted in his stomach when he thought about Sally—as an afterthought. Sally was his girl. Things were serious. They were talking marriage. Tom suspected Sally knew she was his second choice. Sally was like that. She just *knew* things. Always had. In some ways, she was spookier than the house.

Still, Elizabeth had never called, never visited. Tom thought they were friends, but now he wondered. Maybe she couldn't face the house yet. Being here revived his sense of loss over Alan's death. How bad would it be for her?

He stopped in the foyer, leaning the pitchfork against the wall. The house inside looked much like the exterior: a frame of heavy timber beams and plaster walls—a grand house really, not like any farmhouse he'd ever seen. To his surprise, other than dust and cobwebs, the house had suffered little since Elizabeth and the boys had moved away.

A lone oil painting, a portrait of an older woman dressed in vintage clothing, hung on the back wall. Her face was narrow, pale and homely, framed by grey hair, lips drawn tight. Elizabeth hated it. She had never said why.

He heard a faint low beat, like a muffled bass guitar. The sound seemed to come from upstairs, toward the back of the house. No voices, no footsteps, just that steady low-frequency pulse. Given the attack last fall, apprehension tingled in his belly. He didn't need this aggravation and was behind on his fieldwork. Best to walk away—but he couldn't. Curiosity and a sense of responsibility pushed him forward.

As he crossed the foyer and started up the stairs, the *clomp* of his work boots on the hardwood floor echoed in the open stairwell. The pulsing noise persisted. Steady, deep, it could be a heartbeat, he mused. But what the hell was it? A boom box? Where? It seemed to emanate from everywhere at once and bore an uncanny resemblance to the music of Pink Floyd.

Goosebumps rippled up his arm to his neck, the tickle of icy fingers playing over his skin, a creepy, invisible touch of fear and anxiety. Tom hated the uneasiness. A childish feeling, one he should have outgrown.

"Dummy," he muttered under his breath.

Trying to relax, Tom pushed his feet forward, up the remaining stairs, creeping to the left along the hallway, glancing in each open door, seeing nothing but empty, dusty rooms. His senses felt heightened by the musty odor of the old house, the surreal light filtered by dirty windows. The scrapes of his boots on the plank floor resonated about the house in sync with the undulating bass tone.

The house itself stirred, the floorboards coming to life with a subtle beat.

Was he imagining that?

Tom didn't know, but his pulse quickened. His neck ran cold with sweat. His insides churned in a tightening knot. The anxiety grew more intense, almost a full-blown panic. He needed to leave. He felt foolish, but couldn't control the spiraling fear. Deep down, his inner child sensed ghosts and bogeymen in every dark corner of the hallway: hidden eyes, teeth, claws—cold, cold creatures lurking and waiting to pounce.

As he closed the door behind him, another down the hall banged shut, plunging the hallway into darkness.

He froze.

The oak floorboards rattled and the low throbbing sound grew louder and more pressing. The house itself quivered as if tremors had infiltrated the ground beneath it.

Tom stood, gripped by morbid fascination and fear. A dizzy, nauseous feeling swept through him. He bent over, thinking he would throw up.

Another slamming door jolted Tom from his daze. He had to get the hell out of here! Jesus! The floorboards were clattering like a hay-bailer run amok.

He turned and ran down the hall toward the stairs. At the end of the long hallway, a door stood ajar, just an inch or two. Bright sunlight spilled through that crack and the keyhole—a surreal contrast between the calamity indoors and the serene afternoon outside. Cheerful birdsong, from beyond the door perhaps, completed the insanity.

Drawn to the doorway like a drunk to a tavern, he felt powerless to resist the attraction of whatever lay beyond the threshold. Light emanating from the room grew brighter and warmer. He drifted down the hallway, clenching and relaxing his fists, trying to shake the anxiety and regain his composure.

The floorboards rattled along the hallway, the ominous rumbling continued. Danger lurked all around him—but not beyond the door. He just knew it.

He took a deep breath.

Reached for the knob. Hesitated.

Eased the door open—

Two

Present Day

Laura MacKenzie ducked and covered her head as a heavy object crashed to the floor overhead.

There was a mumbled, "Oops," followed by male laughter.

Her husband, Lucas, appeared moments later in the timbered doorway. "Sorry, hon. I hope we didn't freak you out."

"Not too much." She looked up and smiled. He was dirty, disheveled, and handsome—casually sexy with a crooked smile that had caught her eye years ago and held her interest still. Tall, with brown hair tossed to one side and an intense gaze, he looked rakish, but wasn't. Lucas was a considerate, loving husband and her best friend.

"You find anything yet?" he asked.

"Nothing of interest other than an old Bible with a couple of names scribbled in it. Might be something." Laura sat on the floor in the library looking through a stack of books discovered abandoned in a closet. At the north end of the house, the library was bright with four large windows looking out to the woods, the walls inset with shelves and bookcases. Angled bookcases in the corners stretched from the floor to the vaulted ceiling, with intricate carvings on the corners of the bookshelves. Two oil lamps sat high on a corner shelf next to a single dust-covered book.

Laura enjoyed researching family histories, and the house had renewed her interest in the subject and their family ancestry—a welcome distraction from her normal melancholy mood.

"How's it going up there?" Laura said.

"Got the old unit out—as you heard." Lucas rolled his eyes and chuckled. "We'll be ready for the plumbers tomorrow. Where's Nate? We need his help."

Laura pointed to the timbered archway behind her. "Walking the film crew through the plans for the Hall."

Lucas scowled. "Oh sure, we're busting our asses and he's playing tour guide?"

"He's going to be a star, you know." She pursed her lips and shrugged.

Lucas muttered something and walked away.

In the expansive room adjoining the library, Laura watched a film crew follow Lucas's brother, Nate, as he outlined the steps involved in renovating the space at the rear of the house called the *Greate Hall*. Those words, in Old English script, had been carved into the timbers atop the three archways entering the room.

Forty-five feet long, the Hall consisted of three conjoined rooms. The large center chamber had a lofty cathedral ceiling bridged by trussed hand-hewn beams, the walls paneled in a classic recessed style with quarter-sawn oak. Light streamed through large west-facing windows in the imposing rear wall. Flanked by smaller rooms with ten-foot ceilings, a limestone fireplace rose from floor to ceiling on the inside wall of the north alcove.

A moment later, Nate and the crew emerged from the Hall into the library. Nate, bohemian-looking in contrast to his brother, sported a cultivated three-day stubble and shoulder-length hair.

"Hey, Blondie, the guys want to talk to you."

Laura didn't mind Nate's cutesy nickname for her but considered herself a dishwater shade, not a classic blonde.

He was accompanied by a tall, attractive brunette with long hair and large eyes. Her name was Hannah and she looked like a professional newscaster. A twenty-something hipster with a clipped beard and prominent ear stud followed, wielding a handheld video camera. Nate had hired the crew to help document the renovation for HGTV. He had worked with the network on a few projects in the Chicago suburbs, an asset when he pitched this house to the network for a special.

"Can we talk to you for a few minutes, Laura?" Hannah asked tentatively, perhaps aware they were intruding.

"Sure. Why not." She smoothed her hair and scanned her clothing. "Do I look okay?"

"Yeah, you look great," Hannah said.

Laura whispered to Nate, "Keep it short. This is your deal, not mine."

He nodded, looking a bit harried. The television aspect and the film crew? All Nate. He saw the property as a stepping stone to bigger opportunities in his career and a chance to pursue a longtime dream—a major feature on HGTV and eventually, his own show. Laura had come here to escape a memory, the memory of Jacob, their son, who had died a year ago.

Hannah fitted Laura with a small lavalier mic. "There. That'll limit the background noise. We'll do voice-overs as needed."

Laura didn't know how the video crew could work in these conditions. The house was a war zone. Above, roofers were ripping off accumulated layers of cedar shingles and lathe boards and laying plywood decking with a steady din of pry bars, hammers, and shovels. Below them, the heating and cooling guys were ripping out a monstrous old furnace in an assault of hammers, drills, and screeching metal saws.

Hannah, holding a notepad, spoke. "Laura, what's your role in this project?"

"Right now, support mostly. I'm an interior designer, so I'm working on the color schemes, furniture, and decor. As you probably know, we plan to maintain the Tudor character of the house. I'll be looking at reproductions and antiques to that end. I'm also a full-time grandma to a two-year-old."

"Aww." Hannah made a cutesy face. "So where is the little darling?"

"Asleep."

"With all this racket?"

"She's outside, in the RV," Laura said. "It's much quieter out there."

Laura continued, explaining that the old Tudor mansion was a gift of sorts, bequeathed to them by Lucas's mother, Elizabeth. She had died six months before and the house was a complete surprise. Until the reading of the will, they hadn't known it existed. She omitted the remaining details, that Elizabeth had amassed a trust fund for her children worth two millions dollars, the product of insurance policies and a stock-sharing plan through the internet start-up where she had worked for twenty years.

"Are you all going to live here under one roof?" Hannah asked.

"Good God, no." Laura rolled her eyes and laughed. "We'll fix the house and then renovate the barn. Nate and Ashley will live there."

Hannah looked at Nate and raised her eyebrows. "You guys are being relegated to the barn? Isn't the house your baby?"

"It is, but trust me, the barn won't be second prize when we're done," he said. "We plan to restore the original crossbeams spanning a stunning cathedral ceiling. The first floor, about three thousand square feet, will be an open plan with a master bedroom in a loft above. We'll gut the old milking parlor on the lower level and convert the space to an office and workshop. This house is too medieval for me."

"You'll regret those words when I'm done," Laura said lightly.

"Not likely, Blondie. We'll be on the cover of Frontgate." He shrugged. "This place? Not so much."

"Good luck with that." Laura smirked. Looking out the back window, the large grey barn sat like an abandoned prairie schooner in the long grass. It hadn't fared well over the years. Numerous boards were missing from the walls, and a section of the roof had collapsed.

The camera guy asked, "Are we done here?"

"Let's move to the barn." Hannah gestured toward the back of the lot with a wrinkle of her nose. "I'm curious to see how bad it looks on the inside."

As the entourage filed out the front door, Laura followed, but turned right toward a thirty-foot RV parked at the edge of the drive. For now, it was home. An electrician had roughed in power and the plumbers had run water and septic connections to the RV. Nate and wife Ashley had their own RV parked by the barn.

Laura eased the door open.

Dana, her daughter, sat at the dinner table, typing furiously on a laptop. One of two children, she was petite with blue eyes and long dark hair, traits handed down from Elizabeth, who'd had striking dark hair in her youth. Despite her somewhat delicate appearance, she was fit and agile. Both she and Laura had taken *Taekwondo* classes and enjoyed sparring with each other. Twenty-four and single, Dana lived in Naperville, Illinois, but had offered to help with Leah, their two-year-old granddaughter, for a few weeks.

"How's she doing?" Laura nodded toward the back bedroom.

"Good. Still out cold," Dana said.

Leah was asleep in the back bedroom, sprawled on the queen bed and covered with a light blanket.

She was Jacob's daughter and a constant reminder that he was gone. Just the thought of him reduced Laura to sadness and tears. She closed her eyes and tried to will it away, practicing a mindfulness technique—one she had learned working with a therapist—to push back the darkness whenever grief threatened to overwhelm her.

Without a word, Dana stood in the tight quarters of the RV and gave her mother a hug. She seemed to sense when Laura struggled and stood ready with open arms, even though she'd lost a brother and had her own grief to manage. Laura quietly admired Dana's ability to deal with her feelings, convinced she was the stronger of the two of them.

"Okay?"

Laura nodded, took a moment more, focusing on her breathing. Relaxed a little and then said, "How's the paper coming?"

"Five more pages." Approaching her final year of a master's program in psychology, Dana was working on a case study.

Laura squeezed past her. "I'm going to lie down with her. Get your paper done."

"Love you, Mom."

"Love you too."

Laura lay down and snuggled close. Leah had become a haven from the despair she sometimes felt, an emptiness that she could never fill. She tried to push the memory of Jacob away, but he appeared anyway: his inimitable grin and calm manner as he played with Leah in their yard. Mindfulness couldn't contain the melancholy and she fell asleep with tears in her eyes.

Her dreams were often vivid and seldom happy. She dreamt of a funny little man wearing the cap and cloak of a magician, a wand in his right hand, mumbling unintelligibly.

He turned, looked her in the eye, and spoke sternly with an English accent, "Beware the red sky."

Muttering those words, he wandered off and disappeared.

Laura woke with a start, unnerved by the apprehension those words inspired. They sounded menacing. She stared at the ceiling and flexed her fingers, trying to shake the unease. A silly dream and nothing more. Yet, the anxiety lingered.

Sometimes, she wondered if she would ever be happy again.

★   ★   ★

Just after six o'clock, Lucas, Laura, and Nate sat in the Hall on stacks of building materials, surrounded by lumber, tiles, buckets of paint and stain, chatting and drinking bottles of various microbrews from a cooler. The air smelled dusty, filled with dancing motes stirred up by the relentless assault upon every corner of the house. It was quiet though, the contractors gone for the day.

Hannah and the videographer, Zach, who had been filming outdoors, wandered in.

"So where's Ashley?" Hannah said. "We didn't get a chance to talk to her."

"Meeting with some people from *This Old House*. She'll be here tomorrow." Nate tapped the cooler with his foot. "Beer?"

Zack grabbed two bottles and handed one to Hannah. He looked at Nate and said, "I gotta tell you, dude, this is the middle of nowhere. It's literally BFE."

Nate grinned. "I warned you."

Lucas gave a Zach a puzzled look. "BFE?"

"Bum Fuck Egypt, dude. How do you not know that?"

Lucas shrugged and laughed. "Sheltered life, I guess."

Laura grew dizzy as the room seemed to shift sideways and spin. A queasy shiver passed down her spine. Had she been standing, she might have stumbled. After a moment, her dizziness and nausea subsided.

No one seemed to notice.

Low blood sugar?

No.

Something about Lucas repeating the acronym BFE had set her off. She had no idea why.

Laura wasn't superstitious by nature but it felt like an omen.

Three

Hannah and Zack returned in the morning for another day of taping. Laura consciously avoided them while measuring rooms and windows, busy refining her design ideas. By six o'clock, everyone was weary and had gathered in the Hall for beers and idle chitchat.

"I don't feel like cooking," Laura said. "Why don't we grab burgers at that bar in town?"

Everyone agreed enthusiastically except Dana, who stayed behind with Leah.

The road to town, County B, was narrow and serpentine, lined by an assortment of pines, maples, and hickory trees. It was beautiful, a dense wall of lush green that reminded her of her childhood in upstate New York. At heart, she was a country girl, and this felt like home.

The small hamlet of Lost Arrow comprised about a dozen houses, a church, a gas station, and a tavern, all sheltered by older oaks and maples. Lucas braked abruptly and pulled into a parking spot in front of the tavern. Laura put a hand out to brace herself as Ashley and Nate pulled in next to their Silverado.

The White Birch Inn was a casualty of time. A longish one-story building with faded grey clapboard siding and a swayback shingled roof, the usual assortment of neon beer signs extolling the virtues of Pabst, Coors, and Miller High Life adorned the windows. Cool and dark inside, the were walls overlaid with cheap wood paneling. The ceiling, perhaps once white, was the color of old cigarette smoke. The smell of fried food and a danker undercurrent of yeasty beer lingered in the air.

"Beer?" Nate looked at Laura and Ashley.

"Spotted Cow," Laura said. She preferred chardonnay, but this looked like a two-wine bar, white or red.

"The same," Ashley said.

Nate took their orders and walked over to the bar while they headed to a table. In an alcove, Laura noticed a pool table, side tables, and chairs.

Two older men hunched over beers at the other end of the bar glanced at them indifferently.

Laura sat next to Nate's wife, Ashley. Ashley was attractive and petite, with long dark hair, emerald green eyes, and a near flawless complexion. Over the years, they had become close friends, but in the past few weeks, she sensed some tension or distance between them. Stress of the move? The impression that Ashley felt Laura should move on from Jacob's death? Or maybe it had nothing to do with her. At thirty-nine, Ashley was childless, even though they had been talking about children for some time. Laura wondered if a problem existed. Ashley grew touchy whenever the subject arose.

After a brief reflective silence, Hannah said, "So what's the backstory on the house? Why did your mother keep it a secret?"

Laura looked at Nate. "They don't know the story?"

He shrugged and shook his head. "Nope. Never came up."

Zach brought the camcorder up to catch the conversation.

Typical Nate. Nonchalant, cavalier about everything. Laura, feeling self-conscious, swept her hair behind her ear and said, "As you know, Lucas and Nate's mother died about six months ago and left a fairly large estate, including the house and land. She had lived there with her first husband and their father, Alan. He then died in an accident a year after Nate was born. I guess she just boarded the place up, moved away, and never said another word about it. They had no clue it existed.

"Anyway, the four of us came up to look it over and Nate and I fell in love with it. Nate had this vision about renovating the place and sold the concept to HGTV. I wanted to get away from Chicago, live somewhere more rural, and this was perfect. Eventually, the other two came around and here we are."

"On the surface, it sounds crazy," Hannah said. "You just dropped everything in Illinois and moved here?"

"I guess. I had taken leave to take care of Leah, and Lucas had quit his job a few months before. It's a long story and I'm not going into it." No way would she open a conversation about Jacob, nor reveal that she was here mostly to escape her memories of him in Illinois.

"Come on—"

"Sorry. Maybe another time." Laura held firm. "Anyway, as you know, Nate's a contractor and Ashley was already working with him on web design and marketing. I guess you could say this all came along at the right moment."

Hannah raised an eyebrow and asked, "But was why your mom so secretive?"

Ashley spoke. "Apparently, she thought it was haunted."

Hannah leaned in. "Really? How do you know that if she didn't talk about the house?"

"That revelation came from her attorney," Ashley said with a slight head shake. "He didn't understand it either."

"Oh, bullshit." Lucas set his beer down with a dismissive gesture, an edge to his voice. "Mom didn't have a superstitious bone in her body."

"We don't know that." Nate held a hand up, palm out. "And chill, bro."

"She lost her husband there," Laura said. "Whatever she thought or felt about the farm didn't have to be rational."

Lucas sighed. "True, but—"

"People act in many crazy ways when they lose someone they love," Laura said, her voice uneven. An awkward silence followed, and she turned away from the others, forcing back tears. She felt a chilly breeze blow through her as the memory of Jacob surfaced in vivid relief, turning her mood black. He had looked a lot like Lucas and sometimes, a smile or a head tilt from Lucas could trigger these feelings. With the mindfulness exercises, she learned to manage these moments with various degrees of success. It took an effort to regain her composure.

They sipped their beers, thoughtful for a moment. Laura couldn't fathom the mystery surrounding the farm. Couldn't imagine why Elizabeth had kept the property secret all these years. Lucas and Nate had been born there and knew nothing of it. Losing his father at such a young age had always troubled Lucas, and she knew beneath his dismissive attitude lay some anger that his mother had kept a secret from him. Especially since the farm represented a connection to a father he barely remembered.

The conversation had moved on. "—yeah, we were surprised the house wasn't in worse condition," Lucas said. "It's been sitting for what, over forty years? It should've been a disaster."

"The house is exceptionally well built," Nate said. "The main beams are full twelve-by-twelve oak timbers. They're almost indestructible. I was more surprised the roof held up over the years. There were only a few holes in it."

"Any explanation for that?" Zach asked.

Nate shrugged and smirked. "Ghosts? A skeleton crew maybe?"

Ashley elbowed him. "You're a funny man, Nathan, but don't quit your day job."

Their beers ran dry.

Laura said, "We've got this round. Same, everyone?"

Nods all around.

She walked to the bar and ordered. The bartender was a gruff old guy with a craggy face. As he set the bottles down, he said, "Hope you don't mind me asking, but what's with the video guy?"

"Oh, we're renovating a house and they're documenting it for HGTV."

"Really? Here?"

"Yes. Just out of town."

"Which house are you talking about?"

"The MacKenzie place, out on Firelane Eight." Laura extended a hand. "I'm Laura MacKenzie."

The bartender regarded her curiously for a moment and hesitantly shook her hand. He seemed leery of touching it.

"Seriously?" He looked incredulous. "I always hoped that place would burn down."

Laura stared at him. "What? Why?"

He stared back, stone-faced. "You're a MacKenzie. You know why."

He took her money to make change. When he returned, he gave her a suspicious glance, laid the change down, and said, "That place is bad news. You'll be sorry you opened it up again." He turned and walked away.

Laura gathered the bottles and returned to the table. "Apparently, the bartender doesn't like our house."

"What?" Lucas stopped mid-sip.

"He said he'd always hoped it'd burn down, said we'll be sorry."

"Are you kidding?" Lucas said, eyebrows raised. "You ask him why?"

"Yeah. He looked at me and said, 'You know why'." She emulated his gruff expression.

"Ghosts," Ashley whispered, wide-eyed in mock terror.

"It's a small town, not much else to talk about," Lucas said.

This quirk, the superstitious townspeople, only added to the mystery surrounding Elizabeth and the house. The haunting implications piqued her interest, though. What were the origins of the stories? She would soon live in that house and wanted to know. She kept an eye on the bartender. He was talking to the two older guys at the end of the bar in a conspiratorial manner, glancing in their direction, shaking his head with evident disapproval.

"Tell us more about the haunted house stories," Hannah said. Her eyebrows furrowed. "Come on, guys, why would you leave that out?"

"We don't know any stories," Laura said. "Just that Elizabeth thought it was haunted. I'm curious, though. I'm going to research it and see what I can find."

"You're not concerned there might be some substance to the stories?"

"Not even a little," Lucas said with a shrug. "Silly superstitions, nothing more."

"Next time we're up here, I expect a full report," Hannah said in a rush. "Seriously, this is cool stuff. A great story angle."

Nate raised a bottle. "It might be appropriate to toast Mom at this point."

Lucas raised his bottle. "Dear Mom. I wish I understood the secrecy, but no matter. It's ironic your death made this all possible."

"Lucas!" Laura shot him a look. Yes, the secrecy angered him, but he had never been disrespectful toward his mother.

Lucas, looking suitably contrite, said, "Dear Mom. We love and miss you."

The four of them raised their bottles and lightly clinked them together.

One of the old men at the bar shook his head in apparent dismay. No one seemed to notice but Laura, and it left her puzzled and uneasy. When Elizabeth's attorney had talked about the townspeople, Laura assumed he was exaggerating. Now they were here, the superstitions were palpable and she couldn't dismiss them as easily as Lucas.

A wary chill passed through her like a skeletal finger sliding down her spine.

What do they know that we don't?

Four

Kenric Shepherd signed his name and pushed the completed paperwork across the oak desk to the loan officer. Perhaps sixty, the man wore a dark grey Burberry suit, a label Shepherd preferred as well. The sign of a discerning eye. The office was impeccable, stately. Oak furniture and bookcases, muted colors, and two Thomas Moran landscapes. They had similar tastes. In another world, they might be friends. In this world, Shepherd had no friends and preferred it that way.

The banker folded the papers, stuffed them into an envelope, and handed them to Shepherd.

"Do you want to set up online banking for payments and balances?"

"No, thank you. Please send a statement and I'll pay by check. I'm not one for technology," Shepherd said.

"Your accent—a bit north of London?"

"Very good. Stratford-upon-Avon, actually."

"Ah, home of Shakespeare." The banker smiled. "What will you be teaching at the university?"

"Medieval studies. I specialize in the early English languages; Old English from the era of the great epic *Beowulf* to Middle English and

Chaucer."

"Fascinating."

Shepherd doubted his sincerity. His chosen field was boring and esoteric to most, a passion for a few.

"Enjoy the house, Doctor Shepherd. Welcome to Milwaukee."

They stood and shook hands, Shepherd relieved this step was complete. He'd moved many times and found the process tedious. This move was a consequence, in part, of accepting a professorship at Milwaukee University. That was the official story. His true motivations were stranger and still something of a mystery.

Shepherd sauntered out into bright sunshine, hopped in his Range Rover, fished an iPhone from his breast pocket, and checked his email. He smiled at his fib to the banker. He didn't want to stand out and people seldom noticed an older gentleman who was behind the times. A confirmation had arrived. His furniture and gear had passed through customs and was Milwaukee-bound in a moving van. He breathed a sigh of relief; another hurdle cleared in the move from Rome.

Punching the address into the *Touch Pro* system, he drove to his new home, an aging Victorian two-story on the east side of the city just blocks from the Lake Michigan shoreline. The neighborhood was quiet and gentrified. The brick house, with a corner turret, reminded him of a property he'd owned in London long ago. Quite pricey, but worth it. With the closing complete, he hooked a trailer to the Range Rover and drove to the nearest Lowe's with a long list of building materials.

Later, he sat on the porch of his new house in a lovely wicker rocker, sipping an exquisite cup of Twinings English tea, a taste of home. The rays of the setting sun warmed his face. He sat back and closed his eyes, enjoying the sensation, letting his mind wander. He was peaceful and content. In the present—

An odd vibration disturbed the tranquility. Shepherd tensed.

A second, stronger tremor shook the porch.

Bloody hell!

Shepherd dropped the teacup and grabbed his head, trying to orient himself as the porch seemed to tip sideways and spin full-circle. He knew the feeling well, though he had never grown accustomed to it. It was always disconcerting. Always a shock, filled with foreboding and sometimes menace. The vibration, the shifting, the spinning; these were prodromal signs.

A premonition invariably followed.

He laid back, closed his eyes, and concentrated on breathing. Relaxing muscles. Clearing his head. Wriggled his fingers to relieve the tension in them. Waiting for the whirling-induced nausea to ebb.

What now?

When the spinning stopped, three letters appeared in his head in brilliant neon.

B F E

When his head had cleared, he stood and spun his right arm several times, mimicking a bowler in cricket, a silly affectation he found relaxing. He had no clue what those letters meant, but they were important to his journey here. Shepherd walked to the kitchen, thought about brewing more tea, then decided he needed something stronger. He poured a small glass of fine old tawny port wine. Sat at a makeshift table and sipped the strong, sweet wine with hints of raspberry and cinnamon.

He lived life on several planes: as a distinguished Oxford-educated professor who taught medieval studies and languages; as a grey hat hacker skilled in programming and computer security; and from an era that long preceded the information age, as a mystic who trained in the Hermetic traditions, a philosophy that intertwined spiritualism with early scientific study.

Those older beliefs informed the decision to move to Milwaukee. He had received a dozen offers for professorships, several with prestigious European universities. His CV was enviable. Then he had a premonition. More than a premonition. A bone-shaking seizure followed by a vivid message.

Take the Milwaukee offer.

A serious threat exists there.

Thus, he felt compelled to take the position.

The *why* remained a mystery, and this latest premonition was another in a series of clues that added up to—?

Nothing.

A reality in his world; some choices he made on faith. The answers would come. He couldn't rush them, couldn't force the process. He had to be mindful and wait for the universe to reveal the details.

Shepherd clenched and loosened his jaw and fists, trying to dispel the tension, seeking calm.

In the modern era, knowledge traveled at light-speed. To be beholden to this ancient discipline was frustrating. To be fed information in such small doses aggravating.

Patience, Doctor, he chided himself. *Patience.*

He trusted his instincts and premonitions. They were compelling, reliable, and had saved his life more than once. He recalled a last-minute decision years ago to walk off Alitalia Flight 404. The airliner had crashed outside Zurich that night, killing everyone on board.

He needed to be here. There *was* a reason. That he didn't fully understand the reason was irrelevant.

Time would reveal the secret.

Still, an unease lingered. What was summoning him back to the old ways?

★   ★   ★

Shepherd spent the next two days tearing out an upstairs wall, joining two large bedrooms into one large work area. After replacing the old wiring and repairing the walls, he painted the room slate blue and laid carpeting with a thick pad over the old maple floor.

A few days later, two young men delivered three moving pods, lanky fellows with long hair and ill-fitting jeans who insisted upon calling him *Doc*, much to his dismay. A warm sunny day, they unloaded the pods onto the driveway. He had them unpack and set up the sound system first. Now, Beethoven thundered from a half dozen speakers. He wandered around, directing the movers, and alternated between conducting a phantom orchestra and hurling an imaginary cricket ball. Perhaps they thought he was crazy. He didn't care and happily admitted to being eccentric.

As they set the last of three large crates in the garage, the kid with *Tyler* on his name tag said, "Yo, Doc? You want us to open these?"

There were several crates with US Customs and Border Protection stamps, which he had guided through the port of entry at Newark with several sophisticated hacks. The items within weren't stolen; they were old and rare and would have raised questions had they been subject to inspection.

"No. Leave them there for now. I need that desk next. Upstairs, in the study."

The movers struggled with the oak pieces: two large pedestals, a hutch with thirty-odd nooks, a return, and a thick oak slab for the top. The office was quiet and clean with the smell of new carpet. It was here that he pursued his true passion, dabbling in the modern alchemy of computer and system hacking.

When the movers finished, he tipped them well, happy to see them leave.

With his gear unpacked, he finished assembling his workspace: servers, an array of laptops, external hard drives, everything hard-wired to various routers. There was no wireless. He trusted no one and assumed hackers and electronic miscreants were everywhere in a city this size. He knew the dangers of an online presence so he had no legitimate online accounts other than an .edu address at the university.

After testing his array, he sat down and tapped into the dark web with the Tor browser using an anonymized email and IP address. Shepherd spent an hour probing the firewall of a company in St. Louis before breaking in, using a minor glitch in their security coding while Mozart played quietly in the background. He collected several screen captures and wrote his findings in an email to the security officer of the company. He then spent an hour checking out his usual hacking haunts and message boards, looking for new ideas and techniques.

Shepherd poured a glass of port and sipped while he slipped into his pajamas and relaxed.

In bed, he laid back and closed his eyes. Those three letters, **B F E**, danced on his eyelids in cartoonish animation. Farther in the distance, he saw the vague figure of a woman. He could discern no features beyond her dusty blonde hair.

Those letters and that woman represented some grave threat.

Indeed, they were the reason he was here.

Five

The following afternoon, the sun blazed down from a clear azure sky. Cicadas buzzed in the indolent heat and small white butterflies flitted over the tops of the taller grass at the edge of the lawn—an area of clipped field grass in front of the house. The coarse stubble was hard on the feet but a real lawn would have to wait until next year.

Laura stepped outside with Leah and a handful of toys. Leah ignored the toys and played in the grass, picking up leaves and tossing them into the breeze. Dana had driven back to Illinois to meet with her adviser before the fall semester began, so Laura was devoting the day to Leah. Laura sat in a lawn chair, watching the roofers work, jumping up to intercept Leah whenever she tried to shove something into her mouth. After a while, Leah ambled to the drive, picked up small stones and bits of gravel, examining them, and tossing them aside. She was blonde, pudgy—still carrying some baby fat—and looked more like Jacob than her mother, Rachel.

Thank God.

Any thought of Rachel set off an inevitable rush of pain and anger directed at a woman that Laura had grown to hate for her part in

Jacob's death. A pointless and unavoidable mental cascade of thoughts followed.

If Jacob hadn't dated that woman. If they hadn't moved in together. If Rachel hadn't run off with someone else...

But those things happened. And Jacob slid into depression, started drinking, and rolled his car three times one night in a drunken stupor.

If he hadn't met Rachel, he would still be alive.

But he was gone, and she couldn't bring him back. There were so many clichés about burying a child—Laura knew and hated every one of them. Words to describe her pain didn't exist. With Rachel gone and Jacob dead, Leah had become their responsibility and Laura welcomed it. Leah was her one solace, the only piece of Jacob that remained. Neither Rachel nor her parents wanted Leah, thus proving the adage about the apple and the tree.

Jim Mayhew, the roofing contractor, climbed down from the roof, disturbing her gloomy train of thought.

"How's it going, Mrs. MacKenzie?"

"Call me Laura. Overwhelmed pretty much covers it."

Jim Mayhew was near fifty, rather tall, with thinning black hair swept back to conceal a circle of shiny scalp. Lucas found him on Yelp, and Jim, along with his teenage helpers, Alex and Jordan, had become quick favorites on the worksite as an affable, hardworking bunch. Jim was curious and enthusiastic. Laura liked him. He grabbed a lunch pail from his truck and walked over.

"You know, my wife says this place is haunted," Jim said.

"I've heard that rumor."

He raised an eyebrow. "Anything to it?"

"Not that we've noticed."

"That's what I told her. It's old and kinda scary looking, but it doesn't feel, well, you know—haunted."

"You believe in ghosts?"

He shrugged. "Sure. Why not?"

He smiled and shooed away a couple of bees buzzing nearby.

Laura turned and saw Nate walking around the corner and along the front wall of the house. Ashley followed, videotaping every aspect of the inspection. Some days, all this filming, blogging, and scrutiny felt like an intrusion. She would be glad when they finished. She turned back to Jim. "They bothering you at all?"

His face tightened. "Hmm, not too much."

After lunch, Jim and his long-haired assistants continued hammering, tossing shingles, and cursing as classic rock played from a construction radio.

When Leah grew cranky and rubbed her eyes, Laura scooped her up and carried her to the RV. She changed her diaper and lay with her on the bed for a few minutes, whispering grandma-talk in a soothing voice, enjoying the intimacy until Leah dozed off.

Satisfied she would sleep, Laura grabbed the video monitor and her iPad and walked back to her chair in the drive. The noise in the house was deafening; the racket outdoors seemed minor in comparison. Besides, the warm sunshine felt wonderful.

Laura poked around on her iPad on the Ancestry website, trying to open an account, but she was too tired to concentrate. On the roof, the guys had fallen into a routine that seemed automatic and almost mesmerizing to her.

Everything fell away as she watched them work—her surroundings, the bird calls, the sun beating down, the music on the radio.

With the iPad in her lap, lulled by the hypnotic *snap snap* of the nail gun, she leaned back and dozed off. The sounds of the roofing work insinuated themselves into her light sleep and she dreamt of skeletons. A crew of them working on the house, their bones clicking with the rhythmic *snap* of the nail gun. A dark cloud then covered the sun, turning day to night. The cloud grew and swirled and engulfed the house, a violent whirlwind that lifted and carried it away.

Laura awoke with a start. She checked the video monitor. Leah was still asleep.

The roofers had finished the south end and started up the central section of the roof, a more complex span of gables and valleys, moving stepwise across the roof. Jordan laid metal flashing in the valleys while Alex ran back and forth, laying out cedar shakes in rows. Jim then nailed each row down. Laura watched, fascinated by their efficiency. Evidently, Alex was too slow. Jim kept running out of shakes to nail.

Jim yelled to Alex with an exasperated sweep of his hand, "Go prep the ridge for the vent!"

"Okay, boss man."

"Jordan! You're up!"

Jordan ran bundles of cedar with indefatigable energy. Jim nailed shakes as fast as Jordan could lay them along chalk lines while Alex worked above, using a circular saw to open a narrow slot along the roof apex that would allow heat to escape from the attic.

Suddenly, a strange grey cloud billowed from an opening just feet from where Alex was working. Smoke?

Laura shielded her eyes from the sun and squinted for a better look.

Bees!

Angry bees surged from the gap in the rooftop and swarmed toward Alex. Evidently, he'd disturbed a nest in the attic.

Laura jumped up and yelled, "Alex! Look out!"

Startled, Alex windmilled away from the cloud, dropping the power saw in his panic.

He abruptly flung his arms out as if shoved, then lost his balance. The momentum sent him flying and he disappeared on the far side of the ridge. The saw skittered down the roof toward Jim, gaining speed on the steep pitch. He jumped aside but slipped and fell on the roof deck. Sliding headfirst toward the eaves, Jim lunged for one of the roofing jacks, missed it, and fell ten feet to the stubbly grass below with an impact that made Laura wince.

Above, Jordan yelled, "Holy shit! Alex fell off the roof!"

For a moment, Jim was motionless and appeared to be unconscious.

Laura ran over, knelt, and shook him. "Jim! Jim! Are you okay?"

As he rolled over, wearing a confused expression, screams of pain erupted from behind the house. Jim checked his arms and legs and slowly got to his feet. Limping, he followed Laura around the house, down the slope to the backyard. She could hear Alex screaming but couldn't see him in the tall field grass. Laura pushed toward the sound until she found him, lying on his back, screaming in agony.

She nearly gagged.

His right shin had snapped, the bone protruding through a tear in his jeans. A piece of rusty metal protruded from his t-shirt along his left flank, part of some farm implement forgotten in the grass.

Jim pushed in next to her and shouted, "Jesus! Jordan, call 911! Now!"

Laura knelt and tried to comfort Alex to no avail; he continued to scream in pain. A moment later, he passed out. Laura looked closer at the rusty piece of metal poking through Alex's bloodied shirt. It looked like a flesh wound, but turned her stomach anyway.

Hearing movement in the grass, Laura glanced up.

As Jordan approached, Laura spotted a strange man sitting on the chimney.

What the hell?

An eyeblink and he vanished.

With a vague image burned on her retina—a big guy wearing a ball cap—she felt spindly, dead fingers sliding down her spine.

Who the hell was that?

She tried to sidestep the question but an answer popped into her head anyway.

Ghost.

Six

Tom Wolff sat atop the north chimney, gazing over the countryside. The view had an strangely warped appearance, extending only two or three miles in any direction. The edges just fell away. Nothing was visible beyond the low banks of clouds there. He had never walked to the boundary nor did he want to. He belonged here and had no desire to leave. This was his place. Always had been.

Time was meaningless beyond the nebulous passage of days and nights. He didn't know the day, month, or year. Temperature had no effect on him. As if surrounded by a protective bubble, he was impervious to rain, sleet, and snow. He had a vague theory about his existence, that fate had superimposed him on the world like a shadow in some dimension beyond three. It wasn't heaven. No siree. But it wasn't hell, either.

By chance, he had discovered he could occasionally breach those three dimensions with a thought or a gesture. While the thought or gesture didn't necessarily result in a specific action, a crack opened into the living world. Leaves rustled, dust scattered, floorboards rattled, or a door closed. It was just such a gesture, a little nudge, that sent the kid flying off the roof. The motion lacked focus and, as Tom discovered today, was something over which he had limited control. He'd only meant to scare the kid, but had seriously miscalculated and screwed up with alarming results. Worse, he felt no remorse. He wanted to but didn't seem capable of any emotion at all.

As he looked down, he locked eyes with the blonde woman. She blinked oddly and stared.

Had she seen him? Was that possible?

He didn't know so he slipped down the roof, out of sight, and wandered into the woods.

Tom continually discouraged living people from venturing onto the property, approaching the house, or trying to get inside. This was Elizabeth's house, and he was the caretaker. It was his responsibility to watch over the place until Elizabeth and the boys came home. It had been easier before these intruders arrived. With the yard and driveway overgrown with vegetation, the house had been virtually invisible. Now everyone could see it.

Then he wondered: what if Elizabeth had sent these people to ready the house for her arrival? It was possible. They were making repairs. It was a dilemma, and he wasn't sure how to respond. He certainly couldn't ask.

For now, he would lay low. Play a waiting game.

Until Elizabeth returned.

Seven

Desperate for a few hours away from the contractors and the noise, Laura and Dana took an afternoon off and drove to an antique auction in Auburn. The auction hall was once a railway station, a holdover from an era when Chicago and North Western streamliners ran through town. Inside, a podium at the far end faced rows and rows of green folding chairs, the rest of the long terminal packed with antiques, collectibles, and junk masquerading as heirlooms. A sizable crowd filled the seats, and dozens of people stood around the edges, holding their numbers tight to their chests. The room was warm and stuffy and smelled of old wood and dust.

Leah fidgeted and Dana looked bored, but Laura wanted to stay, waiting for an oak wall phone to hit the block. She loved the thrill and atmosphere of the auction, more so with real money to spend. She had already purchased several lamps, boxes of wood utensils to hang in the kitchen, and a beautiful oak hutch and buffet to match a table set she had refinished in Illinois.

The house was now habitable, but construction work continued. The electricians and plumbers were done but the glaziers remained, restoring the leaded glass windows. The HVAC crew was finishing the furnace and air conditioning system. As it stood, they had places to sleep and half a kitchen. Enough for now.

With the renovations nearing completion, her time had come. From choosing paint colors and furnishings to finding pieces and decor that complimented the architecture, Laura had spent hours scouring eBay, Etsy, and other sites for suitable items. She preferred a hands-on approach, and this auction was far more fun than surfing an internet store.

The auctioneer was hawking a wooden box of photo albums. "Yes sir, many fine old postcards and photographs in this box. Come on now, who'll give me five dollars? Come on, give me five dollars."

"Three," said a man quietly with a flick of his number.

From the lack of interest, Laura assumed the contents were junk. Such stuff didn't interest her.

"Okay, I got three. Come on, give me four, give me four. A steal at this price."

Laura suddenly felt queasy, and the room seemed to tilt sideways—

Take the box

"Okay, I got six. Come on now, give me seven."

Laura bit her lip, certain she had blacked out for a moment. She glanced around, but no one seemed to have noticed. A nameless compulsion to win the box possessed her.

The auctioneer rambled on, "—I got six. Who'll give me seven? Come on, give me seven."

Laura stood and yelled, "Twenty!"

The dingy auction hall went quiet. The auctioneer stopped in mid-sentence and stared at Laura. "Lady, the last bid was six."

"So? I said twenty." Laura defiantly stood her ground.

The auctioneer shook his head. "All right, I got twenty. Who'll give me twenty-five? Come on, give me twenty-five."

"Yep!" A tall bearded man in the corner flashed his number.

"All right, I got twenty-five—"

"Forty!" yelled another man.

"Fifty!" came a shout from the back.

The auction ran amok, bids shouted faster than the auctioneer could acknowledge them. Within seconds, the call reached one hundred and eighty-five dollars.

"Two hundred!" Laura yelled.

As quickly as the bidding frenzy began, it died, leaving Laura standing, holding her number up.

"All right, I got two hundred. Who'll give me two-twenty-five? Come on, two-twenty-five." Perhaps sensing the bidding was over, the auctioneer rapped his gavel on the podium.

"Sold! To number sixty-eight." He pointed to Laura and smiled.

As Laura sat down, Dana grabbed her arm and whispered, "What was that all about?"

"Uh, I don't know exactly. Okay if we go now?" Laura was shaking, adrenaline raising gooseflesh on her arms. What *was* that about? She didn't know.

Looking concerned, Dana said, "You feel okay?"

"Yeah, why?"

"You're as pale as a ghost."

"I'm fine. Let's go."

Laura paid for her purchases and made arrangements to pick up the furniture later. Waiting for the box of photo albums, she touched Dana's shoulder. "Listen, can we keep this to ourselves for now?"

"Sure. Why?"

"Because—I don't know. Just because."

Laura didn't know. While she couldn't explain her compulsion to bid on the box, she was dying to rummage through it when they got home.

Why?

She didn't know that either.

Eight

Nate MacKenzie slathered a glob of stucco onto the last stretch of wall on the north side of the house. Worked the wet plaster smooth with a trowel and finished with the arcing flourishes of a skip-trowel texture. Stood back and admired his work.

Perfect.

It was tedious work he could have given to a subcontractor, but few people had his skill in creating a meticulous finish. He snapped a dozen photos for the blog. Another job finished, every detail preserved and documented.

The project looked like a success so far. Their blog had several thousand followers, and they had racked up almost a hundred thousand views on YouTube. Still, he worried closing his successful business in Illinois was a mistake. Felt the constant pressure of deadlines as the HGTV producer pushed him hard to finish. Nate had a great deal riding on this renovation and hoped he would ultimately earn his own show.

He sent a text to Ashley to follow up with video. She was shopping again. The woman loved buying clothes, but he wondered where she'd wear them out here in the sticks. She had expensive tastes and he worried about keeping her happy. Though it was far from certain, Ashley seemed to feel having his own show was a foregone conclusion.

Lighting a Cohiba Mini, he sat and stared out at the lake. The day was beautiful, hot, but comfortable with a soft breeze. He drew a thin stream of smoke into his lungs, closed his eyes and enjoyed the forbidden pleasure. He'd quit cigarettes years ago and saw no harm in the occasional cigar, but Ashley was a virulent anti-smoker and would kill him if she caught him. Thank God she wasn't a vegan.

The view was fabulous, but Nate felt out of place here. Unlike Lucas, he didn't hunt, didn't fish, wasn't much of an outdoorsman. He liked the city: the noise, the crowds, live music at midnight, and fifty great choices when they wanted to eat out. Regardless, fewer people wanted serious style these days, and he had grown tired of remodeling the shitty McMansions that people in the Chicago suburbs favored. This project and the HGTV special were the gig of a lifetime.

For now, the challenge of the job was enough, but he wasn't sure he wanted to live here after they finished it.

Twenty minutes later, Nate cleaned his trowels and grabbed a bottle of Stone IPA from the fridge. It was too early to quit, so he opted to pick off odd jobs until dinner. Nate walked upstairs to the room across the landing, one of five bedrooms on the second level. He was inspecting the floors, tacking loose boards. Two of his guys from Illinois had sanded, stained, and finished the random-width oak floors with polyurethane, but squeaky floorboards remained through-out the house. It was a simple task. He stepped on each board. If it moved or squeaked, a couple of finishing nails tacked it down tight. It was nit-picking, but the TV people insisted upon perfection in every detail.

Outdoors, the harsh buzz of Lucas's chainsaw harried the otherwise quiet countryside.

He stepped down and frowned. Two short boards behind the door lifted slightly and fell back into place. Nate pushed again and whistled in surprise when the floorboards flipped open in a half circle on a concealed hinge.

A trapdoor.

Not just any trapdoor. The edges were so finely sanded that when the door closed, it was invisible. Further, a peg locked the door in place so it wouldn't open unless he pushed on a precise spot behind the hinge. Nate opened and closed it several times, marveling at the construction.

The space beneath looked large, but too dark to see much. Excited, Nate jumped up and ran downstairs for a flashlight. Old houses were famous for hidden nooks and crannies—places where people hid their money and valuables. Nobody trusted the banks back then. He had devoted some idle time to combing the walls for hidden spaces, but hadn't considered the floors.

He laid down and flashed the beam around. The chamber, festooned with cobwebs, extended under the hallway. It was deep, almost two feet down to the dusty floor. With his head on the floor, peering into the corners, he heard a subtle bass vibration in the floorboards, an odd sound. What was that? But he was too caught up in the hunt to question it further.

Directly below, a bulge in the dust caught his eye. He reached, probing gently with fingertips, and grabbed the metal object from the dust.

A cross.

Simple in design with a circle of metal connecting the four arms, it was heavy, cast from iron or lead. It looked old and worthless. Sadly, the space looked otherwise empty. Nate tossed the cross back into the chamber and started when it made an odd clanging noise like metal striking stone.

He swept the cobwebs away and poked into the carpet of dust, his fingers brushing over a surface with a different texture.

Bricks.

They had built the house with timber, plaster, and stone. He hadn't seen a brick in the entire building. Why had they used brick here? It was strange. Nate pushed his head through the opening to look more closely. At first, he thought it was part of the fireplace, but then he saw a fieldstone chimney running upward beside it. The space beneath the brick actually sat *next* to the fireplace.

He stopped, visualizing the floor plan downstairs. There were no doors by the fireplace or in the adjoining sitting room. Evidently, a space with no obvious access lay beneath this chamber.

A secret room. It had to be.

His pulse quickened as he imagined valuable stuff hidden inside. Nate then decided the discovery was his alone. If Lucas knew about it, he'd step in and take over. He always did.

As he peered into the corners one more time, the chainsaw outside revved up with an angry snarl and the droning bass tone grew louder, vibrating the floor. A car with a subwoofer? Out here?

Suddenly, the chamber seemed to close in, constricting and throbbing in sync with the bass and the saw.

Nate couldn't breathe; sweat beaded on his forehead. A cold and nameless anxiety grabbed him and held him until he twisted and jerked away from the opening.

He leaned back, panting, staring at the ceiling in shock.

Jesus! What the hell was that?

A panic attack? He hadn't had one in years.

Outside, Lucas's chainsaw made a growling sound like an angry beast snared in a trap, then revved in erratic pulses.

Over that din, he heard Lucas yelling, the cry of someone in mortal danger. "Nate! Nate! Jesus, Nate, get out here!"

That voice frightened Nate—who didn't easily admit fright—nearly as much as the claustrophobic sensation in the chamber. He slammed the trapdoor shut, ran downstairs and out the front door, expecting to find his brother minus a limb, spurting blood in looping arcs across the yard. Turning at the northeast corner of the house, he plowed into Lucas.

"What the hell is your problem?"

Looking shaken, Lucas turned and pointed to a large maple about thirty feet from the house. Nate stared in shock, fear tickling his insides with spiky fingers. Lucas's chainsaw was cutting slowly up the center of the trunk *by itself.*

"Jesus! What in the hell's happening?"

Mouth agape, Lucas shook his head. "No idea."

The saw veered left out of the trunk and hurtled into the field like a football dropping toward a wide receiver. It buzzed angrily for a moment and quit.

A loud *crack* echoed across the yard. Nate, recognizing the danger, shoved his brother around the corner of the house. A moment later, the tree crashed down right where they'd been standing.

Breathless, Nate said, "That's the strangest thing I've ever seen."

Lucas, wide-eyed in shock, said, "That fucking tree missed us by inches!"

"No shit, Sherlock. What happened?"

"The saw kicked back, threw me, and took off by itself. How'd it do that?"

Nate shook his head. It sounded ridiculous. Staring at the tree sprawled across the gravel drive, he said, "Lucky the car wasn't there, bro."

"Yeah, that too."

"And you're welcome."

"For what?"

"Saving your dumb ass," Nate said sarcastically, but he wasn't smiling. It had been a close call.

Just then, Laura and Dana pulled into the drive, stopped short, and gawked at the trunk in the driveway.

"Let's go up to the car." Lucas, still pale, pushed Nate forward. "Not a word about this."

"Kind of hard to hide the evidence, dude."

"You know what I mean."

★   ★   ★

Laura pulled in and stopped. As she looked at the fallen tree, a queasy feeling rose in her stomach along with an odd shift in consciousness, much like the sensation she felt at the auction hall.

"Mom, you okay?" Dana asked.

"Yeah, fine. Just a little tired." As her anxiety ebbed, she tried to compose herself. She wasn't tired, wasn't sure she could explain it. Didn't understand why that box of junk had knocked her off kilter. Couldn't explain the crazy bidding spree, either.

She felt certain the box contained worthless junk, but Laura suddenly realized she wasn't looking inside it.

The box seemed to emanate sadness, as if tormented spirits lived within. It was a nonsensical thought, irrational even.

Enough!

She took back control in the usual manner, stared at herself in the rearview mirror with mindful resolve, and ended her funk with three unspoken words.

Shut up, Laura!

Nine

Shepherd tapped a key on his laptop and *pleu* appeared on the overhead screen. Two dozen students sat, scattered about the stadium seating in the darkened classroom, taking notes. Some looked bored, others listened raptly.

"This Indo-European root means *to flow*. Some modern derivatives of this root include *pulmonary, pneumonia, flutter, fluster,* and *fly*." He sipped from a water bottle.

"Consider the word *fly*. *pleu* became the Germanic root *fleugan*, which evolved to *fleogan* in Old English. The verb *to fly* is derived from *flegan*."

With his exceptional hearing, he heard the faint pings of a text in progress. He surreptitiously glanced up at the students and saw the faint glow from a screen on Kyle Anderson's face. Kyle then slurped on his coffee, evidently oblivious to the noise he was making. He had talked to the kid twice this month. Shepherd had no interest in the paperwork involved in a formal discipline. He'd love to throw this twit out of his class, but that wasn't possible either. Instead, with an imperceptible flick of his forefinger, he nudged the Starbucks cup on

Kyle's desk into his lap.

Kyle jumped up, jeans covered in coffee. "Shit!"

A ripple of laughter crossed the room.

Shepherd waved a hand in his direction. "Go clean up, Mr. Anderson. You've disturbed class enough today. See you next week."

With a slight chuckle, Shepherd pressed a key on his laptop and a long list of words appeared on the screen.

"As you can see, *pleu is the root of a great many words."

★   ★   ★

Later, Shepherd sat on his porch sipping tea, listening to a cardinal calling and feeling melancholy.

The position at Milwaukee University lacked challenge. His undergraduates were average and there was tension in the staffroom. Professors whined about the quality and the temperament of the students, and complained about the insidious creep of political correctness. The students were overly sensitive and afraid of everything. Some of his colleagues called them *snowflakes,* but it was an overreaction. Some percentage of his students had always been snowflakes. A few were stellar and went on to great things. So it would be with this generation.

Milwaukee didn't thrill him, either. It lacked the allure of a major city and felt provincial after having lived in London, New York, Paris, and Rome. He loved his tenure in Rome, but it had been time to leave. The questions had begun. A colleague noticed he hadn't aged in yearly staff photos. A student found a ninety-year-old photo of him in an obscure journal. Some magic and glib talk defused the situation, but his time in Rome was over.

He sighed.

Truth was, he hated relocating. This move had been the hardest. Was it age? Was he becoming an old curmudgeon?

When he thought about his age, he could no longer recall an exact number. He forever lied about it. His passport said sixty-six, though he was much older. Born during the reign of Charlemagne, his date of birth escaped him and timekeeping then was hardly an exact science. It might have been in July 774 in the English Midlands, or Mercia, as it was then known. The child of pagan parents, he displayed an early aptitude for sorcery and his father, a revered Anglo-Saxon shaman, recognized in his son a prodigy. Kenric then trained for twenty years under Godric, the most esteemed wizard in Mercia, before venturing out into the world.

Beyond good genes, luck, and a considerable skill in magic, he had no explanation for his longevity. There were others like him and they had crossed paths over the years, forming an elite but informal clique called the *Aeldan* or Elders. Those who remained alive occasionally met, though now, he only stayed in touch with Fynn Alden and Lachlan Hayward who had also trained under Godric. They were all skilled in the arts, but they considered him the most gifted of all. He had traveled around England and Europe for centuries performing sorcery. Much of it for good: healing the sick, bringing needed rain, protecting the villages and land of his friends. Some magic had been less than principled: working as a vigilante for hire when wars, conflicts, or personal feuds erupted. Over the years, his growing wisdom and experience had tempered his base urges and tribal instincts.

He had little use for magic now. It was outdated in a technical world. He couldn't cast a spell to hinder terrorists or extremists, but he could frustrate their efforts with the internet, thwart their operations and siphon their funds away, which he donated to charity.

Technology was global. Magic was strictly local. In theory, he could spite someone for cutting him off in traffic. In practice, the years had taught him toleration and mindfulness, and he shrugged off the small slights of life and moved on, the moment today with Kyle Anderson aside.

Shepherd had spent much of his later life teaching, and he'd moved a great deal. He could spend only ten to twenty years in one place before it was necessary to move on. He aged so slowly that questions about his age arose during longer tenures. Occasionally, people asked the questions regardless. Then he used magic to obfuscate the inquiry. In the computer age, it was easier to cover his tracks and confuse the curious. As far as the world was concerned, he was just another in a long line of K. Shepherds. Still, he felt the weight of maintaining a facade increasingly tiresome.

He still had little understanding of his purpose in Milwaukee. No further information had been forthcoming.

Not a hunch. Not an inkling. Nothing. He had all but stood on his head—which seldom worked anyway—trying to coax something from the ether.

Assuming the letters were an acronym, he googled B F E, but the answer was confusing.

Bum Fuck Egypt?

Somehow, a nonsensical pejorative about places in the middle of nowhere and a faceless woman represented a threat?

He sighed. Maybe he was losing his mind.

Or going senile.

Ten

Sunset the following evening was a glorious event. Laura stood at the rear of the Great Hall watching the sun, blood-soaked and engorged, drift beneath the trees and horizon. A band of altocumulus to the west caught the last rays of the sun, glowing brilliant orange, then red, and finally maroon before the drab greys of twilight chased the color away. One by one, Lucas, Nate, and Ashley joined Laura and watched the brilliant spectacle until the room was nearly dark.

"Let's start a fire," Ashley said.

Nate glanced at her. "Why?"

"Why not? I think it would be neat."

"So do I," Laura said. Time to enjoy the house they'd labored so hard over. She sensed a collective sigh fall upon the room. September was slipping by, the first hints of fall splashed in bright red daubs on the maples. This moment had seemed ages away when they arrived. Much of the work now lay behind them and it felt like they had reached an important goal.

As Lucas built a fire, Nate said, "I hate to ruin the mood, but Zach and Hannah will be back tomorrow."

Laura tensed and shook her head. The intrusions were unending. Lucas groaned and said, "How much longer, Nate?"

"Come on," Ashley said. "A couple more times. You guys agreed to this."

"Really? This is what we agreed to?" Lucas stood rigid, eyes narrowed. "The constant invasion of privacy? And what about that wingnut at the door this morning? I thought you were keeping our location secret for now."

"We are." Nate said, defensively. "He got lucky."

"So, how's the barn coming, bro?" Lucas said sharply.

"What's that supposed to mean?"

"You're a smart guy. Figure it out."

Ashley picked up the wine bottle and spoke in a conciliatory tone. "More wine?"

"No, thanks." Lucas set his glass down and walked out.

Laura held out her glass and shrugged, surprised Lucas had been so irritable. "Sorry guys. It's a bit much some days."

★   ★   ★

Almost a week later, Laura parked herself in a comfy recliner in the Hall on a quiet Wednesday afternoon. Sunlight streamed through the west windows. Leah was down for a nap, and Ashley was editing video in the kitchen. Lucas had run somewhere—for hardware or something—and Nate was upstairs doing finishing work. Dana had returned to her home in Naperville, and Leah occupied much of her free time otherwise. This was her first opportunity to pursue something fun.

A laptop perched in her lap, Laura had run searches for Lost Arrow, the Kettle Moraine, and the MacKenzies. The mystery surrounding the house fascinated her. Who built it? How long had the MacKenzies owned it and where did they come from? How and when had the stories about the house start? She was certain those answers lay somewhere inside a Google search, only it appeared the town and the MacKenzies had no history, none Laura could find anyway.

Lost Arrow was an unincorporated township with a generic entry in Wikipedia. The town had no newspaper, no schools, no library—only a church that might prove useful in tracking down Lucas's family. They lived in Auburn County, but that search was equally fruitless. As for the house, it had somehow slipped under the paranormal radar, appearing nowhere on the websites devoted to Wisconsin and Midwest hauntings. Despite the local rumors, she had hit a frustrating dead end.

She joined Ancestry and started a family tree. She entered the requisite information, the names of their parents and grandparents. According to their website propaganda, the software searched through *billions* of records for information about your family. Those bits appeared in your tree as little green leaves. It was *so* clever.

For Laura, that translated into over two hundred hints—birth records, census records, personal entries—most of them connected to her family tree, information she already knew. She received fewer hints for Elizabeth's family and none for the MacKenzie lineage beyond the information she had entered initially. It all added up to nothing.

Then she thought about the box of albums from the auction. Who knew? Maybe there was something useful inside it. But the hair at the nape of her neck prickled. She puzzled over the urge to buy it, the odd reaction she experienced, her reluctance to examine it. Even now, the thought of it unnerved her.

No matter. Laura would look through it regardless, being an advocate of facing anxieties head-on.

The old wooden crate sat where Dana had put it in a corner of the basement. She carried it to the next room by the furnace where the light was better.

Laura plopped down onto the cool stone floor, hesitated, then dove into the old photo albums and scrapbooks inside the box. The first album teemed with black and white photos. Stern looking families. Vacations and summer picnics. Children swimming. First communions. Graduations. Family gatherings. On some, the detail had faded from the photos, leaving faceless groups of people staring at the camera. The scrapbooks contained blue ribbons, awards, diplomas, newspaper clippings. None of it seemed relevant.

On it went, more photographs, clippings, awards and notes of other milestones. Sorting through them was tedious. Still, she carefully checked each book, uncertain of what she was looking for.

She wondered about all these nameless people. The grandparents were long dead now, just fond memories, while the parents had pushed into old age. The children would have grown and had children of their own—all marking time moving in measured steps like the relentless succession of the planets around the sun. Photo albums invariably had this effect upon her. In the larger scheme of things, she was just a tiny cog in a vast machine, a prisoner of time, carried along a dusty and inexorable path. Someday, she would be nothing but a photo in an album, just a memory.

After an hour, with twelve books down and three to go, Laura quit. She tossed the loose books into the box and shoved it next to the furnace. What a waste of time and money. The bewitching moment at the auction? She had no clue what had happened. Indigestion? The onset of menopause—?

Suddenly, the room seemed to twist sideways and spin.

Feeling dizzy and nauseated, she lost her balance and sat down hard. The sensation sent a deep chill down her spine, awakening the unpleasant memory of a childhood illness—

No!

Laura cut the thought short with a fierce bit of mindfulness and determination. She wasn't reopening that chapter of her life.

Nope. It was that simple, part of a well-rehearsed routine.

She cleared her mind and focused on the present and the task at hand.

The last option was good old-fashioned legwork, asking around town, maybe finding a local historian. She decided to go now. Having started this, she impatiently wanted answers today.

She grabbed her purse and popped into the kitchen where Ashley was working. "Hey. Can you listen for Leah for an hour or two while I run to town?"

"Sure. Where are you going?"

"The general store."

"Whoa, girl. Too exciting for me." Ashley waved without looking up. "Have fun!"

Laura hopped into her Honda CR-V and drove to Lost Arrow. After driving a quick loop of the small village, noting the church, the tavern, and a vacant hotel, she parked across the road from Anson's General Store.

It was an old-fashioned country store, a two-story wood frame building, white but spotted grey where the paint had peeled. A wooden staircase ran up the left side. An asphalt drive wrapped around the other side where a pair of gas pumps sat beneath a modern BP canopy. Laura had never been inside; had shopped in Auburn before now. As she walked through the rickety screen door, she noted the worn linoleum flooring and dingy shelves, but the place looked reasonably clean. She pretended to peruse the snacks but scanned the small store furtively. It was otherwise empty and the clerk, buried in her iPhone, ignored her.

The woman was heavy, wearing a dingy white blouse that strained at every seam. Her dark hair was neat but flecked with dandruff. Finally, Laura grabbed a pack of cashews and placed it on the counter between a cluttered display of candy and junk food.

The clerk turned. Her eyes widened a bit. "Will that be all, ma'am?" Her voice was pleasant, rather deep and husky with a hint of an accent. Southern Indiana maybe?

"Yes."

"That'll be a dollar twenty."

As the clerk made change, Laura said, "Do you know anyone who dabbles in local history?"

"Not really."

"I'm new in town. My name is Laura Mac—"

"I know who you are." The woman pushed the change at Laura and turned back to her phone.

Laura recoiled, stunned.

What a bitch!

She grabbed the change and turned to leave.

The woman sighed and swiveled suddenly. "Shoot. I'm sorry. Let's start over."

Hands up in supplication, she seemed sincere.

"Okay." Laura extended her hand. "I'm Laura."

"I'm Carol Anson." She shook Laura's hand. "Again, sorry. Rough morning. How can I help you?"

"I was hoping to learn more about this area. History of the town, stuff like that."

Carol's gaze strayed to an older woman with a grey perm who had just walked in, wearing a tan windbreaker. "Afternoon, Shirley. Lovely weather we're having, huh?"

"It is." The woman joined them at the counter. "Looking for a local historian?"

"I am. That and some information about our house."

"And which house is that, dear?" Shirley smiled pleasantly.

"The MacKenzie place."

"Oh." Shirley flinched slightly.

Carol hesitated, then said, "What about Ted Summers?"

"He's out east, visiting his kids," Shirley said. "How about Janice Foster?"

Carol nodded in agreement, then jotted a number on a Post-it and handed it to Laura.

"Sally?"

Carol shook her head ever so slightly.

"I'd try Janice Foster," Shirley said. "I'm sure she can help."

"Okay, thank you." Laura turned to leave, then stopped. "I'm curious. Why does everyone seem so—so hostile when our house is mentioned?"

Carol shrugged. "We're not hostile, Laura. Superstitious maybe. I guess we consider the house unlucky, that's all."

"But no one will even talk about it. Why?"

"Why?" Carol seemed surprised. "You haven't noticed anything off about that place?"

"Not really."

"Really? That house is bug-ass haunted. Everybody knows that."

Shirley nodded in agreement with a solemn expression.

"But if it's supposedly haunted, why can't I find anything about it online?" Laura felt her stomach tighten with this talk about the house. She had noticed nothing, but these people were serious.

"People come looking from time to time, but they never find the house and we're not about to help them. Things have been quiet here for a long time. We don't want anyone stirring anything up."

Laura raised her eyebrows. "Worried we'll stir things up?"

"Maybe."

"Maybe the ghost has moved on."

Carol frowned. "I don't think it works like that."

Laura shrugged, lost for words. She said goodbye and walked to the CR-V, her mood pensive. It was a strange town, their superstitions palpable, which made the lack of tangible information even more frustrating.

What were they afraid of?

Laura was undeterred. She had two names: Janice Foster and some woman named Sally. She steered toward home, but passing the church, decided to stop. They might have some relevant records—births, deaths, marriages. Worth a try.

The church, the last building on the east side of town, sat to the left of the highway. A cemetery surrounded by a picket fence lay to the right of the church. Tall evergreens stood guard in a row at the rear. *Saint Thomas Episcopal Church* had been carved on a wooden sign with the schedule for Matins and Evensong.

It was a pretty church, Laura decided. A small Norman imitation, built with grey limestone, it had weathered nicely. Narrow stained-glass windows tucked between thick buttresses rose to a square bell tower capped by battlements. The cornerstone dated the church to 1858.

Laura walked through a small picket gate in the stone wall to the adjoining vicarage. Unable to find a doorbell, Laura rapped on the dark wooden door with the iron knocker, a fitting medieval touch. She heard footsteps on wood approach and a tall man with dark brown hair opened the door. Casually dressed in Levi's and a T-shirt with a round, jovial face, he looked like a college student, not a priest.

"Hi. Can I help you?"

"Hello. My name is Laura MacKenzie and I'm new to the area." He didn't flinch at her name. A promising start.

"Great, so am I," he said, smiling. "We have something in common already. I'm Reverend Drew—Kevin Drew. Were you interested in joining the parish?"

"Actually, no," Laura said. "My husband's family is from this area. I was interested in looking through the church records."

"Oh. I'm afraid the records were destroyed in a fire three months ago. Everything we had." He spread his hands and shrugged.

Laura scanned the vicarage, which showed no signs of fire damage or recent repairs. "Must've been a small fire." It was almost an accusation. She couldn't help it. She felt thwarted at every turn.

He drew back a bit at her abrupt tone. "No, you misunderstand. They kept the records in the office of our sister church in Watertown. The office was a total loss. Paper records, microfiche, everything."

"I'm sorry. I didn't mean to snap at you. I just keep running into dead ends with his family."

He paused reflectively and pointed toward the cemetery. "You might try over there."

Laura looked at the rows of tombstones and felt her stomach twist in a tense knot. "Really?"

"Oh, there's plenty of information there," he said cheerfully.

"Like what? I don't understand how that'd help."

"It's hit and miss. Search for the family surname and then try cross-referencing any names you find with the genealogy sites."

"I tried Ancestry and came up empty."

"That's surprising, but genealogy is hard work. Keep at it and don't dismiss the cemetery too hastily."

After a few minutes of small talk, Laura said goodbye and left.

She didn't like cemeteries. Besides, the idea seemed so low-tech. Wandering around a field of dead people, looking for what? She stared at the cemetery, wondering if he was right. Was there something useful in there? She took a step toward the gate, then felt a queasy knot rise in her gut—felt some impending threat beyond that gate. She turned and walked to the car. It was foolish, but Laura wasn't looking today.

In the car, Laura tapped in Janice Foster's number, but the call went to voicemail. She left a brief message, feeling certain Janice wouldn't call back.

Eleven

Tom lounged on a non-existent bench in the root cellar. Leaned back and closed his eyes, trying to rest.

He rested a lot these days. Interacting with the living world was tiring, one facet of many he didn't understand about his situation. Existing somewhere outside the plane of the living, his interactions with their world were unpredictable. Most of the time, he was invisible, silent, nothing more than a cool breeze. He now realized the living saw him occasionally and that he appeared to them as a ghost. A haunting. He wondered if only certain people like the blonde woman could see him. He didn't know. It was so confusing.

As the caretaker, he had been entrusted to look after the place and decided it was helpful these intruders were completing many needed repairs on the house. He could do only so much to maintain the physical structure. Over the years, he had concentrated on protecting the roof.

Still, he saw them as a threat.

One of them had discovered the secret floorboard hatch above the hidden room next to the fireplace, and it worried him. He felt uneasy anywhere near that part of the house. The energy flows were disrupted and bent at obtuse angles, descending into the ground like a gateway to a dark place. Something dangerous dwelt there. Tom had never seen or heard anything, but he sensed a threat regardless. The feeling that hands, claws, or talons might reach out and drag his soul underground, never to see light again. The idea terrified him—fear being the one emotion he still felt in this strange world.

The brick walls of the room seemed to temper and limit its influence and were thus best left alone.

With the roof finished, he wished these people would leave. The house had been quiet for years. Even the kids from town had stopped coming. The thick growths of brush and trees had provided the perfect veil, hiding the old place from the world.

Now, something had changed—the balance disturbed—and Tom sensed trouble ahead.

Twelve

Standing in front of St. Thomas Episcopal Church, Laura stepped through a small unpainted gate into the cemetery. Years of winter frost had tipped and tilted the decrepit stones, and a tall, dense canopy of trees hung over the dead, allowing little sunlight through thick and leafy branches. It was silent, without birdsong, without the slightest breeze to rustle leaves or grass, the atmosphere gloomy, the mood somber.

Still, she felt calm strolling among the tombstones half buried in the long grass. An unending parade of dead people: grandparents, parents, uncles and aunts, children—just names carved into chunks of slate, marble and limestone, many of them forgotten, unknown to any living soul. Here, death prevailed. It was a grim rock garden, mocking the significance of life, a silent reminder of her mortality and the reason she hated cemeteries.

Oddly, she felt only curiosity now.

She found no help, though. Just a random bunch of names but not a single MacKenzie. She chided herself for wasting a perfectly good afternoon wandering among the dead. Laura wanted to leave, but an invisible tether drew her in farther where the grass grew longer and the branches hung lower.

At the back of the cemetery, she found an area cordoned off with small dark boulders. Someone had carved *MacKenzie's Corner* into a stone at the entrance.

It was a lovely little plot.

The tightly bunched tombstones were identical, of simple design, with rounded crowns. Over thirty stones crowded the small patch, and indeed, every one of them was a MacKenzie. As Laura stepped in among them, the air grew cooler and clouds obscured the sun, sending a chill down her spine. She sensed rain nearby and tried to hurry, but couldn't change the breezy pace she adopted entering the cemetery. Onward she walked, passing stone after stone, feeling irrationally calm, wondering why Reverend Drew hadn't mentioned this place. Surely he knew it was here?

Suddenly, she stopped, puzzled by an odd contradiction on the headstones. Some of the souls buried here were older than the church. The stone before her bore the simple inscription:

Peleg MacKenzie
1775-1804

How could that be? She clearly remembered seeing 1858 carved on the church cornerstone. The next stone was barely legible, the whitish marble eroded by years of wind, rain, and snow.

Jeremiah MacKenzie
1713-1751

It wasn't possible. Laura felt certain no settlers had traveled this far west before the nineteenth century. Why were these people here? The absurd image of some ancient MacKenzies dragging all these festering corpses west with them popped into her head. A ridiculous image and yet, she feared it could be true.

One black stone sat alone at the rear of the little plot. Glowing a faint iridescent green, the chiseled lettering was fresh, showing no sign of age or weathering.

Anna Flecher
1481-1516

Laura tensed in fear as an unnerving sensation washed over her. This Flecher woman wasn't a MacKenzie. Why was she here? Why did she find that name so disturbing?

The sky darkened to deep shades of purple. The air was still, but the trees swayed with a slow rhythm, the creaking of the ancient branches growing more insistent. Laura panicked when she realized night was falling. She had to get out!

She *hated* cemeteries. Why *had* she come here?

She looked for the gate, but it was now hidden. The graveyard looked the same in every direction, the picket fence miles away, the distance growing longer; the cemetery multiplying into endless rows of tombstones. Her hopeless sense of direction, normally just a frustrating nuisance, had become a life-threatening handicap. It felt like a dream, but she couldn't wake herself, couldn't escape the terror of this place.

In the twilight gloom, the tree branches looked like arms waving above gnarled faces carved into the corrugated bark of the trunks. Something small and hard hit her on the back of the head. As she swiveled and raised her arms for protection, two more nuts struck her on the back.

Acorns! The oaks were *throwing* acorns!

Laura ran aimlessly as the nuts rained down upon her. Her fear became a finely honed terror when she realized the fence and gate were receding faster than she could run and stumble toward them. She looked down, horrified to find that she was wearing heels. What? Why had she come here? Why couldn't she see the church? Why was she so stupid? She wanted to crawl out of this nightmare, but wishing so couldn't make it happen.

The *why, why, why* in her head intensified into a scream as the trees closed in on her, threatening violence and death. Laura tripped on a stone hidden in the grass. Opening her mouth to cry out, the scream was cut short when her head struck an unyielding chunk of granite. She blacked out with the thought that she would wake in bed like Dorothy returning from Oz.

★ ★ ★

It was dark when she awoke.

The sky was as black as coal, the stars hard, gleaming crystals. Her head throbbed. Checking with tentative fingers, Laura felt a swollen gash over her right eye, a crust of dried blood in her hair.

She lay dazed for a moment as the world came back into focus. The lights of the town shone in the distance, silhouetting the rounded tops of the tombstones before her. Laura turned her head, horrified to see tombstones fading into the darkness in every direction. It was so silent, so still.

Oh God! She was still in the cemetery!

In her abject terror, time crawled and her arms and legs refused her fervent urge to move and escape. Her mind raced on. *Must get out of here. Must get out of here. Must get out of here.*

She struggled to get up—

There was a sound behind her, like a shovel biting into dirt. Laura dared not look around. Her only instinct was to run, but her arms were leaden and barely budged. The sound of more shovels breaking ground spread across the cemetery in a malevolent wave.

The ground was moving! All around her, the dirt came alive as the turf buckled and churned. Gravestones wobbled and collapsed into widening crevices. Faults ran every which way, ripping the ground asunder as tremors freed the dead, imprisoned below. Laura sat rigid, unable to close her eyes, unable to scream, unable to run.

Paralyzed.

Skeletal hands streaked with rotting flesh reached skyward from the soil. Lifeless heads surfaced, hideous shapes without faces, just strips of rotting flesh on their chalky white skulls. They struggled from their earthen confines, filling the air with the smell of death and decay. Gathering together, they staggered like drunks, though they were neither drunk nor human. The decomposing scrum of corpses closed in, surrounding her, moaning a low, raspy chant, "Leave us be, Laura. Leave us be."

Oh God, she wanted to leave them be. She prayed for deliverance but remained frozen in place—an ice sculpture of terror. Cold, lifeless hands, slimy like rotten fruit, touched her arms.

Laura tried to scream, but no sound came.

Tossed and turned and struggled to no avail.

Firmer hands grasped her shoulders.

Laura tensed for the killing blow she knew was coming.

Thirteen

"Hey babe, wake up. Come on, wake up!"

Laura opened her eyes, feeling disoriented and anxious. The bedroom came into focus, dimly lit by moonlight streaming through the windows. A hand—Lucas's hand—gripped her shoulder, shaking her gently. The dead faded away, back into her subconscious.

It had been a dream, a nightmare. She fought back tears in the face of Lucas's sleepy, concerned expression.

"You okay?" He took her hand gently.

She nodded. "Yep. Just a bad dream."

Laura blinked, trying to clear her head, but the cemetery and dead people lurked in the shadows.

"You want to talk about it?" Lucas asked.

"No—no, I'm okay."

Lucas nodded and turned over. Laura rolled onto her side and stared at the wall, heart still pounding, trying to slow her breathing, her body covered in a thin film of cold sweat. What could she say? Lucas would murmur something soothing and that would be the end of it. She didn't want to talk about it, anyway.

Sleep eluded her. Closing her eyes brought the cemetery and dead bodies back to life as vividly as a Wes Craven movie. Laura lay there, eyes open, working a relaxation exercise, concentrating on her breathing, her heart rate gradually slowing to normal. She didn't question the dream. She knew where it had come from. Asking questions about the house, the church, the cemetery—these things had returned to her in the night as a gift-wrapped technicolor nightmare.

Sometimes her rich imagination was a curse.

Instead, she thought about Leah. Walking in the woods. Walking the beach on Lake Michigan. Now and then the cemetery would intrude. She wished it away and slowly, she relaxed. Perhaps she would sleep after all.

★   ★   ★

Lucas slid from bed and mumbled that he had to pee. He wandered into the bathroom, pushed the door shut, reached for and missed the light switch.

"Screw it," he muttered.

He stood, eyes closed, thinking of little but sleep. Nearby, an owl called out. Lucas felt a cold draft from the window, visible as a faint grey square when he opened his eyes. Why was the window open? It was cold outside.

That open window bothered Lucas. Made him feel uneasy, wary. He reached out to close it—

The hand that grabbed him closed about his face so tightly, no sound was possible—at least he thought it was a hand in his blind terror, the feel of it soft and fleshy but cold, as cold as the night air from the window—his mind locked in a silent scream from the shock of being torn from a sleepy state.

It pushed him backwards. Lucas resisted, neck and back muscles straining, his arms flailing to find and strike his assailant. His hands found nothing, and the assailant shoved him into the vanity, his kidneys crashing into the unyielding marble edge. The blow stunned him, but his panic was intense, and his hand found purchase behind, on the sink. He lunged forward and threw a roundhouse punch, but whoever, or whatever it was, had such a long reach that his fist found only thin air.

Losing ground again, he was being pushed slowly backwards toward the door, his neck taut, head bobbing against the force on his face. His hands groped in the darkness, searching for anything he could jerk from the wall and use as a weapon. There had to be something; Laura had hung enough junk on the walls of this place. The fingers of his left hand found the light switch. Lucas flipped it as he shifted his balance in readiness to strike.

The room was empty.

Lucas stared wide-eyed for a moment, seeing only a rustle of the curtains before he fell against the wall and slid to the floor, wheezing and panting from the struggle.

For the longest time, he stared at the empty room in a mindless shock.

Slowly, his breathing and heart rate returned to normal. He pushed away from the wall and shuffled to the sink, washing his face with cold water. Looking into the mirror, he saw pressure marks on his cheeks, marks that were fading rapidly.

A swirl of apprehension tightened in his stomach.

What the hell was that?

There was no rational explanation for it. None.

Lucas sat on the toilet and looked around. Nothing was out of place. Nothing amiss. Had he imagined it?

He looked into the mirror again, but the marks were gone.

Laura called, "Lucas, you okay?"

"Yep, I'm fine."

He wasn't.

He didn't know what to say, what to think. He stood slowly, closed the window, and walked back to bed, flicking the light off with a brief nervous glance over his shoulder. Slid into bed and tried to rationalize the moment in the bathroom with little success.

A ghost?

No.

He inhabited a tangible, logical world free of ghosts. Lucas didn't believe in psychics, hauntings, or the paranormal. Science and reason ruled his worldview, which left room for little else, especially evil spirits.

A panic attack or some sort of vivid waking nightmare? Was that possible?

It sounded ridiculous—though it made more sense than the super-natural, even if it was a reach. Either way, it was unsettling. Haunted house? Or losing his mind?

A strange thought intruded, forcing its way to the forefront, push-ing everything aside.

Laura did it.

She caused the attack in the bathroom.

That was irrational. Crazier than the idea of a ghost in the room. The thought came from somewhere outside his head. Senseless, but insistent.

Impossible.

Maybe it hadn't happened at all.

That he even considered the supernatural fell squarely on his mother. Her secrecy about this house gnawed at him because it didn't fit the woman he knew. He was still angry with her for the perceived dishonesty. Now he was imagining things, having weird waking dreams. Losing it.

He turned over, reached out, and ran his hand over Laura's slender waist and hip. She turned without warning, embracing him and hungrily pulling his mouth to hers.

They kissed and mauled each other with their hands, tearing nightclothes away. Lucas rolled on and into her, led by Laura's clutching arms. They pushed bodies together in ever stronger thrusts, rushing to a mutual climax, then lay breathless in a tangle of arms and legs. They stroked and cuddled each other for a while, without words, before he fell into a deep but uneasy sleep.

Fourteen

Shepherd closed his laptop for the night and poured a small glass of port wine. After a day of classes and an evening spent hacking and crashing the computer network of a Mideast terror cell, he felt weary. More and more, the move to Milwaukee felt like a mistake. He'd come, motivated by a potent premonition, a warning that a significant threat existed here. A situation he was uniquely qualified to handle.

But after the initial premonition and a few vague hints, the trail had gone cold. He wondered if he'd misunderstood, or had somehow misinterpreted the clues and moved here for no discernible reason. He needed to leave Rome, had enjoyed the summer in Milwaukee, but he wasn't looking forward to a harsh northern winter or another relocation. Shepherd slipped into a frustrating round of second-guessing.

Why would a threat from his old life be here in America?

Could his friends from the Aeldan be playing a game with him? The group occasionally engaged in pranks and tomfoolery, though this felt too elaborate. Perhaps he should have been more skeptical, waited for more information before moving. He may have foolishly allowed his intuition to trump common sense, an illogical turn from the rational philosophy he now followed. Still, such thinking wasn't helpful or mindful.

Time to meditate.

He tapped *Chopin Nocturnes* on his playlist, sat in a fat comfortable recliner in the study, and sipped his nightcap. Closed his eyes and drifted, enjoying the music and the pleasant vibe from the alcohol. Shut out doubts and concerns, focused only on the present moment, slipping into a mindful state, accepting the tinge of melancholy in his mood. That was the concept, in theory, but it was too easy to drift back to worry and the trivial, the natural background noise of the brain.

He felt old. Felt he'd foolishly allowed some of his old life into the present day. Worried he'd come here because age and senility had crept up on him and he misread the situation. Thus, the inner battle went until he soothed the anxieties, returned to the present, stayed focused, stopped second-guessing himself.

Peace.

He drank the remaining splash of port. Relaxed and drifted into the first stages of sleep.

Soon, he stood near a house in the woods by a lake. A grand structure, an old Tudor mansion. He had been feeling homesick; it must be England.

No, it was much closer. In the twilight dream state, he couldn't pull a connection until three letters appeared:

B F E

The house existed in **B F E**.

There was something odd about the house. A man wandered the halls of the Tudor manse, a farmer dressed in bib overalls and a dirty cap. Only he wasn't a man but a revenant of some sort. Something darker dwelt there as well, but remained hidden from view.

Somewhat later, he stood in a cemetery, watching the faceless blonde woman being assailed by an army of zombies. He viewed the scene dispassionately. It was dream imagery, not the least bit frightening. A clue of some sort.

Shepherd slept in that comfortable chair all night, the woman, the house, the farmer, and the letters playing in a dreamy loop. His process at work. Piece by piece, a three-dimensional scenario would gradually emerge, and he would understand. He couldn't rush it. Couldn't prod it along.

A house in the woods. The man. The woman. Some hidden entity. They were the reason he was here.

Only one question remained.

Where?

Fifteen

Laura stared out the back window of the Hall, coffee in hand, lost in thought. Fall had come, bringing the first omens of the cold season ahead. At first subtle—a scattering of crimson in the maples—the colors soon multiplied and spread in an explosion of reds and yellows as the poplars, birches, elms, and ashes joined the party. The oaks resisted but soon succumbed to the shorter days and cooler nights, harbingers of the coming winter. On the lake, geese flocked together in anticipation of the day they would fly south.

With the major projects complete, the house was fully habitable. Restored, it was an elegant country mansion that sat agreeably among the trees and the lake. Lucas had tamed the yard and planted a lawn. He was still working around the edges, cutting out deadwood and overgrowth. Mostly, it was quiet—the film crew and photographers gone until Nate completed the finishing touches.

Laura had just laid Leah down for a nap after a rough morning of crying, crabbing, and clinging. She loved the child, but these moments were tiring. Now forty-seven, she had raised two children to adulthood. It seemed easier then. She had more energy, more patience. Thank God

Leah still took naps. Still, she felt guilty when she struggled with the responsibility. Leah was the only tangible piece of Jacob that remained. Even here, she occasionally heard his laugh or remembered a random moment from his childhood. She then wandered off in tears, trying to make sense of his death, knowing there was no sense to be made of it. She felt lost, unable to heal the wounds left by his passing. The move had changed little; there was no escape from the memories. She didn't regret it though. Life was *slightly* better here.

Lucas was part of the problem. He had helped when Dana and Jacob were young, but now he did little but hunt and fish, work in the yard, and disappear most afternoons on unspecified errands. Laura knew he was working through his grief. They both were, but he acted as though his grief was greater and she resented his lackadaisical attitude.

She poured a small glass of wine, plopped down at her laptop at the kitchen table, and logged into Ancestry. Sighed. No new hints today. None for several days now. Her efforts to investigate the house and family tree floundered, starved of information.

Janice Foster hadn't returned her calls. She couldn't figure out who Sally was. As for the ghosts, they'd been here a month and the house seemed fine. Clearly, the townspeople were superstitious throwbacks to the nineteenth century.

The doorbell rang.

At the front door, the UPS lady handed her a package from Ted Summers, Lost Arrow's oldest resident and the town historian. He'd returned from out east and Carol had kindly mentioned Laura's request for information. He then called and promised to mail Laura some material. Laura stopped at Anson's store several times a week and she and Carol had become friends. Carol had recently divorced, and their friends were ignoring her. Laura understood too well how that happened.

She slit the box open and plopped down onto the sofa, but her excitement was short-lived. Filled with photocopies of articles from some long-dead local weekly, most of it was humdrum. Store openings. Store closings. Petty crime. An MD who came and went. Obits. Births. Marriages. A new road. A factory closing—

They had a factory here?

A story about the hotel going bust in the '80s. Local gossip. A few obits that might relate to the house. Even though this was what she'd asked for, nothing felt substantial. Interesting maybe, but not enlightening. Perhaps the rumors of ghosts were just that, rumors.

Laura shoved the box under the sofa.

As she walked past the fireplace, the room seemed to tip sideways. A sensation like lightning ran through her brain, followed by a fleeting, indistinct image. This episode was stronger than any of the others. She stumbled and dropped sideways onto the sofa, muttering insensibly about a woman named Sally.

She sat up a minute later and held her head in her hands.

Spat out a single word. "Shit!"

She couldn't ignore these episodes anymore.

Laura winced at the term *episode,* a word weighted with considerable baggage.

As a child, Laura suffered from a seizure disorder, experiencing momentary absence seizures and grand mal events. Diagnosed with epilepsy, she was treated with the standard medication of the day, Dilantin. When that failed to control her symptoms, the doctors mixed in newer drugs. Several years passed before they found the right cocktail to manage her disorder and the seizures ended. Still, the damage was done. Her nickname was *spazz,* and the other kids tormented her with exaggerated renditions of her attacks, flailing on the ground with comical expressions. Funny maybe—if she hadn't been the target of the ridicule. She had no friends, just a few fair-weather companions who scattered when the bullies appeared.

She learned to live with it and after a while became inured to the taunts, harassment, and teasing. Laura lived a quiet, solitary existence; read incessantly, studied hard, and routinely finished at the top of her class. That also made her a target of the bullies, but she learned to tune them out. Learned to be alone and, better still, to enjoy being alone.

As she grew older, the teasing and bullying faded. She matured from gawky child to attractive teenager, and boys took an interest. The teasing became flirtatious. The girls continued to taunt and dismiss her, but Laura decided they were jealous. By the time she finished high school, her life seemed normal. She buried the memory deeply, but Laura never forgot the pain of her childhood. It shaped her character, a tough, flinty interior seldom visible but ever present. She learned to be mindful before being mindfulness was a *thing.*

There had been a darker side to her seizures, one she refused to examine because it confused and frightened her. Occasionally, as she regained consciousness after a seizure, she would blurt things out. Often, it was gibberish. Sometimes it was a sentence, and not just a sentence, but the answer to a mystery.

"Dad, your hammer is in the grass behind the oak."

It was.

Or, "Mom, you tucked your credit cards under the front seat of your car."

She had.

Most of it was trivial. A little creepy but trivial.

Once, when she was eleven, she muttered, "Billy Mitchell's dead. They'll find him today."

They did.

Billy Mitchell had gone missing three days before. Twelve years old, he had ridden off on his bike on a warm summer day. When he didn't return home by sunset, his parents grew frantic. Friends were called. Teams of anxious and frightened parents searched houses, tree houses, and garages. By day two, with a full-scale ground operation underway, police and volunteers combed the woods and fields around town. Rumors of a sexual pervert in the area, though baseless, spread through schools, restaurants, and kitchens. When they found Billy that day, his demise was much more mundane than a predator. Billy had drowned in the local quarry.

Thereafter, Laura's mother treated her like a leper. The awkward distance between them grew during her teenage years when hormones and the tendency to rebel turned minor arguments into raging battles. By the time she left for college, they were no longer speaking.

Her father, a gentle, logical soul, had a ready explanation for everything. The hammer? She had seen it, and the *episode*—his word for her seizures—had knocked that memory loose. The credit cards? Laura had seen her mother slide them under the seat. Billy Mitchell? Easiest of all. He was missing, people were talking, and she was worried about him. No mystery there. Laura liked his logic, but she didn't really buy the story. A deep-seated fear, exacerbated by her seizures, that she was a—

freak

—never left her.

After five years seizure-free, they weaned her off the meds. She never talked about it thereafter and told no one. Not Lucas, not Dana, not Ashley. It was ancient history. That wasn't an entirely honest assessment. It still hurt to think about it. It hurt even more to talk about it. So she didn't and it remained her secret.

These recent episodes would force her to face it all over again. She would deal with it quietly, and she pondered how she might accomplish that. Lucas wouldn't likely notice. He was often gone hunting, fishing, or running errands. Keeping busy was his way of dealing with things. She missed his companionship, and it was hurting their relationship. They weren't talking enough; weren't spending enough time together. The space that opened between them after Jacob died had grown wider. Lucas became more and more aloof, almost inaccessible. She missed him and the move, once seen as a healing tonic, had done little to remedy the problem.

Discovering that she'd kept this secret all these years might further widen the gap.

Best to say nothing and deal with it on her own.

Sixteen

Lucas woke at six, slammed a cup of coffee, and trekked out to the woods before the others woke. He climbed up to his tree stand and settled in, armed with a compound bow, enjoying the solitude and morning calm in the trees.

As usual, he spent much of his time dwelling on Jacob. Lucas talked to him while sitting or wandering in the woods, caught between anger and despair that Jacob had driven drunk. Sometimes the conversations evolved to bitch sessions, Lucas chiding him for such poor judgement. Jacob returned in vivid and painful flashbacks—this morning, it was the last time they skied Vail, Jacob emerging from a snowbank laughing, face covered in snow after a wild spill. It almost seemed he could reach out and touch him. Then he was gone. Again.

He had baited the nearby clearing with apples, but the deer were having none of it. He sighed. Enough of this.

Lucas walked to the house and spent an hour cutting and splitting wood to burn off his anger and despair. It was therapy, even though it had taken him weeks to trust the new chainsaw after the incident with the last one. Then, under the guise of picking up hardware, bait, or supplies, he hopped into the pickup and drove up the fire lane and along County B to Lost Arrow.

He parked behind the White Birch and walked in, spotting Murphy and Bruce by the pool table, two of a group of people who straggled in and out of the tavern during the day. Most were unemployed or marginally employed. Murphy, in her late thirties, was slim and attractive, with long blonde hair, dark eyes, and a sly smile. She looked tough in tight, shabby jeans and a studded leather jacket, her speech littered with *fuck this* and *fuck that*. Bruce was her boyfriend, but Murphy seemed minimally loyal. She had leaned against Lucas seductively more than once. Lucas couldn't imagine cheating on Laura, but this vixen intrigued him. He felt a stirring in his loins and suspected she was aggressive in bed. Oh, to be single again.

Or not. He wasn't and had no plans to complicate his life.

Lucas put money on the pool table. "What's up?"

Bruce gave him a two-finger salute and took an empty pitcher to the bar.

"Hey, Lucas." Murphy gave him a sultry smile and set the dice cup on the table in front of him.

This afternoon habit had started harmlessly. He'd stopped here a month ago after a grueling day in the yard, cutting through a thick tangle of undergrowth. Lucas ordered a beer and watched three people shooting pool. In college, he'd excelled at the game, so on a whim, he dropped three quarters on the table. One game became five. They were a friendly group and talkative. The beer was cold. He was having more fun than he'd had in years, harking back to his school days before the stresses and commitments of a career, marriage, and fatherhood dominated his life.

Lucas rarely thought about work and realized he didn't miss it, not yet, anyway. Maybe he wouldn't. He had hated work before he quit. After twenty years of dental practice, he'd fallen into a serious funk and recognized the symptoms of career burnout overlapping with his chronic melancholy at the death of his son. His mother's passing had been the final straw. He negotiated a quick exit with his partners, walked away and hadn't looked back.

Still, he was avoiding certain realities, the gaping hole in his soul being one. Trying to grasp the reality that Jacob was gone and would never return. He was avoiding Laura and wasn't sure why, though he still had the irrational feeling she was responsible for the bizarre incident in the bathroom. Right now, he simply felt better on his own. Unless he was here, self-medicating with beer and casual conversation.

He had plans over the next few months. Pheasant hunting opened soon, followed by turkey season, then the November gun deer hunt.

As Murphy lined up her shot, she looked at Lucas, blew him an air kiss and sank the eight-ball. Bold.

Reminded him of Laura when they first met.

Seventeen

On the second Monday in October, Nate awoke at seven, washed a toasted bagel down with coffee, and organized his tools for the day. He spent the morning building drawers and shelves for the bedroom closets. Working quickly, he used reclaimed oak that matched the existing trim well. Ashley called up the stairs just after noon. "We're leaving. Sure you don't want to come?"

"Tempting, but no. I want to get this closet done today." Nate stood at the window and watched the car pull away. Laura, Leah, and Ashley were off on a shopping trip, and wouldn't return until dinnertime. Good.

Lucas left thirty minutes later. He thought he was being sneaky, but Nate knew what he was doing—spending his afternoons drinking at the White Birch. Nate secretly approved. Lucas had evolved from annoyingly responsible to day drinking. The man *needed* to loosen up. The upshot? He would be gone all afternoon.

Until now, he hadn't had an opportunity to investigate the hidden room beneath the trapdoor further. Someone was always home. He imagined finding a stash of cash and valuables within, though the money itself was immaterial. The excitement lay in the arcane nature of the room and the thrill of the hunt. For that reason, he hadn't told Ashley because Ashley would tell Laura, Laura would tell Lucas, and Lucas would take control. He always did.

Unable to detect any access on the first floor, he trotted downstairs. Nate figured the hidden space lay over the far room in the basement, beyond the furnace and utility areas.

The dirty, musty room had been a root cellar once. Old wooden shelves lined the wall, some broken, some still holding empty *Ball* pickle jars. A wine rack draped with cobwebs covered the back wall from floor to ceiling. Overhead, the electricians had rigged a single LED shop light. Nate paused and imagined the room restored as a wine cellar with a tile floor, soft lights and a circular tasting table. He felt a momentary pang of guilt. He should work on the house instead of pursuing this wild goose chase. The show producer was breathing down his neck to finish the project. Oh well.

Nate scanned the walls with a flashlight. The beam fell upon a picture frame in the corner behind the door.

Curious, he stepped closer. It was an oil painting, a portrait of an older woman dressed in vintage clothing. She wore a black gown with a white pleated collar that almost looked like a paper plate around her neck. Her face pinched and pale, framed by grey hair, her expression was grim. Probably some long-dead grandmother.

He shrugged and examined the spaces between the ceiling timbers for evidence of brick. Near the side wall, between two upright support timbers, the wooden underlay had rotted away, revealing rows of mortared brick. Going in from here wasn't the ideal approach, but with care and luck, everything might fall right into his lap.

Grabbing a sledgehammer from the storage room next door, Nate planted his feet and swung up at the bricks in looping arcs. The angle was difficult, his blows ineffective. He paused to catch his breath and was startled by the scrape of wood on stone behind him.

The portrait had moved! What the hell? Originally angled in the corner, the woman now stared at him directly.

Something hard struck a glancing blow off the back of his head and hit the floor with a thud. A puff of wind blew across his neck. Nate froze, feeling a chill in the room. No, more than that. A presence. Behind him.

He swung around.

Nothing. Just an empty room. He stared for a moment, shook his head, and laughed. Wow! He was freaking himself out. A creepy old root cellar, and now he was seeing and hearing things. Next, the old woman would leap out of the frame and chase after him!

Nate wasn't sure he even believed in ghosts, but if they existed, he felt certain this house might be the place to see one—

A glimmer of metal on the floor caught his eye.

"Holy shit!"

A gold coin the size of a quarter lay at his feet. Nate scooped it up, flipping it in his fingers. It looked ancient with a weird figure spearing a dragon on one side and a masted ship on the other. The writing was foreign, Latin probably. He grinned, feeling vindicated, and slid it into his hip pocket.

A brick had fallen, creating a hole in the brickwork. Nate grabbed the hammer and struck upwards, landing a solid blow. Bits of grit fell onto his face and another coin dropped to the floor. He swung the hammer again and caught an eyeful of dust over the top of his safety glasses. A third coin dropped.

Cool!

As he reached for it, a brick fell and hit him on the head.

"Jesus!"

This was too dangerous. The bricks overhead weren't well supported and the entire lot could fall and crush him.

Time for a different approach.

★   ★   ★

Tom finished walking a circuit of the woods near the house, ever watchful for intruders. Did it matter? The trailer-people had moved into the house and it looked like they planned to stay awhile. With them had come furniture, knickknacks, artwork, clothing, and a child. They had invaded his domain and he felt powerless to stop them.

Though he didn't know who they were, one of them looked like his old friend, Alan MacKenzie. He tried to eavesdrop on conversations but heard none of it. Only rarely did he understand the living, their voices murky and muffled, as if under water.

He trudged to the house to complete his loop of the property, a path he'd walked since his arrival here and one he felt compelled to continue despite the people squatting in Elizabeth's house. He stepped through the basement wall and stopped in shock.

Damn it!

One of them stood in the root cellar looking for a way into the brick chamber. The man hefted a sledgehammer and eyed the underside of the hidden room, then swung upwards several times, knocking a brick loose.

Opening that room was a terrible idea. He needed to do something, so he focused on the painting in the corner and gave it a shove, moving it with a satisfying *scrape*.

The guy stopped, startled.

Good.

Tom then watched him scoop up a gold coin from the floor.

Shit!

The man grabbed the hammer, swung upward again and another coin fell. Tom panicked. What could he do? Nothing good would come of this.

Another swing, another coin. A brick then fell and hit the guy on the head. Ouch!

The man stopped and seemed to reconsider.

Good.

Hoping to knock him off balance, to scare him away, Tom shoved him hard, like the push that sent the kid flying off the roof. Nothing happened. Even though he'd moved the picture moments ago, his efforts push the man were now fruitless. It made no sense, like so much in his world.

The man looked determined to get inside, gathering more tools with a stubborn air about him.

Tom felt helpless. His shoulders slumped in defeat. Nothing he tried was working.

Exhausted and in need of rest, he sighed and slipped into the ether.

★   ★   ★

Nate peeked out the window. The driveway was still clear.

Good.

He could be childish and realized he was being childish now. Sneaking around, hiding this discovery was silly. Still, Lucas had a knack of swooping in and stealing his thunder. Though he couldn't prove it, he felt certain Lucas had been Mom's favorite. He skipped college because Lucas went to dental school—chose a trade because Lucas became a doctor. When they were younger, if Nate found something cool, Lucas grabbed it and ran home to show Mom. Nate learned to protect his finds and, all after these years, still guarded them.

Nate considered the room from every angle. The entry from above was too narrow. The left corner of the sitting room was an imposing wall of plaster spread over the brick beneath. A door there seemed unlikely. On the opposite side, the paneled wall of the Hall by the fireplace made perfect sense. There had to be a door hidden behind the paneling. Nate searched every inch of it for a lever or release, but found nothing.

The solution was simple. Carefully remove the paneling and he would be in.

Armed with a small pry bar, Nate worked the joints in the paneling, teasing exposed edges, easing segments free. It was a delicate and tedious operation. The wall was built with hand hewn pieces of wood like a parquet floor, held in place with glue and dowels but not a single nail. It took almost thirty minutes to open a two-by-two section in the woodwork. To his dismay, he now faced a brick wall.

Rather ironic, he mused. Perhaps this wasn't a hiding place. Maybe it was a bricked-up chimney or some other abandoned space of no importance. Still, he'd come too far to quit. He *had* to look inside even if it was empty.

Nate grabbed a chisel and hammer from his toolbox and attacked the mortar between the bricks, a tedious and gritty task. By the time he'd loosened and removed the first brick, ten minutes had ticked away on the grandfather clock.

Jesus, this is gonna take forever!

At this rate, it would be midnight before he finished. That wouldn't do. Time for brute force. He grabbed the sledgehammer and swung a wide arc, striking the center of the bricks. The impact shook the wall; a framed print fell to the floor.

"Jesus Christ!"

Somewhere, a door slammed and he noticed a faint bass tone resonating through the house.

What the hell?

A chill passed through him as he remembered the panic attack he'd experienced upstairs. Then the floor shuddered and a lamp tipped over, landing at his feet. But he was angry and refused to be stymied now.

Sweating, his face pasted with grit and brick particles, Nate swung at the bricks again and again. The center bowed inward as the cracked mortar joints grated against each other. Three looping swings sent the center group of bricks tumbling into the hidden room, and another couple of whacks knocked the rest loose, leaving a jagged opening. Nate let the sledgehammer slide to the ground and leaned on the handle, gasping and wheezing. Another door slammed upstairs.

What was with the doors?

Nate looked around. Fine dust hung in the air, settling on every object in the room. Mortar chips littered the floor, sent flying by the hammer. It would take an hour just to clean up the mess. A vision of an empty room beyond the bricks haunted him. Perhaps the only coins in the room were already in his pocket.

He looked inside but could see nothing. It was too dark. Afraid his work had been for nothing, he reached for the flashlight—

The front door opened and closed. Footsteps sounded on the hardwood floor.

Damn it!

Someone was home.

Eighteen

Lucas strode into the Hall and stopped, staring in stunned disbelief.

The room was in shambles, grit and chunks of brick everywhere. Nate stood, covered in dust near a jagged hole in the wall, a cheesy grin on his face.

"Jesus Christ, Nate. What the hell are you doing?"

"Shut up and listen." Nate quickly outlined his discovery: a hidden room, gold coins in the basement, his conclusion that some treasure lay inside.

Lucas was skeptical. "So, what'd you find?"

"I don't know yet. I was about to look when you came in."

Lucas reached for the light.

"Not so fast, dude. I found it. I'm looking first."

Nate flicked the light on, leaned over, and stuck his head into the hole. The light flashed about, then Lucas heard a grumbled "Jesus Christ." Nate backed out and tossed the light to Lucas, a sour expression on his face.

Lucas knew what he'd find. Nothing. Not a damn thing. Nate was famous for his wild goose chases. In childhood, he was forever looking for buried treasure; then it was money stashed in the old houses he remodeled. He was persistent, given he'd never found more than a few dollars. Lucas leaned in and peered into the dark, flashing the beam about. The space was about three feet by four, the air damp with a vaguely unpleasant odor. All four walls and ceiling were solid brick.

A dusty pile of rumpled fabric lay in the corner, a dark sack or robe perhaps. The room was otherwise empty. No bundles of cash. No gold coins.

Lucas pulled himself farther into the room.

"What are you doing?"

Lucas ignored him, curious about the garment.

"Careful, man."

What was it doing here? Perhaps the coins were under it? Dragging his feet into the room, he crouched atop the loose bricks on the floor and reached to push the fabric aside.

It crumbled to dust and loose tatters. Lucas recoiled slightly, startled. How long had it been here? What was this room? He sifted carefully through the edge of the dust, his fingers brushing across something cold and metallic. He pushed the debris aside and frowned.

It was an old book, leather bound and trimmed with brass corners.

"Hey, take this!" He handed the book to Nate and reached into the dust again as the bricks beneath his feet settled with a slight grating sound.

He continued probing through the dust, feeling other chunks of debris buried there, almost like—

The floor gave way.

He grabbed a hold of the ledge of brick where Nate broke through the wall with one hand; twisted and swung his other hand up, gripping tight as the floor and everything else tumbled into the basement. He yelled, "Nate, grab my arm! Hurry!"

Nate, already reaching toward him, grabbed his arm and helped him through the hole in the wall.

"What happened?" Nate said, wide-eyed.

"The floor gave way, genius," Lucas said angrily. "Might've had something to do with you banging on it with a sledgehammer."

"I told you to be careful."

Lucas threw him a withering look and extended his hand. "Give me the book."

Nate obliged, throwing Lucas an irritated look of resignation.

The dusty leather cover was blank. The inside was filled with faded handwriting in a foreign language, maybe Latin. Lucas had never seen anything like it.

Nate said, "Yeah, well, we'd better clean this mess up."

"We? This is your big adventure, bro. You clean it up."

Lucas sat and paged through the book while Nate pieced the paneling back together, covering the hole and restoring the wall.

"So, what's in the book?"

"I don't know. It's written in a language I don't recognize," Lucas said. "Let's keep this to ourselves for now."

"What? Why?"

"Because otherwise, Laura will take it over."

"Kind of like you're doing?"

"That's different." Lucas shrugged, then glanced at Nate. "When did you plan on telling me about this room, bro?"

Nate shrugged. "Soon."

Lucas gave him a good-natured shove. "Liar."

"Whatever. Come on, help me clean up."

They dusted and vacuumed, finishing as Laura, Ashley, and Leah strolled through the archway.

Laura tossed her bags onto a chair. "What are you guys doing?"

"Uh—fixing an electrical problem. We're just wrapping up," Nate said.

★　★　★

Later that night, after Laura and Ashley had gone to bed, Nate and Lucas sat in the Hall. The room was lit by two small table lamps and a fire, a warm glow radiating from the burning oak and maple logs. There were occasional pops and sparks from the fire, the sparks kept safely within the hearth by a heavy screen suspended from an iron bar. They'd discussed installing glass doors on the fireplace but opted to go with a classic open hearth.

They had arranged the room into three sitting areas. At the far end, chairs and recliners faced a sixty-inch flat screen hidden behind folding panels. The center room comprised two sofas and a love seat set around a large Persian rug facing west out the tall center windows of the Hall, the space accented with various end tables, a coffee table, and several of Laura's Tiffany-style lamps. They sat at the north end, where a semi-circle of comfy stuffed armchairs faced the fireplace.

Lucas paged through the book but could make no sense of it. Other than numbers that could be dates, the writing was indecipherable.

"You figure any of that out?" Nate said.

"Nope. What about the coins?"

"Nothing yet." Nate was busy on his iPad researching them.

"How many did you find?"

"Three. And they're mine."

"You can have them." Lucas rolled his eyes. "Jesus! How old are you?"

Lucas reached for his laptop and flipped it open. He pulled the occasional legible word from the book and searched for it in Google. Some words brought *Not Found* or a generic *Did you mean...?*

Some words came back as *Old English*, but he didn't really understand what that meant so he clicked into Wikipedia, which said:

> *The language of the Anglo-Saxons (up to about 1150), a highly inflected language with a largely Germanic vocabulary, very different from modern English.*

He couldn't translate the book himself, that was clear. Wasn't sure it was worth it, though it raised many questions. How had something this old come to be in the house? Family heirloom? He searched further and discovered that handwritten texts in Old English were rare and valuable. This went beyond a family history. Hidden as it was, perhaps it had been stolen.

"They're Angels," Nate said.

"What?"

"The coins. I snapped a pic and did an image search. They're called Angels or Angelots, English coins from the fifteenth century." He paused and tapped his screen. "It says: *the obverse carried a depiction of St. Michael slaying a dragon, the reverse, a ship. It was a popular coin and often worn around the neck to ward off scrofula,* whatever that is."

"This is bizarre." Lucas said. "This book is hundreds of years old. Those coins are hundreds of years old. Doesn't that seem odd to you?"

"Maybe. I don't know. Must be family heirlooms. Does it matter?"

"I don't know, but you should handle those more carefully."

Nate shrugged and stacked them on the coffee table.

It did matter. Nate had focused on the coins, but these old things were an intriguing puzzle. Had Mom and Dad known about them? It deepened the mystery about his parents.

He had only a vague memory of his father and was still angry with his mother for hiding the house from him. Why had she kept so many secrets? Why had she deceived him? Though irrational, he saw her secrets as lies, a betrayal by someone he had loved and respected deeply. Now he could find no resolution for his feelings—he couldn't confront her and demand an explanation. She could have explained the book and coins had they known. Now she was dead, and the answer was likely lost forever. He then felt guilty for his irritable train of thought. He missed her immensely and it seemed surreal that he'd become the family elder with her passing.

This introspection brought him to the root of his angst—his father. The man was a mythical character in his life, an invisible but ever-present and guiding figure.

Your father would have done this or *your father said* were the words that prefaced the nuggets of wisdom that formed the backdrop of his childhood. Now he wondered how long the house had been in the family. Laura had been researching; he was curious about her efforts. These things—the book and the coins—were pieces of a puzzle. A puzzle he needed to solve. He wasn't sharing this with Laura, not just yet. Lucas needed to figure this out himself and hoped to learn something about his mother and father in the process.

"So, what'd you pick up on your hardware run today?" Nate asked, a sarcastic edge to his voice.

"Why?"

"Because you don't always come back with hardware."

"So? I've had more important things to do." Lucas lit one of Nate's little Cohibas, blowing the smoke into the fireplace. Since when had Nate become the righteous one?

"Like what? Getting wasted every afternoon at the White Birch?" Nate's eyes widened in patent disapproval. "And when did you start smoking?"

"What's it to you? I have a little time off com—"

Somewhere, a door slammed. Then the iron bar and screen covering the fireplace crashed to the hearth with a resounding *bang*.

Nate and Lucas both jumped.

Lucas said, "What the hell?"

"Jesus! That was crazy!"

Lucas inspected the iron supports, which had somehow rotated ninety degrees, allowing the bar to slip free. Nate had used a sledge-hammer on the wall earlier. That seemed like reasonable cause and effect.

Ashley appeared wide-eyed at the archway. "What was that?"

"A door slammed and the fireplace screen fell," Nate said.

"What? Why?"

"The door? Wind probably." Nate pointed to the screen. "This? No idea."

"Let's go to bed. I'll fix it in the morning." Lucas broke the logs apart and sprayed water onto the embers. On impulse, he tried to twist one of the supports, but it wouldn't budge, even when he brought two hands to bear.

He shook his head.

How had they turned at all?

Nineteen

Lucas awoke as the dawn light touched the antique bedroom windows, turning them soft, glowing red. He made coffee, quickly fried two eggs, grabbed his gear, and strolled out to the dock. Loading tackle and bait into the seventeen-foot Alumacraft, he cruised to a spot on the far shore where he'd had some luck, and dropped a line into the water.

He enjoyed the quiet solitude on the lake. The day was windless, the sky clear, the air crisp—a beautiful fall day. It was heaven.

But Lucas could only think about the book, and the more he contemplated, the more he felt compelled to solve the mystery. What was the language? Who had left it behind? Something about the room bothered him, but he couldn't put a finger on it. Curiosity finally trumped the desire to fish. He steered to shore, determined to research the book instead of wasting his afternoon at the White Birch Inn.

At the house, Laura, Ashley, and Leah sat in the kitchen, eating breakfast. He exchanged the usual pleasantries and walked upstairs to their bedroom with his laptop and phone. After several searches, he zeroed in on the Languages Department at Milwaukee University, and pulled a name from their website. Professor Clyde Gregory's listed specialty was English. He tapped the number in and a man with a baritone voice answered.

"Hello, Professor Gregory speaking."

Lucas introduced himself and briefly described the book. He mentioned a few of the words he'd translated, uncertain whether he was pronouncing them correctly.

"It sounds like an older form of English, but it's difficult to say without seeing the book and the text," Gregory said. "You say it's handwritten?"

"Yes, all of it."

"Where do you live? Can you bring it to the university sometime?"

"Um, sure. How about today?" Lucas had nothing better to do.

"That would be good, actually—if you can be here in two or three hours."

"Sure." Lucas jotted down the address and office number. He yelled toward the kitchen. "Hon, I'm going out for a couple of hours."

Grabbing the book, he bounded out the door.

★   ★   ★

Nate also woke early but remained in bed, floating between sleep and wakefulness, thinking about the coins, the room, and the book. Finally, he turned to roll out of bed. A slender arm wrapped around him.

"Where are you going?"

"Nowhere in particular."

"Then what's the hurry?" Ashley said with a sultry grin. She crawled on top of him, kissed him hungrily, and aroused him quickly with her mouth. She then rolled over, pulled him on top, grinding her hips sensuously.

An hour later, Nate slipped out of bed. Ashley had fallen back to sleep. High maintenance or not, her fondness for sex was one reason he loved that woman so. Nate pulled on a pair of work jeans and a grubby T-shirt, quietly left the house, and drove away in the Tahoe.

After stopping for coffee, he went to a coin shop in West Bend, looking for confirmation of their age, origin, and value. He wasn't sure he wanted to sell them, thinking more about mounting and displaying them.

Frazier's Coin and Stamp was a small shop sandwiched between a furniture store and a hair salon, part of a confluent line of small businesses. A clapboard facade ran along the length of the building at various levels like an ill-conceived battlement.

A tall, balding man was busy examining coins with a loupe at the counter. Nate set the gold coins down and waited patiently. The dealer picked up one coin, holding it carefully by the rough edges. He turned it only once, then examined the other two.

"Angelots. These are exceptional pieces—where'd you get them?"

"I found them—in my house." Nate then decided his explanation sounded sketchy. What could he say? It was true. "What are they worth?"

"Four or five thousand, I'm sure. I don't have a market for this type of coin. I can only offer you their value in gold."

"That sounds like a bad idea."

"I'd have to agree," the dealer said.

"How about eBay?"

"Worth a try."

As Nate pulled the seatbelt across his chest, he saw the dealer staring at him intently through the glass door as he tapped a number into his phone.

Something about the guy's expression bothered him.

Hope that's not a problem.

Twenty

The streets around the campus were jammed with parked cars. Lucas parked in a *No Parking* zone because he felt lucky. He walked to the languages building, a bland edifice of brick from the '60s, and followed the directory to the second floor and the office of Professor Clyde Gregory.

An assistant checked his progress and then showed him into the office. An older man sat behind a large desk, wearing a dark sport coat over a turtleneck. He had a bushy white moustache, rather wild swept-back hair, round horn-rimmed glasses with the aura of a mad scientist about him. Framed black-and-white sports prints, mostly related to baseball and football, filled the walls of his office. The aroma of pipe tobacco lingered.

"Mr. MacKenzie?"

"Yes, Lucas MacKenzie."

They shook hands. Gregory waved to a chair.

"Have a seat. Tell me about this book of yours."

Lucas sat and placed the book on the desk. He briefly explained the discovery of the hidden space in the house, the book, and the three

English coins called Angels.

"Angels? I've never heard of them—though I'm not a coin enthusiast." Gregory reached for the book. "May I?"

"Yes, please do."

Gregory opened the book, handling it with great deference, and gently turned the first few pages. He nodded, frowned, pursed his lips, shook his head—it was almost entertaining. Finally, he said, "Germanic, Saxon, somewhere in there."

"What?"

"Anglo-Saxon..." It was almost a question.

Lucas nodded in agreement, feeling only confusion.

"Anglo-Saxon, Old English—I think this is Old English."

"Can you read it?" Lucas asked.

"No. None of it. It's not only Old English, but it's handwritten in a script peculiar to the era. I can read basic Old English if it's printed in a modern font. This might as well be Latin. Actually, I would do better with Latin."

Old English, Anglo-Saxon? Lucas understood none of it. "How old is that book?"

"If it's genuine, perhaps a thousand years old."

"A thousand years?"

"It's possible, though it doesn't seem likely. Texts from that era are extremely rare, though this isn't my area of expertise."

The mystery deepened with no answers in sight. "So it's valuable?"

"Probably."

"But you don't know how to translate it?"

"No. Afraid not," Gregory said. "I know someone who can. I'm certain this would interest him if you wanted to pursue this further."

"I do." Lucas leaned forward. "Who?"

"Doctor Shepherd, the head of Medieval Studies. He's a renowned expert in the old languages of Great Britain. Indeed, he's spent most of his life teaching in Europe. There's probably not a man alive who has a greater knowledge of the old European languages."

It sounded like a sales pitch for the English Department. "Is he in today?"

"I'm afraid not," Gregory said sadly, as if he too would have liked an immediate translation. "Doctor Shepherd is away at the moment. He's a guest lecturer somewhere on the West Coast—UCLA, I think. We expect him back in a week. If you'd give me an opportunity to copy a few of the pages, I'll show them to him when he returns."

"Sure. Thank you."

Lucas bristled as he left the language facility. Having committed to pursuing this, he wanted a quick resolution, and had impatiently expected the answers now. Instead, he would have to wait a week or two before receiving any answer at all.

His mood deepened further when he found a parking ticket under the wiper blade, flapping in the breeze.

Twenty-One

Laura woke early, showered, and then heard Leah calling. Standing at the side of her crib, Leah broke into a toothy grin and threw her arms upwards as Laura peeked through the door, a silent plea to be rescued from the prison that was her crib.

"Good morning, baby," Laura said with a smile. She plucked her from bed, hugging her lovingly, and gazed into her big blue eyes. "You know something, kid? There are times I don't know what I'd do without you."

Leah rewarded Laura with a crooked grin. Together, they marched downstairs to the kitchen.

"Morning," Ashley said absently. She was sitting at the table sipping coffee, playing on her phone. Bright sunlight poured through the windows.

Laura whipped up a bowl of oatmeal and set it before Leah. "Any plans today?"

"Work on the blog for a couple of hours."

"When's this project running on HGTV?"

"I don't know," Ashley said, rolling her eyes. "Nate has to finish it first."

After dressing Leah, she sat in the Hall on her tablet while Leah played nearby. Continuing to research their family trees in Ancestry, her tree had blossomed. Laura received dozens of new hints daily. She had traced several of her lineages back to the Colonies, including an eighth great-grandfather who had sailed on the Mayflower.

On Lucas's side, she remained stuck at his paternal grandparents. Searches yielded nothing. Somehow, his family had eluded county and state records, church archives, and the national census. She found plenty on Elizabeth's side, but she really wanted the MacKenzie history. Who were they? Where had they come from? When did they arrive?

Lucas called from the foyer, "Hon, I'm going out for a couple of hours."

"Okay." Laura shrugged. She knew what he was doing. If that's how he chose to spend his afternoons, fine. He'd sold his practice, spent a couple of intense months working on the house and now, without obligations, he could hunt, fish, and waste a few hours drinking beer and playing pool. She assumed it was a phase that would pass. Soon, he would tire of that routine and head off in search of work or some other adventure. They gave each other considerable freedom in life, and she had no desire to be the controlling wife who questioned her husband's every move.

With her contributions to the house complete, she needed something to do. Laura had pestered Lucas to help her set up her stained-glass equipment and a small play area for Leah in the basement. There was a large room with a stone floor at the bottom of the stairs that had once been a kitchen. It looked like the ideal space for her hobbies, and she decided they were doing it tomorrow before he left for the afternoon.

★   ★   ★

Just after noon, Laura and Ashley sat in the front yard chatting while Leah ambled and stumbled around them beneath the warm October sun.

Nate pulled into the drive and walked around the corner of the Tahoe a moment later. "What's up?"

"Where have you—?" Ashley stopped and gazed up the drive. A light blue squad car pulled into the drive behind the Tahoe, the words *Auburn County Sheriff* printed across the doors. An overweight cop stepped from the car, slid a hat on and walked toward them, sizing up the house as he did so.

He spoke with the official tone cops used for official matters. "Are you Nathan MacKenzie?"

"I am."

"You were in West Bend today, at Frazier's Coin and Stamp?"

"I was." Nate frowned. "Is there a problem?"

"You tell me. The coins, are they yours?"

"They are."

"Can I see them?"

They stepped inside, and Nate led the cop toward the kitchen while Ashley and Laura took Leah to the Hall to wait.

Laura looked at Ashley. "So what's Nate up to? What are these coins the cop was asking about?"

"I have no idea—and I'm not thrilled about it," Ashley said angrily. "Where's Lucas?"

"The White Birch, probably."

"Something's going on here."

A few minutes later, the front door slammed, and Lucas walked into the Hall with a puzzled expression.

"What's going on? Why are the cops here?" He pointed to the corner where Leah was busy pulling the leaves off a parlor palm. "Do you always let her do that?"

"Damn. All right, Leah. Come on, nap time." She turned to Lucas. "Get her some water while I change her, then you can tell *us* what's going on. And *no*, I don't always let her do that."

By the time she had tucked Leah into bed, the sheriff was leaving. They all converged on the Hall at the same time.

"They thought I might be a thief," Nate said, placing the coins on the coffee table. "Apparently, I look a little sketchy."

"Dude, you should be more careful with those."

"That's what the dealer said."

Laura picked up one of the coins. "What are these and where'd they come from?"

"What happened?" Lucas said.

"I went to West Bend to check the coins out," Nate said. "As I figured, they're Angels, worth about five grand each. Turns out someone ripped off a bunch of gold coins in a burglary a few months back. These weren't a match."

"Where did you get these?" Laura said again, a tad sharper.

Ashley said, "Yeah, what's going on here?"

Lucas and Nate shared a brief, knowing look. Laura caught it.

Laura planted her hands on her hips. "All right, guys. What's going on?"

Nate explained how he'd discovered the trap door upstairs, which led to the basement, and finally the hole in the wall—the supposed *electrical problem.*

"So you guys discovered those coins and an old book, and you decided to keep it to yourselves?" Ashley said accusingly. "Excuse me, but—what the hell!"

Pointing to Nate, Lucas said sheepishly, "It was his idea."

"Jesus, how old are you guys?"

"So where's the book?" Laura said.

"Oh, I left it in the truck—"

"The truck? Why in the truck?"

Lucas described his trip to Milwaukee and the meeting with Professor Gregory, then ran to the truck to retrieve the book.

When he returned, as Laura reached for it, her fingers touched the brass binding. A shock jolted up her arm, followed by a brief mental lapse as the room seemed to skew sideways. A subliminal image flashed in her mind and evaporated. A pitchfork? Her fingers slipped off the book and she dropped it.

Lucas caught the book mid-fall. "Jesus, Laura. Careful!"

The episode and his sharp tone left her off balance. She staggered and nearly fell.

Lucas, now concerned, said, "You okay?"

She couldn't speak. Still dizzy, she sat down hard. After a moment, she felt fine.

"I am. I don't know what happened. I got a shock, like static electricity from the book."

Lucas looked skeptical. "Really?"

Laura nodded. She reached for the book, and when she touched it, nothing happened. The dark shadow of her childhood epilepsy intruded again as she opened the book, but she pushed it away. She would deal with that soon enough.

As Laura carefully paged through the handwritten pages, she could read none of it, the text unintelligible. It was old, possibly important, and probably valuable. It wasn't some pioneer diary.

"So what did this Professor Gregory say about this?"

"He said it was old."

"Lucas!"

"He couldn't read any of it. Apparently, it's Old English or Anglo-Saxon or something like that."

"Old what?" Ashley said with a furrowed brow.

"Old English," Laura said. "The language people spoke in England a thousand years ago."

"Well, aren't you a smarty pants."

"I was an English major, sweetie." She patted Ashley's cheek. "So now what?"

"They have a guy who can translate the book, but he's gone all week. They'll call me."

"What are we doing about dinner?" Ashley said.

"Going out."

Laura hoped she'd covered the brief episode while handling the book. A reminder she needed to address the problem soon. She had scheduled a trip to Illinois, ostensibly to visit Dana, but also to see her neurologist for a consultation and an EEG. She hoped the testing would reveal no major issues, but speculation was pointless. Still, she didn't want to deal with that again. Lucas would wonder why she'd hidden it from him. He might be angry and she now realized there had been no good reason to keep it secret. This latest lapse shook her confidence further, and she felt vaguely depressed.

She tried to shake the feeling off as she changed for dinner, but her melancholy gave way to an anxiety that she was losing her mind.

Twenty-Two

Shepherd was about to close his laptop when an email came in from Gregory at the university. Shepherd had flown to San Francisco primarily to attend a hacking conference, the guest lectures at UCSF a convenient cover for this trip. His room overlooked the Embarcadero just north of the Bay Bridge and it was one in the morning, three a.m. in Milwaukee. Why was Gregory awake at this hour?

The email contained two attached photographs. He stared at them, puzzled, until realized they were handwritten documents in an obscure dialect of Old English. The faded script was difficult to decipher. He needed the original, a powerful light, and a magnifier.

Shepherd turned to Gregory's email for further explanation.

The story sounded outlandish. A man had walked into the English Department with a book written entirely in what Gregory correctly had surmised was Old English. The odds of such a thing were astronomical. Books written in Old English did not appear out of the blue. Virtually all known texts were in museums or major libraries. Now, someone had just strolled in with a text handwritten in Old English? The most likely explanation was simple—the book was stolen. He wished he was back in Milwaukee where he could deal with the issue directly.

Kenric studied the photos again. The Old English dialect looked like Mercian, his native tongue. It read like a diary and seemed mundane except for its great antiquity. He dashed off a few emails to friends in England inquiring about any recent thefts of Old English texts. He sent Gregory an email expressing interest, but not his suspicions. With that, he closed the laptop and slipped into bed.

He couldn't sleep.

The documents disturbed him in some intangible way. Something about the dialect, the handwriting. Resigned to the insomnia, frustrated he didn't have the originals to peruse, he poured a small glass of port and sat on the floor in Lotus pose. Closed his eyes. Cleared his mind and quietly repeated his mantra, seeking the calm of a meditative state.

Without warning, a powerful wave washed over him. The room seemed to twist and shudder. Shepherd put a hand out to steady himself as he lost his balance. At first he thought it was an earthquake, but the hanging corner lamp remained motionless. The tremor was imaginary.

A brass and leather-bound book appeared in his mind.

A sign, finally.

Taking a slow, deep breath, he flexed his fingers. Relaxed.

He understood. The book would reveal the location of the house. It was the last link connecting the woman, the house, the revenant, and the hidden entity into a unified whole.

He returned to bed but sleep still eluded him. The nature of that unified whole remained a puzzle, and a tendril of unease twisted in his belly as he pondered that hidden presence. It must be powerful to draw him from so far away. Was this something he wanted to pursue? It felt risky and dangerous, though risk had never deterred him in the past. Besides, this was the reason he'd come to America.

Curiosity slowly supplanted anxiety. He needed to know where this was leading.

Suddenly, he couldn't wait to return to Milwaukee.

Twenty-Three

The next day, Laura awoke with a firm sense of purpose. Having pestered Lucas to organize her workshop for weeks, she grabbed him fresh off the fishing boat and insisted he do it today. They spent half a day organizing a stained-glass work area in the room at the bottom of the stairs. After setting up the workbenches, she organized her glass and tools: soldering irons, glass cutters, and glass trimmers.

The room was large, square, and approximated the footprint of the kitchen and dining room above. A door in the far left corner led outside. On the opposite wall, a door opened on a hallway running the length of the house under the Hall. There were two rooms—one that housed the furnace, water heaters, electrical gear, and storage for boxes from the move, and a root cellar at the far end.

While she worked on smaller details, Lucas found a piece of carpeting and laid out a play area for Leah. He also set up the portable crib so she could nap while Laura worked. They exchanged idle chitchat about the house, the move, the weather, Leah.

Laura asked, "What have you been doing in the afternoon?"

"Oh, a bunch of stuff. Hardware runs—parts, tools, bits. Fishing gear, bait."

Not necessarily a lie, but not the truth either. Laura let it go for now.

Laura raised her eyebrows. "When will we hear more about the book?"

"Not sure. Sounded like Gregory planned to email him some of it."

"Well, I want to know what it says too." Laura pointed a finger. "And no more secrets, okay?"

"Yes, boss lady." Lucas bowed slightly.

With the room mostly complete, Lucas took off for the afternoon. The weather had turned stormy, a steady rain falling, pushed by gusty winds in waves against the windows. Leah started rubbing her eyes, so Laura laid her down and spent the afternoon laying out a lamp she had started in Illinois—almost a hundred pieces of glass she needed to wrap with copper foil prior to soldering.

★　★　★

Later, after Leah was in bed for the night, Laura worked on the lamp for a few hours before retiring to the Hall.

The room was dark. Everyone had gone to bed. She couldn't remember anyone saying goodnight, not even Lucas. Oh well. She opened her Kindle and read for a few minutes, but the book failed to grab her attention. Time for bed. Laura turned the lights off and walked to the kitchen for a sip of soda before heading upstairs.

Outside, the storm had broken. A cold gibbous moon shone through gaps in the clouds, illuminating the kitchen alternately light and dark like a ghostly neon sign. Laura opened the refrigerator and reached in.

There was faint footfall at the bottom of the basement stairs.

Her hand froze on the Pepsi bottle, her stomach churning and fluttering with fear, breath held in tight, as if she had been suddenly cast into stone.

Another muffled footstep. Someone was in the basement, in her work area. Had they come in the back door? They were inconsistent about locking doors at night. Probably not the best policy.

Torn by indecision, Laura wanted to run upstairs to Lucas and safety, but morbid curiosity pulled her toward the stairs, to peek, to see who—or what—was there. If she ran upstairs, she might never know. She tried to rein in her fear.

An owl hooted somewhere nearby.

A faint rustle of fabric. Laura eased her hand from the fridge and took hesitant steps toward the door, willing absolute silence to her movements. She stopped and slid her hand into the partially open dishwasher, finding what she wanted immediately—the solid wooden handle of a carving knife. Thus armed, she crept to the stairs and listened.

Another footfall. And something else, a faint but persistent hum somewhere in the house.

She flipped the light on, knife ready. "Who's down there?"

Silence.

A muted step, and another. They were ignoring her.

Feeling committed—emboldened—she inched down the stairs.

A little louder, she said, "Who's there? I'm armed!"

No breath sounds, nothing. Just that odd humming noise. The furnace?

A faint shuffle of leather on stone.

As she reached the bottom of the stairs and turned—her heart now threatening to leap from her chest—the door to the back hallway eased shut. She hesitated, stuck somewhere between fight and flight, then walked to the door with silent steps. The furnace sound grew louder as she approached.

Placing her fingers on the handle, Laura eased the door open, praying the hinges wouldn't squeak.

At first, the passage was dark, too dark to see. The moon then peered through a break in the clouds, bathing the hallway in grey-white light.

Laura drew in a sharp breath with a barely audible gasp.

She caught just a glimpse of a woman, oblivious to her gaze. She was short, wearing a gathered blouse and a flowing layered skirt that brushed the stone floor. Long grey hair flowed down her back. Whatever Laura expected, it wasn't this little old woman slipping through the far door. The hall fell dark as clouds covered the moon.

Softly, Laura spoke. "Who are you?"

Silence.

A name came to Laura in an unexpected flash: Anna Flecher.

Why did that name sound familiar?

Her anxiety rose, the knife hand quivering. Be it intuition or frightful imagination, Laura wondered if the visitor really was an old woman—or something else. Feared that if the woman turned, her face would be gone, replaced by festering dead flesh, crawling with maggots, a sight that would drive her crazy. The knife suddenly felt worthless in her hand.

She tried to say *Anna* but only a faint "ah" escaped her dry mouth.

The far door closed and the low-pitched hum ceased.

A hand dropped onto her shoulder.

Laura jumped, letting out a sharp scream.

Lucas stood there, his eyebrows furrowed. "What are you doing?"

"Jesus, Lucas! You scared the crap out of me!"

"I can see that." His eyes widened. "What's with the knife? And who were you talking to?"

"There's someone in that room." Laura, still shaking, pointed to the root cellar.

"What?" Suddenly alert, he glanced down the hallway. "Did you see who it was?"

"Not really. It's an old woman."

"An old woman?" He regarded Laura curiously. "Well, she's stuck now."

Nate came up behind them. "What's going on?"

"Intruder, supposedly. Laura says there's an old woman in that room."

"What?"

Lucas shrugged and they walked down the hallway. He pushed the door open, slapped the light switch, and an LED shop light popped on.

The room was empty.

Other than a pile of bricks, the shelving, the wine rack, and an old painting in the corner, the room was empty. The one small leaded window didn't open. Lucas shook his head. There was nowhere to hide, no way out of the room.

The woman had vanished.

Laura stood, dumbfounded. A deep shudder rushed down her spine as the profound realization struck her.

"Oh, Jesus Christ," she murmured. She put her hand to her chest, feeling a second deep chill pass through her. There was nothing rational about this. Nate and Lucas made a pointless search of the room, then looked to Laura for an answer.

"I suppose you think you saw a ghost," Lucas said, his tone keenly skeptical.

"I don't know, Lucas. I saw what I saw."

Nate spoke gently. "What'd you see, Laura?"

Laura described the woman, and Nate looked thoughtful. Not dismissive like her husband. Nate looked to the floor, then the hole overhead, as if pondering something. Laura followed his gaze to a pile of bricks on the floor. Why were they there? She looked up and saw the gaping hole at the bottom of the hidden brick room. She pointed and said, "What about that?"

Lucas looked up, shook his head, and barked. "You see anything up there?"

"No." She didn't like his tone.

"Did you see her face?" Nate asked.

Laura shook her head.

With that, they shuffled upstairs to their respective rooms.

Laura lay in bed, staring at the ceiling. Lucas tossed and turned once and fell asleep.

Just as well.

Her anger smoldered. Lucas had all but accused her of hysteria.

Ass.

He hadn't seen the woman. What did he know?

A ghost? Was that possible? A nameless anxiety in the pit of her stomach said, *Yes. Yes, it was.*

How did she feel about the house being haunted? Why was she even asking the question? She had never given the subject much thought. Still, the old woman had seemed neither dangerous nor threatening. Then she'd simply vanished!

Poof!

Was that what the townspeople were talking about?

Eventually, Laura fell into an uneasy sleep, the vision of the old woman vivid in her dreams.

Twenty-Four

Laura awoke to the sound of Leah crying. She had been dreaming, standing in the hallway, straining to see the face of the old woman walking from her as a tendril of anxiety twisted in her stomach. Who was she?

ghost

Anna Flecher? Who was Anna Flecher?

ghost

How had she disappeared?

ghost

Enough! She rolled out of bed, trying to shake the unease. Leah sat crying and held her arms out when Laura walked in. Together, they went down to the kitchen for breakfast. Ashley sat with a cup of coffee, engrossed in her tablet.

"Morning," she said absently. "See any more ghosts?"

"Not funny. And no."

"Sorry. I think it's kinda cool."

"You would."

"No, seriously," Ashley said. "I have a friend in Chicago who lived in an old house for three years. They had a ghost. They got used to it—even gave her a name."

"Her?"

"Yep, they always saw this woman in a nightgown walking across the hall to the bathroom."

Laura smirked. "Their ghost used the bathroom?"

"You gotta go, you gotta go."

"So what'd they call her?"

"Mrs. Moskopf."

"What?"

"This Mrs. Moskopf lived in the house before them. She died there. They figured it was her." Ashley grabbed her phone. "I should call Hannah and get them back here—"

"No!"

"We could film for *Ghost Adventures*."

"No!" Casually, Laura added, "You're a fruitcake."

"I am. Thank you."

After a hot shower, Laura dressed and dried her hair, pulling it into a ponytail. Maybe Ashley had a point. In the light of day, last night didn't seem so spooky. Ghosts? She had never given much thought to the subject. Wasn't even sure she believed in them.

The day was bright and still, a perfect fall day, an absolute contrast to the dark moonlit hallway last night. Why were things scarier at night? Why did ghosts only come out after dark?

She didn't know. She would see Dana in a few days; Dana was her sounding board for such things, though she felt certain Dana would think a ghost was cool, too.

Laura grabbed Leah, and they walked down to the basement singing a song. "The itsy-bitsy spider climbed up the water spout..."

At one, Ashley announced she was taking a walk and offered to take Leah in the stroller. Laura spent an hour wrapping small pieces of stained-glass with copper foil. She needed to focus on something new and loved making stained-glass lamps. After a while, her fingers grew sore. She stopped and surveyed her progress.

Most of the pieces were ready. Next, she would arrange them on a Styrofoam form and solder them together, creating a Tiffany-style lampshade. She stood and stretched her legs, eyeing the door leading to the back hallway. On a whim, she walked over, opened it, and peered down the hall.

Bathed in the late afternoon sun, it looked mundane. Not ghostly or haunted.

She walked down the corridor and opened the first door, the utility room that housed the furnace and hot water heater. They had painted the walls bright white, the floor industrial grey. Boxes, cartons, and crates lined the walls, remnants of the move from Illinois.

Laura then walked to the root cellar where the old woman had disappeared. Easing the door open, she switched the light on and scanned the room.

There was the pile of brick and debris to the right and the painting of the grey-haired woman in the corner. She looked closely at the painting. She hadn't seen the face of the woman last night, but the hair was the same. Could this be her?

Yes? No? She couldn't tell.

A solitary box sat in the corner next to the picture, the box of scrapbooks from the auction. It wasn't there last night, was it? She remembered putting it next to the furnace, anyway.

Who moved it? Why? Was it a sign?

It still exuded a sinister aura. With no rational reason for believing so, she felt certain she'd missed something important in the box. While questioning her sudden embrace of hunches and superstition, she carried it to the utility room where the light was better. Laura plopped down and delved into the box, tossing the first twelve albums aside. Quickly scanning the next two, she chucked them aside as well.

The last book was bound with heavy die-cut paperboard designed to look like leather. The word **ALBUM**, surrounded by images of antique playing cards, was embossed on the dark cover. Laura had never seen anything like it.

She hesitated before touching it. When she did, she felt a light shock and a moment of dizziness. Saw the hint of an indiscernible image. She didn't want to pick it up, yet felt compelled to hold it—perhaps feeling the contents would reveal themselves in her mind's eye?

Ridiculous. She was contemplating supernatural powers she hadn't believed in a month ago—until the dreams, episodes, and subliminal images returned. Until she saw the old woman in the hallway. Plus the noises, falling fireplace screen, slamming doors, and this strange book.

An inner voice cautioned: *Leave it. Walk away now.*

She couldn't. She wiped the front cover with a rag and opened it.

A bizarre biblical image filled the first page. An angel blowing a horn stood above figures of men and women rising from the ground, the scene captioned with a single word: **JUDGEMENT**.

Time had discolored the heavy vellum pages. A crumbling slip of paper, pasted to the next page, was handwritten with a faded, illegible script. The following seven pages were similar, with two or three small pieces of paper glued to the vellum, the writing equally faded and illegible. While mysterious, it didn't seem relevant to the house.

Four small snips of newspaper, yellowed and crumbling, had been glued to the next page. Though legible, they looked ancient because the typeface still used the long *s* instead of a small *s* in many of the words.

> *On Friday night, around feven o'clock, during the ftorm, a ftack of chimnies was blown down at the handsome and lofty houfe of Mrs. MacKenzie in King Street, Derlinton. The roof on one fide was entirely beat in and the whole made its way through feveral ftories, whereby two fervants were kill'd.*

A cold, hollow sensation washed through her. She nearly dropped the book. Without any rational basis, Laura felt certain this *Mrs. MacKenzie* belonged somewhere in their family tree. It was another sign.

The next two pages held similar, eerie clippings. Some accident, a dismemberment or death; someone named MacKenzie. The locations sounded English.

Flipping ahead several pages, she found the tone gradually evolved even if the subject didn't. The left-hand page held a single undated column of newsprint. The paper was so yellow it was nearly brown, printed with a font from a bygone era.

> *Melancholy Accident and Death — Mr. Thomas MacKenzie of Attleboro was thrown from his wagon on Tuesday, near his farm, and immediately killed. The accident was occasioned by his horse taking fright and running, whereby Mr. MacKenzie was thrown out and dragged some distance. He was so much disfigured as hardly to be recognized.*

Attleboro was in Massachusetts. A pretty little town. She had driven through it once.

Laura turned the page, and a slight shiver passed down her spine. Someone had pasted single articles on the center of each page, stories of death in apparent proximity to the house in Wisconsin. A partial date was visible on one of them, the year 1903.

Auburn Man Killed

Jacob Hellman was killed on the George MacKenzie farm when he was overcome by silo gas. Jacob was 24 and leaves behind a grieving widow and child.

What kind of madness was this?

Creepy, morbid—ghoulish—it spanned centuries. A knot of apprehension twisted in her gut. Page after page, the album documented a legacy of death; a grisly collection of stories seemingly unrelated by any commonality other than surname. Who would assemble such a book? Why?

She turned the page. More clippings, more tragedy. Laura flipped through the album, no longer reading the articles, convinced the book was the work of a deranged person obsessed with the MacKenzie name. And yet, perversely, the book was exactly what she'd been looking for.

Buying the box hadn't been a fluke or a coincidence.

Laura felt certain all these MacKenzies were ancestors. These were the people she had been looking for on Ancestry and unable to find. Within lay an alarming truth: they had all died badly.

Near the end of the book, Laura stopped and peered at an article that filled her with ineffable sadness. The story of Lucas's father, who had died so young, so tragically. She had never known the exact circumstances until now.

Area Farmer Killed

Alan MacKenzie, 32, of Lost Arrow Township, died Friday after a mishap at his farm. MacKenzie was killed when his tractor tipped and fell into a previously undetected sinkhole. He leaves a wife and two small children behind. Funeral services are pending.

After a lingering moment of reflection, Laura turned the page to the next article.

Mystery in Lost Arrow

Auburn—The county sheriff, acting on a tip from a local resident, has uncovered a mystery at a farmhouse in the township of Lost Arrow. Thomas Wolff, an area farmer, has been missing since Friday when his tractor was found deserted near the MacKenzie farm on Firelane Eight. Sheriff Kohler said he is now treating Wolff's disappearance as a missing person's case and has organized searches of the surrounding woods and Lost Arrow Lake.

Beneath it, someone had taped a faded photograph of a man sitting atop a farm tractor, raising his cap as if riding a bronco.

Someone had scribbled a note below the photo.

It ends here!

It did. Those words were the last entry in the book. The remaining seven pages were blank. Laura studied the penmanship of that last entry, noting something familiar about it. A shiver passed through her like an arctic wind as recognition came to her with a stunning jolt.

She was certain it was Elizabeth's handwriting. Laura ran to her workshop, grabbed her purse and pulled a small handwritten note from an inside pocket. A lovely note from Elizabeth welcoming Laura to the family.

There was one common word—*here.* The cursive was identical.

This book, this bizarre collection belonged to Elizabeth? The mystery surrounding the woman only deepened.

Why had she collected all these bizarre stories and articles? Centuries of them!

You know why.

Laura thought she understood. While Elizabeth's beliefs seemed out of character, it was possible to understand her feelings about the house. Elizabeth evidently believed some deeper process was at work. Distraught by the death of her husband, had she spent years collecting this 'proof' of some imaginary evil stalking the family?

Imaginary? These stories were real.

The woman in the hallway last night? The *haunting,* the *ghost,* whatever label she attached, was she imaginary?

Had Elizabeth ascribed this all to a curse? To some unknown malevolence? Was the book an attempt to tie anything that happened to any MacKenzie to some supernatural plot or conspiracy? Or was the book the symptom of a mental disorder?

The simplest explanation was usually the truth—except no obvious truth existed here.

All these years later, Laura felt compelled to buy this box at an auction. Why? Something related to the house? Or something related to Elizabeth? To even consider that, she had to accept that she possessed some psychic ability, and Laura wasn't comfortable with the idea. She certainly wasn't showing this to Lucas. It would send him over the edge. Lucas had little tolerance for the paranormal and he was already angry his mother hadn't told him about the house.

A solution popped into her head, a single word.

Exorcism

Yikes! Where had *that* come from?

This morning she had accepted Ashley's story about harmless old Mrs. Moskopf and now she wanted to call in the Exorcist. She sat, frozen, no longer able to think.

After several minutes in a catatonic fugue, Laura closed the scrapbook and dumped it back into the box and buried it with the other albums. She shoved it into the corner of the room with the painting.

Out of sight. Out of mind. Laura was now glad she'd made plans to visit Dana because she suddenly wanted a few days away from the house.

Soft footsteps in the hall.

She tensed.

"Laura?" It was Ashley.

With a sigh of relief, Laura said, "Yes?"

"Leah's awake. She was asleep when I got back so I laid her down."

"Great, thanks."

"Gotta go. Nate and I are going out for dinner."

★   ★   ★

Having the house to themselves, Laura decided to prepare a nice dinner: lamb chops and a salad. She opened a bottle of malbec. Leah played underfoot while she marinated the lamb. Maybe she would oblige and go to bed early, a thought accompanied by a pleasant tingling in her mid-section.

Her afternoon funk had faded. Maybe she had overreacted. She shook her head. An exorcism?

If anything, Elizabeth had needed one.

Shepherd's Warning 131

Laura then chided herself for thinking badly of Elizabeth. The contradictions were confusing; she wished Elizabeth were here to explain them.

The front door slammed.

Lucas walked into the kitchen wearing a smile. "Smells good. Where is everyone?"

"They went out to dinner. It's just us." Laura finished tossing the salad. Leah sat at the table, coloring.

"And Leah," he said, perhaps sensing her mood. He pecked her cheek. She could smell beer and something else. Smoke.

"She's going down early tonight."

He nodded and set the table.

Dinner was good, the chops grilled perfectly, the wine excellent. Leah sat contently, eating well without fussing.

It felt good, intimate, the conversation easy. A perfect moment until Laura asked, "So what'd you do today?"

"Caught a couple of bluegills this morning. Hardware run in the afternoon."

"What'd you get?" She fiddled with her salad; felt the conversation edging off course.

"Stuff."

Tried to stop herself but couldn't. "Really. I didn't know the White Birch sold hardware."

Lucas stopped eating, fork hanging in midair. "Been checking up on me?"

"Of course not. It's been obvious, and I think it's time for it to stop. You never had any need to sit around in bars before."

"I never had the time."

"Still, what's the deal?"

"I didn't think I had to explain myself." He tossed his napkin onto the table.

"You don't, but—"

Lucas glared at her. "Sounds like I do! What else do you want to know?"

Irked by the turn in the conversation, Laura grew frustrated with Lucas and angry with herself. She didn't want a fight. Wanted Lucas to make love to her, *needed* him close to her. She balled her napkin up and threw it at him playfully. "Settle down. Don't be an ass."

His eyes narrowed. "Then don't be a fucking bitch."

He threw the napkin to the floor and stormed out.

Leah dropped her fork and started crying.

★   ★   ★

Shaking from adrenaline, Lucas drove up the drive toward Lost Arrow, more angry with himself than Laura. He'd never spoken to her like that and didn't understand why he'd gone over the edge so quickly. Still, he made no attempt to turn around, had no urge to apologize. He was driving to the White Birch Inn where he would surely run into Murphy—a relationship creeping perilously close to an affair. Just as he'd been unable to contain his temper a moment ago, he found it impossible to turn around. His phone rang, but he didn't recognize the number.

Area code 414.

Probably a robocall. He stabbed *Ignore.*

Twenty-Five

Late at night, Laura wandered the house like a ghostly apparition, the hallways a maze of shadows and grey moonlight. She heard muffled voices and cries from the rooms she passed but ignored them, afraid to look, imagining disturbing stories from the album playing out in sepia. The quality of the light slowly changed, the shadows and grey tones vanquished by crimson light from the east. Laura walked to the dining room as dawn drew near, stopped, and stared out the east window. The ribbed clouds glowed red, a classic mackerel sky.

Beautiful. Ominous.

As the light grew stronger, the glass itself became luminescent, intensely red, pulsing as if blood ebbed and flowed through the panes. Laura backed away. There was something wrong with the window. Evil seemed to emanate from it. Soon, the entire room glowed red, the light within the glass forming words, a line from a silly proverb:

red sky in the morning, shepherd's warning

The window shattered with a loud crash. Weightless glass showered her like snowflakes—

Then she was awake. Lucas was up and running out the door.

Laura sat up, confused, feeling anxious. "Where are you going?"

"Downstairs to find out what the hell is going on." Lucas sounded angry. Down the hall, a door slammed.

Laura realized the noise had been real and woven itself into her dream. Throwing a bathrobe on and running out the door, she bumped into Nate and Ashley rushing down the hallway.

"What the hell was that?" Ashley asked.

"I don't know, I was sleeping."

"Weren't we all," Nate said.

Downstairs, in the Hall, the bar and screen over the hearth had fallen again despite Lucas's insistence he had strapped the bar to the supports with wire. A framed print had also fallen to the floor.

"The MacKenzie ghost strikes again," Ashley said in a dramatic voice.

"Starting to look like it," Nate said.

"Fuck it!" Lucas snarled and walked toward the stairs and up to bed. Laura followed silently. When she laid down and closed her eyes, the strange proverb again appeared inside her eyelids:

red sky in the morning, shepherd's warning

Wasn't it *sailor's warning*?

She fell asleep wondering what they had gotten themselves into.

★   ★   ★

Laura and Leah left for Illinois a day later on a chilly Sunday morning, rain falling from dark quilted skies that reflected Laura's somber mood. Leah fell asleep, leaving Laura alone at the wheel with her thoughts, the fight with Lucas foremost in her mind. Yes, she had started things, but the way he had spoken to her was inexcusable. They still weren't talking. She was glad she had plans to visit Dana. She missed her daughter and needed a few days away from Lucas and the house.

Anxiety had been churning in her belly the past few days, the sinister return of her epilepsy the source of much of it. She feared the lousy side effects of the drugs, especially Dilantin.

She had conflicting emotions about Elizabeth and her bizarre scrapbook. Why had she gathered all those gruesome stories? Evidently, Elizabeth had been adept at concealing an obsessive and superstitious nature that Laura struggled to understand. What did she suspect?

A silly question. She thought the house was haunted.

Laura wondered if she was right, an unsettling feeling that had lingered since she saw the old woman in the hall.

Ghost. The word kept popping up, unbidden, in her thoughts. Was she being influenced by suggestions from Elizabeth and the townspeople that the house was haunted? What other explanation was there for the old woman, the sudden rash of slamming doors, and the fireplace screen that kept collapsing onto the hearth? For that, she had no answer.

Farther south, the clouds scattered, and the sunshine lifted her mood as they neared Naperville. Dana owned a beautiful, century-old Craftsman house with slate-blue siding and white trim. A year ago, Lucas and Dana had remodeled the kitchen with new oak cabinets and quartz countertops. Dana opened the door and smothered Laura with a hug, then grabbed Leah and pretended to devour her with kisses. They spent the afternoon in the sunny kitchen, gabbing and gossiping, stopping occasionally to entertain Leah when she grew bored with her toys. The change of scenery and simple conversation was a tonic, and Laura felt her anxieties easing. Dana prepared a Caesar salad, and Laura sautéed chicken for dinner.

They laid Leah down at eight-thirty in the portable crib and retired to the living room with their glasses and a bottle of chardonnay. Dana had arranged a grouping of sofas, chairs, and tables in a rough semicircle, focused around a Sony 65-inch flat screen like a miniature amphitheater. The walls were rather bare, decorated with a few small prints and mirrors. It felt, despite the abundance of furniture, like the room wasn't quite finished.

Dana set her wine down and leaned forward. "Okay, Mom, let's have it."

"What?"

"I'm glad you came, but you obviously have something on your mind. You're doing that thing with your lip and playing with your hair."

"That obvious, huh?"

"Afraid so."

Laura sat, nibbling on a fingernail. She was a churning mess of emotions. Driving down, she had decided to say nothing, but now felt a powerful urge to talk. Dare she let this out? While she debated internally, Dana tuned in a soft rock station and sat patiently, sipping wine. Laura did a quick breathing exercise. Played with her hair. Gave Dana nervous side glances

Then she talked.

The house. The album. Lucas. Everything. Once started, she could not stop until she had spilled every detail. She seamlessly transitioned to her childhood illness. The telling was cathartic.

Dana sat there, alternately frowning or wide-eyed, her mouth agape. Taking it all in. Silent. Letting her mother talk until Laura stopped and said, "That's about it."

"That's it?" Dana looked astonished. "Jesus, Mom! That's crazy! And amazing."

Laura felt exposed. Her darkest secrets revealed. She hadn't realized the weight she still carried from her past. She stood and wanted to run from Dana's incredulous expression, feeling she had made a mistake, but Dana grabbed Laura and drew her into a comforting hug.

"Holy shit, Mom! You kept that inside all these years?"

Laura wiped her eyes with the back of her hand; hadn't realized until now that her eyes were damp with tears. She nodded.

"Jesus. Why?"

Laura shook her head. She had been afraid to tell this story, a fear that now seemed foolish. It didn't sound so awful now. It felt good to have it off her chest. "I—I don't know. I had such a miserable time in school. Now it seems so—inconsequential."

"Shit. You don't have epilepsy—well, maybe you do, I don't know—but you're genuinely psychic, lady." Dana gazed at her with sincere wonderment.

Laura frowned. "I doubt that."

"What? It seems clear to me from your story."

"I don't believe it." Nor did she want to—though that wasn't entirely true. She was reluctant to acknowledge it, to give it a name. It felt safer to keep it hidden in the dark, pretending it didn't exist. She couldn't even imagine trying to explain this to Lucas. It had driven her mother away. What would he think?

"Okay, so maybe I don't understand what it would be like," Dana said. "Maybe I'd feel the same way."

Laura crossed her arms in a hug and shrugged.

"How have you kept it at bay for so long?"

"I don't know. Willpower, dogged stubbornness?"

"And you were just telling me how weak you felt? It took a lot of courage to deal with all of that." Dana stared at Laura with rapt affection. "I've always known you were strong, but I'm in awe."

Laura smiled self-consciously. She didn't feel strong, but having shared this with Dana, she felt free, unburdened. Why hadn't she trusted anyone before now? Perhaps Lucas wouldn't have understood, but why hadn't she trusted Dana or Ashley?

"Well, you didn't give it to me." Dana said wryly.

"You can have it." Laura waved her empty glass at Dana.

Dana refilled their glasses and they settled back into the cushions.

"I just don't understand why it's come back," Laura said.

Dana looked thoughtful. "I think the answer is obvious."

"What?"

"You guys moved into a spooky old house with some sketchy history," Dana said with tipsy animation. "It's probably loaded with psychic energy or whatever they call it. Have you thought about bringing in a ghost hunter?"

"No!" Laura snapped.

Dana looked taken aback. "Why not?"

"You sound just like Ashley. It's nonsense, parlor tricks—unless you believe in that stuff."

"You don't?"

"I don't know. I've never thought about it."

"What are you afraid of, Mom?" Dana put a hand on Laura's arm.

"What do you mean?"

"You have a rare and marvelous gift, and you're running from it." Dana said. "Maybe you just need to learn how to use it."

"I wouldn't know where to start. And yes, I am afraid of it. It doesn't seem natural." Laura leaned back and crossed her arms. "What good is it?"

"I don't know." Dana then smirked. "Maybe you just need to meet other psychics."

"Really. How could I have a child with so many bad ideas?"

"I'm serious!" Dana protested.

"Hmm." Laura was thoughtful. "Far as I know, no one's formed a support group for confused and troubled psychics."

Dana raised her eyebrows. "Then you'll just have to start one."

"Psychics Anonymous? Hold it—if we're psychic, no one would be anonymous, right?"

Dana clapped. "Very funny, Mom."

Laura giggled. She was tipsy. She fell serious again, wanting to talk this out. "So, what's your theory about the old woman I saw?"

"Maybe it's just like Ashley said, a harmless haunting like what's-her-name? Miss Moskopf?" Dana smiled. "I think it's kinda cool. I've gotta come up to Amityville and visit."

"Oh, you're funny, kid." Laura kicked Dana playfully in the shin.

"If it really bothers you, what about an exorcism?"

Laura eyed Dana critically. "Seriously?"

"Why not?"

"It sounds crazy." Laura wrinkled her nose. "Makes me think of that movie and the girl spewing vomit."

Dana snickered. "Sounds like fun. I'll bring the popcorn."

Laura pondered the idea of exorcism, until now, an abstract idea from an old movie to her. Did the church still perform exorcisms? She decided it wouldn't hurt to ask Reverend Drew when she returned home. How would she broach the subject?

Silent for a moment, Dana said, "What about the epilepsy?"

"I have an appointment tomorrow with my neurologist."

"Oh, so you didn't really come to see me." Dana feigned hurt feelings.

"A little maybe." Laura shrugged.

"Love you too, Mom." Dana reached for the wine bottle. "So, Ms. ESP, what am I thinking right now?"

"That we should get pleasantly drunk."

"God, you're good."

Laura laughed, but her unease returned.

Lucas was still an ass. She still had epilepsy and some freaky psychic thing, and their house was probably haunted.

Perfect.

Twenty-Six

The following morning was cloudless and warm, unusually so for October.

With an end-of-month deadline from the show producer bearing down, Nate was rushing to finish the exterior, completing repairs on the stucco beneath the eaves on the south end of the house. Only one section remained, at the apex of the gable next to the chimney. Out back, a crew was putting finishing touches on a new roof for the barn. Jim Mayhew had declined the work.

Knocking material loose from the damaged section, Nate noticed lettering carved into the adjacent beam. Neat, professional carving. Nate pulled a hammer from his work belt and knocked away more of the old stucco for a better look. It was a name.

GEFFREY CLARKE MDXIV

The builder of the house, Nate suspected, though he wondered why he had hidden it here. He pulled his phone from his pocket and snapped a photo of the inscription. Nate felt certain MDXIV was the date the house had been built, but couldn't remember what D stood for. Ashley would know.

Just then, his phone pinged. A text and photo from Hannah, the video producer.

Hey, somebody photobombed one of our pics! Who is this dude?

It was a photo of the Hall. A tall guy in bib overalls and a ball cap stood in the far archway. Weird. It wasn't anyone he'd hired. Maybe Ashley would know that, too. He took a step down the aluminum ladder, dropping his foot to the next step. It felt spongy. Assuming he'd misstepped, he shifted his foot and put his weight on it.

The rung gave way with a *ping.*

Nate slid down ten feet of ladder, lost his grip, and fell another ten feet to the ground.

Ashley, who was taking photos, rushed over. "Nate! Are you okay?"

Thoroughly winded, he wasn't sure. Quick inventory: arms and legs worked. Back hurt. Otherwise okay.

"Yeah, I think so."

He looked up the ladder at the gap in the steps.

The ladder was only months old. No way a rung should have failed. Man, he was going to sue someone.

"Shit. My lucky day. I better buy a lottery ticket."

Twenty-Seven

Laura and Leah returned home a few days later on a dreary fall afternoon, steady rain falling from ashen clouds hanging low over the trees of the Kettle Moraine. The house looked like a haven from the weather, a plume of smoke pushed at a steep angle from the chimney by the blustery wind.

The EEG and consultation were uneventful. The neurologist declared her normal but suggested she see her primary care doctor for a complete physical. An undiagnosed heart arrhythmia could cause similar symptoms.

Nate, Ashley, and Lucas were sitting in the Hall. The TV was on, but no one seemed to be watching it.

Lucas gave her a warm smile. Good. The fight was over. Laura settled in next to him.

Ashley said, "Hey, you guys want to play a game?"

There were vague murmurs of assent. Ashley disappeared, returning a few minutes later with a bottle of shiraz, four glasses, and Scrabble. She arranged everyone around the coffee table in the center of the Hall and poured the wine. Leah skirted back and forth around the furniture, playing hide and seek with whoever would make eye contact.

The game crawled and Ashley struggled to keep everyone engaged. "Are we going to play? Nate! *Brung* doesn't count. It's not in the dictionary. You know the rules."

"Sure it does. Bring. Brung. Duh."

"It's bring and brought, genius." Laura slapped his knee.

There was a clatter from the kitchen.

Ashley rolled her eyes. "The freaking knives again."

"What?"

"Two days ago, knives started falling off the magnetic bar in the kitchen. I took them off the bar and set them on the counter. They still fall onto the floor."

"Why?"

"Mrs. Moskopf, of course," Ashley said.

"Who?" Lucas asked.

A pine knot exploded in the fire, sending cinders flying against the screen. Laura looked up and saw duct tape wrapped around the supports, binding the bar and screen in place. It was an unsightly mess.

Laura pointed. "What's with that?"

"It won't stay up," Nate said.

"What?"

"It keeps falling down," Lucas said. "There's something wrong with the supports."

"Yeah, they're haunted." Ashley smirked as she placed her letters.

"Oh bullshit," Lucas said.

"You have a better explanation?" Ashley met his skeptical gaze. "I did some reading. The thing with the knives sounds like a poltergeist. The bar is probably the same thing."

"You believe that?" Lucas said.

"Again, do you have a better explanation, given the evidence—*stuff falling by itself?*"

"It's an old house."

With this exchange, Laura thought more about her conversation with Dana. Driving back, she had decided to consider the exorcism and talk to the reverend. Maybe tomorrow. Then she remembered that she and Ashley were going shopping. The day after then. Give her time to frame her case.

Outside, the weather had turned ugly. The gusty wind rattled the windows and produced an eerie assortment of moans and whistles in the eaves and bare branches of the trees around the house. Rain pelted the glass, punctuated by sharp taps of sleet.

★   ★   ★

Laura awoke at six.

Lucas was already gone. Hunting probably. She walked to the window and caught her breath. It had snowed. Not much, an inch or two, but enough to paint the landscape ghostly white in the moonlight. It was beautiful, serene. The house was otherwise quiet. Looking at the monitor, she saw Leah sleeping in her crib, so she went back to bed.

Somewhat later, she heard Leah crying for rescue.

Carrying Leah down the stairs, Laura smelled bacon cooking and found everyone gathered in the kitchen eating breakfast. She poured a cup of coffee and joined the others at the table.

"What's the plan, people?" Lucas asked.

"Going shopping," Laura said without enthusiasm.

"Big sale at the mall today," Ashley said.

"Jesus, who goes to the mall anymore?" Lucas shook his head. It was more a statement than a question.

Nate said, "I'm finishing up last-minute projects before the film crew returns. I could use some help."

"No problem. I'll be here all day."

Nate raised his eyebrows but said nothing.

After breakfast, Laura showered, dressed for a day of shopping, and packed a bag for Leah.

She had grown weary of Ashley's incessant need to shop. After today, she was done for a while. She had finished the first lamp, started another and planned to open a store on Etsy. She would prefer to spend the day in her workshop.

Finally, Ashley announced she was ready after an inordinate amount of time on hair and makeup.

"We're leaving!" Ashley yelled from the top of the stairs.

"Have fun, ladies," Nate yelled back.

His voice sounded oddly distant. Feeling dizzy, Laura stepped down the first few steps. There was something she needed to remember. Something important. It felt just out of reach...

Then it came to her. "Nate, be careful, okay?"

She sensed a brief lapse of time, a second or two. Laura tried to shake the feeling off. Nate and Lucas were staring at her strangely. When she looked up, Ashley was too. She must have sounded crazy. Trying to recover, Laura said, "You too, Lucas."

Only it sounded like the afterthought that it was. Nate quietly said, "Yeah, sure."

Lucas just stared before turning away to go about his work. Laura retreated up the stairs in embarrassment.

"That was cute," Ashley said snidely. "What was that about?"

"I don't know why I said that."

$\star$ $\star$ $\star$

Laura felt adrift at the mall. There was nothing she needed but Ashley strolled through every store, regardless. Perhaps sensing her mood, Leah was cranky as well. Laura was relieved when they finally took a break and sat on a bench. She pulled a packet of Goldfish from her purse for Leah. Ashley spent a minute inspecting her bags and looked up.

"You didn't buy anything. How come?"

"Not in the mood, I guess. Maybe I need a break from shopping."

"Okay. Whatever." Ashley was always so nonchalant. In a week, she'd forget this conversation and beg Laura to go shopping. The honeymoon was over. Laura needed a break from Ashley. Some new friends, anything. Tomorrow, she was stopping at Anson's and talking to Carol about meeting other women in the area.

Laura said, "What's with the knives falling on the floor in the kitchen?"

Ashley shrugged. "A poltergeist, I guess."

"And that doesn't bother you?"

"Not really." Ashley shook her head. "It's just a few knives falling down."

"You're very blasé about it."

Ashley shrugged. "It doesn't seem all that spooky to me. I think it's kind of cool."

Laura looked at Ashley curiously. How could anyone be so casual about such a thing?

"Come on, let's go."

They stood and stepped into the stream of shoppers strolling up and down the main aisle.

Laura turned to say something to Ashley when she felt a dizzy swoon. The long mall slid sideways as a sensation like electricity surged through her brain.

Laura staggered and fell to the floor, barely conscious. A pair of hands caught her halfway, saving her head from a hard landing. Moments later, she lay there muttering the only thought rattling about in her head: *"Red sky in the morning, shepherd's warning, red sky in the morning, shepherd's warning..."*

Laura slowly regained consciousness, shaking her head and blinking in confusion. She saw Ashley. Her eyes flew open.

"We have to go! Something's wrong at the house!"

"What?" Ashley looked alarmed, confused. "What happened to you?"

"I don't know." Laura shook her head, trying to clear the fog, thinking: *Oh no, grand mal seizure, drugs, ridicule...*

She felt another swoon and thought she was having another seizure. Then it was gone. By sheer force of will, she pushed her anxieties and queasiness back and focused on making a dignified retreat.

She struggled to get up. A man reached out to help her up. "Are you okay?"

"Yes, I'm fine, thank you." Disoriented, she stood and brushed herself off, feigning composure. She took Leah from Ashley's arms and politely pushed through the crowd to the exit. Halfway to the car, the aftershock of the seizure welled up in a nauseous wave. Laura set Leah down, keeled over, and threw up.

Ashley helped her to the car, looking flustered. "God, Laura, what's wrong with you?"

"I don't know." Her hands were shaking. She felt empty. Couldn't think.

"Something you ate?"

Laura shook her head.

"What's wrong at the house?" Ashley put a hand on her shoulder.

"The house? I don't know."

Ashley clicked the door locks open and helped Laura into the passenger seat. "You said something was wrong—"

"No, I didn't. Can we just go, please?"

Twenty-Eight

Lucas and Nate spent the morning in the basement insulating the sill plate where the outside walls met the foundation. At noon, they broke for a lunch of ham sandwiches and beer in the kitchen.

"So you're done hanging at the White Birch?" Nate said skeptically.

"It was getting old." Lucas shrugged. "What are we doing this afternoon?"

"We should clean the gutters. Make sure everything is spiffy for next week."

Lucas's phone rang with the classic old-school *ring*. An unknown number: 414 area code. He then realized it was probably Gregory calling.

"Mr. MacKenzie, this is Professor Gregory from the University. I've been waiting for your call. I left a message."

"I'm sorry. I never got the message."

"Oh well, I've finally reached you regardless. Doctor Shepherd looked at the pages from your book and he's quite excited. It is indeed Old English. If you have time, he'd like to meet with you to look at the book and discuss the possibility of translating the work. He feels this might be a significant find."

Lucas's interest quickened. "Absolutely. My schedule is open."

"Good. Could you manage short notice like last time? Today, perhaps? Doctor Shepherd will be in until five."

"Can you hold a moment?" Lucas relayed the gist of the call to Nate.

"Go. I can handle the gutters."

Lucas promised to be there within the hour and ended the call. He changed, grabbed the book, and ran out the door minutes later.

★   ★   ★

Nate finished lunch and rigged a ladder up the back of the house. Under clear skies, the morning snow had melted, and it felt more like August than October with a warm southerly breeze.

He climbed the ladder onto the roof with agile grace, no fear of the height, a thirty-foot drop from the eaves. On the deck, he stepped carefully. The shingles were dry, but the accumulated leaves were wet and slick, ready to send the careless skittering off the roof to a hard landing below with a single misstep.

Working from the top, he swept the leaves from the roof and fished thick clumps from the gutters with a gutter scoop. Of course Lucas had weaseled out of this job. The call from Milwaukee had been timed perfectly. He *had* to rush right down there. Like it couldn't wait a day or two. Lucas knew he was under pressure with the film crew returning next week. As expected, he was micromanaging the book. Nate was surprised Lucas hadn't demanded the coins as well.

Ass.

It took an hour to work around the house and clean the various gutters. In that time, storm clouds brewing to the west blotted out the sun. He rigged a hose and dragged it up the ladder. Spent another twenty minutes flushing the remaining debris from the gutters while thunder rumbled in the distance.

Nate tossed the hose off the roof and stopped to watch the dark clouds beyond the lake. It was probably the last storm of the season and looked fearsome. Towers of dark cumulus billowed skyward as a roiling wall of cloud approached the lake. Lightning spiked to the surface of the water, followed by a sharp clap of thunder.

Jesus, that was close! He had to get off the roof.

Nate then noticed an eerie and iridescent bluish glow around the chimney. It looked like St. Elmo's fire, the phenomenon that lit the masts of ships in stormy weather. With that thought came a terrifying realization. Nate threw himself flat halfway down the roof and covered his ears, heedless of the fall. What was coming was far deadlier.

His hair stood on end and a lightning bolt struck a nanosecond later with a deafening blast. After a moment, Nate realized he was still alive and terribly lucky.

Holy shit!

A moment of hesitation and he would've been dead. Nate scrambled for the ladder and scurried down while vivid images of his charred, smoking corpse raced through his mind.

Jesus! That had been *way* too close.

Nate collapsed the ladder and carried it to the barn. After the storm, he would need to check for damage.

He sat with a sigh and realized he was shaking—a delayed adrenaline rush from his near-death experience.

Damn. He needed a beer.

Nate slid the barn door closed and walked toward the house. The yard seemed sullen now, the trees bare, devoid of life; the birds silent, gone to cover as the storm approached.

Nate bolted for the lower rear door as the sky opened up and rain fell in torrents. Walking through Laura's workspace and up to the kitchen, he grabbed a bottle of beer from the fridge. Sat and stretched out. Closed his eyes. His heart still racing, he took a long drink from the bottle and tried to relax.

As his breathing settled, he heard that odd bass hum again, coming from somewhere in the house. Nate then noticed the thermostat in the hallway flashing an error code.

Shit.

Had the lightning strike damaged the system? The furnace and the chimney weren't connected, but Nate had no idea where the lightning had gone to ground. Metal ductwork snaked around the base of the chimney and, theoretically, some voltage might have jumped to the metal and gone through the furnace. Maybe the breaker just needed to be reset. He set his beer on the table, walked down the stairs, and into the back hallway to investigate.

He caught a whiff of something. Propane?

As he stepped through the doorway, he automatically reached for the switch and flipped the light on.

In that instant, Nate realized his mistake.

Twenty-Nine

Lucas met Professor Gregory at his office and they walked down the hall to meet Doctor Shepherd. Gregory walked with a slight hunch and looked eccentric with his wild swept-back hair. Shepherd was a small man, perhaps five-six, slightly built, in his mid-sixties. Dressed in a tailored grey pinstripe suit, he spoke with an articulate English accent as he politely asked them to sit down. Lucas sat in one of two rattan chairs and looked around the room as Gregory sat and fussed with a handkerchief.

The office was impeccably neat and smelled faintly of incense, one wall lined with books from floor to ceiling, arranged by size to give a uniform appearance to the eye. Shepherd sat behind a beautiful oak desk that was equally neat, his books and papers stacked in perfect piles. He had decorated the wall behind the desk with numerous degrees and a bizarre painting that Lucas discovered, with a little squinting, was called *The Bewitched Man* by Goya.

"Goya was fascinated by witches and witchcraft," Shepherd said. "But he wasn't superstitious. His art was mostly a protest against the Inquisition and religious tribunals."

"Fascinating," Lucas said, somewhat insincerely.

"Quite." Shepherd stared momentarily with piercing green eyes, idly stroking his clipped grey moustache. "May I see the book?"

Lucas handed the book to Shepherd, who spent a moment examining the cover, the brass edging, and the binding, raising his eyebrows twice. He opened it and lingered on the first page. He appeared to be mumbling the text silently as he turned a few pages, then a few more, slowly leafing through the book without a word. His expressions were almost comical: frowns, raised eyebrows, a few smirks. After nearly ten minutes of this silent perusal, Shepherd closed the book and carefully set it on his desk.

"Where did you find this?"

"We found it hidden in our house," Lucas said.

"Really. Most interesting." Shepherd seemed lost in thought. "Do you have any idea who hid it?"

"No idea. I was hoping the book would reveal that. Does it?"

"Not really. Please, tell me about the house and the space where you found this. I'm curious."

Lucas briefly described the house, the room, and the circumstances that led to the discovery. Rather than appeasing Shepherd's curiosity, his description brought a flurry of questions about the house, the layout of the rooms, and the space where they had discovered the book. He then had Lucas draw a diagram.

Exasperated, Lucas put his hand up. "Hold it. What does the book say?"

Shepherd waved off the question impatiently. "We'll get to that. It's all about context." He pointed to the crude floor plan. "Why do you call this room the Great Hall?"

"Because that name is carved into the lintel over the entrances to the room. Actually, the word 'great' is spelled with an 'e' at the end."

"Fascinating. Your description sounds exactly like an English country manor from the Tudor period, around the sixteenth century. A house that might have been owned by a baron or a lord. I would love to see it. Surprising to find such a house in the Wisconsin countryside."

"It's a remarkable reproduction. I've been to England so I'm familiar with Tudor construction."

"I see. And how long have you lived in the house?"

"A few months. Anyway—the book?"

"Yes, the book. It's written in Old English, the language of the Anglo-Saxon people of England from roughly the sixth century to the eleventh century. Modern English evolved from this venerable language which itself arose from the Germanic tongues of the Angles, Saxons, and Jutes who settled Britain in the fifth century. This book doesn't belong to that early period. It was written somewhat later I think."

"So how old is it?"

"I'm not certain, but I would guess about four or five hundred years old."

"Five hundred years?"

Shepherd looked thoughtfully into space for a moment. "It's certainly possible."

"How can that be?"

"I don't know. This book is an anomaly and will almost certainly require a full translation to reveal that secret."

"Why would something like that be in my house?"

"That's the question, isn't it?" Shepherd was thoughtful for a moment, then said, "I think Occam's razor applies here."

"What is the simplest explanation?"

"I would assume the book was handed down over the years by successive generations of your family. There is no other reasonable answer at this point."

"So, what does it say?"

"I don't know yet," he said. "It's handwritten, of course, not always legibly. It's an odd dialect, so it could take weeks to translate enough of the text to determine that. From what I've read, it seems a mishmash of things. Part diary, part medical text. A list of cures with a few spells tossed in for good measure."

"Spells?"

"Harmless stuff, really. In that era, medicine and spells were often the same thing, along with leeches and bloodletting." He smiled, the first Lucas had seen. "So, there it is."

"You'll need to keep the book?"

"We would, yes. Written texts from that era are rare. This book may be a significant find. It's certainly valuable. Are you comfortable leaving it with us?"

"Will it be safe here?"

"Absolutely. We adhere to a strict set of guidelines for borrowed materials regarding security, environment, fire protection, and handling. It will also be insured. We'll draft an agreement covering all these details that will also be your receipt and acknowledgment of the arrangement. The book will be kept under lock and key in a controlled environment."

It took another two hours to draft and sign the paperwork and to find the dean to take possession of the book.

★   ★   ★

Lucas arrived home as night fell to a frightening scene, one that sent a deep chill through him. Red and blue lights flashed everywhere, the drive filled with fire trucks, squad cars, and an ambulance. The road was littered with the curious, likely summoned by police scanners and Facebook posts. As he tried to turn into the drive, a cop stepped forward and blocked his path.

"What's your business here, sir?"

"I live here. What's going on?" His tone was curt, a mask for his rising fear. Where were Laura and Leah? Nate and Ashley? What the hell was going on?

"Do you have any identification?"

Lucas thrust his driver's license at the cop.

"Seems in order, Lucas." His tone softened. "There's been an accident. I believe your brother may have been involved."

"Nate?" Lucas grew frantic, eyes darting in every direction. EMTs pushed a stretcher carrying a prone form to an ambulance. Lucas pushed the door open. The cop, as if reading his mind, put an arm out to stop him.

"That's not your brother. A firefighter was injured in a fall. They took your brother to Auburn Memorial an hour ago. His condition was stable at the time."

Lucas needed to hear no more. He gunned the engine, threw the shifter into reverse, and flew backwards, narrowly missing some looky-loos on the road. He grabbed his phone to call Laura, then saw she had called five times and left as many messages. Damn! He'd turned the ringer off at the university. Her voicemails were incoherent. Something about an explosion, the furnace, and Nate. None of it made sense. He called her, but it went to voicemail.

He sped to Auburn in a reckless, emotional panic, imagining the worst.

Laura, Ashley, and Leah were sitting in the emergency room when he ran in. Ashley was crying silently and Laura was doing her best to manage Leah, her face a study in anxiety and fear.

"What's going on? Where's Nate?"

"Thank God you're here. He's in surgery." Laura said. She tried to hug him but he pushed her away.

"What happened? How is he?"

Laura's eyes were damp and red; she'd been crying. "It's bad, Lucas, very bad. They haven't told us anything, but I know it's bad. They said the furnace exploded."

"What? That's not possible."

An older man dressed in surgical garb, a mask hanging around his neck, walked up to them, his manner formal and grave.

"Mrs. MacKenzie?"

Laura and Ashley nodded in unison.

"Are you all family?"

Lucas said, "Yes. How is my brother?"

"Please come with me."

The doctor led them to a small room off the main lobby labeled *Consultation*. There was a small conference table surrounded by chairs and a couple of nondescript prints on the wall. The room was otherwise bare. Soulless. A place where doctors dispensed bad news.

He motioned for everyone to sit down. His face remained fixed and dour. His bedside manner wasn't the least bit comforting.

Lucas felt his insides twist into knots. He murmured, "How is my brother?"

"He's still in surgery, but his condition is stable. His left arm has multiple breaks and four ribs are fractured. He has minor burns. From what we understand, he was thrown through a basement window by an explosion. His head may have struck the foundation in the process."

He paused and clasped his hands together. "As a result, he also has a head injury, a subdural hematoma—bleeding around the brain at the injury site. The surgeon is working to relieve the pressure now. Assuming the procedure goes well, it may still be several days before we know if there are any other neurological issues. First, we need to see if he regains consciousness."

"Why wouldn't he?" Lucas asked, fearing the answer.

"The injury is that severe. I want you to be prepared for every possible outcome."

Thirty

Laura watched Ashley pack the Tahoe from an upstairs window on a dismal grey afternoon. The surgery had successfully relieved the pressure from the subdural hematoma, but Nate remained in a coma. After three days, his doctors recommended a move to a facility that specialized in head injuries, and Ashley agreed. She opted for a specialty clinic in Illinois near their old home. They had kept the house until the renovation was complete and they were certain they wanted to stay in Wisconsin.

Laura walked downstairs to say goodbye. Ashley had scarcely spoken to her since the accident and, as she approached the Tahoe, Ashley turned on Laura, her face a mask of pain and anger.

"Stay away from me!"

"Ashley—"

"You knew something was wrong that day. How?"

Laura took a step back, stunned by her ire. "I didn't know—"

"You knew! And you did nothing!"

Palms up in supplication, Laura said, "Ashley, please—"

Ashley jabbed her finger at Laura like a spear. "There's something wrong with you, Laura. You're a freak!"

In tears, Ashley jumped into the Tahoe, slammed the door, and spun her tires pulling away. Her words were like a physical blow, and Laura stood rigid, too stunned to speak. Watching the vehicle disappear, Laura cried and wished bitterly that she had never come here. So much had gone wrong. She went into the house, snatched Leah from her crib, and hugged her as if she were the last person on earth.

Lucas had barely spoken since the accident. He remained aloof and unreachable. Cold. She tried to comfort him, but he pushed her away and refused to discuss any of it. A traumatic event like this could ruin a marriage and she feared their relationship was in mortal danger. They had survived Jacob's death, but Lucas had handled it differently. They had drawn together and talked; fought the urge to be alone, to wallow in silence. Now, Lucas refused to discuss anything, refused to seek counseling, and Laura realized she could only do so much. Beyond that, time might be the only cure for his near catatonic state.

She tried to be patient, mindful, but she needed his companionship. Wracked with guilt and wounded by Ashley's anger and accusations, she couldn't stop dwelling on Nate, his injury, and the coma that might become a permanent condition. Between Lucas, Ashley, and Nate, she couldn't handle the sense of loss she felt.

Laura knew Nate's injury was her fault. The warning signs had been there, the danger clear. She had failed to act and now Nate was in a coma. Had she heeded her feelings, she might have prevented the accident.

How?

She didn't know. It was immaterial. It was her fault. Ashley blamed her. Lucas blamed her, too.

Unable to rely on Lucas for even simple tasks, Laura hired a contractor to repair the damage to the house and replace the furnace. The fire marshal determined the lightning had traveled down an old copper lightning rod next to the chimney. Some of the voltage ran along a cold air return and through the furnace, destroying the control board, exiting along the flex-steel propane supply line. The heat melted holes in the thin metal pipe that had been improperly grounded.

Propane leaked into the room and the hallway. Heavier than air, it pooled near the floor, so Nate probably didn't smell it. A spark from the light switch ignited the gas. Focused by stone walls and thick timbers above, the blast followed the path of least resistance, throwing Nate backwards through the window and fifteen feet out onto the lawn.

The gas line was a known issue and attorney letters followed, filled with dollar signs, urging them to sue the contractor. Offended by the crass nature of the letters, Laura shredded them, knowing Lucas would go postal if he saw them. Ashley could decide later if she wanted to pursue that course. There had been no fire and only minor structural damage, a testament to the sturdy construction of the house. Nate had just been in the wrong place at the worst possible moment.

Oddly, the house had been quiet. The bar and fireplace screen remained in place even after she removed the tape Lucas had used to secure it. Doors stopped slamming randomly. The knives sat motionless on the counter. She finally put them back on the magnetic bar where they stayed, mocking her. She scarcely noticed, mired in a melancholy so thick and brooding, it might have spilled into a full-blown depression it wasn't for Leah.

Leah was a refuge from her overwhelming sadness. The sight of those big blue eyes and crooked grin made her smile and eased the pain. They played together, read stories, watched movies, and spent most of their waking moments together. Learning to talk, a distinct personality was evolving, and Laura found the process fascinating. So different from raising her children. She felt so much more relaxed and patient.

It wasn't enough. She missed Lucas. She missed Nate and feared she might never see him again. Most of all, she missed Jacob with a keening ache. This house, where she had hoped the healing would begin, had only compounded her pain and left her longing for her old life in Illinois.

Thirty-One

Shepherd typed the next line of Old English into a Word document:

Ic hine cuðe cnihtwesende. Wæs his ealdfæder Hæreðes haten.

He considered the words for a moment, then entered the translation into a second document:

I knew him when he was a young boy. His father before him was called Haereth.

Shepherd sat in his second-floor study, translating the pages of Lucas MacKenzie's book. He didn't have the original text. That was under lock and key at the university. Instead, he worked from high-res images on a thirty-two-inch monitor. The process was painstaking. Line by line, he deciphered the faded and scrawled handwriting and made a best guess as to its meaning. Old English was structurally different from modern English, so any translation required a degree of creative interpretation. Attaching specific meanings to words and preserving the nuance of the text was an inexact science, even for an expert who spoke fluent Mercian as he did.

His initial assessment had been correct. The first part of the book was a diary, mundane and personal, written by a young, affluent woman. That was surprising. In sixteenth century England, reading and writing were almost solely the province of men. Women who could do either were rare. Oddly, the author's name appeared nowhere in the text. Most of the incidental names appeared only as initials, giving the narrative a secretive air.

The middle segment was medical—not a textbook—but a series of remedies interlaced into the narrative. It read more like the work of *cunning folk*, practitioners of spells and medical remedies prevalent in the Middle Ages. Rarely even semi-literate, most would have been unable to write a text of this complexity, especially in Old English. If this was the work of cunning folk, the book was a true oddity. He had seen nothing like it.

At first, he thought it was stolen. Then he considered forgery. Having seen the book, held it in his hands, he knew it was genuine. Somehow, the book had traveled from medieval England to the Wisconsin countryside unscathed. Was it a carefully protected family heirloom? Or something darker?

From an antiquities point of view, it was a remarkable find and would create a buzz when word of it circulated. He wanted no involvement in that aspect. He preferred a discreet profile in the academic world lest it invite scrutiny into his past.

The curious question? Why was it written in Old English? It was clear from the cultural and social references the book had been written in the fifteenth century. Old English had evolved to Middle English by then. Who would still be writing in the ancient tongue?

It was a rhetorical question. He knew the answer with uneasy certainty. It was the language of medieval witches and sorcerers, and somewhere within lay the reason he was here. He was certain of it.

Unfortunately, he had no idea what he was looking for. Might be a chapter, a page, a paragraph, a single sentence. His translation would need to be thorough and methodical. It might take weeks to answer that question.

There was also something familiar about it. He had an inexplicable feeling when he first held it: a brief shock accompanied by a vague subliminal image. Had he seen or read something like this in the past? He couldn't remember, his brain cluttered with the accumulated memories of a millennium. These days, specific memories were harder to find. Nothing useful surfaced.

In the full equation, he had the elusive location of the house and the mystery woman. He needed to visit, view the setting, complete that piece of the puzzle. Which was more important? The house or the book? Why had the book been hidden there? What role did the blonde woman play?

The book felt like the critical clue. Within lay the answers to all his questions.

Answers that would be forthcoming when he completed the translation.

Thirty-Two

Dressed in bib overalls and a greasy Purina cap, Tom wandered the woods and fields around the house. He was the caretaker and that was his job. Watch the house. Keep strangers and the curious away. Allow no harm to befall the place. He had grown tired of the responsibility, though. While he had little temporal awareness, it seemed years and years had gone by and an endless future here stretched ahead of him. It felt more like a life sentence than a job.

Tom heard a car with a faulty muffler approach and knew at once who it was. He wandered over to the old logging trail and watched the car park out of sight on the disused forest road. A teen stepped out and looked about furtively. Tall and thin in stature, his clothes hung loosely on his frame. He looked like a scarecrow, and that was the name Tom had given him. He was a frequent visitor.

Scarecrow grabbed a rifle and walked into the trees, stalking the forest for small game. Armed with a .22, a powerful scope, and a keen eye, he felled small animals—often rabbits and squirrels—maiming and killing them out of what appeared to be pure malice.

When he seemed in good spirits, a last shot to the head finished his brutal work. Otherwise, he left the injured animals to be devoured by other predators. Today, he looked angry and miserable and hadn't stirred up so much as a mouse.

Breaking through dense brush, Scarecrow stopped and stared at the MacKenzie house. He didn't normally come this way and Tom imagined he saw that big old house as a vision out of a horror movie. It looked empty, too. No lights, no cars in the drive; Tom knew they weren't home. The kid slowly raised his rifle and put his eye to the scope. Those panes of leaded glass had to be tempting targets.

Tom approached, trying to rustle the brush and make noise—or better yet—materialize and scare the shit out of the little bastard.

Lowering the rifle, the kid turned, eyes narrowed, but there was little evidence of fear in them. Tom, feeling sleek and grey, sidled through the woods, leading him away from the house.

The boy crouched and stalked him like an animal. He raised the rifle, brought the scope to his eye, and fired two quick shots. Tom fell out of sight in the underbrush; waiting, gathering his energy for the big shock.

Scarecrow approached carefully and, as he stepped forward to deliver the killing shot, Tom willed himself to materialize as he reared up with a terrible howl, yelling, "Little bastard!"

The kid yelped as he jumped back in fright. Dropping the rifle, he lost his footing, stumbled, and scooted backwards on his ass into the brush.

Tom snatched a pitchfork out of the ether and jabbed the tines at the boy with clear malice.

Rolling and scrambling away, Scarecrow ran headlong through the brush. He lost a shoe but barely slowed, thrashing through briers, scratching his arms.

Tom gave chase, but the kid never looked back. He kept running until he reached his car, dove in, and locked the doors, still shaking in abject terror, looking like he had just seen a ghost.

Ha! That was fun!

Scarecrow would have one hell of a story to tell—if anyone believed him.

Tom watched the little creep gun the engine and careen backwards down the road, scattering gravel and dirt, leaving his gun and shoe behind. Tom laughed a ghostly laugh, quite certain he'd never see that troublemaker again.

Standing in the woods, he looked with longing toward his old property. The house had burnt down years ago and the had fields reverted to wild prairie and woodland. He had no family and had willed the land to the Kettle Moraine State Forest to preserve the natural character of the property. He never imagined they would get it so soon.

He turned and wandered toward Elizabeth's house.

Whoa!

The house was glowing slightly. The roof shimmered an iridescent green, especially around the central chimney. He closed his eyes and shook his head. Looked again, but the aura was still there. In all his time there, he had seen nothing like it. The cause seemed obvious. The people in the house had opened that disused brick room and now the roof was glowing.

Whatever it was, it felt like an omen.

Nothing good would come of this.

Thirty-Three

As night fell over Lost Arrow, Lucas walked into the White Birch Inn and sat on his usual stool at the far corner of the bar. Two older men sat in the middle, talking to Jake, the bartender. The place was otherwise empty, though the usual crowd would soon filter in. The nights here had a constancy Lucas found reassuring. As one of the regulars, he drank and played pool as they all pissed and moaned about life and politics in a daily ritual that often ran past midnight.

Behind a feigned mask of composure, Lucas was a churning mess of grief, despair, and regret. Somehow, he had lost control of his life. He didn't understand why he spent so much time with these drunks. Or Murphy. He hadn't slept with her, though she was clearly available. He was attracted to her raw, seductive manner, her lithe and sexy movements, but she was rough around the edges. An internal voice suggested he was better than this, that a relationship with her was beneath him. Besides, he was married, though that seemed less and less compelling lately.

Most days, he wandered the woods around the house with a bow or sat on the lake in the Alumacraft. He otherwise whiled away the hours at the White Birch with Bruce, Murphy, and other interchangeable characters.

Much of his malaise stemmed from an inner dialogue that ran incessantly in his head. Nate's accident was his fault. He'd left Nate alone that day and therefore, the blame fell on him. Simple cause and effect. Had he stayed home, Nate would be fine. He had put his own interests over his brother's safety and now Nate was paying the price.

He also imagined a darker outcome. Had he stayed home, he might have been injured as well. Instead, he was fine and Nate was in a coma. It had a name—survivor's guilt—but giving it a name did little to ease the haunting burden he felt.

Lucas wallowed in his unrelenting guilt and saw no reason to discuss the issue so he ignored Laura and her persistent nagging on the subject.

The final irony? The trip had been a waste of time. Shepherd had no answers. None would be forthcoming for weeks, if at all. The book was a worthless relic if Nate didn't recover. Lucas was often abrupt and dismissive toward Nate, but beneath that good-natured contempt lay a deep love and admiration for his brother. He felt Nate slipping away and would never forgive himself if he didn't recover.

Some of his angst stemmed from the strange comment Laura made that day.

Nate, be careful, okay?

Was it a warning? Had she somehow foreseen the accident? But that was stupid. He didn't believe in premonitions.

Then Ashley pulled him aside and related the story of Laura's seizure and ramblings in the mall. Reflecting further, he wondered why Laura hadn't been more emphatic in her warning. How did she know?

Was she somehow responsible? Lucas recognized these thoughts as irrational, but they continued to nag him.

This he knew: since the accident, her every word grated on his nerves. She sounded more and more abrasive as she poked and prodded him to talk, to seek help, to open up. At least no one at the White Birch bothered him beyond brief inquiries into Nate's condition. Still, some deeper connection remained between them, perhaps the only reason he hadn't slept with Murphy.

Yet.

But he was wary of Laura and sensed something sinister about her. He also realized he was being paranoid and irrational. He didn't believe in the paranormal, a fantasy world of good and evil inhabited by angels and devils living in fanciful places called heaven and hell—superstitious nonsense for the simple-minded.

So why was he thinking that way?

He didn't know.

And he couldn't stop.

Thirty-Four

With a kiss to the forehead, Laura laid Leah down for a nap and stood in the hallway, feeling lost. Hours of silence lay ahead. Her life was accursed with silence, an emptiness that grew greater every day, magnified by the sprawling house.

She donned a white *dobok,* tied the red belt around her waist, and jogged downstairs to the Hall. Pushing the coffee table aside, she performed a stretching routine, and then practiced her *Palgwe* forms, a *Taekwondo* technique of fighting an imaginary opponent in precise steps.

Stand to attention. Turn right and punch, step and snap-kick. Turn left, punch, step, snap-kick...

Laura missed the discipline of classes and needed to find a local *dojang* to complete her training for the black belt. After forty minutes, tired and sweating profusely, Laura took a shower and dressed in black sweats. Leah remained asleep.

Returning to the Hall, she sat at the Steinway and played scales and simple progressions to loosen her fingers.

The brisk sunny days of October had yielded to the dull grey skies of November. The last holdout leaves fell from the trees, and wintry winds brought snow squalls from the north, painting the landscape with patches of white. It was a sad, faceless passage of time. Nate remained comatose. Ashley hadn't spoken to her since. Lucas had all but deserted her. He spent his mornings hunting or splitting wood, fleeing every afternoon to the White Birch, often till after midnight—unless he drove south to visit Nate. She had gone once, but Lucas had been silent the entire trip and Ashley left without a word when they arrived.

Lucas had quit shaving and looked pale and gaunt. He was curt when they talked and refused to discuss their failing relationship. They hadn't made love in over a month. Instead, he pushed her away when she tried to touch him with various ironic excuses: *I'm tired. I have a headache. Not tonight.*

She wondered if he was seeing someone else—though he had never given her reason to doubt him.

Laura knew he was in pain and tried to be supportive, but her sympathy had soured to anger and resentment. She was hurting, too. Nate was like a brother and she couldn't stand to see him in a hospital bed, looking near death. With the loss of Lucas's companionship and the apparent end of her friendship with Ashley, she felt alone in the world.

Working a new strategy, Laura lived a life apart from Lucas. Perhaps ignoring him would draw him back. She moved a bed into Leah's room and slept there, made meals on her own schedule, came and went as she pleased.

She doted on Leah, playing and having adult conversations, Leah's big eyes intent, as if she understood every word. Perhaps she did. They had a routine. She and Leah ate breakfast, then walked when weather permitted. Otherwise, they played indoors. Leah napped for a few hours every afternoon and sat quietly in her play area, engrossed in her toys, while Laura worked with her glass. Laura had now sold two lamps on Etsy and had orders for more.

Playing a simple chord sequence, she broke into dreamy variations, losing herself to the music. The progressions morphed into more complex patterns with an aggressive edge. She could disappear into the chords *and* vent her frustrations.

It was the Sunday before Thanksgiving, and Laura had thought about a turkey, but couldn't see Lucas sitting down for dinner. No, he would go to the White Birch, and that would leave just her and Leah. The thought of spending Thanksgiving alone filled her with deep and longing sadness.

Her phone rang. Laura stopped and looked at the screen.

It was Dana. After some initial small talk, Dana said, "I was wondering if you'd mind if I came to visit for a few days?"

"No, I'd love it," Laura said, almost desperate for meaningful company, but she detected a tone. "Dana? Is anything wrong?"

"Oh, nothing—"

Silence.

She then realized Dana was gone.

Dropped call. The signal out here was iffy—not that anyone ever called. A moment later, the phone rang.

"Hi, Mom."

"What's the matter, hon?"

Still silent. Laura checked her phone again and Dana finally spoke. "My communications professor hit on me last week. Blatantly. I told him no—I was polite—I thought I was, anyway. I just got my last exam back with a failing grade. There was nothing wrong with it, Mom.

Nothing!" Dana was almost yelling. "I may have to retake the freaking class!"

Laura clenched her fist. How did that shit still happen? "What's the little bastard's name—"

"No, Mom, you can't go off on him. I'm appealing. In the meantime, is it okay if I come?"

"Of course. When?"

"Tuesday."

"Perfect. I can't wait to see you."

She hung up and sat staring into space. With Dana coming, she had to clean the house. She would do a turkey, stuffing, the works. Dana couldn't have called at a better time. Lucas could go to the bar; she no longer cared. She, Dana, and Leah would have a Thanksgiving feast.

Then she remembered the party tonight at Brenda Anson's. Laura contemplated canceling, but decided against it. She needed to get out of the house and meet people, and a Pampered Chef party sounded like a good place to start.

The invite had come from Carol at the general store. Laura had been running there for sundries—butter, half and half, eggs—and often lingered, chatting with Carol. In passing, Laura mentioned her need for a babysitter.

Carol had said, "You could ask my daughter. She's laid off and I know she's looking for something to do. You'll have to bring her to town, though. Brenda won't go anywhere near your house."

Laura was hesitant to leave Leah with a relative stranger.

Carol may have sensed her reluctance. "Brenda's hosting a Pampered Chef party day after tomorrow. You're welcome to come. You can meet my daughter and see the house."

"I'd love to." Though she wondered about being asked. Lost Arrow hadn't been particularly welcoming.

"There'll be a few women your age as well."

"That sounds wonderful. I need to get out more." It sounded like a perfect opportunity to meet some women from town. She would welcome help with Leah so she could attend auctions, pick up glass supplies, or simply get out of the house for a while.

A knife fell to the floor in the kitchen and clattered on the tile. Laura trudged to the kitchen, picked the knife up, and set it back on the counter. A moment later, a door slammed somewhere upstairs.

"Mrs. Moskopf! Whoever you are, knock it off!" Laura yelled to the empty room. This nonsense with the knives and doors had started a few days before. It wasn't scary. It was annoying. Were they trying to tell her something?

More and more, she thought about leaving and returning to Illinois. She loved Lucas, wasn't seriously contemplating divorce, but she couldn't stand being ignored much longer. Maybe she needed bolder action to grab his attention, but that sounded desperate and cynical, and in a moment of candor, Laura realized she was becoming cynical about many things. In a moment of melancholy, she'd written a conciliatory email to Ashley, but had received no answer.

So it was good Dana was coming, and good she was going out tonight.

Otherwise, Laura feared she'd lose her mind.

Thirty-Five

Brenda Anson lived three doors down from the store. The house looked like a smallish Cape Cod with stone steps and a covered entryway, flanked by mature spruces. Laura was inexplicably nervous. She could still drive by and go home, but she forced herself to stop. She walked up to the house, lugging Leah on her left hip, a diaper bag and purse hanging from her right shoulder.

Carol opened the door, wearing navy-blue stretch pants, a dingy white sweater, and a big smile. "Hi, Laura. Glad you came. Come on in."

Setting Leah on her feet, Laura took off her coat as Brenda rushed to the hallway, smoothing wrinkles from her sweatpants. She looked much like her mother: heavy set with jet black hair, a pale white face—though her eyes were brighter, not as puffy as Carol's. Two young boys, perhaps four and six years old, trailed shyly behind. Two other women sitting in the brightly lit living room in animated conversation paused to give Laura a quick appraisal.

Laura followed Brenda into the living room. Leah dropped to her knees and crawled to a pile of toys scattered on the taupe carpeting along a hallway leading to the bedrooms. The boys plopped down next to her and began playing. Laura smiled, but the boys only stared at her.

She sighed and sat in a small brown armchair with a view of the front door and the guests as they arrived. The room itself was subdued in color, mostly whites and greys, but enlivened with an abundance of greenery: spider plants, philodendrons, and ferns.

The doorbell rang, the door swung open and three women burst in, giggling like schoolgirls. They were briefly quiet, but giggled again as they surged into the living room.

An attractive blonde sauntered in, snapping her gum. "Hey, Bren. Got anything fun? Vibrators? Dildos? Oops. Sorry, Mrs. A, didn't see you sitting there."

Carol threw her a withering look.

Laura remembered seeing her before at the White Birch wearing a studded leather jacket, projecting the same cocky attitude.

Brenda struggled up and introduced everyone. The blonde was Murphy. The other two, mousy-haired and nondescript, were Kelly and Erica.

Murphy turned to Laura, smirking. "So you're Laura MacKenzie..."

That dangling sentence was so laden with implications, Laura felt she could reach out and grab it. The other two women exchanged a glance. Laura felt uncomfortable and out of place.

Why was Murphy so smug?

An answer rose from her subconscious, that Lucas was having an affair and they knew about it. Laura dismissed the idea. Lucas may have been distant, but an affair? No way. Especially with the likes of Murphy. Then her conviction wavered. She didn't feel entirely sure of herself.

The tension passed as more people arrived. Within ten minutes, the room was full of boisterous women trading the latest gossip and bitching about their husbands or their children. No one engaged Laura in conversation and she questioned the decision to come, feeling bored and uncomfortable.

Leah disappeared. Laura went to find her, surreptitiously checking the rooms and the housekeeping. The house was reasonably clean. Maybe she would leave Leah for a few afternoons. Brenda seemed nice enough, and her boys behaved well. Leah was content playing with the other children so she let her be.

Walking back to the living room, Laura caught a snippet of conversation cut short when the women saw her. "That Laura MacKenzie is pretty enough—"

She pretended not to notice and sat, feeling uneasy about the undercurrents in the hidden shoals of this party.

The doorbell rang. Brenda escorted a woman into the room who looked near seventy and walked with a cane. Her face was pleasant, clearly pretty in her younger days, her straight grey-brown hair framing her face in a schoolmarmish fashion. Older than most of the women, she seemed out of place, and yet everyone greeted her warmly. Her name was Sally.

She stared for a moment with large, intelligent eyes and extended her hand. "Nice to meet you, Laura."

Laura shook her hand. Was this the Sally that Carol had mentioned?

She sat on the other side of the adjoining maple end-table, in a matching brown armchair, which had remained empty, as if reserved for her.

"We were sorry to hear about your brother-in-law," Sally said. Condolent murmurs passed around the room. "How is he doing?"

Laura grew uneasy with this line of conversation; curious about the obvious respect Sally enjoyed.

"It's been hard. He's still in a coma. Nothing's changed," Laura said. Sadness and guilt welled up inside, and she struggled to conceal her feelings.

Perhaps sensing her discomfort, Brenda passed around the latest kitchen gadgets, demonstrating a few of them as she went. It was noisy and chaotic as the women examined and played with the items while carrying on various conversations, mostly local gossip and upcoming events. Laura joined in the cooking conversations and ignored the gossip, the usual mix of fact and fiction, envy and contempt. Knowing none of the players, it was mostly meaningless. Sally talked little but observed intently. A catalogue and order form made the rounds.

Brenda stepped over to check on them. Sally asked for a cup of tea, and the tea arrived a few minutes later during a lull in conversation.

"So, Laura, how is that house treating you?" Sally said, her voice pleasant, almost hypnotic.

Laura turned with a start. The question, innocuous as it seemed, felt loaded with implications Laura could only guess at. She heard whispered murmurs: "Don't know how you can live there..." and such.

Laura was now the center of attention. The chatter faded.

Head cocked inquisitively, Sally waited for an answer.

"How is the house treating me?" Laura asked, puzzled by the odd question. Felt her stomach tighten with a wary sensation.

Fingering the handle of her cane, Sally said, "Yes. I'm curious. I wonder if you've heard any of the stories people tell about that house."

She tried to act nonchalant. "Not really." Wasn't sure she wanted to.

Sally stared with penetrating eyes. "People around here believe the MacKenzie house is haunted. Most of them wouldn't go near the place if their lives depended on it. Maybe it's foolish superstition, maybe not, but since you're here, I wondered how you felt about it."

"It's fine. We haven't noticed anything," Laura said unconvincingly, chilled by the question.

Sally had preternatural knowledge about the house. Laura could see it in her eyes, feel it emanating from this strange woman in a wave. The room was so quiet, the whistling of a falling pin might have been audible. Sally placed her hand on Laura's. A sudden surge of warmth traveled up her arm. She grew lightheaded.

"I lost a dear friend there, you know," Sally said. "Forty-some years ago. Such a long time in the past, but I still remember that summer well because of the heat."

Sally's expression became dreamy, her voice soft but fervent. Laura heard the voice of a younger woman, saw her face as it was that summer, a young woman in love. The room faded from view.

"Tom Wolff and I started dating that year. He was in love with Elizabeth MacKenzie—everybody knew that—but when she left, I was happy to step in. He was a good man, and I thought he was going to propose on Labor Day."

Sally smiled briefly at the fond memory, then her expression darkened. "And then for whatever reason—I don't know—chasing vandals maybe, Tom went over to the house that day and found trouble. I *knew* he was in trouble, so I called the sheriff."

She stopped, near tears, the memory and pain of that day still clearly vivid.

Laura leaned in and murmured, "What happened to Tom?"

"He parked his tractor near the house, but they never found him. Haven't to this day."

Sally's hand slipped from Laura's and as it did, Laura felt a brief lapse of consciousness as the room seemed to skew sideways. Subliminal images, like video in ultra-fast forward, flashed through her mind far too quickly to comprehend.

In a vacant monotone, Laura said, "I know what really happened."

Laura looked up as the room came back into focus. The faces of the women around the room had paled, their mouths agape, as they stared at Laura and Sally with a collective expression. Fear? Awe? Laura couldn't decide.

"I don't know why I said that." She had vague impressions, as in the past, but nothing tangible. If she could have slipped out on the breath of the wind, she would have, but she felt trapped here and unable to move. Feeling drained, a headache probed at her temples.

Sally looked weary. Laura heard Leah yelling in one of the bedrooms. She jumped up to find her, grateful for an excuse to leave the room as it erupted in an excited jumble of voices. Laura found Leah struggling with an older boy who was trying to shove her into a closet.

With an angry glare, Laura pushed him aside, scooped up Leah, and walked back to the living room, praying for the strength to leave with her dignity intact.

The room quieted. Sally stood and Carol helped her with her coat. Sally then put a hand out to Laura, who took it hesitantly. "I'm going to go. I suddenly feel tired."

"Me too."

"It seems we have something in common." Sally looked at Laura with a piercing gaze.

"I'm not sure I understand."

She leaned in. "I think you do."

"Can we talk again?" Laura said, though she couldn't explain the urge.

"Yes, if I can help. I live in the brick house next to the old hotel." She squeezed Laura's hand. "Some of what you're looking for is up the road in the cemetery. I'm not sure why. Just a hunch, but I've learned to trust my instincts over the years."

Laura said her goodbyes. Everyone remained surprisingly cordial after that strange, intense moment.

She drove home, shaken and confused by her meeting with Sally. She didn't understand it; couldn't even describe it lucidly.

It seems we have something in common.

Laura tried to ignore the implication. The seizures she could live with. The other thing? She didn't want it. Still, she hadn't forgiven herself for missing the clues about Nate accident even as she continued to deny she was psychic at all.

Was she psychic? She didn't know but Sally seemed to be.

I knew he was in trouble.

Her ramblings about the house were disturbing. Was it superstitious nonsense? It sounded ridiculous.

The disappearance of Tom Wolff was a fact, that story the last clipping in the bizarre album. That alone meant nothing. People disappeared all the time without help from the supernatural. Tom Wolff was probably long dead and resting in the woods or at the bottom of the lake. Why blame the house?

But Sally did. And there were Elizabeth's enigmatic words: *It ends here.*

Elizabeth evidently blamed the house, too.

What ends here?

Truth was, Sally and Elizabeth, the rumors about the house, the album, the falling knives, the slamming doors, and the disappearance of Tom Wolff? They all added up to something. Something important. Until now, Laura had been in denial. That needed to stop. Time to face this head-on and figure out what that *something* was.

How? She didn't know.

The house was quiet when they walked in. Laura didn't want to be alone and missed Lucas acutely, but he was gone. It was just the two of them, so she pushed her anxieties aside and focused on Leah. On the sofa, she tickled Leah. They both laughed and giggled while she changed Leah into warm onesie pajamas. They played peekaboo, followed by their daily word game.

Leah pointed, pursed her lips and said, "Ga-ma."

Laura pointed at her and said, "Le-ah."

She turned her finger on herself and said, "La-la."

Back and forth they went, saying simple words. Soon Leah rubbed her eyes. Laura cradled her in her lap and read from a book. When she finished, Leah was asleep. Laura carried her upstairs and tucked her into the crib, giving her a soft kiss on the forehead. All this served as a diversion from events at the party earlier. A little downtime. Tomorrow she would start digging further into the mystery surrounding the house.

Laura grabbed a comforter and pillow from her bed and walked downstairs. After pouring a glass of wine and stoking the fire, she curled up on the sofa in the Hall and read a book, waiting for Lucas. Sleep came and she vaguely remembered Lucas walking in and tossing a log on the fire before stumbling upstairs to bed.

Near dawn, she dreamt of a carnival, a tent, an old woman in vivid Romany clothing, dealing cards—Tarot cards—in a descending line.

The Magician

Death

Wheel of Fortune

The Fool

Judgement

The cards were labeled, but Laura knew nothing of Tarot and didn't understand what they signified. Janice Foster would probably know, but Janice had never called back.

Without turning, the woman shook her head and said, "This is bad."

Thirty-Six

Laura awoke with a start, certain someone was watching her.

Right there, on the sofa. Except the sofa was empty.

She looked around. The room was dark; the fire reduced to a few dull embers, the baby monitor silent. She smelled coffee. Laura slid off the sofa and shuffled to the kitchen.

Lucas sat at the table, his back to her, cup in hand, staring into space. She walked up behind him.

"Morning."

He didn't move. She put a hand on his shoulder. "Lucas?"

He jumped suddenly, spilling his coffee. "What?"

"Were you sleeping?"

"Uh, I don't know." He turned to look at her. His eyes reddened and glazed, he seemed confused.

Laura said, "Rough night?"

"Guess so."

Laura poured herself a cup of coffee, added cream and sweetener, and sat at the table. "Been awhile since we've had coffee together in the morning."

"Yeah."

Why did she feel like she was sitting here with a stranger? He didn't even look at her, just stared into space.

"Going hunting today?"

"Yep."

"Going to the White Birch later?"

"Probably." He shrugged, still avoiding her gaze.

Her anger swelled, but she tried to rein it in. She wanted to open a line of communication before it was too late, draw him back before they grew too far apart and their relationship passed the point of no return. It wasn't anger so much as loneliness and desperation stealing over her. She felt lonely, even with Leah in the house. She wanted comfort, advice, strength, and most of all, a sense of family—the three of them, together. There was something wrong in the house and she didn't want to face it alone.

Laura stood and walked behind Lucas, leaning against him, running her hands lightly up and down his chest. His shoulders tensed.

"How about something different tonight? A nice dinner, some wine, and then—"

"Nope. Big game tonight. Maybe tomorrow." He shrank into the chair, avoiding her touch.

Football? She was being pushed aside for Monday Night Football? Her anger flared again. Laura took a deep breath, forced her resentment aside even though she felt cheap pushing so hard to gain his affection. She didn't want to fight. Then she thought, why wait? She pressed against him. "Maybe we shouldn't wait until tonight."

He shoved her away. "Christ! Is that all you think about?"

Laura flushed. "Screw you, Lucas! That isn't all I think about. At least I think about something besides myself all the time. I understand that Nate's situation has been tough—"

"You don't know shit," he barked, staring into his coffee.

"I know you've been taking it out on Leah and me. You wander around the woods all day and then go drink all night. You have a family, Lucas, or have you forgotten?" She defiantly put her hands on her hips.

"Yeah, and if you had your way, when I wasn't servicing you in bed, I'd be scrubbing floors and playing nanny."

"Fuck you, Lucas!"

"Truth hurt?"

God, he looked so smug she wanted to slap him. "That isn't even close to true and you know it! What the hell is wrong with you?"

"Maybe I'm tired of being nagged."

"Lucas, we've hardly spoken in the last month. When have I had time to nag you?"

"Oh, you've managed. Like now. Blah, blah, blah. Nag, nag, nag. Jesus!"

Laura jabbed a finger at him. "If you were a little more—"

"If you were a little more *this*—if you were a little more *that*," he mocked. "Fuck you, Laura. I don't need this." He grabbed his coat off the back of the chair, stormed out of the kitchen and down the stairs. A moment later, the lower door slammed.

Laura stood, petrified by shock, wounded by his cruel words, his tone, his angry body language. While the man who stormed out looked like Lucas, it wasn't the man she married. Lucas had never spoken to her like that. Well, that wasn't entirely true. The change had been evident since Nate's accident and had worsened in the past week. She thought of the women at the party, the talk, the looks.

Was Lucas seeing someone?

She didn't know.

Laura put her coffee down and walked to her bedroom in an aimless shuffle, forcing back tears, feeling miserable their conversation had gone so awry. Between the house and Lucas, maybe it was time to pack her things and leave. Still, Dana was coming tomorrow. She would have someone to talk to. Maybe Dana could talk to Lucas.

Unable to push past the sadness, she crawled into their bed—tired of the single in Leah's room—and fell asleep.

An hour later, Laura woke to a familiar sound, Leah crying for rescue from her crib. It was just after eight, and her sleep had been deep and dreamless. Her earlier melancholy had mostly dissipated. She slid out of bed and walked to Leah's room. The little blonde scamp smiled and jumped up and down at the side of her crib when Laura walked in.

"Ga-ma, ga-ma!"

"Come on, you. Let's go get some breakfast."

Laura made grape jam on wheat toast, cut into squares, and marveled that Leah never refused them. While she ate, Laura mulled over the strange meeting with Sally last night. It almost seemed like a dream now.

It seems we have something in common.

No denying it anymore. Sally seemed so calm and casual about it. No big deal. Maybe it wasn't. Perhaps she had been running from her own shadow all these years. Still, the *gift* had never been useful to her.

I know what really happened.

Except she didn't; had no clue why she said that.

At face value, Sally's story seemed whimsical. The man she loved had gone missing and that despondent young woman had evidently turned an inexplicable but natural disappearance into a supernatural event. Certainly, it was easier to blame the house. But haunted houses, while scary, never actually killed people. Or did they?

Why was she asking such a silly question? An accident was the most logical explanation. Perhaps his body remained hidden in the woods or at the bottom of the lake. Such things happened often enough and the paranormal had nothing to do with it. According to Sally, he had no enemies, so murder seemed unlikely. Suicide was another possibility.

If only she could remember the string of images that accompanied that strange moment last night.

The vague feeling a woman had been involved? The ghost she saw in the basement hallway?

That connection felt tenuous, useless.

She needed to brave a trip to the cemetery. Part of her dreaded the prospect, driven by a silly fear of cemeteries. Despite that, she felt compelled to go.

Why? Because of a few words from a woman she barely knew? Illogical?

Yes. But she was going anyway.

A quick hot shower and she felt even better. She jumped into a pair of jeans and a white sweater and dressed Leah for the day.

She needed a sitter and wondered how Brenda felt after last night. She had nothing to lose in calling. Laura punched the number into her phone and chewed on a nail until Brenda answered.

"Brenda? This is Laura MacKenzie."

"Hey, Laura. How are you?" Brenda's voice betrayed no hint of misgivings.

"Fine, just fine. Uh, I was wondering if you could watch Leah for a few hours today?"

"No problem. Bring the little doll over. She's adorable."

"Great, I appreciate it." Laura paused a moment. "About last night, I was wondering..."

"You're wondering what I thought, right?"

"Yes."

"I felt lucky to be there. Sally has a gift—I guess that's what you'd call it. She just *knows* stuff, always has, and people around here feel she's special—respect her for it. Then you come along and you both connect like that, saying all that weird stuff. It was like a séance or something, so I figure you have it, too. Makes you special too, you know?"

Laura wasn't sure she felt special.

"I guess so. Okay if I bring Leah over in half an hour?"

"Sure, see you then."

"Awesome! Thanks."

"Janice Foster is going to call you. She asked for your number."

"Okay. Thanks for the heads up."

Laura was halfway down the stairs when her phone rang. The number looked vaguely familiar.

The voice, rushed and breathless, said, "Laura. This is Janice Foster. I have to talk to you. I heard what happened at Brenda's. I'd like to help."

Laura made a slight clucking sound with her tongue. So Janice Foster had heard about her meeting with Sally. She'd called Janice months ago. The woman had never returned her calls but now she wanted to help? Laura suspected that Janice Foster might be a crass attention-seeker.

"Janice, I called you three times. You never returned my calls."

"I know, and I'm sorry. I didn't feel I had much to offer before now."

"I'm really busy right now—"

"Laura, this is important. It was in the cards."

The cards? Tarot cards? Jesus! Bunch of silly, superstitious nonsense. But the thought nudged a memory loose. Something about Tarot but she couldn't pull it.

"What is it?"

"You need to see them," Janice said.

"I was just going out. Can I call you later?"

A moment of silence. Laura thought her phone had dropped the call, but Janice then said, "Don't wait too long, Laura. Please call me back as soon as possible."

"Sure," Laura said, thinking *maybe, maybe not.*

She stabbed the red phone icon and went to fetch Leah.

Thirty-Seven

Laura stopped at Brenda's, staying and chatting over coffee about the children, Sally, Carol, and life in Lost Arrow. She liked Brenda, more so now they'd talked one-on-one, and felt comfortable leaving Leah there.

Laura swung the car around and drove back to the church. Sat for five minutes, nervously eyeing the tombstones. On the right of the church, the cemetery swept over a slight rise to a decrepit picket fence marking the outer perimeter. Old oaks scattered around the graves, the branches bare and skeletal, formed a canopy of interwoven branches above. Patches of snow dotted the grass. A mangy arborvitae hedge lined the rear boundary of the churchyard.

Enough procrastination.

Laura stepped out of the car and walked across the highway—the main street of Lost Arrow—to a gate next to the church. The graveyard looked harmless, but memories of her nightmare lingered and magnified her silly fear of cemeteries, an inexplicable, irrational phobia. She struggled through funerals and often concocted excuses to avoid them.

Steeling her nerve, Laura pushed on the gate and nearly choked with fright when the hinges let loose and the gate fell to the ground with a dull *thud.*

Jesus!

She clasped her chest, then looked around furtively. She grabbed the gate and set it nonchalantly against the church wall, deciding that God had a sick sense of humor. Her stomach fluttering with apprehension, Laura stepped into the cemetery.

The oldest stones sat next to the church. Walking cautiously, searching for MacKenzies, Laura found three in the first row. She snapped a pic of each stone with her phone and continued searching, checking each stone, snapping pictures of any names she deemed relevant. She soon realized the limitations of this haphazard process. With a bunch of names and no system to organize them, what good were they? She'd lost faith in Ancestry. If these people hadn't turned up there, how would she know where to place them in the MacKenzie family tree?

The task grew tiresome by the time Laura reached the newer sections along the fence and she felt foolish. Sally had a hunch, but she hardly knew Sally. Why had she taken her so seriously?

She walked faster, her concentration waning. Laura would have missed the small marker—it was partially buried under a crusty drift of snow—had she not tripped over it. She pitched forward like a drunk, grazing her head on the rough marble edge of a tombstone.

The world swirled with a crazy burst of stars.

Laura sat up and touched her fingers to her forehead. It was bleeding slightly. She wiped the bruise with a handkerchief and looked around nervously, but the cemetery remained peaceful, the sun visible through a thin stratus haze.

With an uneasy laugh, she assured herself the fall was a coincidence, nothing more. Laura stood, shook the snow and dead grass from her clothes, and retrieved her phone. She kicked the snow from the small angled marker irreverently, feeling cold, tired, and foolish. Stopped abruptly and frowned.

Kneeling, she wiped the rest of the snow away and stared at the stone inscribed with only a name.

Anna Flecher

That name. Where had she heard it before?

She pushed herself up, then sat down hard, remembering the connection. The hair at the back of her neck tingled.

The woman in the hallway. The glowing tombstone in her nightmare. That name had now come up twice. Who was Anna Flecher? Why did her name keep popping up like a ghostly omen? Laura snapped two pics of the stone, feeling off-kilter.

The grave of Alan MacKenzie stood nearby, followed by a long, fruitless stretch. Her head hurt so Laura moved quickly, anxious to be done and away from there. An uneasy feeling was stealing over her. The time spent there had been a waste of time. She had a bunch of photos, but nothing that looked like answers to her questions. No magical resolutions.

Turning down the last row of grave markers, Laura found a stone with a familiar name carved into polished granite:

ELIZABETH MACKENZIE

She stopped and gazed thoughtfully at it. The tombstone was neither attractive nor ugly, just a bleak chunk of reddish stone, an inadequate tribute to a woman who was once uniquely alive and vital. Seeing it opened tender wounds. For a moment, she saw Elizabeth's face, heard her voice, her laugh. Laura broke the spell of her reverie before becoming too deeply mired in sorrow. A damp breeze had sprung up, and the sun disappeared behind a dark wedge of clouds. A few snowflakes fell, driven by the wind.

Laura, happy to be finished, ran for the car. She opted to run home first, to treat the bruise on her forehead before returning to Brenda's. Not until she turned off the highway and onto Firelane Eight did the realization dawn, striking with such force that Laura slammed on the brakes, skidding to a stop on the gravel just short of the ditch.

They had buried Elizabeth in Illinois!

Laura grabbed her phone and flipped through the photos until she found the pic of Elizabeth's stone and checked the dates. They matched. It *was* Elizabeth.

What was she doing here?

Thirty-Eight

Kenric Shepherd stared at the MacKenzie house in awe.

This was B F E?

The acronym seemed misguided. The property looked beautiful, idyllic.

It was the house from his dreams and the heavy wooden structural timbers were authentic, not simply dark planks nailed to the exterior to emulate the Tudor style, the common practice now. The roof lines, the stucco exterior, the heavy oaken door and leaded windows? A reproduction? Nonsense.

He felt certain the house was genuine even though finding an English Tudor home here seemed as improbable as stumbling across an Egyptian pyramid. Adding to the illusion, the house sat in beautiful surroundings reminiscent of the countryside north of London.

There were two reasonable explanations for the presence of this house in Wisconsin. One, some family had moved their home from England to this place. Disassembled the house, board by board, and re-assembled it here. Possible, but why would anyone go to such lengths?

Two, an English master carpenter had settled here and built this home as a nostalgic turn to his homeland. Why not? If he had sufficient money and labor, it was plausible.

He considered a third possibility: the mere presence of this house implied preternatural forces at work, that the building had not arrived by conventional means. Like the book, the house aroused some buried association, but he couldn't retrieve the memory. He had seen something like it before but then thought, of course he had. There were dozens of fine Tudor homes just like this all over England.

A faint stream of negative energy emanated from the building. An ultra-low frequency hum, vibrating in the planes and wavelengths of his old life. He felt it probing, evaluating him, seeking answers, just as he sought answers. The energy arose from an entity within, but he could discern nothing beyond that. He fingered an amulet in his pocket that projected a protective field to counter the negative energy.

One thing was clear. He was in the right place even if he wasn't sure why.

Shepherd imagined the room layout as best he could ascertain from the exterior and snapped several photos with his iPhone. This piece of technology still amazed him; a camera, a communication device, a compass and mapping tool, a library with access to a world of knowledge, an instant source of news and current events, and a storage device for music, pictures, and ideas. Long ago, people would have seen this device as magical or the work of the devil. Now children owned them.

The front door opened and an attractive blonde woman holding a small child stepped outside and walked to a Honda CR-V in the drive. The blonde woman from his dreams. Another confirmation. She put the child into a car seat, buckled herself in, and drove away.

Every clue had come together, yet he felt only vaguely enlightened.

He scurried to the entry and surreptitiously scraped some wood slivers from a beam near the door into a small envelope for later testing. Touching the house, he felt a strong sense of déjà vu, a feeling he had seen *this* house somewhere long ago. The probing energies here were stronger, insistent, trying to bore into his skull like a titanium bit.

Time to leave.

He hurried to the Range Rover, floored the accelerator, and raced down the fire lane, pursuing the woman. She was important in some way he still didn't understand. Her connection seemed the most tenuous of all. The book and the house fit together meaningfully. A book of Old English, an old Tudor mansion—an obvious association. Still, the woman mattered.

A hunch.

It sounded so unscientific, so implausible.

Hunches for most people were random ideas that popped into their heads, ideas they then called intuition.

In his case, the hunches—his intuitions—were prescient and almost always accurate. He couldn't explain why. It wasn't a subject amenable to rigorous scientific study. While he was truly psychic, even he couldn't deliver reproducible results for a study. Further, he had no intention of submitting to testing or ridicule when most scientists considered the subject on par with divining and carnival magic, unfit for serious study. Contrary to his scientific training, he knew there were things in the world that couldn't be explained empirically, couldn't be measured, couldn't be controlled with technology. His precognition was one of them.

Slowing as he approached the highway, he looked at the corner street sign, blinked, and screeched to a halt. Reflective green with white lettering, the signs marked the intersection of two roads:

County B—Firelane Eight

He slapped the steering wheel.

Bloody hell!

This was B F E?

Shepherd felt certain it was. He had been directed here all along. Why had he never considered the letters might point to a specific location? It wasn't a metaphor, it was a map point!

He sighed.

So much for his fabulous intuition.

★   ★   ★

Parked fifty feet behind the Honda, Shepherd watched the woman stumble about like a klutz. What was she doing? What did she hope to find in the cemetery? A family tree? Had she never heard of Ancestry or any of the other genealogical sites?

He sat there for almost thirty minutes as she wandered around the cemetery. Then she fell. The woman was no study in grace. He thought about walking over to help, but she seemed unharmed, and he didn't want to give himself away. Not just yet.

Her name was Laura. Intuition again.

Having left this world of magic and omens long ago, he was surprised to find himself drawn back to it, almost against his will. He couldn't always summon answers on a schedule. Three hundred years ago, when the world moved at a glacial pace, if the answers came a day or two later, it rarely mattered.

It mattered now. He felt frustrated and perplexed—by the book, the house, the source of energy within, the compulsion to follow this woman. A frustration that compelled him to drive here to establish the definitive link between those things, hoping to discern the reason fate had drawn him to Milwaukee.

Instead, a new set of questions arose. How did the house get here? Who built it? Were they the authors of the book? Why was this situation commanding so much of his attention? Why had he been unable to intuit the significance of B F E?

Bloody hell!

He was missing something important and he worried people might die if he didn't figure it out. The energy source within was the most puzzling of all. Beyond sensing a presence, he could discern nothing about it. Felt baffled by his inability to solve that mystery.

He watched Laura climb into the CR-V. She reminded him of Laila. Laila was his first wife, and remained, even after all these years, his one true love, his soulmate. She had also possessed great longevity, but he could not save her from the plague in the fourteenth century. There had been women and wives since, but none had possessed her grace, her charm, her intelligence.

Over the years, he grew to fear love, always fated to watch his partner grow old and die. He could slow the inevitable, but he couldn't stop it. Alas, it had been a long time since he'd been with a woman. He had almost forgotten what it was like. Such was the curse of his solitary existence. Feeling melancholy, he turned a half circle and pointed the Range Rover toward Milwaukee and home.

His progress on the MacKenzie book had been glacial. Still, more than halfway through the book, a darker thread had crept into the narrative. The woman was evolving from healer to dark sorceress, the first hints that the revealing passages were near.

When he arrived home, he prepared a light dinner, poured a glass of cabernet, and walked up to the office. He looked at his computers and felt his pulse quicken. Adventure awaited there. Then he glanced at the book page displayed on the other monitor—the translation in progress. Important but not fun.

He sighed and sat, reaching for the keyboard and mouse, seeking the elusive words in the diary that would justify his presence here.

And explain his rising anxiety.

Thirty-Nine

At the house, Laura walked up to the bathroom and, in an absent frame of mind, washed the dried blood from the bruise on her head. There was no logical explanation for Elizabeth to be here. She had watched the casket disappear into the ground in Illinois. Several illogical reasons came to mind. Lucas and Nate, for reasons known only to themselves, had her moved, tombstone and all. A hidden clause in the will? Another aspect of Elizabeth's arcane life? Why wasn't she buried next to Alan? None of it made sense.

After touching up the bruise with concealer, Laura grabbed her tablet and sat at the kitchen table. She logged into Ancestry to enter the names she had discovered in the cemetery, hoping to reveal some significant mystery about the family. To justify what otherwise felt like a wasted trip.

Referring to her photos, Laura entered the first name, *Henry MacKenzie*, only to discover he already had a profile. She typed in the next name, *George MacKenzie*. He also had a profile. Laura clicked to the *Tree View*, surprised to discover the MacKenzie paternal lineage now extended back four generations—six unknown names she hadn't entered. Henry was Lucas's great-grandfather, George his great-great-grandfather.

Something was wrong.

She hadn't made these entries. She had only entered Lucas's father and paternal grandparents on the MacKenzie side, and Ancestry didn't automatically populate family trees. Each hint, photo, or document had to be approved in a simple *Yes, No,* or *Maybe* format. A sense of dread crept over her, an empty sensation in the pit of her belly.

George MacKenzie, the oldest entry, sat on the far right side of the tree. She clicked on the arrow to expand that branch of the family tree, and four more generations appeared, going back to Joseph MacKenzie. Joseph was Lucas's sixth great-grandfather, born in 1710. He had lived and died in Attleboro, Massachusetts with his wife, Sarah Smith. Both had died in their forties.

She hesitated, afraid to click on Joseph's arrow to extend the tree back in time. She had searched for this information for months. Now it appeared unbidden in her Ancestry tree. Feeling compelled, she clicked on the arrow and four more generations appeared back to the birth of Edward MacKenʒie, in 1590. He had lived and died in Derlinton, County Durham. The town sounded vaguely familiar. Where had she heard that name before?

It was time to quit. To log off, close the computer, and leave this be. She could live with some harmless ghost hanging around the house, but she couldn't handle someone or something who could infiltrate her Ancestry page and fill in the blanks. Haunting a house and hanging around flicking knives onto the floor was one thing. Logging into her account and making data entries? Could a ghost do that?

The answer was no. No way.

Yet the entries were there.

A morbid compulsion to see how far this madness went possessed her. Like a gawker at a lurid crime scene, she couldn't look away. How far back did it go?

Her pointer hovered over Edward's name. She closed her eyes, clicked on the arrow, and opened her eyes.

Three more generations appeared. She had reached the end and felt relieved—until she saw the last entry on the right.

Anna Flecher

Laura nearly choked. Who in the hell was Anna Flecher?

She grabbed her phone and searched frantically back and forth through her photos, but the stone bearing the name of Anna Flecher was missing. Instead, she found two pics of a small marker which read:

Audra Fletcher

Had she misread the stone?

She wasn't misreading the family tree. Anna Flecher (1481-1516) was the first wife of Edward MacCoinnich (1478-1529). After Anna's death, he had remarried. Edward and Catherine MacCoinnich were Lucas's thirteenth great-grandparents according to Ancestry, though she didn't understand the odd surname. She typed *MacCoinnich* into a Google search and discovered it was a Gaelic name, pronounced *mac-co-neesh*. The page also listed anglicized name variations, including *MacKenzie*.

So who was Anna Flecher? Why did it matter? Anna and Lucas weren't even related.

There was an explanation for this, she realized. Nothing sinister but malicious nevertheless: a practical joke.

Perfect too. She nearly fell for it. Someone was messing with her. She suspected Lucas. He knew her email address, her favorite passwords; it would be easy for him. The why was less clear. Trying to rattle her? Gaslight her? Make her question her sanity? She checked the sources for the earlier MacKenzies and they looked legitimate. If this was a ruse, it was thorough and believable.

Then she saw the clock on the range. Jesus! It was after four! She had forgotten about Leah. Laura jumped up and ran for the car, hoping Brenda would understand. At the front door, she stared out in surprise. Fog had developed while she was indoors, the yard and trees now shrouded in a ghostly mist.

Ten minutes later, Laura pulled up to Brenda's house as night fell in fading shades of grey. Checking her phone, she saw a weather advisory for dense fog with freezing fog developing by nightfall. The words sent a chill through Laura. An apprehension that her life was about to unravel.

Brenda was waiting at the door, visibly upset as Laura walked up the steps. She had been crying. The storm door swung open and a dark foreboding ran through her. She wished she could turn and run, wanting to hear no more bad news, but it was too late. The unraveling had begun, and Laura knew whatever Brenda told her would only draw her deeper into the uncharted territory her life had suddenly become.

"Brenda, what's the matter?"

"It's Janice Foster. She's in the ICU and they don't know if she'll make it. I just got the call. I've got to go over there. Mom's all shaken up—they've been friends since high school."

"What happened?" Laura felt numb. First the strange phone call this morning. Now Janice was near death?

"Heart attack, I don't know—they aren't sure. I've got to go. I'll call you later when I know something."

Laura zipped Leah's coat as Brenda bundled her children in winter gear. Then she watched them drive away, disappearing into the fog. Strapping Leah into the car seat, she sensed imminent danger, a feeling that had been growing and swelling all day. Events were rising to a climax.

On the highway, Laura strained to see. Even with fog lights, the road was seldom clearly visible, and Laura struggled to concentrate. This morning she shrugged off Janice Foster's call. Now it haunted her. Janice had something important to tell her, and now she was in the ICU.

A coincidence? A sad but meaningless fluke? Or a sign of a darker nature, of a nameless menace set free when she and Sally had touched hands, or Nate opened the room, or—?

Stop it!

The road was a foggy blur as Laura turned onto Firelane Eight, but they were nearly home.

A dark shape loomed ahead. A vague impression, an animal or something. She squinted. Was there something on the road? Laura swerved and slammed her foot onto the brake, heedless of the danger on the slick road. The car slid out of control.

Laura let out a yelp as the Honda bucked and bounced, nose up, into the ditch. For a moment, she stared in a daze at the wipers clicking back and forth; at the fog illuminated by the headlight beams tilted skyward like airport beacons.

A giggle from behind broke the trance.

Laura looked at Leah, grateful she was unhurt. She thought it was a game. Feigning composure, Laura leaned back and kissed her lightly on the cheek. For a wistful moment, Laura envied Leah. Life was so much simpler for children.

Gently pressing the accelerator, she tried to ease out of the ditch, but the wheels just slipped and spun in place. She pushed harder, softer, harder, softer, trying to rock the car, hoping to coax it back onto the road. It was no use. The car was stuck and showed no inclination to move. If anything, they were sliding deeper into the ditch.

Grabbing her phone, Laura tapped in the number for emergency roadside help.

Silence. Zero bars. How the hell did this happen in this day and age? Jesus!

She tried rocking the car again, but it stalled. Then it wouldn't start. She cranked the CR-V again and again. The battery ran down and the lights dimmed as she drained the battery.

Suddenly, her anger, frustration, and an impending sense of panic boiled over. Laura slammed the steering wheel with her palms and yelled, "Damn it!"

Leah yelled, "Gama!"

Being admonished by a child was like a slap. Laura pulled her from the car seat and rocked her gently. "It's all right, baby. Grandma's sorry."

They would have to walk.

Though nervous at the prospect, Laura was afraid to stay in the car. She worried about the cold. Worried about things lurking in the woods. It was a crazy thought, she realized, and Leah didn't need crazy just now. Laura struggled to be mindful.

Holding Leah with one arm, she climbed from the car, slipped in the mud, regained her footing, and side-stepped up to the road and turned toward home.

Only then did she realize how dark it was, how dense the fog had become.

Laura was blind, the road only evident through her boots as she inched forward. Leah whimpered in her ear. She imagined at any moment something horrible would materialize out of the mist, and she worried about missing the house or walking in the wrong direction. None of this was enough to distract from the cold, bone-chilling fog that slowly drenched every inch of them. Soon, her hair was dripping, and the road was freezing beneath her feet.

She sensed something behind them.

A feral presence. It was only a feeling—she hadn't heard a thing—but the sensation was powerful and frightening.

Trying to control her panic, Laura ran. Stumbled. Scrambled to her feet and ran again. They were being stalked by something she could neither see nor hear, a creature evident only to her sixth sense.

Or she was imagining all manner of nonsense and suddenly afraid of harmless night shadows.

But the tremulous feeling in her gut said they were in danger. She couldn't be mindful. Blind in the fog and darkness, the anxieties stacked up and up. Her fear spiraled out of control.

Her innards churning, her heart racing, she felt death following behind, stalking them.

Then she imagined long talons reaching for her slender neck.

Forty

A light!

Someone ahead beckoned with a lantern or flashlight, signaling the way. Difficult to discern in the fog, it looked like a man in bib overalls and a cap. The creature behind them faded, receding as she followed this stranger, this good Samaritan, leading them home. A name popped into her head.

Tom. His name was Tom. A neighbor? They didn't have neighbors. At that moment, it didn't matter.

She saw light in the distance, weak in the dense fog.

It was the house! The windows grew brighter with each step, like the eyes and teeth of a grinning monster. Laura jogged, heartened; ecstatic to be almost home.

When they reached the front door, Laura stopped and looked back, but the man was gone.

"Thank you!" She yelled into the fog.

Weary, damp, and cold, she peeled their wet outer garments away, marched upstairs to the bathroom, and ran a hot shower. Laura pulled Leah in with her, and they luxuriated under the powerful stream of water. Washed their hair, soaped up, laughed and giggled as they played with the bubbles. After donning pajamas and drying their hair, they went to the kitchen where Laura prepped a bottle of juice for Leah and brewed strong coffee for herself.

Lucas wasn't home. She felt alone and vulnerable. Laura carried Leah to the Hall, laid her on the sofa, and built a fire, watching the flames lick at the wood and then consume it. The fire was soothing, a talisman, holding back the darkness and—as her ancestors perhaps felt—warding off the creatures lurking there.

The *what ifs troubled Laura*—Janice, the fog, the *thing* in the dark. Leah, unperturbed, slid off the sofa and wandered over to her toys.

The slide into the ditch was her own fault. She should've known better, but why hadn't the anti-lock brakes worked? Had something loomed up on the road? She didn't know, the fog too dense to reveal that secret. Had something stalked them, or did she have an overactive imagination? The guy with the flashlight? How did she know his name was Tom?

Janice Foster needed to tell her something and now, Janice was fighting for her life. An unfortunate coincidence? More like unbelievable. Laura suddenly questioned everything, the situation laden with dark possibilities. What was Janice Foster's story? Not knowing drove Laura crazy.

It was in the cards.

Tarot cards? Her life was devolving into lunacy.

Still, the timing of Janice's illness—

The grandfather clock, chiming the hour, intruded on her muddled thoughts.

Leah!

Gone. Disappeared.

Laura jumped off the sofa and began a frantic search.

"Leah!"

She heard a giggle toward the kitchen.

Nope. Not in the kitchen. She then glimpsed blonde hair halfway up the stairs. Another giggle. The little shit thought she was funny. Leah scrambled higher, looking back and giggling as Laura charged up the stairs after her. She was mischievous, turning on lights as she went. Leah topped the staircase and stopped.

"Stop, you little gremlin!"

Leah shrieked with delight. She beelined across the landing and disappeared into the bedroom, her footsteps padding on the wooden floors.

As Leah pushed the door shut, she let out an anguished cry. Laura ran up the remaining stairs two at a time.

She found Leah behind the door, one leg stuck in the floor. When she tried to pick her up, Laura realized her leg had snagged in some sort of trapdoor. She lifted the opposite edge of the hatch and pulled Leah free. Laura rubbed the leg, which appeared to be fine, and soothed Leah as she carried her to the bedroom.

Time for bed.

Laura changed her diaper, laid her in the crib, and quietly read a bedtime story. Ten minutes later, Leah was asleep.

Laura poured herself a glass of wine, grabbed a flashlight from the junk drawer, and walked upstairs. She sat and pressed on the floorboard and popped the trapdoor open. She closed it and marveled at the way it essentially disappeared into the surrounding floorboards. Only because Leah's foot was so small did it trip open. This had to be the trapdoor Nate found.

Peering inside, she spotted a cross in the dust and recognized its antiquity at once. Cast from grey metal, either pewter or lead, it was slightly wider at the end of each arm. A circle of metal inset at the center of the cross ran through all four arms. Casting the light about, the chamber appeared otherwise empty.

She reached for the cross. As her fingers touched the dull metal, a charge surged up her arm, and the chamber disappeared.

She was trapped and blind in a dark place...

Hungry, starving. And thirsty. Dying. She was dying. No escape. Delirious, afraid. Most of all, she was angry. Venomously angry.

Vindictive—

Laura threw herself backward, breaking the spell. Flat on her back, panting, her heart racing as she tried to erase the sensations of that awful place.

What the hell was that?

She fought the urge to panic. Stared at the ceiling light. Forced herself to relax. Took a deep breath, then another and another. Slowly, calm returned. As did her curiosity.

Grabbing a pencil from the bedside table, she reached down and flipped the cross, careful not to touch the metal. She noted a single word carved into the crossbar in old English script.

Dryhtdōm

Laura slipped a piece of paper from the nightstand and wrote it down, slammed the door shut, and jogged down to the Hall. Pulled her iPad into her lap and typed the word *cross* into the search box, then clicked on *Images.* She quickly learned it was a Celtic cross, a religious symbol that arose in Europe eons ago.

Laura wasn't sure how to translate the word with that odd letter before the 'm'. With a further search, she discovered the ð was an obsolete letter from early written English. Substituting that letter into her search, the word came up as the Old English word for *judgement.*

That word jarred a memory loose. Where had she seen that word? She remembered and felt her insides tense and twist with anxiety.

The album.

Laura ran downstairs and grabbed the album from the box in the root cellar. Flipped it open. An image filled the first page. An angel blowing a horn stood above figures of men and women rising from the ground. Beneath the picture was a single word:

JUDGEMENT

She carried the album upstairs and sat by the fire. On a hunch, ran an image search for Tarot cards. Clicked on the image of the card labeled *Judgement.* The card and the album were almost identical.

The implications? She didn't know, but this was no coincidence. A connection existed. Disparate strands were coming together, revealing—?

She had no clue.

Maybe tomorrow this would make sense. Tonight, she was too tired to think.

She shoved the album under the sofa and checked on Leah, opting to sleep in her own bedroom tonight. Laura slid into bed and contemplated the word *judgement,* a word laden with dark meaning.

Retribution. Punishment. Damnation.

Falling asleep, Laura feared judgement coming for them.

Just as it had come for every MacKenzie in the past.

Forty-One

Lucas sat at the dimly lit bar of the White Birch Inn, casting idle glances at Murphy, the TV, his beer, and the motley crew of drinkers in the bar. It was Monday night, and the Packers were playing the Bears.

The crowd in the bar roared as Green Bay scored.

He thought it was a touchdown, but he hadn't really been watching. His concentration had deteriorated in the past few days, his muddled thoughts continually returning to the dangers of living under the same roof as Laura. There was something dark and disturbing about her. Mostly, he dwelt on Nate's accident and her apparent seizure and premonition in the mall. That incident had scared Ashley away and formed the core of his distrust.

The announcer was droning on the TV, "—there you have it, the incredible running talents of—"

At that moment, the tavern disappeared. He stood in a field surrounded by a cheering crowd, the people dressed in clothing from a bygone era, like a Renaissance fair. Before him, two horses charged at each other, the horses decked in bright woolen prints. Knights in armor atop the horses wielded jousting spears. They collided—

Lucas looked up to see a cornerback plow into a receiver.

Like a waking dream or a hallucination, the vision was brief, but so vivid, Lucas had to shake his head to clear it.

Jesus! I'm losing my mind!

He chugged the rest of his beer, trying to wash away the feeling of impending insanity.

Murphy turned to him. "Hey Lucas, you okay? You don't look so good."

"Yeah, I'm fine. It's nothing."

He wasn't fine and knew it.

Stress? Was that it?

Had to be. First Jacob, then Nate, now the marriage. What could he do? Laura was driving a wedge between them with her bizarre premonitions. With her obsessions about the house. Her suspicions and accusations. The pestering. The nagging. A woman whose every word grated on his nerves like the keening howl of a coyote.

What could he do?

The answer was obvious.

Laura had to go.

Forty-Two

"Laura! Wake up!" Lucas shook her shoulder roughly. "Leah's crying, and I'm leaving."

Laura opened an eye and peered over the comforter. Lucas loomed, dressed in hunting gear.

"What happened to you?" he said. "You look like shit."

"Huh?"

"The bruise on your forehead?"

Bruise? Her tumble at the cemetery. "I fell."

"Klutz." He was eyeing her neck and it felt creepy.

She sat up and snapped, "Not so fast. I want to talk to you."

"I've got to go. Leah's crying—"

Her anger swelled. "Why don't you take care of her? She's your granddaughter, too."

"That's your job. That was the deal."

"The 'deal' never included ignoring her. You've hardly acknowledged her since we moved here."

"Whatever." He turned and clomped down the stairs.

"Lucas!"

As she climbed out of bed, the front door slammed.

Laura laid down and cried. She had been afraid to cry, afraid if she did, she would never stop. Instead, the tears relieved her pent-up emotions, her anger, and broke the gloomy mood with she had awoken with. Laura realized she could remain there sniveling, but doing so would change nothing. She shook off the self-pity, slid from bed, and walked to Leah's room.

Bouncing at the side of the crib, Leah yelled, "Gama!"

Leah's smiling face worked magic on Laura, and she hugged her lovingly, grateful for this oasis of comfort in the surrounding discomfort. After making breakfast, Laura stood at the window of the kitchen, soaking up warm rays of sunlight. Outside, the sun was brilliant, glinting off the spindly bones of the trees and the shrubs petrified by a rime of ice.

The icy glaze reminded her of another problem. The Honda. Laura called the roadside assistance hotline and gave them the location of the vehicle. Laura and Leah dressed, then sat reading a book until someone knocked at the door. A skinny young man stood there, needing a signature for the tow. Laura tipped him and left a few minutes later for Brenda's house with Leah.

★   ★   ★

Laura stopped at the small brick house next to the motel and rang the bell. No one answered so she drove the short distance to the church. Laura hadn't been to church since Leah's baptism and only randomly before then. Uncertain why she'd neglected her faith, she regretted it now, longing for the comfort and security of a higher power. Then her contrary voice mocked: *you're only here because you're in trouble, Laura.*

If there was a problem with the house, some sort of haunting—

If? Why was she clinging to if?

The house was haunted and this seemed the logical place to seek advice. She banged on the door with the stern-looking knocker and waited, rubbing her hands together briskly. A smiling Reverend Drew answered, wearing his gown and collar. He was an attractive man, she decided, even in his vestments.

"Mrs. MacKenzie, hello. What can I do for you?"

"May I come in?" Laura asked sheepishly. She felt nervous. In his formal attire, he seemed more official, less accessible.

"Please, silly of me. It's cold out." He stood aside and waved Laura in. "Did I see you in the cemetery yesterday?"

"Yes. That's what I came to talk to you about—if you have time."

"Surely. I've dressed early; I have a funeral in an hour. Let's go to my office."

They walked down a corridor lined with closed doors, the walls unadorned, the old plaster crazed with cracks like tiny fault lines. His office, a cubbyhole at the end of the hall, was a study in chaos. The shelves on the walls were chock full of books, loose-leaf binders, and stray bits of paper. The small desk was cluttered, the floor littered with boxes filled with more papers and books. He moved a box from a straight-back chair and motioned for Laura to sit.

"Sorry, I wasn't expecting company. Did you find what you were looking for?"

"Yes—and no." Laura felt nervous, unsure where to start. "The tombstones are in good condition. That helped."

"They are. They're mostly marble or granite." He sat at his desk. "I wish I could say the same for the headstones in back—"

"Headstones? What headstones?" Laura looked up from her fidgeting fingers.

"Behind the arborvitae hedge. I never thought to mention them to you. The stones are badly weathered and illegible anyway." He leaned forward. "The townspeople tell some interesting stories about that plot."

"Like what?"

"They say it was already here when the first settlers arrived." He chuckled. "I love these small-town superstitions."

"I need to see it," Laura said reluctantly, feeling compelled but dreading what she would find.

"Okay, but I won't join you. You can use the door over there."

Laura let herself out and trudged through the icy grass, around the tall arborvitae wall. Stopped dead in her tracks.

Thirty or forty weathered stones sat huddled together, snow caps on their rounded tops, looking like a platoon of dwarf soldiers. Enclosed by a small stone wall, *MacKenzie Corner* wasn't carved on any stone but it was the same place, a vision from her dream. The names were no longer visible, erased by centuries of wind, rain, and frost. No matter. Laura knew who was buried here. They were all MacKenzies, every one of them. She squatted by one stone, touching it gently in a trance, her finger tracing faint grooves in the worn stone, letters that were barely discernable.

M A C...

Why were these stones here?

You know why.

The answer seemed too incredible, even for her vivid imagination. Laura felt certain none of these people had died in Lost Arrow. She was equally sure none of these stones belonged here.

A growing dread whispered: *There's no escape. Run away. We'll drag you back here to rot just like we dragged Elizabeth back.*

Laura shook her head.

Stop it!

Still, she sensed it was so. The insight chilled her more than the coldest January night. This plot was a ghost—of the past and the future—a twisted Dickensian ghost of the MacKenzie family going back generations. The wind moaned through the bare trees in a plaintive wail, and Laura knew she had come to the right place. Feeling alone, her future suddenly seemed bleak. She stood and trudged back to the rectory.

Reverend Drew stood as she stepped through the door. "What did you—are you okay, Mrs. MacKenzie? You look pale."

"Not really. It's part of what I came to talk about." Laura shed her coat and sat down.

"Let's talk, then. That's what I'm here for," he said gently. He crossed his legs and clasped his hands on his knees.

Laura dropped her gaze to her fidgeting fingers. This was more difficult than she imagined.

"Take your time."

After a quick breathing exercise, Laura told her story methodically—the explosion and her episode that day, the doors slamming, the falling knives and the fireplace screen, her meeting with Sally, the album, the cross, the woman in the hallway, the rumors about the house. Spoken aloud, it sounded absurd.

Reverend Drew sat silently, face impassive, listening to every word, fingers steepled. Laura finished and waited nervously for a response. He maintained steady eye contact. "It seems you have some mild psychic abilities."

"I've known since I was six."

"How do you feel about it?"

"I've never liked it."

"Do you feel guilty about your brother-in-law?" His gaze was sympathetic. He was good at this.

"What do you mean?"

"Having foreseen his accident to some degree?"

"No—yes. I don't know."

"Have you been depressed?"

Laura saw the path of his reasoning. "You think it's all in my head, don't you?"

"I don't doubt your psychic abilities are genuine. I'm a fan of the subject and you tell a convincing story. As for the rest of it…"

Here comes the you've-been-under-a-big-strain routine.

He clasped his hands together nervously and set them on his knee. "I see someone who's dealing with a great deal of stress. The death of your son. Caring for his child. Your brother-in-law's accident and losing your friendship with his wife. The breakdown of your marriage. Most people would have difficulty handling that amount of stress. I think you're coping fairly well, but it doesn't surprise me you've transferred some of the guilt and anxiety you feel onto the house. A little counseling—"

"You think I'm crazy."

He shook his head. "I didn't say that."

"But you don't believe me either," she said with a trace of sarcasm. She couldn't help it.

"I'm looking for the obvious answers here. You haven't actually said so, but you've implied your house is haunted."

"I guess so, yes."

"I'm trained to steer clear of the supernatural when psychological issues might be involved. That seems to be the case here." He leaned forward, spreading his hands. "You may also be telekinetic. That would explain the falling and shifting objects."

An interesting point, one she hadn't considered. "And if the obvious isn't at work here?"

"True hauntings are rare, Mrs. MacKenzie." Hands clasped together on knees, his eye contact unflinching. "Most cases have conventional explanations, so it would be difficult to accept that there's a genuine haunting in my parish. Do you understand?"

"I do. What about the album?"

"I don't know. Death is a part of life? It sounds macabre, I agree. Your mother-in-law's approach to dealing with her grief wasn't healthy, but it wasn't supernatural either."

Laura couldn't disagree, but then realized she had something tangible. "What about Elizabeth? We buried her in Illinois. What's she doing here?"

"That's fairly simple," he said, and ferreted through a box next to his desk.

"Someone in the family made the arrangements. I have the paperwork here somewhere. I talked to a woman on the phone about it."

Laura wondered if Lucas had pulled something behind her back. Given his attitude, anything was possible. If so, she was about to look like a fool.

"Here they are." He lifted his head from the box and perused the document. "As I said, a member of the family—Anna Flecher, listed here as Elizabeth's mother—made the arrangements."

"Anna Flecher?" Laura said, her voice rising.

"What?"

"That name—Anna Flecher. She has something to do with all of this. The name came to me in a dream. The woman in the hallway? Her name was Anna Flecher, too. In the family tree, she's the first wife of Lucas's thirteenth great-grandfather. Now this?"

"I don't know. Sounds like a quirky coincidence," he said, eyebrows raised.

"Elizabeth's mother has been dead for years and her maiden name was Culver, not Flecher." Laura sat up straight, feeling vindicated.

"This is very unusual." He continued fiddling with the papers. "There must be some explanation. You can't just go to a cemetery and have someone disinterred and moved—not without identification and the proper paperwork."

"Someone did."

"I intend to investigate this carefully."

"Do you still think I'm crazy?"

"I never said that," he said defensively. He looked into her eyes. "I'm concerned you may have some stress related issues that would be amenable to therapy. I promise you one thing. For now, I'll keep an open mind. I'd like to see the album and anything else you might have, and we'll go from there. If it turns out I'm right, will you consider seeing a therapist?"

"Sure," Laura said. "I'll drop those things off in the morning if that's okay."

"Perfect."

She stood and they walked down the narrow hallway to the door. "Thank you for your time."

He opened the door and put his hands out, taking hers in a reassuring grip. "Laura, I'm sure everything will work out. Thank you for coming to see me and placing your trust in the church. I wish more people would think of us when they run into trouble."

At that moment, Lucas drove by.

Laura froze, stunned by the angry look he threw her.

Forty-Three

"Any news on Janice Foster?" Laura asked when she stopped to pick up Leah.

"Nothing good," Brenda said, looking distraught. She then rushed them out the door.

The talk with Reverend Drew had done little to settle her anxieties. As she walked to the car, she worried that Janice's sudden illness was no coincidence.

What then? An omen? A warning? And who was Anna Flecher? What was the significance of that name? Was it a part of an elaborate plot to drive her away? Who would do that? Lucas?

Possible, but quite paranoid.

Regardless, it was working. Laura didn't think she could stay in the house much longer. If she told Lucas how she felt, he'd call her crazy—if he talked to her at all. Maybe he'd welcome her leaving.

Laura buckled Leah into the car seat and drove home while Leah jabbered away. She smiled; the kid was good for her mood. Turning into the driveway, the sight of Dana's car surprised her. Jesus! With all that had happened in the past few days, Laura had forgotten she was coming.

Dana pulled a suitcase from the trunk as she walked over, Leah in tow. They hugged, spent five minutes catching up, and Laura then took her on the grand tour of the house. Dana hadn't been back since they finished the project.

"God, Mom, the place looks amazing. So whatever happened to the HGTV special?"

"Not sure. Ashley was handling it, and we haven't spoken."

Dana knitted her brow. "Still? That seems so unlike Ashley."

"I know. I've basically written her off."

They spent the rest of the afternoon talking. About Dana's problem at school. Laura then described the events of the past few days. Dana, ever the attentive listener, sat silently until Laura finished.

"I don't know, Mom. The reverend makes sense. There has been a lot of stress in your life," Dana said. "The telekinesis thing is spooky, though."

"Tell me about it."

"So maybe a little therapy wouldn't be a bad idea?"

Laura shrugged; wished it were that simple. She and Dana talked through dinner, then retired to the Hall with a bottle of wine and Scrabble. Laura remained distracted by the idea that Anna Flecher might be an elaborate ruse to scare her away. Nothing else made sense. She avoided discussing Lucas until Dana could spend time with him, though he hadn't come home for dinner. Perhaps she wouldn't have the chance.

Around ten, Dana announced she was exhausted and went to bed in the guest room. Laura slipped into Leah's room and stood there, staring at her angelic face, before planting a kiss on her cheek. At times, she felt overwhelmed by the responsibility of raising this innocent and trusting child. Was Leah safe here? Reverend Drew and Dana seemed to think so. Maybe she did need a counselor, not an exorcist. That was the logical, reasonable explanation.

Lucas? Laura no longer understood him. What was driving the unraveling of their marriage? Grief? Anger? Infidelity? She didn't know, and he wouldn't talk about it. Giving him time no longer seemed reasonable. He grew more distant every day; the marriage felt like a lost cause.

Too anxious to sit and read, she walked downstairs to her workshop. The lamp she was making, an order through Etsy, remained unfinished. She was approaching the deadline and hadn't worked on it in days. It felt like things in her life were piling up, becoming unmanageable.

She heard a shuffling sound in the back passage. Jesus! Enough of this! She wasn't afraid, just angry. She flipped the light on and peered down the hallway.

Empty.

She walked down the hall to the utility room. Also empty.

The root cellar?

Empty.

She turned to leave and saw the pile of brick, dust, and debris on the floor. She peered up at the ragged hole in the ceiling, into the brick room where Nate had discovered the book and the coins.

The book.

Laura had forgotten about it. Like the album, she was convinced it was a link to the things happening in the house. She angrily assumed Lucas was keeping the information about it from her. Damn him anyway! Only anger did no good. Sweet, sexy, serious; none of it opened a dialogue. Frustrated, resentful at the sad state of their relationship, she kicked the pile, scattering debris and a few bricks.

Looking down, she noticed a dark, rounded object protruding slightly from the pile. The shape was vaguely familiar. She knelt for a closer look, then tugged at the object. At first, it resisted. When she moved a couple of bricks, the pile shifted slightly and she pulled it free.

A bone.

She wasn't a doctor, but it looked like part of a human arm bone. She held it for a second, transfixed, then dropped it in revulsion.

Curious, she picked at the bricks, pulling them away one by one, then she sorted through the dust with a stick. Found another chunk of bone.

She teased the stack apart, pushing bone fragments right with the stick and stacking the bricks on the left. There were lots of broken pieces of bone in the pile, some she recognized, some not. The long bones were broken. There were fragments suggestive of a skull and a few teeth. Laura pulled the phone from her pocket and snapped several photos for Reverend Drew.

A shiver ran down her spine. You didn't have to be Sherlock Holmes to solve this mystery. The room was a tomb, and it took little imagination to ascribe everything that had happened since to Lucas and Nate breaking into it. Evidently, they had never recognized its true nature.

No matter. She was going to bed and giving this stuff to the reverend tomorrow. If he decided she needed help, she was accepting the offer. As a concession to her anxieties, she opted to sleep in the guest room with Dana.

Forty-Four

Shepherd stared at the words for so long, they faded to a blur. In anger, he slammed his fist on the keyboard and kicked the wastebasket. He couldn't believe this was happening and yet, the book, the house, and the evidence suddenly formed a coherent whole.

A picture of frightening clarity.

Something he had done long ago had returned to haunt him. Five hundred years ago, to be exact. The handwritten answer lay on the last page, though his sense of dread had been rising through the previous dozen pages.

The text had evolved from a diary, to healing folklore and magic, and finally, to a *grimoire*, a text of magic, spells, and invocations. Witchcraft. And not just any witchcraft. The woman had matured from practicing harmless magic to malignant evil; became skilled, dangerous, and feared. He sensed the answer before he read the actual words, but the absolute proof he'd been seeking now lay before him.

The book belonged to a woman named Anna Flecher, and the story began in England with a friend, Edward MacCoinnich. Edward was a baron with substantial landholdings, in favor with King Henry VII and a cousin to the King's wife, Elizabeth of York. His marriage was arranged, as was common with the rich and powerful in that era, to the daughter of another wealthy landowner, William Flecher.

Over the next decade, Edward had a compelling run of luck, with his land holdings and farms, in his business ventures, and in his personal life. Deals broke his way with uncanny regularity. Opponents and competitors suffered from ill-timed accidents and other misfortunes. In battle, he was invariably victorious. His luck became legendary, and many whispered that he had sold his soul to the devil.

The truth was darker. He had married a monster.

At first, Edward had no clue his wife was the architect of his great fortune and unaware that she practiced the black arts. A rumor circulated that Anna wasn't really William Flecher's daughter, but a mistress. William had grown tired or wary of her. The stories varied, but her skill as a sorcerer was unrivaled and people feared her.

Armed with the truth, Edward confronted Anna. She laughed and, in an arrogant tirade, boasted of her skill in sorcery and claimed credit for his every success. She treated him dismissively and boasted she was too powerful to be stopped by anyone. He was merely a respectable figurehead, useful only as a front for her malign ends. He was to play along and stay out of the way, or die badly. She brooked no arguments.

Afraid for his life, Edward chained Anna to a beam in the root cellar of his house and placed guards outside the door, intending to have her tried and executed.

With a powerful spell, she escaped the locked room and murdered his father. As her actions grew more audacious, Edward realized he needed to act before he too became a victim. She was crazy with power—so arrogant she believed herself invincible. In that, Edward saw her weakness. She believed he was too frightened to act after his father's death. Anna needed to die, but he feared her spirit would return to exact revenge. She had become that dangerous.

At a jousting tournament, Edward, in obvious fear of his life, cornered Shepherd and pleaded for help.

Shepherd knew about Anna Flecher. He was a member of a community of practitioners in the arts of sorcery and magic and her name had surfaced more frequently as her schemes grew more brazen. They saw Anna as a dangerous and growing threat. Eventually, reckless fools like her provoked a backlash, leading to witch-hunts and trials. Dozens of eccentric innocents, women mostly, were invariably arrested and burned at the stake.

Shepherd agreed to help. He would bind Anna and her remnant spirit to protect Edward, but he was adamant on one issue—he wouldn't be an accomplice to murder.

Edward agreed and followed Shepherd's instructions for burial—or so he said. To keep a watchful eye on his dead wife, Edward sealed the body in a meticulously mortared brick tomb hidden within his house.

With a binding spell, Shepherd created a powerful field around the mausoleum to prevent Anna from haunting Edward from the grave. A Celtic cross, cast in *fine metal* by Shepherd, held the spell in place. The idea sounded ridiculous in the twenty-first century, but in 1516, the technique was widely used to contain evil spirits and demons.

One that hadn't worked, he realized.

Somehow, Anna had continued to wreak havoc all these years later from the brick tomb the MacKenzies had opened. Before him were the words explaining everything.

Edward hadn't killed Anna.

He'd buried her alive.

Adding insult to cruel fate, Edward left three gold coins for the toll to cross the River Styx, sending Anna straight to hell—or so he thought. Instead, he'd given her the opportunity to cast a final invocation that haunted his descendants still. The MacKenzie house was Edward's house; the same house where Edward interred Anna Flecher five hundred years ago in the north of England. How it arrived in Wisconsin he couldn't imagine, but it implied powers greater than his.

Anna should be eternally dead and forgotten. Instead, her evil legacy lived on. It wasn't possible to make amends now, but he could prevent further deaths by confronting and destroying her.

He was deeply disturbed it taken so long to make these connections. Alas, he knew the reason.

Time.

Five hundred years had passed. It was hard enough to remember details from forty or fifty years ago. Five hundred years? It was incredible he remembered it at all! Advancing age added to his forgetfulness. Still, it was a disastrous lapse. He had been translating the book for weeks and only now had it come to him, though really, there had been few clues until deep into the book. She never mentioned Edward by name. Her name appeared nowhere in the narrative. When he suspected, he rushed to the end and realized the awful truth.

He recalled Edward had died badly years later, attacked and devoured by wild boars during a fox hunt. He'd assumed simple bad luck had befallen him, but now he wondered. Edward had several sons by his second wife. Over the years, the name MacCoinnich had evolved to MacKenzie. Everything fit perfectly.

His binding spell had sealed her fate and led to her death. Anna had to know Shepherd had a hand in her murder and likely harbored considerable malice toward him. It wouldn't matter that he hadn't known Edward buried her alive. Anna wouldn't care.

And somehow, this woman or her dying invocation had persevered for five hundred years, remained potent, and had evolved beyond death into a dangerous force. Her anger had to be intense, and he worried about the retribution her angry spirit might be planning.

Shepherd now regretted getting involved, but Edward had been a trusted friend, and Edward had deceived him. He'd have never taken part in such a gruesome undertaking had he known.

He knew one thing with certainty: the problem was his and only he could fix it.

Problem was, his skills were rusty and hadn't been seriously tested in a hundred years. Confronting Anna would require considerable thought, planning, and bravado. While he prepared, he needed to convince Lucas MacKenzie that he and his family were in grave danger and needed to leave the house.

Now.

Forty-Five

Lucas lay naked on the bed in the dark bedroom of the small apartment, enjoying the afterglow of lovemaking. Next to him, Murphy inhaled on a cigarette, the embers glowing brightly, then fading to a soft glow.

He fondled her bare stomach.

"Good, huh?"

"Yeah."

In the distance, a train whistle called out to the night over the rumbling music of steel on steel and the pulsations of the diesel engine. It was otherwise quiet.

"Are you staying over?" Murphy asked.

"Yeah. That okay?"

"Sure. That won't cause trouble with wifey?"

The question disturbed the tranquility of the moment. He had forgotten about Laura, and while Murphy was neither bright nor sophisticated, she was wild in bed and filled a void in his life. The root of that emptiness was a collection of woes: his lack of purpose and direction, his brother's injury, Jacob's death, the disintegration of his marriage, and the feeling he wasn't entirely well. There were moments when he blacked out, periods of time he couldn't account for.

"She don't seem so bad. I met her, you know."

Lucas turned toward Murphy, leaning his head on a crooked arm. "Where?"

"At a party. She's kinda spooky, though."

"What do you mean?"

Murphy inhaled on her cigarette. Outside, a modified car roared up the street. "It's hard to explain. There's this woman in town—Sally. She has this gift; she knows stuff before it happens, you know, like ESP?"

Lucas nodded.

Murphy shifted to her side, propped her head on her hand. "Anyway, Sally and your wife started talking, and suddenly, the whole place went weird. Dude, it gave me the creeps. They were talking about your house and some guy that disappeared there years ago. They never found him and never figured out what happened."

She touched Lucas's arm. "So things were weird and Sally was talking and then your wife says in a creepy voice, 'I know what really happened'. It was like a séance."

Lucas felt dazed. This was further proof he was no longer safe under the same roof as Laura. He took the cigarette from Murphy and inhaled deeply.

Time to act.

Forty-Six

Laura drifted between sleep and wakefulness, chasing a phantom, the specter of Anna Flecher. If she saw her face, she would understand, but Laura couldn't catch her. Anna disappeared through the basement wall.

She woke and listened to Dana snore softly next to her. Maybe Anna Flecher was the least of her worries. Her marriage felt over. Lucas had become so distant, they could no longer manage a civil conversation. She recognized her part in their problems but feared he was seeing someone else. Perhaps if she threatened to leave, he would come to his senses, but Laura saw the futility of coercion. To plead or threaten was nothing but desperate. An anxious thread ran through her mind, worries about being alone, trying to start over.

A lot had happened in three days. Meeting Sally at Brenda's. Discovering Elizabeth in the cemetery. Janice Foster's call and sudden illness. Finding the older cemetery. The album. The bones and the implications they created. Anna Flecher—the inexplicable name that might tie it all together. All in three days. Far too quickly to make any sense of it.

As a story, it sounded patently absurd in an age of computers, the internet, and smart phones. All the ghosts and goblins of the medieval era were dead, along with the ancient superstitions. Maybe Reverend Drew was right. Maybe she needed counseling to see through the clutter in her head, to see it was all nonsense—or some harmless old ghost lady who didn't want to leave their house.

In the primitive region of her brain however, in the realm of fears and superstitions, Laura *felt* something dark and twisted in the house that science alone couldn't dispel. That what she'd experienced *was* real and every bit as dangerous as it appeared. Laura believed this to be true, and though she'd ignored such feelings in the past, she intended to follow her instincts, heed the warnings, and get out.

Decision made. She would see Reverend Drew to show him the evidence—which seemed painfully thin—and inform him of her decision. A stop at Sally's to satisfy her curiosity about the other night.

It seems we have something in common.

Then would come home and pack. She wouldn't threaten Lucas. She was leaving without a word. If he wanted her, he would come find her. Laura showered, plucked Leah from her crib, and walked down to the kitchen. She fired up the Keurig and made breakfast for Leah. As she sat at the table with her coffee, Dana wandered in, wearing pajamas, looking sleepy.

"Morning, Mom."

"Morning hon." Laura looked over the top of her coffee cup. "Sleep okay?"

"Like the dead."

"I think I'm going to move out of the house for a while."

"Something I said?" Dana popped a cup into the Keurig.

"I'm serious. There's something wrong with this place. You haven't been here long enough to feel it. I don't feel safe here."

"Aren't you going to wait to see what the reverend does?" Dana sat across from Laura, looking concerned. "Or consider a little therapy?"

"In either case, it'll take weeks or months."

"What about Dad?"

Laura, pensive for a moment, said, "Things aren't going well between your dad and I right now."

"Huh? What's going on?"

"We're barely talking." She paused. "I think he's seeing someone else."

Dana stared, mouth agape. "No way. Dad wouldn't do that!"

Laura remained mute; knew she had to tread carefully.

Dana sharpened her gaze. "Seriously? Are you sure?"

"No, I'm not sure." Laura held her cup defensively.

"So you're just assuming he's cheating?" Her disapproval was palpable.

"Yes. Even if he isn't, I can't talk to him anymore. Maybe we just need a break."

"And where are you going?"

"Your house?"

Dana shook her head. "I'm not getting in the middle of this."

"I don't want you to."

They discussed the issue for a few more minutes, but Laura refused to be dissuaded from what Dana obviously considered a rash decision. Laura grabbed her phone and punched in Sally's number.

"Hi, Sally, this is Laura MacKenzie. Can I stop over today?"

"Sure, Laura. When?"

"In an hour or two. I have to stop and see Reverend Drew first."

"That'll be fine."

Laura grabbed her fur-lined parka and looked at Dana. "Sally's home. I'm going to stop there after I see Reverend Drew. Would you mind watching Leah for a few hours?"

Dana nodded. "No problem. I've missed this little lady."

As Laura was walking out the door, her phone rang. Ashley. Laura hesitated, then stepped back inside and tapped the green icon.

"Laura?" Her voice was soft, almost haunted.

"Ashley?"

"Yeah. How have you been?"

"Okay, I guess." Hesitant, Laura didn't know what to say. Ashley's parting words still hurt.

"Laura, thanks for the email. I should've answered sooner." A moment of silence. "I'm sorry. I didn't mean what I said when I left."

Ashley sounded miserable. Laura softened. "I hoped you didn't mean it. I just didn't understand. How are you doing?"

"I'm hanging in there."

"And Nate?"

"Nothing's changed." She started weeping.

Try as she might, Laura couldn't stop herself from crying too. God, she missed Ashley. "Do you want me to come down there?"

"Actually, would it be okay if I come back for a few days?"

"Of course. It's your house too." As she spoke, Laura felt torn by the decision to leave and the desire to mend her friendship with Ashley. "Just so you know, things have gotten weird here."

"Mrs. Moskopf?"

"And some. I was planning on leaving in a few days."

"And it's still okay that I come?"

"Absolutely. Why don't you plan on Thanksgiving dinner with Dana and I. Okay?"

"I will, thank you. I'll drive up in the morning."

Laura tapped the red icon and walked out to her car, feeling happier than she had in days. Happy about fixing things with Ashley. Deciding to leave.

Outdoors, the air was bitterly cold, the sun a pale disk in a haze of cirrus clouds. At the door of the vicarage, Laura felt nervous, worried the reverend considered her crazy; that he was waiting for the right moment to commit her and send her away in a padded truck to a place where old ladies wove imaginary baskets.

Stop it!

Reverend Drew opened the door in formal attire, his face somber.

"Good morning, Laura. Let's go back to my study."

They walked down the passage in silence. He gestured to the straight-back chair and sat at his small desk. The clutter was better organized today. He pointed to the bag Laura held and said, "May I see what you have?"

Aimlessly reading titles on the bookshelf, feeling foolish, Laura wished she hadn't come. There were times—despite all she knew and had seen—when she doubted herself, as she did right now. In the light of day, the haunting of their house seemed silly, ludicrous even.

Laura opened the bag and handed him the album first, allowing him to page through without interruption. He raised his eyebrows occasionally but said nothing.

Laura nearly choked when he turned the last page and she saw a new article taped in place.

LOST ARROW MAN INJURED IN EXPLOSION

"Did you put this in here?"

"No! It wasn't there the last time I looked." Another element of a crazy story. She realized Lucas might have added it, harking back to her paranoid theories. Reverend Drew looked at her with an indeterminate expression between concern and disbelief.

"Honest! My husband must have done it."

"Why would he do that?" His look verged on condescension. She was losing his trust.

"He doesn't believe any of this. He's mocking me. As I explained last time, we aren't getting along."

He took a deep breath. "What else do you have?"

She handed him a printout of the family tree with the name Anna Flecher circled.

"A curious coincidence but probably not supernatural."

She then handed him a list of events in the house: the old lady in the hall, the knives, the doors, and the fireplace screen. He perused the list and paused, looking thoughtful.

"There's another thing," Laura said. "I found bones in the basement last night. Human bones."

He turned and locked eyes with her. "You're sure they're human?"

"I am. They were under the room Nate broke into. I think it was a burial vault."

He sat up and spoke more formally. "That may be, but you need to report them to the police. Now."

"What?" Laura hadn't even considered that.

"It's the law. You need to call immediately." His gaze was insistent. Was he testing to see if she was lying about the bones?

She pulled out her phone and said, "Nine-one-one?"

"No. Just a sec. I have the sheriff's number here."

Laura dialed and explained the situation to an officer. Concluding it was probably an old burial and not a recent event, they told her to leave the site undisturbed until they could investigate. Someone would stop by the house later today.

"Satisfied?" Laura said.

"Is this all of it?"

"Yes. Is it enough?"

He studied her thoughtfully, then glanced at the list again. "It's a good start. I'm just asking myself the same questions the bishop will ask. As I explained yesterday, people who come forward with stories like this occasionally have psychological issues, and the phenomena they describe have conventional explanations. I'm not sure what the bishop will think, but for what it's worth, I think the case has merit. You'll have to give me time. There are strict procedures to be followed. I'll need to keep these things, of course."

"I expected you would."

"The bones might be the compelling reason for an exorcism, or at least blessing or purification ceremony, depending upon their age and the circumstances of their interment." He added offhandedly. "One question. If you're convinced the house is haunted, why are you staying there? Aren't you worried about your safety?"

"I am. I'm planning on leaving in a day or two until this is resolved."

"Okay. I'll see the bishop later today. We have a meeting scheduled. I'll bring this up then."

"Thank you." Laura studied his shoes, which were black and scuffed.

He stood and said, "I want you to think about therapy as well, okay? We should explore every avenue."

"I'll do that."

"I have to go," he said. "Another appointment."

Laura stood also, but balked, looking him squarely in the eyes. "So will it work?"

"What?"

"The exorcism, blessing—whatever. Will it work?"

★   ★   ★

Kevin Drew donned a confident face. "If one or the other is necessary, I think so—yes."

Beneath that positive statement, he felt an aching doubt. While he professed an interest in hauntings and possession, he never truly believed such things existed beyond abstract religious thought.

After Laura's last visit, he had asked around and heard a plethora of stories about the MacKenzie house. Though archaic and silly like most local folklore, he sensed something darker here, a strange apprehension, compelling and illogical in the same breath—the presence of evil. His mind returned to childhood fears, imagining creatures lurking in the shadows of unfamiliar halls and doorways. Though he never actually *saw* the monsters, he sensed them reaching out to grasp and harm him. He'd fight the feeling, tell himself it was nothing but nerves and silly superstition, yet he would quicken his step and his fragile beating heart would race until he was safe.

Laura MacKenzie—her house, her books, her stories made him feel that way, an irrational swell of fear his faith couldn't erase. He was glad she planned to leave, convinced the threat at the house was real.

He wanted no part of it.

Forty-Seven

Sally's house was a small brick house surrounded by the bare frames of oaks and thick, green spruce trees. As Laura strolled up the walk, Sally opened the door and waved her in.

Sally took Laura's parka, gestured to a small settee, and said, "Would you like some tea or coffee?"

"Tea, please." Laura sat down as Sally walked into the kitchen through a café door, using her cane for support.

The living room was small, papered with a dated floral print. Sally had filled walnut cabinets flanking the windows with small antiques: coin purses, old cameras, pocket watches and clocks, a chess set, silver dollars, and small tools. An old RCA floor radio sat next to a tall bookshelf filled with hardcovers. A small flat screen TV was tucked in the corner.

Sally returned with two cups of tea and sweetener and set the tray on the maple coffee table. She sat in a fat stuffed rocker, tucking an iPad under the table.

"I love your cabinets," Laura said.

"Thank you. I used to love shopping for those things. Going to auctions and flea markets was always fun." Sally took a sip of tea. "How can I help, Laura?"

"I'm not sure," Laura said, hesitantly. "You mentioned stories about the house?"

Sally settled into her chair. "Where do I start? According to an Indian legend, the house just appeared out of the blue."

Laura almost dropped her cup. "What?"

Sally nodded. "It's true. They considered it evil and gave it a wide berth. It's only a legend, of course, but I'd be concerned if my house figured into Native American folklore. Over the years, a good many people have lost their lives in or near that house. Tom's disappearance was the final straw for me. It may sound irrational to blame an inanimate object, but I do."

A Native American legend? Laura shivered at the thought. "I found bones in the basement last night. Someone was buried in the house."

"Oh my. That might explain a few things."

Laura nodded. "How has this all remained a secret? Why has no one ever investigated the house?"

"TV people and ghost hunters come looking occasionally, but they never find it," Sally said. "Never will. Folks here don't want anyone snooping around."

"I'm starting to understand why." Laura sipped at her tea. "You heard about Janice Foster?"

"Of course."

"She called me the day she fell ill. I cut her off. Maybe I shouldn't have. The timing was spooky."

Sally pursed her lips and exhaled dismissively. "Janice is fifty-nine and sixty pounds overweight. Her heart attack doesn't sound unnatural to me."

Sally was probably right but the timing still seemed suspicious. Laura set her cup down. "So, tell me about Elizabeth."

"Didn't you know her?" Sally asked, clearly puzzled.

"I did, and I didn't." Laura said. "I thought I knew her until she died. She had all these secrets. We didn't know about the house until the reading of the will."

"If Elizabeth hadn't died unexpectedly, you'd have never known the house existed."

"What?"

"Elizabeth had planned to tear the house down and donate the land to the state." Sally seemed to be staring into a different plane.

Laura leaned in. "How do you know that?"

"We stayed in touch. She visited now and then to walk the land and visit Alan. Elizabeth never got over losing him. I think that's why she kept the house so long."

"Then why tear it down? Why not pass it on to her children?"

"Because she knew there was something wrong with it," Sally said. "She not only planned to tear it down, she wanted to have the site blessed."

Laura cocked her head. "What? Like an exorcism?"

"Not really. Gentler than that."

"So why didn't she?"

"I think she was torn between wanting to be rid of it and losing her last connection to Alan."

Laura became more confused, and her memory of Elizabeth faded a bit more. She had hidden so much behind a careful facade. "Why did she marry Alan then? Why live there?"

"Love. Simple as that. As a young woman, she was stubborn and didn't believe the stories about the house. Then Alan died. She packed up and moved out the week after and never set foot in the house again."

It suddenly felt like she never knew Elizabeth at all. "I found an album, a strange book with all these clippings about MacKenzies who died over the years. The story about Tom was in there."

"Is there a strange drawing on the first page with the word—what was it—?" Sally looked off into space.

"Judgement."

"Oh my." Sally knitted her brow in consternation. "I saw Elizabeth toss that book into the trash forty years ago, right here at my house."

Laura cupped her elbows with her hands. "So it was Elizabeth's?"

"No. Someone sent it to her. She drove up one day with it. It had upset her." Sally shook her head, a look of distaste crossing her face. "Understandably. It was perverse, twisted."

"In the book, under the picture of Tom, Elizabeth had written, 'It ends here!' Do you know what she meant?"

"I don't know. I don't remember that."

"All I want to do right now is pack and leave."

"I don't blame you. Is your husband going too?"

Laura cast a glance at Sally. It was an odd question. "I don't know. He hasn't been himself. There's been a lot of stress in our lives, especially with his brother. I've tried to give him time and space to heal, but I think he's seeing someone else."

Sally said nothing, which Laura found disconcerting, further confirming her feeling that Lucas was cheating. This was getting too personal and she had learned nothing useful.

"I can't believe this is happening."

"Unfortunately, I can." Sally sipped her tea. "I understand you're talking to Reverend Drew. My feeling is he'll be of little help."

"Why do you say that?"

Sally opened her eyes and leaned forward. "I don't know. It's just a feeling. Over the years, I've learned to trust my feelings."

Laura was suddenly more curious about their common ability. "When did it start for you? This—thing?"

"I don't know." She shrugged, turned her palms up. "I've always had it."

"How do you feel about it?"

"How do I feel?" She looked vaguely confused. "It's part of me. I don't feel one way or another about it. It's like asking how I feel about having blue eyes."

"I don't like it." Laura stared off into space.

"I know. I sense you've been running from it."

"Absolutely. How can you be so calm about it?"

"I accept it, that's all." Sally gave her an inquisitive look and a casual shrug. "Mindfulness. Isn't that what you call it?"

Laura nodded, feeling particularly unmindful.

Sally held her hand out. "Here, take my hand."

"Why?"

"We both have the gift. Together, who knows what we'll come up with?"

Laura took the hand hesitantly. There was a surge of warmth, just like at Brenda's. Sally closed her eyes; Laura did the same. For Laura, there was nothing but a random stream of consciousness. Sally was silent.

After a minute, Laura let go. "This isn't helping."

Sally grabbed Laura's hand. "Try harder!"

Try harder? "What are we trying to do?"

"I'm not sure yet." Sally shrugged, but gripped her hand intently.

Laura did what she knew best: cleared her mind, relaxed, focused on her breathing; mindful like martial arts.

A silly proverb appeared in her mind's eye: *Red sky in the morning, shepherd's warning...*

Then Laura stood in the auction hall, bidding on a box. Moments later, she was trapped in the cemetery. Night had fallen. The dead were escaping their coffins, chasing her away. Leah appeared and walked away from her, into a fog.

Leah! Wait!

But the fog was swept away by the house at sea, cutting through the waves like a stout clipper ship. Then she saw a skeleton lurking in the basement hallway of the house. The procession of scenes and visions was incoherent, senseless.

Sally gripped her hand tighter and said, "The bones. The bones are Anna Flecher."

Laura's eyes snapped open and pulled her hand away, the connection broken. "How do you know that name?"

"I don't know. It just came to me. Who is she?"

"I wish I knew. Somehow, she's at the center of all this," Laura said. "Did you see anything else?"

Sally looked befuddled. "Nothing that made any sense. You?"

Laura shook her head. Two evidently wasn't better than one.

Sally touched her arm. "You're wrong. It just didn't work this time."

Laura looked at her curiously.

Sally shrugged. "I sensed your feelings, I guess. Work at it and you could too."

"How?"

"Just leave yourself open to it. From what I've seen, your ability is far stronger than mine."

"I don't feel strong right now." Laura stood, disappointed. She slipped into her parka. "I've got to go."

Sally touched her arm. "What does the shepherd proverb mean?"

"I don't know. I can't figure that out either. It's just a silly proverb, isn't it?" She snugged her zipper. "Thanks, Sally."

She smiled. "Hang in there, Laura. I'm here if you need me."

★   ★   ★

Laura returned home in a sullen mood. She had learned nothing useful. Whatever was going on in the house seemed too incomprehensible to fathom. It no longer mattered. She was leaving. Laura walked toward the Hall but retreated when she saw Lucas sitting by the fire.

She found Dana and Leah sitting in the kitchen. "What are you doing in here?"

"Uh, it was warmer here. What's with Dad?"

"I don't know. Why?" Laura popped a pod into the Keurig.

"He's grumpy. And he sounds drunk."

"I don't know what your father's problem is, but I've had enough." There was so much she wanted to explain to Dana, but she had neither the energy nor desire to talk. There would be time after they left. "I'm going to pack. Ashley's coming tomorrow to visit. After that, I want to leave. Is that okay with you?"

"Anything you say." Dana said with an edge. Laura felt the wary look that followed her out of the room. Was that what Sally was talking about?

Laura found the suitcases in a closet upstairs and tried to decide what to take, what to leave behind, but accomplished nothing. She was exhausted. The meeting with Sally had drained her. Maybe after a few minutes of rest, she would feel better.

Laura lay on the bed. Despite the nebulous clutter of anxieties in her head, she fell asleep. As her mind drifted to the unconscious, she was aware of a vague unease, silent and brooding, like storm clouds in the distance, growing darker and more menacing.

Sometime later, she startled from deep sleep and sat upright in bed, her neck wet with sweat. Someone had been chasing her, a shadowy figure, a faceless dream creature. The room was dark. How long had she been asleep? Her phone rang. She reached and clicked the green icon.

"Laura, it's Sally." Her voice excited, her words rapid fire. "I figured something out."

Laura felt groggy. It took a moment for the words to sink in. "What is it?"

"I can't tell you over the phone. You wouldn't understand—well, no—you wouldn't understand."

Very much awake now, Laura said, "Sally, tell me! I need to know now!"

A brief pause; a sharp intake of breath. "You need to watch out for your sister-in-law."

"Ashley? Why?"

"I don't know. That's all I have. If I get more, I'll call you back."

Laura sat for a minute, stunned. That was the craziest thing she'd ever heard. Ashley a threat? Sally was losing it. She had just talked to Ashley. No matter. Time to pack. As she stood, she felt dizzy, felt the room twist sideways in the all too familiar sensation. Laura lost her balance and fell to the floor.

Here it comes—

The image was more than a flash, longer than subliminal. It was technicolor vivid. In it, Sally lay bloodied and dead on her living room floor.

Laura lay dazed for a moment before her thoughts crystallized.

Sally was in immediate danger, the nature of it unclear to Laura. She needed to warn her. Now.

Laura tapped Sally's number. She answered after two rings.

"Laura? What is it?"

"Get out of your house, now!"

"What?"

"Leave! Go to the White Birch."

There was a crash in the background and muffled sounds of struggle.

"What are you doing here?" Sally was no longer speaking into the phone.

"Get out of here! Laura, it's—"

Sally's phone fell with a loud *thump* followed by a piercing scream, vivid and chilling—almost childlike.

Then silence.

Stunned and terrified, Laura stared at her phone and screamed frantically, "Sally! Answer me! Sally!"

Dana came running up the stairs. "Mom! What's wrong?"

"I don't know," Laura said, nearly hysterical. "I was talking to Sally, then she screamed—"

"What?"

"I—I think someone hurt her—killed her."

Forty-Eight

Shepherd tapped Lucas MacKenzie's number into his phone. The call went to voicemail, so he ended it. A voicemail was a poor means to relay the urgency of the situation that Shepherd considered critical.

He changed his mind, called again, and spoke in a breathless rush. "Mr. MacKenzie, this is Dr. Shepherd. We spoke several weeks ago about your book—the translation. I've completed it and I need to speak with you urgently. It's something of a warning. Information in the book suggests that you and your family may be in danger. I have further questions about the house as well. Please call. As I say, it's urgent. If need be, I can meet you at the house."

Shepherd rang off and decided he'd sounded a tad loony.

★   ★   ★

Lucas sat in his tree stand, watching a four-point buck in the distance. His phone vibrated twice, but he let the calls go to voicemail.

He was in a better mood. More focused. Sleeping with Murphy had fixed something within. He also saw Laura more clearly. There was something abnormal about her. Murphy had provided the last clue; Laura had a dangerous, unnatural power. Something amplified by the house. He never believed in such nonsense before, but it explained the attack in the bathroom and Nate's accident perfectly.

Laura had to go, but would a divorce be enough? That was the question. He had imagined slipping his fingers around her neck and squeezing the life out of her as a preferable alternative to divorce.

A few hours later, he walked into the lower level of the house, stamped the snow from his boots and peeled away the layers of his cold weather clothing. Grabbed his phone and checked his voicemail.

Lucas stared at his phone. The message verged on crazy. A warning?

Still, he needed to retrieve the book; what harm was there in talking for a few minutes? Lucas hit the callback button and heard Shepherd's clipped English accent moments later. They agreed to meet in an hour.

Lucas changed into clean jeans and a flannel shirt and drove away in the truck.

★   ★   ★

Shepherd looked up as Lucas knocked on the open door. "Mr. MacKenzie, good afternoon. Please, sit down."

As Lucas sat, Shepherd walked around the desk and closed the door. He already sensed the skepticism. This might not go well.

"So, what's the story with the book? Your message was—strange."

Shepherd sat behind the desk. "Indeed. Sorry about that. Regardless, you're here. Let's jump right in."

He set his hand on the book. "The first half of this is the diary of a young noblewoman. Mundane day-to-day stuff. Then medicine becomes the main narrative. This woman fancied herself a healer. The title for such people then was *cunning folk,* their medicine a combination of roots and herbs, spells and magic, invocations and amulets. An unusual profession for a noblewoman."

"Interesting, but how is that relevant to the house? You said something about a warning?"

"Indeed, I'm coming to that. This book has a dark ending." He ran a finger along the edge of the cover. "It seems the woman's husband buried her alive as punishment for some transgression."

Lucas leaned forward with a curious expression. "Seriously? How do you know that?"

"She wrote about it. It's the final chapter, so to speak."

Lucas shook his head. "That's grim—and ironic."

"Indeed. So, consider this." Shepherd fixed an intense gaze on Lucas. "You're buried alive and wish to leave some message for posterity. Or words of anger over your predicament. What language would you use?"

"English, of course."

"Precisely. And yet, this woman wrote her last words in Old English. Furious words, in a language that had been dead for hundreds of years when she wrote them." He eyed Lucas cautiously, knowing they were entering difficult terrain. "Significantly, you found this book in your house."

Lucas looked pensive for a moment. "As an intellectual exercise or historical oddity, it's interesting. Otherwise, I don't see the significance."

"You're not curious about this?" Shepherd sensed something off about Lucas, a change in his affect, but couldn't put a finger on it.

"What are these angry words? What's so urgent here?"

"I'm coming to that," Shepherd said. "You see, a small group of individuals continued to use Old English after it ceased to be a spoken language."

"Who's that?"

He set his pencil down. No matter how he framed it, the explanation would sound ridiculous, but he forged on. "Witches, Mr. MacKenzie."

"Witches? Are you serious?" Lucas looked incredulous, somewhere between abject shock and an urge to laugh.

"Quite serious. Does sorcerers sound more palatable?"

"Not really." Lucas shook his head with skeptical disdain. "To be honest, I don't believe in any of that nonsense. I should be going."

"Please, hear me out." He stood and paced in the small office. "Your concepts about witchcraft and sorcery are informed by European ideas on the subject, ideas driven by a truly dreadful treatise, the *Malleus Maleficarum*. That rubbish set off a witch hysteria that lasted two hundred years. Thousands of people—eccentric spinsters, mental defectives, various and sundry church enemies—were tried and burned at the stake."

"Interesting, but—"

"No true sorcerer ever faced a trial or inquisition. They were much too powerful to be exposed and tried."

Lucas stared with a look of incredulity. "You believe that?"

"Absolutely. I know the subject intimately." Though he had no intention of sharing his back story, he said, "You could say I'm an expert. The practice of sorcery is universal, woven into every known culture since antiquity."

Shepherd opened the book to the last page and pointed to the last paragraph. He read it aloud in a flawless Mercian accent for impact. Turning to Lucas, he said, "Essentially, it's an invocation."

"A what?"

"An invocation. A spell. A hex if you like."

Lucas appeared to be biting his tongue. Regarding him hawkishly, Shepherd removed his glasses and closed his eyes, searching for the right words. Locking eyes with Lucas, he said, "Given that you discovered the book hidden in your house, I believe you and your family are in danger. This incantation—and don't laugh—is terribly harsh."

"You said this was written five hundred years ago. How could it possibly affect us now? Sorry, but it sounds crazy." His tone carried a clear implication: *and so do you!*

"I imagine it does. But understand this. The invocation remains in force until revoked." He raised his eyebrows.

"What?"

"The woman who wrote this is dead. She can't undo it. Therefore, the invocation is still in force."

"If this happened five hundred years ago, then clearly, it happened somewhere else."

"Immaterial. The invocation isn't on the house." Shepherd locked eyes with Lucas. "It's on you and your family."

"How could you possibly know that?"

There was no good way to explain his insider knowledge of the subject. Instead, he said, "This book almost certainly refers to your ancestors."

"Lucky them."

The man was a lost cause. "The room where you found the book—did you find anything else?"

"A few coins. We didn't find a body, if that's what you're asking."

"I was."

"Doctor, thank you for your time. I need to get going." Lucas stood to leave.

"Yes, of course." Shepherd frowned. "You don't believe me."

Lucas laughed. "No. Sorry. Not a bit."

"You're making a mistake, Mr. MacKenzie."

"Whatever. I gotta go, Doc." Lucas edged toward the door, giving Shepherd an amused, dismissive glance.

"Please consider what I've said. I believe the situation is dangerous. If you change your mind, call me." He tucked a card into the book and handed it to Lucas, unhappy to see the book go. Lucas MacKenzie would probably sell it. He favored burning it to destroy the evidence of his failure.

Lucas tucked the book under his arm. "If I run into trouble, I'll get a cross and some silver bullets to protect myself."

"You've been watching too many late-night thrillers, Mr. MacKenzie."

"That may be, but that's rather ironic coming from you after the whole witches bit." With that, Lucas marched off.

Crosses and silver bullets won't protect you from this, my friend!

Shepherd shook his head. The man was an idiot, though who could blame him? It was a ridiculous story.

Unless you knew the truth.

Forty-Nine

Dana stared at Laura in disbelief, then horror. "Oh my God!"

"I don't know what to do," Laura said, nearly hysterical. "What if she's dead?"

"Call nine-one-one. Now!"

Laura dialed 911, telling an agitated but lucid story. There was a pause; Laura placed on hold. The woman returned and said, "We've notified the county sheriff, ma'am. They're sending a squad."

Laura jumped up and grabbed her coat. "I need to go over there! I have to know what's going on."

Dana stood, eyes wide, jaw set in an expression of fear. Laura scarcely noticed. "Mom, I'm coming too."

"No! I can't wait." Laura started toward the door, but Dana grabbed her arm and said, "Mom, slow down!"

"What?"

"You're acting nuts. Slow down. Leah and I are coming too! *Just wait!*"

Ten minutes later, Laura grabbed her parka and ran out the door with Dana and Leah trailing. No longer warm, the Honda sputtered to life and roared as Laura slammed her foot to the floor, careening in a wide circle onto the fire lane.

"Mom! Seriously! Chill out!"

Laura took a deep breath and tried to slow down, but it was no good. The trees raced by on either side, meshed together like the rocky cliffs of a river gorge, but Laura only saw them within the subconscious pilot that controlled the car. Blurred high speed pictures played in her mind as Laura imagined what she would find at Sally's, every muscle in her body taut with dread.

On the highway, the lights of the town shone dimly in the distance, like the stars of a faraway galaxy. They might as well be, Laura thought, suddenly fearful for the fragile fabric of her world. Threatened by some unknown entity, she felt it shattering like a delicate ornament, never to be made whole again.

A squad car racing by, red lights flashing, shook Laura to the present. The car joined others clustered on the roadway ahead in a scene reminiscent of too many disasters to be lost on her. A crowd had formed in front of Sally's house. Pulling to the side of the road, Laura switched the engine off and watched, shivering with a strange mix of emotions that left her ready to collapse in tears.

"Mom, this looks bad."

Laura just nodded, afraid her voice would betray her.

More people joined the crowd and an ambulance arrived, bringing hope, but only momentarily. There was no rush to the house, just talk, and the spreading ripples of rumors and whispers among the crowd. With this realization, all hope died. Sally had the answer and Sally was dead.

Within the anonymous heads and hats of the crowd, Laura picked out Brenda and Carol Anson talking quietly to each other, their vaporous breath rising into the red glare of flashing lights. Laura slipped out of the car and walked toward them, her hands tucked tightly into the pockets of her parka.

A head turned. Someone said, "That's Laura MacKenzie."

More heads turned. Laura felt conspicuous, naked. Carol turned and walked over to meet her, her expression pained and fearful. She kept looking over her shoulder. Taking Laura by the arm, Carol pulled her in close. "Feelings are running a bit high here. Might be best to stay away for now."

"What about Sally?"

"She's dead." Carol started crying. "Jesus, Laura. What's happening here?"

Even though she suspected the worst, the confirmation still stunned her. Voice weak, uneven, she said, "I don't know. I just saw her today."

"You should go, seriously. I'll call you later—when I know something." Carol nudged her toward the Honda.

There were dissonant murmurs in the crowd. A few people took menacing steps toward Laura as she retreated to the car. No uniforms, no signs of help were anywhere in sight. Carol grabbed Brenda's arm and walked away from the crowd toward the store.

Someone yelled, "This is your fault!"

"No—" Laura spoke in a whisper. There was nothing she could say to these people. Nothing. She felt tiny and alone.

"Get out of here! Leave us alone!" Several voices barked at once as the crowd grew unruly.

Stepping backwards, Laura felt for the edge of the car with her hand. Ran around the fender as the first snowball struck her on the back, winding her. Laura tore at the door as more snowballs splattered against the car. A rock bounced off the windshield.

Dana yelled something she didn't understand and Leah was crying. Laura pressed Start but nothing happened. Then she remembered the brake, stomped on the pedal, and started the car. Fear hobbled her every move.

"Mom! What the hell is going on?"

"They seem to think I had something to do with Sally's death."

"That's crazy!"

Laura could see fear in her daughter's eyes. Fear of the animalistic mood that had taken over the crowd—their fear turned to mindless anger by an inexplicable event. Her foot hit the accelerator, tires spun, then found purchase as Laura forced the vehicle into a sharp turn and sped out of town, shaking from a powerful rush of adrenaline.

As the town receded behind them, she cried, scarcely believing Sally was dead. Everything was collapsing, shredding into meaningless bits, the weight of it bearing down on her.

Dana placed a hand on her shoulder, offering support as they rushed home. As she drove, the adrenaline and a chaotic rush of random feelings gradually forged a new and stronger emotion within.

Anger.

Anger at the crowd. Lucas. The universe.

Who killed Sally? What did she know?

The house came into view, the door, the kitchen, her actions mechanical. She felt almost robotic.

Dana, holding Leah, followed her into the kitchen. "What happened back there?"

"I don't know. Sally's dead and they blame me." Her anger suppressed every other emotion.

Dana slumped into a chair in shock. "Jesus!"

"I doubt He'll be much help," Laura said, tossing her coat on the table and pouring a glass of wine.

"Mom, this is getting out of hand." Dana looked deeply troubled.

Laura's anger reached a white-hot flash point. She reached for the sugar bowl, meaning to smash it. As her fingers touched the ceramic finish, the bowl flew off the table and shattered against the wall.

Laura and Dana looked at each other with stunned expressions.

"How'd you do that?"

"I—I don't know." Laura then reached out and touched the salt shaker. Nothing happened.

"Mom, what's going on here?"

"I don't know. I met with Sally today, and now she's dead."

"So? You didn't do it."

"She knew something, something about the house."

"You're not making any sense!" Dana eyed her suspiciously. "What's the house got to do with it?"

"I don't know, but it does. I'm packing now. We're leaving in the morning."

Laura had one other obligation or confrontation to handle first. She had planned to leave without a word but decided Lucas wasn't getting off that easily. Their relationship had never been perfect, but they had been happy. Now the marriage was in ruins and Lucas was oblivious to the problem—or didn't care.

Was he cheating on her? Perhaps it no longer mattered.

As Laura reached the arch of the Hall, she saw him sitting by the fire, drinking a beer, working on his laptop. She stopped, nervous, inexplicably afraid of him. Why, she didn't know.

He looked up. "What's going on? What's with all the yelling?"

"We need to talk."

He turned back to his laptop. "Later. I'm busy right now."

"Lucas, I have something to tell you, and you'll sit and listen until I'm finished, even if you think I'm crazy."

"I'm not—"

"Not a word, Lucas!" Laura felt like bolts of lightning were flying from her fingers. Anger. Fear. Frustration. "You'll listen, or Leah and I will walk out the door and never come back. Do you understand?"

"You've got a minute," he said with a resigned look. Or was it a wary expression? She couldn't tell. He set his laptop aside.

Laura paced by the fire, looking for the right words, worried she could no longer reach him, fearing failure meant the end of them. Who was this man? She hardly knew him now, so wide had the gap between them grown. Was there anything to save? The prospect of divorce cut deep like a stab wound. Lucas was an enormous part of her life. She still loved him. Couldn't imagine a world without him.

"What's happening to us, Lucas?" She tried to soften her tone and was only partly successful. When he didn't answer, she said, "Are you seeing someone?"

He continued to stare at her with a flat, wooden expression. She feared he was.

"Lucas! Say something!"

He spoke like a father addressing an unruly child. "Why are you freaking out? Do you even hear yourself lately?"

"I'm not freaking out," she said, throwing her hands up. She then decided maybe she was.

"You have an unpleasant tone. And no, I'm not seeing anyone." His body language was off. He broke eye contact.

She stared him down. "I don't believe you."

"Nice. So now I'm a liar *and* a cheat."

"I think you might be."

"Then there's nothing to talk about." He slammed the lid of the laptop.

She put her hands on her hips. "Lucas, there's something wrong with this house and I think you know it."

"Bullshit." He spat the word out.

"Hear me out. I can't live here anymore. I'm afraid we're in danger if we stay."

"A few nightmares and now you're convinced the place is possessed. Sounds like you're freaking out to me."

"Unless it's true!"

"God you're pathetic."

"And you're an insensitive bastard. It's more than nightmares. It's the knives and the fire screen and the woman in the basement."

"Yeah, I know. You saw a ghost—only you. The problem isn't the house, Laura, it's *you*."

The doorbell rang.

They both froze. The sound shook Laura out of her angry fugue. Lucas, poised to speak further, evidently thought better of it and walked to the front door. Laura followed, curious and nervous about who might be there. She peeked out the window of the sitting room, worried she would see a mob with torches, but spotted a squad car instead.

Lucas opened the door and a male voice said, "Good evening. I'm Sheriff Greene and this is the coroner, Dave Henson. I understand you found human remains in the house?"

Lucas looked confused. "No. Not that—"

"Yes. I did," Laura said, stepping up and flashing a look of vindication at Lucas.

She led the two middle-aged men down the stairs, through her shop, and along the hallway to the root cellar. Laura flicked the light on and pointed to the pile of bones next to the stack of bricks.

The coroner donned latex gloves, knelt, and carefully picked through the pile.

Laura saw Lucas pale when the coroner said, "Yep, they're human. Old though. I'd guess over a hundred years old."

Dave spent a few minutes looking around the room, peering into the brick room above with a flashlight, then pulled a cell phone from his pocket and snapped a dozen pics. "The bones come from up there?"

Laura nodded.

He turned to the sheriff. "Looks like an old burial. A little strange maybe, but nothing criminal."

"Okay. We'll need to process the remains," Sheriff Greene said. "When, Dave?"

Dave stared at the ceiling for a moment. "After the holidays. Monday or Tuesday at the latest."

"You folks need to stay out of here until Dave comes back to finish." The sheriff shooed them out and covered the doorway with crime scene tape. He whistled and appeared to be enjoying himself.

"You guys did a marvelous job on this place," Dave said.

"I'd say," the sheriff said. "Find any ghosts in the woodwork?"

They both laughed.

Laura and Lucas remained conspicuously silent. They walked the men to the door and wished them a happy Thanksgiving.

When Laura shut the door, she turned to Lucas, who still looked pale. "What's with you? You look like you've seen a ghost."

Lucas spoke, his voice a monotone, his head shaking with a tremor of disbelief. "It can't be true. Shepherd's nothing but an old fool."

Laura felt a shock wave rip through her.

Shepherd.

Shepherd was a person!

Laura grabbed his shirt. "Who is Shepherd? *What did he tell you?*"

Fifty

Kevin Drew left his dripping boots outside the office and slumped into the chair at his desk, shocked and nauseated by what he'd seen. Sally had been a dear friend, but the slashed and mutilated body to which he administered the Last Rites had barely looked human. After one awful glance, he rushed out to vomit in the snow. He had spoken the prayers with eyes closed, but the cloying smell of blood that pervaded the house remained vivid in his mind, even now.

Watching the crowd chase Laura MacKenzie away, he felt humiliated by his inaction, his fear of the mob. The talk was rampant afterward, about Laura and the MacKenzie house. Murmured threats to burn the place down, Laura with it if she refused to leave. Good God! It was the twenty-first century, and these people were acting like medieval peasants on a witch hunt!

After Laura left, he tried to reason with the crowd to little effect. He recognized many as parishioners, but they weren't interested in the message, bent on some sort of vigilante justice. Hopefully, cooler minds would prevail tomorrow.

He wished Laura MacKenzie had never come to see him but that ship had sailed. Her book and notes sat on his desk. The bishop had been unimpressed by the story and didn't feel it warranted further intervention.

Reaching for the album, he paged through it aimlessly, hoping to see some plausible explanation or discordant note. A deep, disturbed shudder ran through him as he turned the page after the Nate MacKenzie story. A nearly blank piece of newsprint stared at him, faint letters visible, growing bolder:

LOST ARROW WOMAN MURDERED

The article was writing itself before his eyes!

He flung the book to the floor with fear and loathing, afraid to touch it, willing it to disappear. Kevin realized he would need to see the bishop again and make a more fervent presentation after his half-hearted efforts today. Something genuinely evil was at work here in Lost Arrow. And somehow, Laura and the house were connected to Sally's murder despite the rational absurdity of such a thing.

The parish phone rang.

Hard, cruel words rushed at him. "Stay out of it, motherfucker, or you'll end up dead—just like Sally."

Click.

He knew he would heed the warning. Frozen in fear, humiliated by his inability to act decisively, Kevin Drew felt paralyzed.

Impotent.

Fifty-One

"Who is Shepherd? *What did he tell you?*"

"Nothing." Lucas shoved her hands away and retreated to the Hall.

"Lucas! Who is Shepherd?" Laura pursued him. He'd known something all along. "What did he tell you?"

Lucas stood rigid and silent, his face impassive as she approached. He tried to sidestep Laura. Laura shifted and blocked his path.

"Tell me!"

Lucas regarded Laura dispassionately. "He said we're cursed. The guy is bat-shit crazy."

"How would he know that? The old book you found?"

Lucas nodded.

"Lucas!" Laura yelled, angry beyond reason. "Tell me what he said! Every word!"

"He told me some guy buried a woman alive in the room Nate found and then she cast a spell on the MacKenzie family. I saw him today. He wanted to 'warn' me." Lucas gestured with air quotes and an eye-roll.

It was true. As ridiculous as it sounded, Laura believed every word.

After everything that had happened, everything she'd experienced, she believed.

Lucas stood, hands in his pockets, staring into the fire. Laura quietly said, "Lucas, you believe it. I know you do. You looked like you'd seen—"

"Seriously? Shut up, Laura!" His face was livid, color back in his cheeks, a dangerous gleam of scorn in his eyes. "If you believe that shit, you're as crazy as he is!"

"You believe it, I know you do! You couldn't hide it!"

Lucas barked a humorless laugh tinged with lunacy. His expression, taut and menacing, pierced her like the steely tine of a pitchfork. "Never! I listened, that's all. I wanted to see how far your delusions have gone. You're fucking crazy, Laura. Certifiable."

"Fuck you!" She raised a hand to slap him but withdrew. Thought better of it.

"We're done. Take your shit and get the fuck out!" He stormed out of the room. The front door slammed moments later.

So that was it. They were finished.

Dana poked her head around the arch a moment later. "Mom? You okay?"

"No. Not okay. Gimme a few minutes."

"I heard everything. Are you guys—?"

"Dana! Just give me a minute!" Her tone was sharp, rude. Looking startled, Dana turned and walked away.

Coming off her earlier adrenaline rush, the pain and confusion in her head was overwhelming. Laura laid on the sofa. To rest her eyes, to think, to regroup before she went upstairs to pack. She felt so tired. Exhausted. Almost drugged. The grandfather clock, ticking away time, seemed entirely too loud because the house was so deathly quiet. She closed her eyes. Just a few minutes' rest.

Moments later, she was asleep.

When Dana later shook her, Laura barely stirred. She couldn't reach consciousness. Dana gave up and walked away.

Vivid dreams haunted her sleep.

She stood on the beach in Chicago, the lake water cold and refreshing. Lucas and Leah were with her, and they were having fun, laughing and playing as they had before the house came into their lives. It felt fabulous to be there, so good to feel normal.

A tap on her shoulder. Laura turned around and screamed.

The woman from the hallway stood there, her long, grey hair partially concealing a skeletal face, the face of Anna Flecher.

"Go away and leave well enough alone. Forget Lucas. He's mine." Her words were a hiss, followed by dead laughter that lingered after she faded into the haze.

Laura then walked alone on a desolate stretch of sand, the whistling wind kicking up clouds of dust and pushing tumbleweeds off to infinity. A small man appeared out of the dust, a caricature of a wizard dressed in a flowing blue robe covered with stars and crescent moons, carrying a bag.

A doctor's bag.

He mumbled as he vanished into the dust. "The sky is red, that's why. The sky is red, that's why."

Her later sleep was deep and dreamless. The stoned slumber of overwrought emotions. The sky outside first grew wan with the early light, then vivid red as the sun rose towards the horizon.

★   ★   ★

As sunlight first touched the leaded glass in her room, Leah awoke and stared at the ceiling, content for a few minutes with a soggy thumb. She grew bored and stood, making a circuit around the crib before she yelled, "Gama!"

She shook the gate at the edge of her bed and gaped in surprise when it fell into the open position. That had never happened before. She lay down and turned until her feet were sticking out over the floor and slowly lowered herself to the carpet. Two and fearless, excited by this newfound freedom, she forgot about Gama and her wet diaper. She bounced from toy to toy as each one grabbed her attention.

She pulled the closet door open. There were more toys in there, she knew. She worked her way through them—a stuffed bear, a naked Barbie, a xylophone—until she reached the far corner.

As she reached for a toy car, the floor suddenly shifted and dropped downward into the joist space above the kitchen. It was another trap door, long forgotten, simple in design: either open or closed. She fell through the floor, through a weak section of plaster lathe that gave way with little resistance, sending the frightened child down upon the dishes and glasses strewn across the quartz countertop.

★　★　★

A loud crash of breaking glass startled Laura awake.

She sat up, fully alert, vigilant. Listened, but heard nothing. Something was wrong, terribly wrong, and Laura felt a crushing anxiety in her chest. She stood and roamed around the Hall. Didn't remember falling asleep here—oh, maybe she did. She and Lucas had fought and she had lain down. Why hadn't Dana woken her? Where was Leah?

She stepped past the fireplace into the library.

Nothing out of place.

That sound. What was it?

Walked through the arch to the sitting room. The house was silent—her breathing and a clock ticking the only audible sounds. Eerie. So very eerie.

She stepped into the foyer, looked up the stairs, saw nothing. Took a few more steps until she could peer into the kitchen.

Something red sat on the island among the broken glass and dishes. Laura slowly walked forward, not comprehending what she was seeing until she realized it was Leah and the red color was blood.

Uttering an anguished cry, Laura ran to her.

She slipped and fell in olive oil pooling on the floor from a broken bottle on the counter. Her head struck the edge of the quartz countertop followed by the stone floor, all in a rapid blur of motion before the world went dark.

Fifty-Two

Laura was lost.

She had tumbled through the stone floor of the kitchen into a cavernous space filled with dry, swirling fog. Laura wandered aimlessly, searching for Leah, the steady rhythmic clicking of her heels echoing around her. Nebulous shapes crossed her path. She heard sounds, voices perhaps, low and distorted, speaking in tongues. Time was an abstract. Perhaps this was the afterlife, but it was neither heaven nor hell, just a murky void. Cold. Painless. Indifferent.

Then breaks appeared in the fog, like the sun burning through a morning haze. The light came and went like intervals of day and night. Her dreams were vivid; fragments of the house, a pitchfork, Sally, Lucas, and Anna Flecher woven into frightening collages. Occasionally, Laura saw Leah, but she invariably disappeared into the haze. As the fog dissipated and Laura edged closer to consciousness, she fought it, preferring the anesthetic numbness of the swirling mist. There was no reason to wake up.

Leah was gone.

She heard muffled voices and felt hands manipulating her body.

They physically moved her; then she was rolling and moved again. Unwillingly, Laura opened her eyes and focused vacantly on a room both white and bright. A machine towered above. An intravenous pump clicked steadily beside her.

Confused, she twisted and struggled in a panic, sending angry spears of pain through her head.

"Where am I?" Laura cried.

"Auburn Hospital, ma'am."

Then she remembered. Leah was gone. She felt hollow and disconnected from her body. Tried to find her way back to the fog, away from the suffocating pain and grief that awaited her in consciousness. She wanted to sleep forever.

"Annie, page Doctor Ellerton. Stat."

She fell back onto the gurney, slack like a lifeless doll.

"Mrs. MacKenzie, the doctor will be right in."

A young woman, dark-haired, plain-faced, and dressed in white, put a hand on Laura's arm, either as reassurance or in restraint. It wasn't clear. Laura recoiled from the hand.

"Relax, Mrs. MacKenzie. We're going to perform a CT scan."

What was this place? A hospital? An asylum? Why did she need a scan? Nothing made sense. She only remembered the bloodied body on the kitchen counter. Could think of nothing else.

The door of the room swung inward. Two doctors in blue smocks, a middle-aged man and a younger woman, strode in and quickly circled the table.

"Mrs. MacKenzie, I hear you've rejoined the living."

Laura remained silent, eyes closed, trying to slip back into the fog and away from these people, to wallow in her pain and misery.

"Laura?"

Someone lifted an eyelid and flashed a light into her left eye. Laura twisted away from the light.

"Laura, I'm Doctor Ellerton," a man said. "Laura, I don't know how much you remember. You fell and hit your head. You have a nasty bruise and a concussion. There may a small bleed in the lining of your brain. It's important for you to lie still so we can complete the scan."

He put a reassuring hand on her shoulder. "If you're worried about your granddaughter, Leah was doing just fine when I checked this morning."

Laura's eyes flew open. "She's okay?"

The male doctor nodded.

She struggled to hold back tears of relief but cried anyway. With the image of Leah's inert bloody form forever emblazoned in her mind, it felt like a miracle. It didn't seem possible she could have survived.

Laura relaxed while the woman, a radiologist named Greenway, performed the CT scan. Ellerton then tested her reflexes and asked a bunch of seemingly pointless questions. Images appeared on the viewer in the corner. As the doctors studied the images and conferred in hushed tones, Laura dozed.

One of them spoke to her? She rolled over. "What?"

Doctor Ellerton turned and looked inquiringly.

"Did you say something?" Laura asked.

"No. We're still studying your scans."

"Something about me being lucky?"

"Neither of us said—" He stopped and exchanged an indeterminate look with his colleague, shook his head, and turned back to the scans on the viewer. Their silence puzzled Laura. If she was all right, why didn't they say so instead of behaving in such a conspiratorial fashion?

They walked to her bedside.

"You're making a remarkable recovery," Ellerton said. "You've been unconscious for two days, and initially, you had a small bleed in the lining of your brain—a subdural hematoma. Today, your scans are virtually clean. If all goes well, you should be able to leave tomorrow. The nurse will return you to your room. I'll stop by to see you later. Okay?"

She nodded.

A nurse wheeled Laura on a gurney along a confusing maze of hallways to her room. The building was silent but for the faint hum of machinery. The air smelled medicinal, clean, sterile.

She was settling into bed when a thin bearded man in a baggy green scrub suit breezed through the door. "Mrs. MacKenzie?"

Laura nodded.

"I'm Doctor Lewis. I'm taking care of Leah. How are you feeling?"

"Okay, I guess. How's Leah?"

"She's doing great. She had a couple of nasty lacerations that required sutures." He spoke with animated gestures. "Other than that, her injuries weren't serious."

Laura flashed again to the image of Leah bloodied on the kitchen counter, knew she would never wipe it from her memory. "But there was so much blood—she looked like she was dead."

"Leah was unconscious and she had a deep scalp wound. Scalp wounds bleed profusely and look worse than they really are." He put a reassuring hand on her arm. "As for the fall, small children are lighter and more flexible than adults. They often escape without serious injury. She was unconscious for several hours and, given the delicate nature of the suturing, we've kept her sedated. She should be ready to go home tomorrow."

"Can I see her?"

"Absolutely. But later. She's sleeping and Doctor Ellerton wants you to rest, so let's wait until after lunch. I'll send a nurse down for you. I have to finish rounds. If there's any change, we'll let you know." He breezed out the door with a wave.

Laura lay back on the pillow, warmed and relieved by the knowledge that Leah wasn't seriously injured. Burying Jacob had nearly killed her. She wouldn't have survived had Leah died. Accusing thoughts then pointed an ugly finger. How could she have been so stupid, so careless with the life of that child? She should have left the house sooner—though she never imagined Leah would become a target.

No more.

Tomorrow, she and Leah were leaving and never going back. How Lucas reacted no longer matter. Things felt irrevocably broken between them. It was another pain she wasn't certain she would survive. Thank God for Dana and Leah. The love and support of her daughter and the unconditional love of her granddaughter would surely help see her through.

As Laura drifted to sleep, Dana poked her head through the doorway. She looked tired and unkempt. "Hey Mom, I heard you were awake. Sorry I wasn't here. How are you feeling?"

"Okay. Have you seen Leah?"

"Yeah. She's doing great. When I saw her that morning, I thought—" Dana fought back tears. "How did she get there?"

"I don't know. I can't even imagine." She took Dana's hand. "Where have you been?"

"I went to the house to get my stuff."

Laura sat up. "What? Are you leaving?"

"No. I've slept here the last two nights. Since you're doing better, I'll stay at the hotel in town tonight."

"Not the house?"

"I'm not staying there. Period." Dana stared into space, near tears. "I'm scared, Mom. Leah could've died. And Dad is totally weird. He hardly talks to me. He looks angry all the time."

"Has he been here?"

"No. Not once." Dana nibbled on a fingernail. "You're not going back there, are you?"

"No." Laura shook her head. "As soon as I'm discharged, I'm taking Leah and leaving. Can we stay with you for a while?"

"Of course. Don't be silly."

"I need a favor."

"What?"

"Please stay and watch Leah for me just in case she's released before I am." Laura gave Dana her best pleading face. "A day or two is all I'll need."

"I don't know, Mom."

"Please...?"

Dana looked to the window and her shoulders relaxed. "Of course I'll stay. I don't know why I'm being so—I guess I'm just scared. Just don't ask me to go anywhere near that house."

"Don't worry. I'm not going there, either," Laura said, shaking her head.

"Two days, Mom. Then I have to get back to school. Jesus. You can scratch what I said about toughing it out here," Dana said solemnly. Then her forehead furrowed. "Did Ashley stop by?"

"No. Is she here?"

"Yeah. She said she was coming up. She looks terrible. Like she's aged ten years."

"If you see her, tell her I want to talk to her."

"I will. I'm going to get a room. I'll let you get some rest." She set Laura's parka and purse on the Naugahyde recliner. "I brought these. I didn't know if you'd need them."

Dana turned to leave, hesitated, and said, "Two cops are asking questions about Leah's accident. I think they're coming to see you."

"Great, just what I need."

"Right? Anyway, I'll see you later." Dana disappeared through the door.

What the hell did the police want?

She decided there was no point in worrying about it, though until that moment, she hadn't actually considered the question: how *had* Leah fallen onto the countertop? How had she gotten out of her crib? As she pondered these questions, fatigue overtook her and she fell asleep.

Fifty-Three

Lucas tapped the red icon and dropped the phone into his pocket.

Damn!

Laura had regained consciousness. He preferred her dead.

If Dana hadn't run down the stairs so quickly—if he had recognized the opportunity sooner—he could've bashed Laura's head against the floor a few times and finished things.

For now, he needed to play it safe and kick her out. A permanent solution was best, but any attempt was too risky now. The police had been asking questions about Leah's accident and personal aspects of their lives. If something happened to Laura, he would be the prime suspect. They always blamed the husband. If she moved to Illinois, that would be enough.

For now.

There was a thorny issue in divorce, though.

The house. He wasn't relinquishing the house, but buying Laura and Ashley out would be difficult. He might have to work again. Right now, he was more concerned about the dangers Laura posed, certain she was responsible for the grief in his life. Nate remained in a persistent vegetative state and might as well be dead. Leah had nearly died after a mysterious fall. Laura was clearly closing in for the kill.

He needed to be vigilant until he decided how to handle the situation.

The guy who buried his wife alive had the right idea.

Lucas threw his coat on and smirked as he sauntered out the door. Headed for the White Birch Inn, he felt confident the answers would come to him.

Fifty-Four

Laura was dreaming. Walking in the basement, following the old woman gliding silently along the hallway. Laura grabbed her shoulder to turn her around, to see her face—

"Mrs. MacKenzie?"

—a face she knew?

Laura opened her eyes. A plump nurse in bright cartoon print scrubs stood at the foot of her bed.

"I'm Jean. Would you like to see your granddaughter?"

Laura closed her eyes and searched for Anna one more time, but she was gone.

"Mrs. MacKenzie?"

"Sorry, I'm still half asleep. I'd love to see my granddaughter." Laura struggled up and tried to get out of bed.

"Take it easy. Doctor Ellerton said you have to go up in a wheelchair."

"What?"

"Sorry, those are orders."

After slipping into a bathrobe, Laura acquiesced. She did feel weak.

The nurse took Laura up one floor to a brightly colored ward littered with stuffed animals. Cheerful pictures adorned the walls. Small children dressed in pajamas played in the hallways. Some looked remarkably healthy while others were tethered to machinery by tubes taped to arms, legs, even noses.

They reached Leah's room and Laura felt a compelling stab of guilt seeing her lying in the tall hospital crib. Leah's head and right arm were bandaged, her left leg bound with adhesive tape securing an intravenous line tethered to a blue pump at the bedside. Laura struggled to hold back tears.

Leah's eyes lit up when she saw Laura, but she then sulked as if to say, *Where were you while I was going through this?*

The nurse lowered the side rail, and Laura leaned over, talking softly and stroking her forehead. Leah responded to her touch, smiling, then struggling to reach her.

"You can hold her if you like," the nurse said.

"Please, I'd like that."

The nurse sat Laura in a rocking chair, picked Leah up, and placed the child in her arms, carefully situating the tubing. Laura had difficulty holding her, her arms weak and unresponsive.

They rocked. Leah smiled.

Laura cried.

Leah dozed off, and Laura, after her arm had fallen asleep, called for help to lay Leah in bed. She wanted to walk to her room, but a nurse was lurking with the wheelchair and nabbed her as she stepped out the door.

Two men were waiting when they reached her room. One looked fiftyish, wearing a cheap suit, the other man younger, wearing standard police garb. He looked attractive in a cop sort of way.

"Mrs. MacKenzie?"

Laura nodded.

The suit spoke. "I'm Lieutenant Jensen, Auburn Police. This is Sergeant Thorpe." He flashed a badge and dropped it into his pocket. Jensen looked bland and humorless and held a fedora in his left hand.

"I'm tired. What do you want?" Laura snapped.

"Just a few questions. We understand you've been through quite an ordeal."

She nodded and sat in the lone chair, exhausted and feeling hostile without knowing why. Why didn't they just go away? She felt foolish for snapping at them. "I'm sorry. I'm just tired."

"We just need a brief statement from you about the events of that morning," Jensen said.

"I don't remember much."

"What do you remember?"

"I was asleep in the Hall and heard a loud noise in the house. It was about 7 a.m. maybe?"

"Do you normally sleep in the Hall?"

"Um, no. My husband and I were fighting." Laura stared out the window at the grey sky, trying to remember. "I walked to the kitchen, saw Leah—I must've slipped and fallen. I don't remember anything else."

"Nothing?" Jensen remained a blank slate.

"No. I don't even remember falling."

"Let me get to the point then," he said. "There are some unanswered questions about your granddaughter's accident."

"Like what?"

"The crib was left open."

Laura thought for a moment. "No, it wasn't. I remember pulling the side of the crib up and locking it. It's a habit."

"Did you know about the trapdoor in the closet?"

"There's a trapdoor in the closet?"

"There is." Jensen fiddled with his hat nervously. "Any idea how she got out of her crib?"

"I—I don't know," Laura said hesitantly. She looked out the window; noticed it was snowing lightly.

"She would've needed help," Jensen said cautiously, his face expressionless.

Laura reflected, then realized the implication. Anger rose in her like a righteous sword. "What in the hell are you suggesting? That I had something to do with her accident? I said I latched the side of the crib and I did."

"Your husband said you've been having emotional issues. That you did this to—to prove your house is haunted."

Laura tried to quell her rage, afraid she might lash out. She needed to project calm. Sanity. She took a deep breath, then another, let it pass. "That's ridiculous. He knows I wouldn't hurt Leah. My husband is having an affair and wants me out of the way. Did you ask him about that?"

Jensen jotted down a few notes. He was tight-lipped, like he'd heard it all before. Thorpe stared out the window.

How could she explain it? What would she say? Hmm. Somehow, an old house and an angry dead lady grabbed Leah and pushed her through a hole in the floor. A story that would surely convince them of her emotional issues and earn her a ticket to an asylum.

"Sorry, Mrs. MacKenzie," Jensen said gently. "We have to investigate your husband's complaint. We came to hear your side of the story."

He slid his hat on, opened the door, and paused. "We also talked to your daughter. She seems to feel your husband is overreacting."

Jensen filed out. Thorpe followed, but turned and looked at Laura searchingly.

"Is the house haunted?"

Laura's eyes met and held his gaze. "I don't really know anymore."

Thorpe shrugged and closed the door as he shuffled out.

Laura was stunned and tired, but not too drained to feel bitter anger toward Lucas. The accusations were outrageous—a betrayal—and he knew it. The rotten, miserable bastard. How could he? She would find the best attorney money could buy to tie him up with court orders and injunctions and make his life a living hell. Enough of this. She was taking Leah, moving back to Illinois, and filing for divorce. Time to walk away and start over. Lucas and that wretched house could go to hell.

Her rage soon crumbled into depression.

Things couldn't get much worse. Nate was in a coma. Sally was dead. Everyone and everything seemed allied against her—Lucas, the house, the town. Carol had never called. Ashley hadn't bothered to stop by.

Thank God Leah was safe and Dana was here.

They had always been close, more so than she and her mother had ever been. Still, she wanted her husband back, the one taken by the house or some faceless woman from town. She wanted her friends back. Wanted her life in Illinois back. She wanted to cry but couldn't find the tears.

Fifty-Five

The rough prodding of a nurse woke Laura from deep sleep.

The woman wrenched her arm for a pulse, then jabbed her forehead with the thermometer.

Laura protested, "Hey, take it easy!"

"You take it easy, honey. I'll be gone in a moment." The nurse's manner was cold in contrast to her earlier friendliness. After she left the room, Laura noticed other members of the staff just down the hall at the nurses' station, talking and glancing toward her room. They weren't very subtle. She heard fragments of conversation drifting down the corridor.

"—police came to see her."

Disapproving murmurs followed.

"—bet it was no accident."

Laura soon understood. On the weight of circumstantial evidence, they believed she had caused Leah's injuries. It had been a long and miserable day, but this was too much. Laura wasn't staying another minute. Tomorrow, she would strike back, see an attorney, and deal with Lucas. Take Leah and leave. Her doctor in Illinois could examine her in a day or two.

She grabbed her phone and called Dana.

"Hey, Mom, how are you feeling?"

"Okay. Where are you?"

"What's the matter?"

"I'll explain later. Just tell me where you are."

"The Auburn Inn, room one-thirteen, but—"

"I'll see you in a little while."

Laura slammed the phone down and buzzed the nurse. She climbed out of bed looking for her clothes and found them hanging in the closet. She heard a nurse pad in behind her.

"What are you doing?"

Without turning, Laura said, "I'm leaving."

"You can't do that. The doctor was quite specific; you need to stay until tomorrow—"

Laura turned, angered and frustrated. "I said I'm leaving, and as soon as I'm dressed, that's exactly what I'm doing."

"We'll see about that! I'm calling the doctor!"

"Call whoever you like. Just get out of my room. I want to get dressed."

As the nurse stormed out, Laura tossed her gown and pulled her clothes on with angry thrusts. She was doing the right thing. The doctor said she was making a remarkable recovery, and she preferred the idea of a hotel bed over a hospital bed. Leah would be safer here at the hospital than anywhere else. She was slipping into her parka when the nurse and an older woman barged in.

"Mrs. MacKenzie, please stop and reconsider. You have a serious head injury." A slim figure, her face was stern, her hands locked on her hips.

Laura stared at her coolly. "I know my rights. I'm leaving. Do I need to sign something?"

"You'll need to sign an AMA form."

"If you have it ready, fine. If not, send it to me."

Laura marched down the hall to the stairs. She went up to see Leah, found her asleep, but lingered for a moment just to watch her, then kissed her forehead. She left Dana's room number with the night nurse, called a cab, and knocked on the hotel room door thirty minutes later.

Dana pulled the door open. "Hey, Mom. What happened?"

Laura walked in and tossed her coat onto the bed. "The police all but accused me of tossing Leah through a trapdoor in the closet after your father told them I was an attention-seeking psychopath. Now the nurses think I'm Attila the Hun." Laura described the police visit and the attitude of the nurses later in the day.

Dana shook her head sympathetically. "Are you sure you're okay?"

"Yeah."

"What are you going to do?"

"First, I'm going to find an attorney and deal with your father—he's gone crazy. He knows I'd never hurt Leah."

"Divorce?" Dana said tentatively.

Laura struggled with her tears for a moment, then forced them back. She nodded.

"I'm sorry, Mom. It's sad." She gave Laura a hug. "Are you sure?"

"I'm afraid it's gone too far for anything else."

"Then what?"

"We'll pick Leah up and get out of here," Laura said. "Can I stay with you for a few weeks?"

"Absolutely. You don't need to ask."

Laura tapped on Ashley's name in her contacts, but the call went to voicemail.

"Where's Ashley staying? I want to call her."

"I don't really know."

Laura called the other local motels, but couldn't find her. Around eleven, Dana fell asleep, leaving Laura watching an old movie on cable called *Dark Passage*.

Exhaustion soon took her, leaving the room lit ghostly grey by the TV.

Fifty-Six

Shepherd watched Lucas drive off in the pickup.

The house was dark and he felt certain it was empty. Stepping out of the woods, he followed the edge of the trees to avoid leaving suspicious footprints in the snow. He jogged down the drive to the front door.

That Lucas MacKenzie was a skeptical twit complicated the situation, but it wasn't his fault. It was a ridiculous story and, after all this time, one he scarcely believed himself. Still, he was partly responsible for the problem and only he could resolve it. The village idiot in the equation, Edward MacCoinnich, had been dead for almost five hundred years. Now, his ugly death didn't seem punishment enough.

Shepherd didn't yet have a plan. Over the past three nights, he had driven up and observed the house, becoming familiar with family routines. He soon recognized a nightly pattern.

Lucas left each night between seven and eight o'clock and returned late, often after midnight. Curious, he'd followed Lucas to town the night before and discovered he was frequenting a tavern, drinking heavily, and cheating on his wife. He did not see Laura come or go

296

and had the impression she was gone. Maybe she had taken a trip for a few days. Or left Lucas. That would be better. Lucas was a bastard.

Mostly, he came to observe and assess as he formulated a remedy to rid the house of Anna Flecher. He had detected no hint of her yet. She had to be here, but had somehow concealed her presence. It would be a game of cat and mouse as they appraised each other, searching for weakness. Anna would know he meant to destroy her and she would have revenge in mind.

He tried the front door and it opened. Unlocked, no alarm sensor. Lucas was obviously a trusting soul—or daft.

The house looked almost exactly as he remembered it. The colors and decor were different, more contemporary, but this was almost certainly the same Tudor house inhabited by Edward MacCoinnich and Anna Flecher five hundred years ago.

He removed his boots and walked a slow circuit around the first floor, performing a quick inspection of each room. In the Greate Hall, he examined the paneling on the right side of the fireplace and noted subtle tool markings left behind when they opened the wall to access the tomb.

It was uncanny. Somehow, this house, built in England centuries before, had been transported here by forces he could scarcely imagine.

A flash of insight jogged his memory. He had placed an object here long ago that would confirm Edward had interred Anna in *this* house.

He walked up the stairs and across the hall to a bedroom and searched the floor behind the door. He pushed down, and the trapdoor flipped open. Inside, the cross tailored to enforce his binding spell still lay there, identifiable by the word he'd engraved on it five hundred years ago.

Dryhtdŏm

Judgement.

Ironic. In the end, judgement had come for Edward MacCoinnich, not Anna Flecher. It would be doubly ironic if she exacted a revenge on him as well. He pocketed the cross.

He sensed an ultra-low frequency resonance in the house, a deep bass *thrum*. It was a sensation felt more than heard, a vibration caused by the dissonant conflict between his presence and the house—or Anna herself. He fingered the protective gold amulet over his heart, an unconscious reflex. The tension grew steadily. She was here.

Time to leave.

He wasn't ready for a confrontation. Tomorrow, he would return and finish the job he'd started eons ago.

Feeling brazen, he spoke in his ancient Mercian dialect, *"Ic i ongéan-férede."*

The equivalent of *I'll be back*, he smirked and walked out, slamming the door behind him.

He climbed into the Range Rover and breathed a sigh of relief. A second amulet rested on the dashboard. Disabling a means of escape was common. Once it was killing or maiming horses; now, it would be vehicle sabotage. He took no chances, understood the risks. With amulets, he protected his person and vehicle, but he then thought about the cross in his pocket. That hadn't worked. Not even a little.

The thought sent a chill down his spine. He was walking a dangerous path to fix this. It would be much safer to run, but his ethical sense of duty outweighed any thoughts of flight.

That failed cross? A warning. To stay focused, to avoid reckless or rash approaches.

Driving home, he worked through feasible solutions to end this nonsense once and for all.

Fifty-Seven

In the woods one hundred yards from the library, Tom sat on the fallen bole of a tree struck by lightning years before.

He stared at the house, transfixed. In the last few days, the faint, iridescent green aura that appeared weeks ago had spread from the roof to envelop the entire structure. He didn't understand the phenomenon and assumed it was an omen of trouble ahead.

Tom couldn't imagine what dangers lay ahead but knew he was to blame. He had failed to keep the intruders out of the brick room. Something dangerous had been locked within and they had foolishly set it free. That presence, the probable source of the creepy green aura, now filled the house with a hostile energy that had chased him outdoors.

Was this all preordained? Had fate brought him here to protect the house until these people came and released this thing from bondage? That made little sense. Whatever the cause, an evil story was unfolding, directed by the dark and dangerous presence, a threat to everyone living in the house. He worried they were about to reap the whirlwind and Tom felt an overwhelming sensation almost like fear.

More than ever, he longed for death. Not the twilight consciousness he now occupied, but blessed oblivion. He was tired of being a prisoner. He was also certain Elizabeth was never coming back. Maybe she was dead.

He had no reason to stay, but he didn't know how to leave. An invisible tether kept him close to the house. Physically, he seemed indestructible. The bullets Scarecrow fired at him had passed right through his body. Maybe silver bullets would do the trick? Or a wooden stake through the heart? An exorcist? Tom grimaced at the irony, reduced in this miserable existence to praying for an ugly demise.

Tom needed to grab and take hold of his destiny. Otherwise, a hundred years would pass and he'd still be here, dithering, unwilling or unable to act—truly a fate worse than death.

Things had to change.

Soon.

Fifty-Eight

Laura and Dana woke just after eight. After showering, they ate breakfast at the motel restaurant, a small alcove with four tables and a diminutive menu. Laura was at peace with her decision to leave, but felt a powerful undercurrent of unease, much like the day Sally died. Worried about Leah, she called the hospital, but Leah was fine and would be ready for discharge by noon. Laura called several local attorneys, finding one willing to see her today. Tapping the red icon, she turned to Dana.

"Will you come with me? I'm nervous."

"Of course," Dana said. "Are you sure you want to do this?"

"I am. Your dad is going through something. Maybe this will bring him to his senses."

Dana merely nodded.

More than nervous, Laura was downright apprehensive, but attributed her unease to starting the process to end her marriage. Broken or not, it was still painful to consider letting go. Flashbacks of happier times played in her mind: Dana's birth, the trip to St. Lucia, their wedding day.

Now all seemed lost. Laura was certain he was seeing someone. The thought of him holding another woman—touching her, making love to her—felt like a dagger through her soul. She had doubts. Filing might be a mistake, might push them apart forever, but to protect herself, to protect Leah, it was the logical course. If he came to his senses, she would reconsider pursuing the divorce.

The attorney worked from an office building three long blocks from the motel. Laura and Dana walked but soon wished they hadn't. The sky was dull and dark, the color of washed slate, the air bitterly cold. The bank thermometer stood at a frigid seven degrees.

After a brief wait, they were shown into a spacious office. A big man jumped up from behind the desk to greet them with an outstretched hand. "Morning, ladies. Bill Wexler."

Wexler was a tub of a man with a moustache and soul patch, dark bushy eyebrows, and an energetic manner. His suit looked trendy and custom-made. He listened to Laura intently and then said, "What do you need from me?"

"I want a divorce and I want custody of our granddaughter. Can you handle that?"

"Heck, yes. Do you want the house?"

"No."

"Wisconsin is a no-fault state. However, if we file first and get the jump on him, you'll get temporary custody of Leah. Meanwhile, we'll tie him up in paperwork so completely he'll need court approval to use the restroom."

Laura didn't care for Wexler but retained him regardless, based on his promise to tie Lucas in knots. She suspected he was unscrupulous, but decided a tawdry approach was just the ticket for this situation. Wexler asked numerous questions and took copious notes. At length he said, "That should do it. There's one more matter to attend to before I get started."

"What's that?"

"I'll need a retainer plus filing fees for the paperwork. Two thousand dollars should do it. Is that a problem?"

"I don't know. I hadn't thought about money. Let me check." Worried that Lucas may have frozen the accounts, Laura logged into the bank app and confirmed the accounts remained opened. "It's not a problem."

"Figure out what you'll need for the next month or two. Go to your bank and draw it out in cash or a cashier's check. Drop off the retainer and I'll start the paperwork."

Laura and Dana walked to the bank and spent an hour making the arrangements. They delivered Wexler's retainer and ran back to the motel. Laura grew more anxious. This was taking much too long—it was after one o'clock.

Laura packed the few items she had while Dana went to fetch the car. A few minutes later, Laura's phone rang. Dana.

"Mom, my car won't start. It won't even turn over. I called for help, but they said it might be two hours. I can't get an Uber either."

"We don't have that much time. I'll call a cab."

Laura summoned a cab, impatient to discharge Leah from the hospital. She called Ashley while they waited, but the call went to voicemail. When the driver arrived, they grabbed their purses and phones.

It had started to snow. The cabby, a congenial man with an unruly mess of grey hair and a big weathered nose, warned that a big snowstorm was on the way. The radio soon echoed his forecast in dire tones. A winter storm was approaching—a *panhandle hook*—swinging northward from Texas. Apparently, it was a particularly bad sort of storm.

"Here we are, ladies." He coasted to the entrance.

Laura paid him, stepped out, and said, "Could you have someone pick us up in an hour? We'll need a ride back to our motel."

"I'll wait for you in the coffee shop."

"I don't want you to go to any trouble."

"It's no trouble. I'm due for a break. Might as well take it here."

Laura and Dana rushed through the revolving door to escape the cold. The lobby was devoid of people or noise beyond the faint hum of machinery. The elevator door was open and waiting. Laura shivered, trying to shake off the cold and a growing sense of dread. The apprehension was more acute, a premonition of danger and confrontation, a sense her life was about to unravel in a bad way, a feeling approaching panic.

Stop it!

Laura silently cursed her morbid imagination and stepped out at the third floor. Everything would be fine. They would pick up Leah, drive to Illinois, and Wexler would handle the rest. She walked briskly to Leah's room, leaving Dana behind, her steps loud on the hard floor, faster and faster, Laura unable to control her spiraling anxiety. Something was wrong. She just knew it.

Stop it!

The corridor smelled of disinfectant. Two small boys clad in pajamas raced past her, giggling. Laura tried to smile, slowed the last few feet to the door, and stuck her head around the corner.

The room was empty.

Fifty-Nine

Shepherd ate a light breakfast, a concoction of roots and grains high in complex carbs. Normally, he was comfortable eating alone, but this morning he felt melancholy. He missed Laila with longing sadness. Her memory invariably surfaced in times of stress. Her calm manner, her dulcet voice, had always been an antidote for tension. The burden to end the problem in Lost Arrow weighed on him heavily.

He thought about Laura as well. She reminded him of Laila, but there was something more. She exerted a powerful pull. Why? Though not certain, he suspected she was like him, a natural. She might not know it—might sense she was different, but not why. If so, she would have little training and her skill would be a raw, untamed thing. It was good she had gone away. The house was a dangerous place for her.

As he ate, he checked the forecast, dismayed to see a winter storm warning in effect. Still, tonight was the optimal time to confront Anna Flecher. She would prepare to meet his challenge and he dared not give her too much time to ready a defense.

He hadn't sensed her presence in the house and assumed she was cloaking herself. But he worried about a darker possibility. Perhaps she'd invoked some malignant energy or demon to exact a revenge before she died. If she was sufficiently powerful, it was a possibility and it would complicate the remedy.

One by one, Shepherd ticked all possibilities off a mental checklist until satisfied he would arrive at the house prepared for every contingency.

Shepherd spent an hour packing supplies and the tools and accouterments of his profession into the Range Rover. The garage was heated and that allowed him to work at a comfortable pace. No need to hurry. He would wait until Lucas left the house, giving him at least five hours to work. A thread of anxiety ran through the mental preparations. How had she sustained a presence for so long? She was dead, entombed in brick, and yet somehow, she persevered. Five hundred years later, Anna Flecher remained a threat—or had left some dangerous legacy in her wake.

He walked down to his basement workshop. Unlike the advanced technology in the office two floors above, the tools and raw materials here harkened back to a simpler, more primitive era: roots, herbs and medicaments, amulets and talismans, the spoken word. He had spent little time here lately. He'd embraced technology at every turn and had become a wizard of a different persuasion, a sorcerer of technology—the only logical path in the modern world. But now, improbably, a dangerous manifestation of that primitive era had found him. Regardless of his reservations, he needed to send it back where it belonged.

Tackling the last and most vital preparation, he encased a wax carving of his favored talisman in high temperature plaster. When it set, he placed the plaster cylinder into a furnace. The wax within melted and vaporized, leaving an impression of the object in the plaster. He melted pure gold over a burner and poured it into the mold.

It was a simple, ancient weapon, and yet potent in practiced hands. While the amulet protected him as a force field might, this talisman magnified and projected his energy, weakening his opponent. It was very effective at close quarters.

He sighed. Weapons now were far more sophisticated, but people were still primitive creatures at heart. Despite tremendous advances in technology and medicine that had given people longer, fuller lives, the primal urges remained. The tribal need to fight and kill, to persecute and exterminate; the evil present in every person, which, under the right circumstances, led to anger and violence, from domestic abuse to genocide. Life had become easier over the centuries, but not necessarily better.

Shepherd shook his head in dismay, trying to shake his melancholy.

Why hadn't he taken an apprentice?

That was the way, but it hadn't been a conscious decision or one born of laziness—rather, a lack of suitable candidates. Laila had been unable to bear children. He had no living offspring of his own to teach the ancient ways.

He spent an hour trimming and polishing the gold figurine. Then he milled four runic letters into the metal and spoke the words—in Mercian—of an old incantation to empower it. Sliding the talisman into an inside pocket of his parka, he climbed into the Range Rover, reasonably confident he was ready.

Shepherd drove north out of Milwaukee while the fury and passion of Beethoven's *Ninth* thundered from the Meridian sound system.

Victory lay ahead.

The alternative was too awful to imagine.

Sixty

Laura stared at the empty room—the bed stripped, the cabinets bare—as the implications struck with blunt force. She fought panic, tried to rationalize that they Leah had moved to a different room but couldn't slow her racing heart, nor could she keep from running to the nurses' station.

Dana stopped, open-mouthed. "What's the matter?"

Laura accosted a young blonde at the desk. "Where's Leah MacKenzie?"

The nurse looked at her for a bewildered moment, then cheerfully said, "Oh, your husband came for her. He said you weren't feeling well."

Laura saw the curtain rising on a disaster worse than she imagined. She cried in desperation, "What? Where'd they go?"

The nurse blinked. "Home, I guess."

"Oh, my God. Dana, hurry! Your father took Leah!" She ran past Dana who stared in disbelief, a look of dread in her eyes.

Dana turned and followed. "Mom! What's gotten into you? And where's Leah?"

Laura plowed blindly through a young couple stepping off the elevator, almost oblivious of her actions.

"Your dad took her! We have to go get her." She pushed the button for the lobby and gnawed on a fingernail. "Oh God, I hope she's okay."

Eyes wide, standing rigid, Dana looked like a mannequin carved from a slab of oak.

Laura said, "Say something!"

"Mom, I can't go to that house! I'm scared to death of that place. Call the police, but don't go there."

Dana was right. Call the police and let them handle it. No, that wouldn't work. They would say Lucas taking his granddaughter was no crime, and by the time she explained—*if they believed her*—it might be too late. Wexler wasn't filing the paperwork until tomorrow morning. She had no legal standing.

"Technically, your father has done nothing wrong. We have to get her ourselves." Laura spoke quietly, but her voice was intense, reflecting the smoldering rage beneath. Lucas had done this to spite her. He had no interest in Leah. He wanted her to grovel and beg. The bastard. The rotten, miserable bastard.

"How, Mom?"

"I don't know."

"You're both acting crazy and I don't want to be in the middle of it!"

"I know and I'm sorry."

"How do you intend to get Leah back?"

"Right now, I'd kill if that's what it took, but that won't be necessary. He doesn't care about Leah—he's doing this to hurt me. If you come with me, he's less likely to make a scene. I know I'm asking a lot—"

"You are," Dana said irritably.

Laura nodded and slowed her breathing trying to appear calm even though panic and hysteria threatened to send her running through the hospital screaming. It was difficult but Dana seemed to draw strength from her apparent determination.

The elevator door opened.

"I'll come, but if *anything* goes wrong, we leave and call the police. Okay?" Dana gazed at Laura intently. "And no fighting! Just grab Leah and go."

"Thanks, Dana," Laura murmured. "I hope that cab driver is still waiting."

They rushed through the lobby to the coffee shop. The cabby sat at a small table littered with cellophane wrappers and a paper cup. He looked up, surprised.

Laura said, "I know you're on break, but can you take us to Lost Arrow? It's an emergency."

"No problem. The coffee's bad here, anyway. Hope it's nothing serious."

"So do I."

He cleared the table and struggled to keep up with Laura and Dana. Outside, snow fell and a thin blanket had settled on the cab. The driver opened the rear door, jumped in, and started the car.

"Where in Lost Arrow?" he said, looking over his shoulder.

"The MacKenzie place. It's on the other side of Lost Arrow, on Firelane Eight. Please hurry."

The transmission clunked into gear. "Good enough. I'll find it."

He drove along a rough road through a neighborhood of older clapboard houses to the highway, gathering speed as they left town. The old Chevy rattled over every bump and the wipers squeaked, setting Laura's teeth on edge. Country music played quietly on the radio. Her mind was a blur of conflicting pictures and emotions.

Laura feared the approaching confrontation. Lucas wouldn't hurt her, but how difficult would he be? Would he just hand Leah over? Would they fight? With that thought, Laura saw herself lashing out with feet and hands, punching and kicking Lucas until he fell, then striking him again and again—

Stop it!

Laura tried to be optimistic, willing things to work out, but her anxiety was more compelling. She sensed a showdown coming, a battle with not only Lucas, but with Anna and the house itself. Laura took a deep breath.

Just take Leah and get the hell out of there.

She thought about the story Shepherd told Lucas. An invocation? A curse? How could such a thing exist? It sounded like medieval nonsense, yet evidence for its existence surrounded her: the book, the album, the slamming doors, the accidents, the long trail of death, the graves, the house itself.

How could such a thing exist?

She had no answers. Only her deep love for Leah and fear for her life kept Laura from turning and running. But she would avoid any confrontation. She was taking Leah and leaving. From a distance, perhaps this situation would make sense, seem less insane.

The falling snow made the wooded landscape look surreal, a world populated with cardboard houses and trees from a strange dream. The view was hypnotic, and for a while Laura stared out the window, absently wishing she could slip into a crack of that fantasy landscape and wake up with Lucas at her side, Leah in her bed, her world safe again.

Passing through Lost Arrow, Laura looked for but didn't see Lucas's truck parked at the White Birch.

They turned onto Firelane Eight, the rear of the car sliding as they did so. Suspense and worry closed in like a strangler's hands about her throat. Dana sat tense and rigid next to her. The car bounced over a slight rise, her stomach lurching with a giddy rush.

"Sure is a creepy-looking place," the cabby said.

Every muscle in her body drew taut as the house grew to fill the windshield.

Icicles hanging from the eaves looked like the fangs of a great white shark. The wind pushed smoke from the chimney at a sharp angle over the snow-covered roof. The house could be a great dragon crouched in a lair, the broad dark beams crisscrossing the whitewashed plaster forming the skeleton of the beast.

Laura put her hand on the door handle.

Dana said, "Should we have him wait? Just in case?"

Laura hadn't thought about it. "No—yes, until I get Leah. We'll take the Honda when we leave."

Laura slid out of the car and stood in the soft snow, willing herself to be strong amidst her anxiety and fear. She was here and hoped to God she was ready to handle the approaching encounter.

The loud cry of a bird over the lake startled Laura from her gloomy reverie—only the lake was now hidden beneath a broad expanse of white, ringed by snow-cloaked trees. A solitary black bird lofted in the air above.

She turned to Dana and said, "Stay here for now. Let me try diplomacy first."

Dana nodded.

Walking to the front door, Laura saw an old blue Chevy parked by the truck but scarcely registered the car as important. She was preoccupied with a singular thought—to get Leah away from here safely. Nothing else mattered. Nothing.

But the door was locked and she didn't have her keys.

Laura gave the knocker a stern beating, irked to be knocking on her own door.

Footsteps approached. Then the heavy iron handle moved downward. The thought of the cab driver and Dana looking on gave her strength as she prepared to meet Lucas.

She nearly gagged in shock when a woman opened the door. Whoever Laura expected, it certainly wasn't the blonde standing there, holding her granddaughter!

After a confused moment of growing recognition, Laura put a name to that snarky face.

Murphy.

Sixty-One

"Lucas said you might come here," Murphy said. "He told me to call the cops if you did."

The sheer fury of her anger eclipsed any rational thought Laura had. As Murphy tried to slam the door, Laura forced her leg through the opening, lunged forward, and snatched Leah with her left arm in a swift move that surprised them all. She swiveled and punched Murphy in the solar plexus with a tight fist, knocking her to the ground, and then moved in, kicking her in the stomach with a leather boot. Murphy lay winded and cowering.

"Get out of my house, you bitch!"

When Murphy didn't move quickly enough, Laura gave her a hard kick in the ass. "Get out!"

Murphy scrambled to her feet, grabbed her coat, and ran out the door, yelling, "Lucas is right! You're fucking crazy!"

Laura sat down hard and cradled Leah, who was sobbing, frightened perhaps by her grandmother's rage. Rocked and soothed her until she settled into hitching whimpers, careful to avoid the bandages on her head.

The realizations swept through Laura in an ugly wave. Lucas *had* been seeing another woman.

Sleeping with her in their bed.

For all that Lucas had done, the blow to her dignity and whatever love remained was more than she could bear. The pain stabbed like a steely blade to the heart. She fought back tears, but they came anyway, and Laura broke down, sobbing bitterly. She didn't deserve this. Couldn't understand how they had come to this.

She distantly registered the sound of a car revving and roaring away. Leah was crying again. Laura fought for control, wiped her face on her sleeve, and tried to calm the child. She felt less tense, no longer frightened. Though shocked by her quick leap to violence, Laura was happy she had literally kicked Murphy's ass.

Moments later, Dana peeked through the doorway. "What happened? Who was that?"

"I—I think we just saw the last of your father's girlfriend," Laura said as she soothed Leah. She let out a humorless chuckle hoping to cover her aching grief.

"Are you okay?" Dana stared wide-eyed.

"Yeah, I'm okay."

"So, where is he?"

Until that moment, Laura hadn't considered the question. He was probably hunting, but even if he was home, she was no longer afraid.

"Lucas?"

Silence.

"Lucas!"

No answer. Laura stood and said, "The truck's here, so he's out hunting somewhere."

"Great. You've got Leah. Let's go."

"Wait a minute. I want to grab a few things."

"Jesus, Mom, let's get out of here!"

"Just a minute. Please?"

Dana agreed reluctantly and nestled Leah on her shoulder. Laura ran upstairs and threw armfuls of clothing into a large suitcase, filled another with Leah's clothes, and ran them out to the Honda CR-V past Dana's nervous scowl.

The cab driver waited patiently, his wipers clicking back and forth, the engine rumbling with a low reassuring sound. They didn't need the cab. Things had turned out perfectly. Now she had cash, clothes, a vehicle, and a few personal effects to sustain them until the courts straightened out the mess. By the time Wexler finished with him, she wanted Lucas to hurt as badly as she hurt now.

Laura rushed by Dana and said, "One more thing."

"Jesus, Mom, let's go!"

Laura ran to the Hall; not just to appease Dana, but because she could feel the house stirring. There were sighs and groans that sounded eerie and unnatural, unrelated to the rising wind outdoors. Several knives clattered to the floor in the kitchen.

"Mom!"

Laura grabbed her iPad, turned to leave, and stopped dead, letting out a small yelp.

The wall was open and Anna's tomb gaped at her like a dark, maleficent eye.

An ice-water chill ran down her spine. Her insides tightened. Laura ran from the Hall, giving that opening a wide berth, fearful that icy hands would reach out and grab her. Dana ran out the door ahead of her, holding Leah. The snow, heavier now, flew in waves and swirls, driven by the wind. Dana opened the rear door and strapped Leah into her car seat. Laura walked around the Honda toward the cab when Dana yelled, "Mom, start the car first! Just make sure, okay?"

Laura stopped. Dana was right. She hopped in and the Honda started immediately. She ran to the cab.

"What do we owe you?"

He checked the meter and said, "Twenty-five ought to do it."

Laura found two twenties and tossed them onto the seat. "Thanks for being so patient. Keep the change."

She slammed the door and ran to the car. In a minute, they would be out of here, away from Lucas and that wretched house. She kicked the snow from her boots and sat in the car. A brief smile crossed her face. Mission accomplished. Leah was safe. Laura shifted into reverse and punched the gas; the Honda lurched backwards. Shifting to drive, she twisted the wheel and fishtailed up the driveway. As she turned onto the road, the Honda stalled with a jolt.

For a moment, Laura stared at the dash, confused. She pushed *Start* but nothing happened. Looked down, realized her mistake and shifted to park.

The wipers swished back and forth while Pearl Jam played on the radio.

Laura stepped on the brake and pushed the ignition button. The starter coughed and whined for a moment and quit. She pushed it again, but the starter just clicked this time.

Laura had a sudden, awful feeling. She shifted to neutral and let the Honda roll backwards. Stopping in the center of the drive, she pressed the button and the Honda roared to life. She pressed the gas and jerked forward. As they reached the road, the Honda died again.

"What's the matter?" Dana said with a rising pitch.

The dash lights went dark. The wipers quit. The radio fell silent.

Laura rolled back into the drive. "It won't go. I think it's the house."

"Mom! Look under the hood. Maybe something just came loose."

It was a silly suggestion, but Laura had none better. She motioned for Dana to pull the lever inside the car, and as the hood cracked open, Laura pushed it upward until it clicked. She managed only a cursory glance at the confusing tangle of wires and hoses. It was the top of the engine that caught her attention, her eyes drawn to a message scrawled with a finger into the grease and dirt on the valve cover above the word **iVTEC**: *you're dead bitch*

Laura gasped and nearly doubled over in shock. Dana let out a short, piercing scream when she saw the words through the gap between the hood and the dash.

"Do something!" Dana's voice verged on panic.

The truck! She ran to the truck and grabbed the door handle.

Locked. She yelled to Dana, "Throw me my key ring!"

Laura caught it and fumbled with the keys, trying each one in the lock in a frantic struggle. None fit.

Damn it!

Why had she wasted so much time in the house? Why had she let the cab go?

"Dana! Call the cab back!"

A second later, Dana yelled, "I don't have a signal."

Jesus! Laura was angry, frightened, near her wits' end. She grabbed her phone from her pocket. No signal.

Damn it!

Laura charged toward the house in a blind panic. She'd find the keys to the truck—no, screw the keys, she'd call the cab back on the landline. They could reach him by cell or—

I'm going to kill her. I'm going to kill that fucking bitch. I'm going to bash her fucking brains in. I'm going to kill that fucking bitch—

The evil and menace in those thoughts, those words, struck Laura with such force, she nearly fell over. Movement at the periphery of woods caused her to stop and look out in that direction. The trees were visible as a faint dark outline in the falling snow, but Laura was sure she had seen something moving.

Lucas!

His bright orange hunting gear grew clearer as he walked from the far edge of trees toward the house. Only he wasn't walking. He was running, charging like an angry bull. Her chest seemed to collapse with crushing pressure as she watched him, suddenly certain they were in grave danger, convinced Lucas intended to harm them.

Sixty-Two

Laura hesitated for a moment before she understood perfectly what they had to do. She ran to the car and yelled, "Lucas is coming, and he's lost it! Take Leah and run! Get to the road, call the sheriff, flag a car down, *anything*. Just get her out of here!"

She looked at her phone; still no signal.

Dana looked distraught. "Oh my God, Mom. Why? What about you?"

"Just go! Hurry, so he can't catch up and take Leah! He's lost his mind. I'll hold him off until you get help."

Looking into Leah's big, inquiring eyes, Laura hugged her and whispered, "I'll see you later, baby. I love you."

"What are you going to do?"

She kissed Dana on the cheek. "I love you too. Don't worry about me. Go, get help."

Dana, looking lost and confused, didn't move.

With tears in her eyes, afraid she wouldn't see them again, Laura nudged Dana and said, "Go!"

She longed to go too but someone had to hold Lucas back. He had gone crazy and this seemed the only way to keep Dana and Leah safe.

Tears gave way to determination as Laura watched them disappear into the swirling snow. She ran to the house with only a vague notion of how to stop Lucas. If she could hold him off for five or ten minutes, Dana would reach safety and summon help. Frightened more for Dana and Leah than herself, Laura felt certain fear for her own life would come soon enough.

Laura flung the door open and ran to the closet where Lucas kept his guns. A gun was the only threat Lucas would respect and the only weapon that might keep him from killing her. Would it? He had a rifle too and knew far better how to use it. Her only edge was surprise.

Her eyes darted across the gun rack; there were a dozen rifles and shotguns. Which one?

A slim rifle stood alone at the end of the rack. She recognized it, a Marlin 30-30 she'd used the few times they had gone hunting together. A box of shells sat next to it. Laura grabbed the rifle and the box, tipping shells into her quivering hand. Found the chamber and pushed a shell in.

It fit. She slid three more into the gun and dropped the remaining shells onto the floor. If four wasn't enough—?

Gripping the gun so tightly her knuckles blanched, Laura stumbled forward and fell onto the deacon's bench in the foyer. She now had an unobstructed view of the front door and the basement stairs. She reached for the phone. Thank God for landlines.

Laura punched in 911 with a shaky finger, holding the gun in her lap with an elbow. It rang and rang.

Nearly crying, she muttered, "Hurry, damn it!"

"Nine-one-one, what's your emergency?"

"Police! Hurry!"

"Your name and address, please?"

Laura sat, perplexed for a moment, then said, "What?"

"Your name and address, ma'am."

Laura started to speak, silently cursing an idiotic protocol that was wasting precious seconds. Didn't they realize it was an emergency?

The line went dead.

No hiss, no dial tone, just silence. Laura didn't redial, certain Lucas had cut the line.

Instead, she set the receiver down slowly while her heart thumped crazily in her chest. Wary, hyper-vigilant, her eyes fixed wide open, she had virtually stopped breathing. It was deathly silent except for the sound of the wind. She couldn't believe Lucas wasn't already in the house. Had he gone after Dana and Leah?

The rear door at the bottom of the stairs crashed open and slammed into the wall.

Lucas stormed in, panting hoarsely as Laura swung around, slid to the floor, and pointed the rifle down the basement steps.

Sixty-Three

"Lucas, if you come near me, I'll kill you! I mean it!"

Lucas stood at the bottom of the stairs, gun at his side, staring at her curiously like a big, dumb parrot. He looked ill, cheeks sunken, eyes dark and hollow, his beard white with frost. Laura sat rigidly, her finger straining at the trigger. Could she kill him if she had to? Would she?

"Laura, what's the matter with you?" He spoke in a gentle tone. He seemed confused by her behavior. Or was he playing a calculated game with her?

She faltered.

He took a step.

"Lucas! I mean it! Don't move! Tell me where the truck keys are."

Would it matter? Could she run to the truck quickly enough to escape?

Best to stall, buy time until help arrived.

He seemed convinced she might use the gun even if she wasn't sure she could. He was still holding his rifle. That wouldn't do.

"Put your gun down, *now!*"

Lucas slowly set the rifle, butt down, by the stairs. "Relax Laura, the keys are in my pocket. Why do you want them?"

"I just want to leave. It's obvious things are finished between us."

"What's with the gun?"

"I—I was afraid you might try to hurt me."

"Have I ever hurt you before?" His eyes looked as cold as snow.

"No—but you've been different lately. Angry. You said we were finished. And why did you accuse me of hurting Leah?"

"I don't know. It seemed like the only answer at the time." He gave her a look that fell somewhere between concern and pity. "I hate to tell you this, Laura, but you're the one acting strangely. I'm beginning to think you've lost your mind. You need help."

Great, Reverend Drew had said the same thing. Laura remained wary. Something was off. Lucas seemed conciliatory, and a part of her wanted to believe, but she resisted. He was too rational. Still, he was talking. If she could stall a little longer—

He moved toward the first step. "So, what do you think?"

"Don't move, Lucas! Right now, I'll talk, but that's all I'll do."

"Okay, okay." He raised his hands in a conciliatory gesture. "What do you want to talk about?"

"How about that *slut* you've been sleeping with?" Plenty of venom on *slut*.

Lucas dropped his eyes in a reasonably sincere gesture of regret and humiliation. Laura felt moved by it, foolishly. So easy to be duped by emotional signals like that from people we love. Except Lucas didn't love her now. He was cheating on her. It was a ruse. She steeled her resolve.

"I'm sorry. Murphy was an inexcusable mistake. I can only ask that you forgive me."

Laura winced at the name *Murphy. Her* of all people; the thought made her nauseous—them kissing, Lucas lying on top of her and—

Stop it!

Lucas slipped out of his parka and set it aside.

"Forgive you? Why the hell should I? She was in our house!"

He considered, then said, "I screwed up, badly. But we had a good marriage—"

"Were you fucking her in our bed?" Her finger tightened on the trigger.

"No!" He feigned shocked and pressed on. "Yes, things have been rough lately, but I think the marriage is worth saving."

"I don't know if I can anymore."

"We should try. Let me come up and talk to you."

"No." She wiggled the rifle barrel in his direction. "I like you fine right where you are."

"We'll go somewhere else then," he said casually.

"Where?"

"The White Birch? I don't know." But his eyes belied the offhand manner.

"I don't know either, Lucas. You accuse me of trying to kill Leah. You bring your slutty girlfriend into our house, and now *you* want to talk? Fuck you."

"Yes, I want to talk."

"Just so you know, I filed divorce papers on you."

"Whatever." He was losing patience. She didn't want to push him too far. How long had Dana been gone? How long before help arrived? Seconds stretched into minutes, minutes felt like hours. How much longer could she hold him there?

"Okay, I'll talk. But not here. Not like this."

Lucas slowly put his foot on the first step.

"Stop!" Laura raised the gun. "You're going to have to accept that I don't trust you right now. We go separately, me first. Throw me the keys to the truck."

Lucas was playing a deceptive game with her. For a moment, she imagined a way out. She had no intention of talking to him. If she could get the keys, back away slowly, fire a shot over his head if need be, she'd have about a five or six second lead on him. It might be enough. But what if the truck stalled like the Honda? Maybe Dana and the police would be here by then.

"Why don't you trust me?" he said.

"How about the note under the hood of my car?"

He looked confused. "What?"

"Oh, you know. What in the hell did I ever do to you?"

"Seriously. I don't know—"

"Liar!"

He looked ready to say something, then thought better of it. He took another step.

"What are you doing? Stop!"

"I'm bringing you the keys."

"Throw them to me."

"I can't do that." His expression hardened, his eyes narrowed, glossy and snake-like, concealing a darkness beneath. He no longer looked like Lucas. Was he crazy? Possessed? No time to ponder.

"Lucas, I'll kill you if I have to," Laura said in a shrill, rising voice. Could she? The thought set off an insane mental cascade of emotions: fear, anger, a sense this would end badly. The man she loved had lost his mind.

He started up the stairs with slow, deliberate steps, never taking those eyes from her.

"You won't shoot," he baited. "You don't have the nerve."

Laura felt a rapid, rising dread, a crushing pressure in her chest.

He kept coming, staring at her, step by step, pushing her—pushing them to the brink, coming until she felt compelled to act.

Closing her eyes, Laura squeezed the trigger.

Sixty-Four

Dana ran awkwardly, holding Leah tight with her right arm, up the drive and along the road, praying help was near. She glanced back, seeing a vague image of her mother running for the front door. Moments later, the house vanished in the blowing snow. A blast of adrenaline and pure terror fueled her, a rush of energy feeding an illusion she could run forever.

Eyes forward, searching for help, she was only dimly aware of the trees on either side of the road. Her pounding heart, measured breathing, and the steady *thump thump of* her feet on the snow-covered pavement merged into a primitive rhythm Dana found comforting, spurring her on. The running was a good distraction from the panic and fear lurking beneath the surface. In her grasp, Leah was docile and quiet.

The wind was a howling animal in the trees, icy torture on the road. Her body contracted within her clothes until they felt too large to protect her shivering frame. The road, swallowed by the enveloping greyness of the storm, never changed as she ran forward. In her mind, the highway was only a mile away, eight or nine minutes at this pace.

Soon, she would find a signal for her phone or flag a car down and summon the police. Perhaps they were on their way.

After a while, Dana questioned her progress. How far had they come? Without visible landmarks, she could be running in place in this storm. Lugging a child was a greater burden than her legs could bear. Her muscles cramping with pain, her side ached, and her arm felt numb from Leah's weight. She couldn't maintain the pace. Dana stopped to catch her breath and walked, convinced the highway was near.

Fear and anxiety rushed at her and couldn't be held at bay. Why had she left Mom behind? Was her father dangerous? The house, yes, but Dad? She couldn't comprehend it. He was the coolest guy she knew.

But what if he was? How would Mom fend him off? Morbid images played in her mind: her mother lying in a pool of her own blood, eyes open and staring sightlessly—

No. Dad wouldn't do that. Dana realized with a painful longing just how much she loved her mother. How had things devolved to such insanity between her parents?

But if he had hurt her, was her father now pursing them? She felt trapped in a conflict between the memory of father she knew and the stranger he'd become. She had to get help before anything happened. It was the only tenable solution.

She drove her legs to a slow and pitiful run, more attuned to the surrounding sounds. The cold tree branches creaked and groaned as the wind howled through them and played a mournful dirge in the wires above. A lonely sound, Dana imagined they were the only people walking the earth, that nothing existed beyond this stretch of road. The snow that concealed them was also an enemy, slowing their progress and gnawing at every gap in her clothing.

As she neared the brink of exhaustion, Dana saw a flickering of light in the distance, uncertain at first, growing brighter in the dusky greyness of the storm.

The highway!

It had to be, but the lights were stationary. Indeed, they looked like multifaceted squares floating in the blowing snow.

Dana blinked and stared.

Windows.

The house!

How in God's name had she ended up here, at the house? She had run in circles!

What was happening?

In her fear, she didn't rationally examine the question, instead flailing herself with bitter self-loathing. Besides, the answer was too terrifying to contemplate.

Over the keening storm, she heard a single gunshot, a sound muffled by the wind. Dana stifled a scream at the implications and bolted again, fueled by a second shot of adrenaline.

Her stride was wearied but as straight and true as she could visualize within the raging blindness of the storm. The stride of the hunted, the stalked. Though exhausted beyond any imaginable bounds, she didn't falter, certain any misstep would be the death of them. Her only concern was getting Leah to safety.

Then she heard a voice calling her name. But who would be out in this weather?

It called again, growing louder, a female voice. At first, Dana thought it was her mother. And with that thought, a rush of elation.

Mom got away!

But the voice sounded cold and ethereal like the wind. It wasn't her mother.

Looking back, Dana saw a mirror image of the scene ahead, the road disappearing into swirling curtains of snow. Within the storm, her fear and imagination were playing tricks on her, taunting her.

Or something was following them. Not her mother. It could only be—she dared not think it, but the name popped into her head, anyway.

Anna Flecher.

Sixty-Five

The rifle wouldn't work.

Laura squeezed the trigger harder, but the gun refused to fire. Sensing her disadvantage, Lucas charged up the remaining stairs, yelling with a throaty growl, "I'm going to fucking kill you!"

She stared wide-eyed at the gun.

The safety! She hadn't flipped the safety!

Laura fumbled, clicked the button, and fired, but pulled up on the barrel. The shot went high, sending plaster raining down on Lucas, the explosion deafening in the confined space. He hesitated, a flash of shock in his eyes, then charged again.

In the last instant, Laura rolled and dodged his lunge, but lost the rifle. Lucas, surprised and off balance, crashed into the deacon's bench, sending the phone clattering across the hardwood floor, the bell ringing randomly as it bounced away.

Laura leaped over him and ran. He grabbed the hem of her parka. It slid off her back.

Thank God she hadn't zipped it!

"Bitch!"

She bolted through the sitting room and the library into the Hall, too frightened to scream, looking for a weapon, a place to hide, any chance for a reprieve; wanting to live and praying Dana had found help. Her eyes lit upon the brass poker by the fireplace as footsteps closed in from behind—

Lucas plowed into her, sending Laura sprawling into an end table, knocking the wind from her lungs. He leapt upon her, mashing her face into the hardwood floor, panting like a feral animal in her ear. Laura tried to scream; only a muffled croak escaped.

He spoke quietly with clear menace, "Now I'm going to kill you."

Awful images flooded her mind—her body splayed out, head lolled, her neck broken—and she couldn't make them stop.

Laura struggled, twisting and straining to escape his grip, pleading through clenched teeth, "Lucas! Don't! Please!"

He grabbed her hair and jerked her head back, nearly breaking her neck. Searing pain ripped down her spine to her toes. He struggled to stand, pulling and lifting Laura by her hair, then grabbing her roughly by the shoulder, keeping a distance between them, evidently wary of her. Laura fought harder, writhing every which way to break loose.

"Let go, you bastard!"

Laura didn't want to die; not now, not like this. If she could hold out a little longer, surely help would come. She fought her panic, trying to relax enough to use her training to fight back.

Without warning, she dropped to the floor and lashed out at Lucas's leg with a hard-heeled boot, striking his kneecap hard but off-center.

"Ohhhh shit!" Lucas staggered, lost his balance, and fell. She rolled and vaulted to her feet, managing a single step before Lucas snagged her ankle and yanked her into a fall.

He grabbed her ponytail, snapping her head back and quickly snugged his arm under her chin, jerking upward with the crook of his elbow.

Bright lights flashed, the room spun, the taste of bile filled her throat. Her body was numb except for her neck, which throbbed as if broken. Her knees buckled. Weak, consciousness fading, passing out—she was going to die. Dana would be five minutes too late. Laura should've run with them into the relative security of the storm. Nothing of her life flashed before her. Nothing but a fading picture of Leah and the grim certainty that her own stupidity had been her undoing. She fought hopelessness but tears came, anyway.

Lucas jerked Laura to her feet, pulled her spine tight against his chest, turning so she faced the hole in the wall.

The tomb of Anna Flecher.

Her neck aching, her head woozy, Laura saw the threat with intense clarity. The jagged brick maw gaped at her like a predator and she understood. The realization frightened her to the brink of insanity.

All this had been preordained. Lucas knew she would come. Knew the mistakes she would make: the fight with Murphy, sending the cab away, trying to flee in the Honda—the thoughts drove her to despair. It was the reason he had taken Leah—to force her to return here.

Lucas pushed her toward the hole.

"No! Lucas! No!" Her screams were hoarse, her damaged throat raw. The room blurred with tears and she nearly gagged on his animalistic scent of stress sweat and stale beer.

Why did he hate her so?

"I've got the bricks and mortar downstairs." He whispered into her ear, "You'll be buried alive."

Threatened with that awful death, desperate to escape, her will to live surged back. If she could stall, buy time, get lucky, anything. She squirmed fiercely, seeking any weakness in his grip.

Off balance, Lucas stumbled. His forearm slipped up near her mouth.

Laura bit as hard as she could, shaking her head like a rabid dog— barely aware she was growling from deep within—as the taste of his blood mingled with the tang of sweat.

Lucas cried out in pain. "Fuck!"

He yanked his arm free from her frenzied bite and lost his grip on her hair. As she pivoted away, he shoved her shoulder, knocked her off balance and punched her in the face.

"Bitch!"

His fist smashed into her cheekbone in a cosmic explosion of pain. The blow sent her sprawling backward. She slammed into the wall, the room whirled, and she felt consciousness slipping away, a sickening feeling that threatened to suck her back into the fog beneath the floor. Fog that beckoned sweetly, promising an end to her fear and pain. Laura drifted away.

Reason and desperation pulled her back.

Wake up, Laura! Wake up!

She fought and struggled to open her eyes against the immense weight dragging her toward oblivion. Had to stay lucid, stall, time an escape. Run. Hope for a break.

Lucas was standing three feet away, wiping blood from his arm. Face soaked with perspiration, he had foam at the corners of his lips. The man looked sick and rabid.

She made a sudden move, rolling toward the archway.

"Not a chance!" He hissed.

Laura glanced over her shoulder, trying to anticipate his move as she clambered into an unsteady crouch. He pounced, grabbed her, and dragged her to her feet, pushing her toward the gaping hole in the wall.

She struggled, but locked in a bear hug, his grip was too strong to break.

Twisting her, he seized her hair and forced her head into the brick opening.

"Take a good look. It's the last place you'll ever see."

His voice exuded evil, deep and primal, with a tone as frightening as her imminent death. He pressed her harder against the wall, and Laura could feel him swelling against her.

"But not before I fuck you one more time," he said roughly. He lifted her, spun her around, and grabbed her breast. His face, hard, red, and angry, was almost touching hers. "You fucked everyone else in town, you bitch!"

Laura spat in his face. She couldn't even imagine where he got that awful idea. He was insane!

Momentarily shocked, Lucas clenched his teeth and slapped her. Forced her against the wall, trapping her there. Reached down and ripped at her jeans, pulling them open and trying to force his hand down and between her legs. The humiliation was intense, a helpless, degrading feeling that sent her shuddering toward tears.

Lucas was livid and crazy with rage. "It was the priest, wasn't it? I saw you—you were fucking the priest!"

In this frenzy, he loosened his grip just a little, but just enough.

Laura dropped like a rock, wrenching her arms free and pushing him as she slid down the wall to the floor. As Lucas came back at her, Laura coiled her right leg and kicked upward and outward as hard as she could with deadly and practiced aim. The moves were focused, with little conscious thought, drilled into her by a *Taekwondo* instructor months before. Lucas doubled over as the leather-soled heel slammed into his groin.

"Ohhhh Jesus Christ!" His face, at first surprised, buckled in agony as he swiveled and dropped to the floor, wobbling back and forth, clutching himself. He retched in pain.

Enraged beyond reason by his assault, his murderous intent, his attempt at rape, Laura lunged for the end table, grabbing the decorative glass ashtray filled with potpourri and lifted it high before swinging it down sharply, slamming the ashtray onto his head as leaves and petals rained down.

He jerked and was still.

Laura knelt over him, panting in loud and ragged gasps, ready to bash his head again.

He didn't move.

She remained crouched there, suspended in time as her maniacal thumping heart and labored breathing eased. For a while, she had no thoughts at all. Laura then realized she was crying, tears running silently down her cheeks. She wanted to find Dana and Leah, leave, and never look back.

Was he dead?

She sat hard; felt hollow, like a character in a vivid nightmare. Unmoving, Lucas didn't appear to be breathing. Laura didn't know how she'd feel if he was dead.

She set the ashtray down and reached to touch the carotid artery on the side of his neck, feeling for a pulse.

His eyes snapped open. He twisted and grabbed her by the throat, his eyes wild, teeth clenched in a feral grimace.

She screamed, sharp and wounded, as he threw her to the ground and clawed at her jeans and ripped her blouse. It happened so quickly she felt momentarily paralyzed by terror and panic. He struggled with her thrashing arms as he tried to force his way between her legs.

What had once been so beautiful between them was now ugly and repulsive. She dreaded the thought of him taking her, panting and thrusting into her, and fought it with all her will.

Concentrated on her training. Pictured the outcome.

Suddenly relaxing the muscles in her hips and thighs, her legs cleaved open.

As he dropped on top of her, Laura jerked a hand free and stabbed two fingers—locked rigid like a spear—into his eye.

He rolled away, screaming.

Laura grabbed the ashtray and slammed it down on his head.

Then raised her arm and struck him again.

Sixty-Six

Shepherd rode comfortably into the rising storm. In the Range Rover, with four-wheel drive and winter radials, the weather posed no threat to his plans. The opulence of this vehicle—the heat, the cushioned ride, the leather seats and concert level sound system—was unimaginable centuries ago when walking was often the only mode of travel.

Yet he met people daily who complained of unbearable torments in their lives. Heavy traffic, flight delays, dropped calls, bad weather. People were soft with no concept of history. Their problems were frivolous. And the catalysts of so much anger, shortening their lives with needless stress.

The blueprint to eliminate Anna Flecher wasn't definitive, the situation only modestly amenable to planning. He had assembled a mental list of strategies that had worked in similar situations in the past. Which to use, when to implement, was trickier. As always, he would improvise, or as the Americans so colorfully put it, shoot from the hip. His improvisational skill had once been phenomenal, but he hadn't faced a situation this dangerous in many years.

Still, he hadn't lived all this time on simple luck either.

As he drove, Shepherd consciously meditated to prepare for the conflict, striving to avoid underestimating his opponent. Her presence, her spirit, her magic had persevered for *five hundred years*. Powerful and deeply rooted, she wouldn't be easily sent packing. Anna Flecher knew he was coming and would fight his every effort. Anticipate his moves as he sought to anticipate hers. Plot his demise as he plotted hers.

Icy fingers of apprehension ran up and down his spine.

Good. Complacency would be fatal.

Then vivid lightning ripped across the sky.

An omen? No.

It was thundersnow. Breathtaking, but hardly supernatural. The storm was intensifying in scientifically predictable ways. He liked the symbolism though.

The world he was about to enter existed in dimensions that modern technology could neither detect nor examine. Harking back to a bygone era, the gift of extrasensory perception, extensive training, and special skills were the requisite keys to these age-old realms. They were otherwise invisible to ordinary people, to science, to discovery.

Without proof, he felt certain Laura had the gift. That she was a natural.

Just a hunch.

In other circumstances, he would love to meet and talk with her. But it was better she was gone. The house needed to be empty and, despite the weather, Shepherd felt certain Lucas would be drawn to the tavern and his mistress like iron to a magnet.

He drove north, wary of fools flying by, believing themselves invincible in their SUVs. Shepherd slowed to fifty in deference to the strengthening wind and accumulating snow as the Range Rover occasionally slipped and broke traction.

The highway narrowed to two lanes and the traffic dwindled to a few hearty travelers. Snow blew across the headlight beams, hiding the pavement behind a blur of white. Perversely, he enjoyed the drive. In the Range Rover, he was equal to the storm, no longer a lone figure bent against the wind, harried by the elements.

He turned toward Lost Arrow and the road narrowed further. No one had attempted to plow here. A few vague tracks faded into the darkness ahead.

A powerful wave emanating from the MacKenzie house passed through the vehicle, shocking him to attention. Acutely alert now, he sensed violence and chaos afoot, preparing to visit the MacKenzies.

How? Why? The house was empty, wasn't it?

That was the plan: Lucas at the tavern, Laura safe and secure elsewhere.

But no, the final chapter was already underway, wreaking havoc just five miles ahead, rushing to a conclusion without him.

Bloody hell!

Shepherd clutched the talisman in his pocket.

He had waited too long.

Sixty-Seven

Dana ran in fear, following an imaginary line in the snow that would take them far away from the house. The voice called to her, but she tuned it out, no longer trusting her senses. Cold and frightened, Leah cried loudly in her ear. Enveloped by the storm, Dana imagined creatures materializing at any moment out of the snow and darkness, sent by Anna Flecher to kill them. She tried to reason them away, but then worried they were doomed to wander in circles until they froze to death.

Panic fueled her terror while hopelessness and exhaustion weighed her down. Maybe if she just laid down and rested for a few minutes? Then she noticed a small sign in the ditch at the edge of the road.

LOST ARROW
Lost Arrow Snowmobile Club

Beneath the lettering, an arrow pointed left into the woods. Afraid the road formed an unending circle, she prayed it was a shortcut to town. Dana took a chance and plunged into the gully and onto the trail, but lost some resolve at the tree line. She gazed at the forbidding landscape of gnarled trunks, swaying branches, and swirling snow with primitive fear. A bird called somewhere within the woods in a frantic screech, barely audible over the whistling wind in the trees. Sinister looking or not, her fear of the house was greater so Dana ran into the woods.

The trail was easier to follow than the road. Blue reflectors on aluminum poles marked the way. At first she jogged, but soon slowed to a walk, no longer able to push her legs to run. She felt safer surrounded by trees. Protected.

As she relaxed, fatigue overwhelmed her. The woods became a frightening place with night falling. The knurled boles of the trees donned hideous faces, the branches like giant arms, waiting to grab and squeeze them to death. Small evergreens and snow-covered bushes became crouched animals, rodent-like creatures watching from beneath white lairs. The forest, of which there seemed no end, was masked in horrid costumes. Snow swirled around her as the wind howled through the branches. Lightning flickered above like the strobe in a haunted house.

She heard a voice again, calling her. "Dana!"

The voice seemed to surround them.

A trick. Had to be.

No one knew they were here. She ran again, renewed in her panic. Someone—or something—was chasing them. She heard or imagined footsteps on the trail behind her.

She ran faster; the sound drew nearer.

Terror seized her, but she had depleted her reserves. Her stride slowed no matter how hard she pushed. She stumbled and almost dropped Leah. Stood, took two steps, and tripped again. She refused to quit, but felt the sharp sickle of death swinging inexorably towards them.

Dana wobbled and fell. Stayed down, clutching Leah, panting, crying, unable to go farther. A silhouette materialized out of the snow. Dana leaned away from the figure, a figure that looked spectral in the half-light of the woods. The apparition moved toward her and resolved into the last person Dana expected to see.

Ashley.

Dana stared in disbelief, then grew suspicious. In the past hour, she'd come to mistrust everything—her sight, her hearing, the house, her father.

"How'd you find us?"

"I followed your tracks." Ashley huddled close to comfort them and for warmth.

Dana didn't pull away. It was Ashley.

"Looks like I got here just in time. You look terrible."

"I feel terrible. You wouldn't believe—" Dana grabbed Ashley's arm. "Have you been to the house?"

"Yeah. Everything's okay."

"What?"

"Laura's holding Lucas at gunpoint. She just called the cops. They had one hell of a fight."

Ashley stood and brushed snow from her clothes. Dana did the same, cold and too tired to feel anything but vague relief. They shuffled down the trail and, a few minutes later, walked onto the road and toward the house, heads bent, buffeted by the blizzard. Dana grew anxious again, worried the police would never arrive in this storm. More worried the weather was a manifestation of some evil emanating from the house.

Most of all, afraid once they arrived, they would never leave again.

Sixty-Eight

The ashtray broke into two bloodied fragments as Laura struck the second blow. She dropped the jagged piece from her hand, seeing nothing beyond the horror of Lucas's battered head. Only dimly aware she was spattered with blood, a powerful wave of nausea rolled through her. She leaned over and heaved a thin stream of bile, then coughed in misery.

Laura sat up and wiped her mouth with the back of her hand. In shock and exhausted, she vaguely expected Lucas to roll and pounce again, but the side of his head was a bloody mess. He had no pulse. No, Lucas wasn't getting up again. Ever. Her anger spent, she slid into despair.

The cold, hard consequences of her rage struck with blunt force—as clear as a brilliant, faceted crystal.

She had murdered Lucas.

Her hands streaked with his blood, disgust and bile rose in her throat. She couldn't erase the last few moments from her memory, the sight of the ashtray bashing his head with primitive violence.

Boom! Boom!

She shivered, feeling cold and vacant, her mind in a daze. Laura could scarcely form a coherent thought but knew no justification would alleviate her guilt even though it was self-defense, even though the crazed man she fought with had intended to kill her. Laura couldn't comprehend why Lucas attacked her and now she would never know. Lucas was dead.

Random memories played in her mind. Their first date, his expression of awe when Jacob was born, their last trip to Aruba. It was all gone, lost, destroyed forever. How could she live again? The most precious part of her life was gone.

As despair and anguish took hold, Laura, overwhelmed by visions of the past and a future stolen, leaned on his shoulder and wept bitterly. Something of her still loved him, despite all he'd done. Now he was dead.

Then she remembered Dana and Leah. They were still out, wandering in the storm. Maybe they had reached safety but she needed to know for sure.

Laura stood unsteadily and buttoned her jeans, tearing up again, trying to suppress the fear and helplessness she felt as Lucas attacked her. She buttoned and tucked her tattered shirt in. As she stuck her hand into Lucas's pocket for the truck keys, the front door flew open and footsteps sounded on the plank flooring.

Dana called out, "Mom? Where are you?"

She felt a tremendous surge of relief. Dana and Leah were here! The keys to the truck were in her hand. Together, they would leave this place and never look back. It was over. She looked at Lucas, his broken skull. Dana shouldn't see that.

"Dana! Don't come in here!"

Too late.

Ashley and Dana—with Leah snuggled on her shoulder—walked into the Hall, windblown and flecked with snow. Dana stared at Laura, unable to conceal her shock.

"Oh my God, Mom, you look terrible."

Laura rushed over, hoping to distract them by pulling Leah and Dana into a hug. "Thank God you guys made it!"

Laura turned and grabbed Ashley's hands, happy to see her friend again. "When did you get here?"

Dana's brow knitted into a puzzled expression. "I thought—where's Dad?"

As Laura closed on Ashley, a powerful wave blasted through her. *Get your hands off me, you bitch!*

Laura yanked her hands away and stepped back. "Ashley?"

Ashley seemed to fade slightly, her face and body morphing into someone—or something else for an instant, like a micro-expression. Laura stood, stunned and baffled, grave fear exploding inside her. Who? What?

"Mom? What's the matter?"

In a daze, Laura eyed Ashley. "Who are you?"

Dana looked at Laura in shock and surprise. Ashley stood there for a moment, her face a grimace of contempt, then she briefly morphed into the woman in the painting in the root cellar. Just a flash, nearly subliminal.

Craziness. Insanity.

The feelings washed over Laura in a sickening rush.

Dana glanced at Laura with a nervous scowl, as if she too questioned Laura's sanity. "Mom. It's Ashley,"

"No it's not!" Laura shook her head, queasy with fear and confusion.

Dana glanced sideways, gaped in shock and stepped backed, gripping Leah, staring at Ashley in abject fear. She had finally seen the change, too.

Just above a whisper, Laura said, "Who are you?"

"Where's Dad?" Dana said, voice rising in pitch. "I thought—"

Her eyes focused to the right, where Lucas lay bloodied and still. Dana clapped a hand to her mouth as if to stifle a scream.

Another wave passed through the woman, blending and mutating the visage that was Ashley. A tight grin crossed her face. She laughed unexpectedly. "Don't you know by now?"

Staring at that iniquitous creature, a blinding terror paralyzed Laura and rendered her mute.

In an awful realization, the answer to that question appeared in her mind.

Brightly. In neon.

Anna Flecher.

Sixty-Nine

Dana screamed, wide-eyed in terror. Inching backward, she bumped against the sofa and tumbled onto it. Her eyes rolled up, and her head lolled back as she lost consciousness. Leah fell from her arms and rolled onto the floor, howling with fear. Laura took a step toward her.

"Leave her!"

Laura froze, stunned by the power of that voice. Evidently Leah was too. She jerked, found her thumb, and settled into muted whimpers. The woman stepped forward and swung her arm, striking Laura backhanded across the face, knocking her to the floor.

"You stupid bitch! I wanted to kill Lucas!"

Nearly hysterical, Laura lay there, her mind teetering on the edge of madness. Was this a dream? A dreadful nightmare? Her mind was locked in mortal conflict between real and unreal, sane and insane. As much as she'd felt a presence in the house, a part of her had refused to believe it.

Anna Flecher was dead!

But in her soul, Laura knew this could only be Anna Flecher. Why did she look like Ashley? Was it Ashley? Had she somehow become warped and crazed by grief? She was so angry when she left.

"Confused, are we?" The woman spoke with an English accent.

Laura stared, mute.

"No matter. I'm going to kill you so slowly, so horribly, you'll wish Lucas had done it for me."

"Who are you?"

"I think you know, but by all means, let's talk." She spoke casually in Ashley's voice. The woman crossed her arms, resting her chin on one hand in a mocking parody of a concerned friend. "We have time. I'm waiting for someone to arrive."

Laura sat up and shivered, arms wrapped tight across her chest. Her earlier will to fight had evaporated, leaving her weak and defenseless. If she had any rational thought in her head, it was sheer wonder her heart didn't simply evaporate into the nothingness of a moonless night and blow away.

In the English accent, she said, "I'm Anna Flecher. My husband buried me alive in this house."

Anna pointed to the hole in the wall. "Left me for dead. I think you figured that much out. With magic, I've persevered, but only after suffering an awful, lingering death. I've been settling the score with the bastard ever since."

"What's that got to do with us?"

Pointing to Lucas, she said, "That useless twit is the thirteenth great-grandson of my husband and the harlot he married after he murdered me. Look it up. I filled in your family tree since *you* were getting nowhere. Anyway, I had this lovely little plan to kill you all, one by one, and you've gone and buggered it up!"

"I did nothing—"

"You killed Lucas, you stupid cow."

"It was self-defense."

"Blah, blah. Talk, stall, see if I care. You're still going to die."

A sudden, dark awareness dawned in Laura's mind as Anna kicked her, knocking her sideways.

Anna smiled. "Things will work out, regardless."

Laura hardly noticed. She fell into a trance, a razor-sharp focus provoked by a growing comprehension of the things Anna had done. Her anger rising, the urge to lash out and strike possessed her. She sat up and narrowed her eyes to slits. "You killed Sally."

"Yes."

"Turned Lucas against me?"

"Yes. Wasn't hard."

"Murdered Ashley?"

"Yes yes yes! Enough!" Anna's expression was savage, cruel. The image of Ashley shimmered and gelled, concealing Anna. "What does it matter? After I kill the three of you, the house will be mine again, as promised centuries ago. The authorities will see nothing but a ghastly family murder and a suicide—yours. As Ashley, it will all be mine. Nate left me everything."

"Nate's still alive—"

"Nate's a zucchini, dimwit." She waved a dismissive hand. "I saw to that."

Hearing those words, something snapped, fueled by uncontrollable rage. Laura leapt up, launched off her left foot, kicked out with her right leg, and drove her heel squarely into Anna's solar plexus. Laura felt a grim satisfaction as Anna's eyes opened wide in surprise and pain. Her body toppled backwards into the wall and she collapsed into a dazed heap.

Her eyes snapped open, her expression focused and cunning. With a sweet smile, she hissed, "Is that the best you can do?"

As Laura eyed the woman, the sofa to the left of the fireplace rumbled and shook violently. Anna twitched her index finger. The sofa levitated and flew at Laura. She dropped to the floor as it sailed overhead, crashing into the wall and collapsing like a lifeless corpse.

Fighting was useless, Laura knew it, but she grabbed a piece of the broken ashtray and flung it sidearm at the woman. The heavy glass sailed true, but Anna deflected the projectile with her hand.

Anna raised her arms. The room shook with her ire, a seismic wave of hatred. The walls trembled, pictures and wall hangings crashed and clattered to the floor. Plaster dust fell like rain. Leah howled in terror. Dana's body rocked and rolled off the sofa, narrowly missing Leah.

Sensing movement above, Laura glanced up and jumped clear as a large chuck of plaster crashed to the floor where she had been standing.

She faltered, then reached back, grabbing the brass shovel from the fireplace and hurling it at the woman.

Anna snatched it out of the air.

An arrogant smile crossed her face as she taunted, "I've been teasing you. Now I'm going to bury you!"

Anna threw the metal shovel like a spear, straight at Laura's throat. She shoved her palms out in a futile defense.

The shovel slammed into an invisible barrier just inches from her hands, falling and clattering to the floor.

How—?

No time to ponder.

Laura grabbed a ceramic lamp and threw it across the room with preternatural force. Her strength seemed to be growing, but the lamp flew wide. She plucked pillar candlesticks from the mantle and pitched them in a barrage across the room. Anna deflected them with her hands, the heavy glass smashing and exploding against the wall and the floor.

Her anger flamed white hot at this awful creature and the damage she had inflicted upon them. Laura hurled a thick glass hurricane lampshade fast and true, striking Anna on the forehead with a wet *thwack*, opening a gash on her temple. Anna wobbled and fell against the wall, momentarily dazed.

Sensing an advantage, Laura charged, but Anna thrust her hands forward, palms out. Laura slammed into an invisible barrier, bouncing backward like a rag doll and falling to the floor in a graceless sprawl.

Laura lay stunned, her rage tempered by the sheer absurdity of the situation.

She was fighting a dead woman!

How could she overcome such forces? Still, as she pondered this, her hand reached for a brass table lamp, firing it at Anna with deadly aim and strength.

Anna reacted too slowly. The lamp struck her in the chest, knocking her to the floor.

Laura charged as Anna struggled to her feet. Grabbed a pewter sconce and swung, smashing it against her head. Anna fell into the wall, but before Laura could strike again, she lunged and shoved Laura, sending her stumbling to a hard landing on the oak planks in front of the fireplace.

"Bitch!" Anna hissed.

They eyed each other with hatred, panting in ragged gasps, exhausted, each searching for weakness in the other. Blood ran in a rivulet from Anna's temple. The sofa to the right of the fireplace shook and rose a foot, then fell to the floor.

Anna was struggling!

With that knowledge, Laura grew stronger. The urge for revenge filled her heart. She became a deadly predator fueled by hate and adrenaline, her primal fight-or-flight response running at full throttle.

Laura ran two steps, leapt and side-kicked the woman in the chest. She landed and swiveled, landing a roundhouse kick to the head, knocking Anna to the floor. In a mindless frenzy, she kicked again and again while uttering animalistic grunts. Anna curled up to fend off the blows, then jumped up when Laura paused, throwing an arcing punch, her fist striking Laura just below the eye.

Laura staggered backwards, stumbled over an end table, rolling and falling, her weight landing on her twisted left arm.

It broke with a dry *snap*. Pain shot up the arm and into her shoulder, a lightning blitz of agony that brought tears to her eyes and a rush of bile to her throat.

Anna fell to one knee, near exhaustion and collapse. With Ashley's face and voice, she spat at Laura with venomous loathing and said, "I've hated you from the moment I met you."

Momentarily confused, Laura whispered, "Ashley?"

"I'm not Ashley, you bitch."

From the far side of the room, she charged at Laura, her face contorted in rage. Laura rolled backwards, ignoring the grinding pain in her left arm, her hand grabbing the handle of the brass log poker, ready to swing it sharply, hoping for something, anything. A stunning blow, a reprieve, deliverance from this nightmare.

The overhead lights flickered. The air at the center of the room shimmered, drawing in diffuse vapors that condensed into a cloud. The sudden change was disturbing enough to stop Anna in her tracks.

Laura dropped the poker in abject shock, unable to comprehend the portent of this phenomenon.

A big man materialized out of the fog.

What the hell...?

But Laura knew.

It was Tom. Sally's Tom, who had disappeared so many years ago.

Six feet tall with curly black hair, a greasy Purina cap, and a pitchfork in hand, he swung the implement and skewered Anna Flecher through the abdomen as she backpedaled away. Lifted her and slammed her impaled body, tines first, into the hardwood planking. She coughed up a few bloody bubbles and died, eyes locked open forever in surprise.

He brushed his hands clean of some invisible stain and spoke to the room. "Now we're even."

Tom tipped his hat at Laura and evaporated into thin air.

His appearance capped the insanity of the night. It couldn't be real. A nightmare? Hallucination? A complete psychotic break? Anything was possible.

Laura stared at the dead body of Anna Flecher in a stupor. It looked like Ashley, but now she would never know the truth. Had Anna assumed Ashley's shape? Stolen her body? Regardless, Laura felt certain the creature who looked like Ashley was dead.

With the Hall silent, the storm outside held at bay, it felt over. Finished.

As her heartbeat slowed, she crawled to the sofa. Dana was still unconscious, and Leah lay next to her, whimpering. Somehow, they had remained safe during the chaotic fight with Anna. Laura carefully scooped Leah up with her good arm and smothered her in kisses.

At that moment, the large center window behind her imploded with a deafening blast, showering the room with glass.

Seventy

Shepherd drove through Lost Arrow in a blizzard of biblical intensity. Snow blew in angry lines across the headlights, the road all but invisible. Lightning flashed in sporadic bursts, a godsend really, vaguely illuminating the trees lining the road, providing some reference for the way forward. He missed his turn, almost slid into the ditch, and had to back up. Nearly blind, he crawled down the fire lane. He might as well have been walking.

A dark feeling, a mix of anxiety and dread, grew within. A steady stream of negative energy flowed from the house, pressing at his temples like a painful vice. No longer hiding, Anna Flecher seemed very much in evidence and eminently powerful. More dangerous than anything he'd confronted in a century or more.

With these anxieties came a primitive emotion long absent.

Fear.

A visceral, heart-pounding, gut-wrenching cacophony of adrenaline coursed through his arteries in the primal response to danger, born from a deep existential fear he might not survive this battle. He could turn back, but he wouldn't. His ethical code was deeply ingrained. As an author of this mess, honor demanded he fix it.

He saw flickers of light ahead, specters that resolved into the faceted windows of the house. Turning the headlights off a hundred feet from the driveway, Shepherd navigated using an internal sense to avoid drawing attention to his arrival.

The house was ablaze with light. Two vehicles sat in the drive, Lucas's truck to the left and the Honda abandoned in the middle, one door hanging open. Lucas and Laura, it seemed, were home.

Bloody hell!

The night was fast careening off the rails. There was something evil at large in the house and the MacKenzies were trapped in the middle of it.

He eased down the drive and pulled in next to the truck, keeping the Range Rover mostly hidden from the house. Closed his eyes and scanned the house and the nearby environment. Stationary and no longer fighting the storm, the negative energy emanating from the house was intense. Images assailed him. Visions of death, murder, and mayhem. Past? Present? He didn't know. An insane rush of information flew by too quickly to discern. It was overwhelming.

Taking a deep, calming breath, he meditated. Settled his anxieties, closed out the noise, and prepared to meet the challenge ahead.

He decided to walk a circuit around the house while he finalized a plan and an entrance. Shepherd touched his talisman, then dropped several amulets and various Celtic crosses into his pockets. Pulled ski goggles over his eyes and snugged the hood tight around his face. He walked toward the back of the house, through deep snow, thankful he'd worn waterproof boots. It was dark here, no light visible in the lower level. As he turned at the back corner of the house, brilliant light spilled from the upper floors, illuminating the chaotic face of the storm.

He sensed a child inside. Another complication. He sensed something striking about the child, that she was just like Laura, though it wasn't relevant now.

An image flashed through his mind and lingered, the body of Lucas MacKenzie, his head battered and covered with blood. He was dead.

Bloody hell!

He had arrived too late for Lucas. Maybe Laura, too.

No. She was there. Injured, but alive. Plus another woman. A family member? And something else, something dark.

Anna?

Lucas's death weighed on him. He had approached this too cautiously, waited too long, waffled when the situation clearly demanded a daring, calculated response. A sign he was getting old. Growing soft. Worst of all, losing his edge. He hadn't walked in this world for a long time and suddenly felt ill-suited to meet it.

No matter. He was here now.

Shepherd winced as an especially powerful wave emanated from the house. It was confusing. Anna Flecher, but not Anna Flecher. Some presence acknowledging his arrival. Gathering strength. Anticipating. Lying in wait.

Time to end this.

Holding the gold talisman, he whispered a chant to invoke a binding spell on Anna and the house. Closed his eyes to visualize the energies bending to his will.

As he fought the negative energy within, the large window overhead imploded with a thunderous roar.

★　★　★

Kneeling at the altar, Kevin Drew traced a sign of the cross on his chest, stood, and ran to his office.

It was time to act. God wanted him to intercede at the MacKenzie house.

He grabbed and zipped his parka and pulled a woolen cap over his head. Checked his pocket for the key fob. Touched the cross at his neck, slipped thick mittens on, and stepped out into the night.

The storm attacked every millimeter of exposed skin at once, but the cold Jeep Wrangler started without hesitation. He shifted into drive and turned left onto the highway. He shivered nervously even though he felt protected by an invisible shield emanating from above. Nervous because he was stepping into the unfamiliar and frightening territory of the supernatural and felt out of his element.

The road was a frightening vision—a furious, twisted wall of wind and snow, assailing the few trees he could see. He drove slowly, letting the navigation system guide him, occasionally fondling the cross on his neck.

"Turn in two hundred feet."

"Turn in one hundred feet."

Thank God for the GPS. He would've missed the turn; the sign had gone down in the wind. As he swung to the right, he saw a faint set of tire tracks rapidly filling with snow. According to the map display, his destination was almost two miles up this zig-zaggy stretch of road.

Farther up, the tire tracks veered to the right near a big house occasionally visible in the snow. Nice to know there was another house on this stretch of road if he ran into trouble.

The drive grew more harrowing. The Jeep bucked against invisible drifts littering the road, pushing him right, then left, threatening to send him into the ditch. Still, he was almost there—

Without warning, the car broke into the open. No trees on either side of the road, the wind fierce and unremitting.

Whiteout.

Had he taken a wrong turn? The navigation system insisted the house was near, but a sense of dread crept over him. Something was wrong.

A dark circle loomed ahead.

What the—?

He slammed his foot on the brakes. The Jeep bucked and slid sideways as he realized in horror the exact nature of that dark circle. Careening, sliding out of control on the ice, the Wrangler pitched over into open water on Lost Arrow Lake. On its side and sinking fast in the perfect darkness of the storm, Kevin Drew couldn't find a handle or grip, couldn't orient himself in the vehicle. Knew with absolute dread there was no escape from this watery grave. He prayed to God to save his mortal soul as the cold water rushed in.

So cold.

So very cold.

Seventy-One

Laura reflexively threw an arm up to cover her head and crouched over Leah while glass rained down upon them. Numb physically and mentally, she remained in that position long after the glass stopped falling, cowering until she felt cold air from the broken window creep along the surrounding floor. She also felt the distinct sensation of eyes watching her.

Laura didn't look. She was exhausted. Mentally drained beyond rational thought.

Ashley was Anna? Anna was Ashley? It was so confusing.

Regardless, Lucas and Anna—or Ashley—were dead. It should have been over, but Laura felt someone or something staring at her and knew with sickening certainty it wasn't finished. Another battle loomed. A fight for which she had no stomach. One she saw no chance of winning. She was done. Spent. Finished.

The room was deathly quiet—other than the sound of the wind outside and the ticking grandfather clock that had somehow survived the maelstrom. Afraid to look, frightened of the palpable presence, Laura lifted her head anyway.

The room appeared empty.

She focused, searching the Hall. Every pane of glass in the center window had shattered, the lead camework bent inward and ruptured, forming an ovoid hole. The room was in shambles. Tables overturned, a sofa destroyed, lamps broken, glass everywhere. Ashley or Anna lay near the fireplace, staring with sightless horror into space, the handle of the pitchfork pointed upward from her chest. Dana remained unconscious. Lucas lay near the center of the room, the battered side of his head dark red. Leah was silent, snuggled next to her.

Beyond the destruction, Laura saw nothing, but felt eyes gazing upon her nevertheless.

The lighting seemed faulty as well. The overhead lights and a lamp that had survived flickered, brightened, then faded as if some force was drawing the energy out of the room.

Scanning the Hall again for some detail missed, her eyes settled on a point near the broken window.

Though nothing was visible, Laura sensed something disquieting and evil there, a cold, fathomless blackness—perhaps the threshold of an abyss into which she could fall forever and ever.

Laura shivered, cold with weariness and fear—the primitive fear of a child lying in bed at night, awakened and searching the darkness for the creature stalking her. It might be hiding under the bed, within the closet, or even crouched by the bed, its reddened eyes boring into her back. The terror would grow until paralysis made it impossible to roll over and dispel the monster. She would lie there and imagine a long-clawed paw settling slowly upon the bed. Would close her eyes so tight, blood vessels threatened to burst. Remained rigid until she fell into an uneasy sleep, waking the next morning with an unsettling memory of her nightmare.

Though she longed for it, she wasn't in her childhood home, nor her bed, and didn't have the reprieve of sleep to dispel this beast. No, it was here in this room, nameless and invisible, intent on harming them.

She distantly registered the sound of the front door opening, then slamming shut, feet stomping boots free of snow. The police? What good would they be? They would stumble upon a scene of incredible violence and Laura would finally get the rest she craved—in a jail cell or an asylum.

No flashing lights. Not the police.

A voice in her head spoke. "Hello, Laura."

Who—?

But with that thought came the answer.

Shepherd. He had come to help. She carefully laid Leah between two cushions, stood, and brushed the glass from her clothing as he walked into the room, a black satchel in his hand. Dressed for the weather in a heavy parka with a fur-lined hood, he was an older man, slight in stature. Laura could think of nothing to say. She then noticed the room was humming, a low bass *thrum* that sounded menacing—if one could infer menace from just sound.

The sorcerer named Shepherd spoke. *"Hwæt! Hēafod-mægum, þæs þū in helle scealt werðo drēogan, þēah þīn wit duge!"*

The low frequency hum became a vibration, an agitation in the air, resisting Shepherd. Or so it seemed to Laura.

He continued to speak fervent, incomprehensible words. A crack appeared in the wall by the window. Dust and plaster fell from spreading cracks in the ceiling. He didn't acknowledge Laura standing nearby. It didn't matter. His words seemed to counter the presence in the room, an antidote perhaps. Or just her deluded longing for the madness to end. Slowly, the vibrations ebbed. The lights grew brighter, the air clearer, the sense of peril receding through the damaged window. Shepherd spoke for a few minutes, then closed his eyes, raising his head slightly as if testing the air.

Finally, Laura said, "Is it over?"

He held a finger up to silence her.

She eased over to Leah, who had miraculously fallen asleep between the cushions. The adage about children sleeping through anything had just passed a crazy test. Laura scooped her up with her good arm and tried to brush the glass from her hair with limited success. The broken bone shot sharp pains up her arm with every movement.

Dana stirred and slowly sat up, looking befuddled. Stared, mouth agape, at Shepherd. Screwed her eyes shut, shook her head and looked again. She must have seen Ashley, lying there dead, impaled with the pitchfork. Her eyes rolled back, and Dana collapsed against the sofa with a sigh in a dead faint.

Shepherd spoke. "No. It's not over. Get the child out of here now! Put her somewhere safe and place this next to her. Then hurry back!"

He handed her a small, heavy silver object. An amulet.

"What?"

"Don't argue!" He looked anxious, his brow knitted with worry lines.

"What's the matter?" Her voice quavered. What could possibly happen now? Her anxiety returned in cascading waves. A nameless dread, sleek, black, and deadly, stalked her.

A resounding crack ripped through the relative quiet. As she recoiled from the noise, she glanced up and saw a large lamp dangling from the beam above. It tore loose and fell. Shepherd sidestepped to dodge it, but the heavy lamp seemed to anticipate the move, falling in an arc and striking a glancing but substantial blow to his head.

Shepherd dropped like an eighty-pound sack of Idahoes.

Seventy-Two

Laura hesitated only a moment.

Shepherd was unconscious or dead, she didn't know which, but opted to follow his instructions to the letter. She stood and ran awkwardly from the room, trying to balance Leah on her hip with her good arm, the amulet clutched in the other hand.

Through the sitting-room window, she saw the Range Rover in the driveway parked beyond the truck, still running, a cloud of exhaust driven at a sharp angle by the wind. Thought about running, taking his vehicle and fleeing—a fleeting thought born of desperation. But she couldn't leave Dana behind and Shepherd had come to help. She couldn't leave him to deal with this alone. She just couldn't. Laura bounded upstairs, grabbed pillows, and ran to the kitchen. Made a small bed with the pillows in a corner and laid Leah down. She was asleep, oblivious to everything, and for that, Laura was thankful.

The amulet was solid silver, given the weight. Round, a series of pikes and tridents radiated from the center, surrounded by runic symbols. Laura set it next to Leah, trusting it would protect her, but then thought about how irrational that sounded. She barked a humorless laugh. Little of what had happened today was even close to rational. Laura stayed, watching her sleep, trying to stave off his command to return to the Hall. She stroked Leah's hair for a moment and stood wearily.

The house was silent. Perhaps Shepherd was wrong. Maybe it was over.

Laura walked warily through the sitting room and the library, pausing at the entrance to the Hall.

Shepherd lay prone, the room quiet beyond the sounds of the wind. Occasional wafts of snow blew into the room. Dana remained unconscious on the floor. She should move her, but couldn't imagine how she would with a broken arm.

She knelt beside Shepherd, saw a gash on his temple. Found a pulse. She gently shook his shoulder.

Awaking with a start, he shook his head. Focused on her. "Laura."

She nodded, feeling an odd kinship with this man. "How do you know my name?"

"I've been observing you. Watching the house, your husband, all part of a long story. We mustn't dawdle. Please help me up."

She took his arm and he rose to his feet.

Laura looked at him searchingly. "Everything seems quiet now."

"It isn't over. She's just toying with me."

"She?"

"Why yes I am, Kenric." The precise British voice came from behind. Laura turned and saw Ashley standing there, suspended really, like a puppet, her face dead and blue. Three dark puncture wounds crossed her abdomen, accented with rings of drying blood. She held the pitchfork and dropped it to the floor with a clatter.

Laura edged back, hand over mouth, but she couldn't stifle her scream, a long, piercing reaction to that unbearable sight. She felt faint and willed herself to pass out, but could find no reprieve from the insane image of dead, talking Ashley.

"I've been waiting for you, Kenric." The dead woman glared at Shepherd. "Five hundred years I've been waiting for this moment, you bastard."

She uttered a string of guttural sounds, words perhaps, and thrust her hands out.

Laura felt a wave pass by, but it failed to affect either of them physically.

Anna looked surprised—if one could infer surprise from a dead face. She spoke in guttural tones with a grand wave of her arm, but nothing happened. The body looked like a grotesque marionette. It was awful.

"That isn't your friend," Shepherd said.

It looks like my friend. Laura struggled with that cosmic contradiction. What had happened to Ashley?

"It's the ghost of a monster, manipulating the body of your friend."

Shepherd spoke a few unintelligible words and the abomination that was Ashley collapsed into a shapeless heap.

He pulled an object from his bag, a slender silver cross with a pointed tip. "Here, stab her in the chest."

"What?" Laura stared in shock. "Are you nuts?"

"Hardly. It'll prevent Anna Flecher from re-animating the body."

"I can't—"

The corpse sat up and said, "Sorry Kenric, but your time is up."

Shepherd threw the cross and nailed the dead creature with deft aim. It flailed in spasms before falling limp, the cross protruding grotesquely from its chest.

Laura thought she had seen everything tonight, but this monster inhabited a nightmarish plane far worse than Laura could imagine. Fighting with Lucas, with Anna, and every awful event this long night had left her numb. Adrenaline depleted. Exhausted. She ached everywhere. Her cheek, her neck, the broken arm, her shoulder, her hip. She wanted to curl up and crawl into the fog. Anywhere but this horrid otherworld filled with talking corpses, pitchfork-wielding dead men, and ghostly apparitions.

Finally, Laura said, "How was she buried here, five hundred years ago? Before Europeans arrived?"

"She was buried in this house, in England. I don't know how, but something very powerful carried it here." He seemed to contemplate that mystery, then raised his eyebrows. "Clearly, it followed your family. I've never heard of anything like it."

Laura said. "What do we do now? Hold hands? A united front or something?"

He smiled and shook his head. "Hardly. This isn't a film."

"What then?"

He gave her a silver amulet. "Put this in your pocket." He then handed her a silver Celtic cross. "Focus your energy through this."

"What? How?"

"You don't know?" He rolled his eyes, took a deep breath and sighed.

"No. I don't know what you're talking about."

"Use your abilities, my dear." He spoke as if coaxing an addled child.

"What abilities? I don't have any *abilities*," she said irritably.

"You're wrong—and very gifted. You have the ability to channel the forces of nature to your advantage—I feel it strongly. You're a natural. With the proper training, you could accomplish great things."

Laura stared at him with conviction. "I don't want it."

"You have it. Why fight it?"

"It's unnatural—"

"Daunting perhaps, but also a marvelous gift, bestowed on very few."

That she might possess powers like those she had seen in this room was too frightening to consider. Still, the evidence was there. She'd stopped that shovel in mid-air. Fought off a dead woman.

"What does the cross do?" Laura asked.

"It's a talisman. It focuses the fundamental energies like a lens. It has no particular religious significance. For some reason, that shape is simply the most effective. You and the cross will act as an amplifier to focus my magic."

He took her shoulders and turned her slightly. "Stand here and hold it like so."

He arranged the Celtic cross in her hands, held up high. She dropped her hands, unwilling to hold the pose.

"Do it!"

"I feel stupid."

"You would rather be dead? Now do it! We're running out of time." He was trying to help but sounded exasperated. Laura sensed a powerful undercurrent of anxiety.

"My arm is broken."

He reached and gently took her left arm, placed his hands over the break, and spoke a few words in his strange language. With his index finger, traced a pattern over the break and spoke again. The pain faded and disappeared.

"It's fixed?" Laura was incredulous.

"Somewhat." He said, a bemused smile on his face. "It's mending but I also shut down your pain response."

Shepherd reached into his satchel and pulled out a container that looked like a big salt shaker. He sprinkled a circle of bluish powder around her, then outlined a second blue circle around himself. He gazed intently at the fireplace. The logs burst into flames and burned, filling the room with warmth and orange light. It grew brighter as the lights above faded.

Reluctantly, Laura held the cross up. Tried to focus, to be mindful.

Silence fell upon the room. A silence laden with unspoken threats of violence and death. The rumbling returned, subtle at first, then shaking the floor, growing in intensity until the wall behind Shepherd crumbled. Paneling and plaster crashed to the floor.

Shepherd swayed, struggling to maintain balance. He spoke rapidly in his ancient tongue, raising and lowering the cross as if appealing to the gods. Perhaps he was. Tremors shook the house, seemed to radiate from the focus of darkness by the window, an invisible but palpable malignancy. Another of the large windows imploded, showering the room with glass. Shepherd never faltered, his voice rising in volume and pitch.

Laura stood rigid, holding the Celtic cross, feeling energy, electricity perhaps, coursing through her. She sensed immense conflict in the room, a cataclysmic confrontation; a collision of matter and antimatter, life and death, light and dark, good and evil—the clash of two immutable forces bent upon destruction and annihilation of the other. A battle between an invisible entity and a slight man, a man who looked like he should be playing chess instead of slaying the monsters or dragons that inhabited the room.

Shepherd spoke rapidly, an impassioned chant that sounded other-worldly. Beams above creaked and groaned. Plaster fell in chunks from the ceiling. The fire in the hearth waxed and waned and flared brightly again. The rumbling intensified until it felt like the foundations were crumbling.

The old man reached inside his parka and pulled out a gold cross. Swapping the gold for the pewter cross, he triumphantly held it high. It was beautiful. A polished gold Celtic cross, it glowed brightly with its own light.

The turbulence near the window reached a frenzy, the air condensing into a dense fog, a diminutive storm filled with snow and dazzling arcs of lightning. The floorboards beneath it cracked and splintered and were sucked into the maelstrom. His cross was brilliant, filling the room with light. The fire in the hearth flared into an inferno.

Shepherd shouted the ultimate words of an ancient incantation in a booming voice. *"Gæð ā wyrd swā hīo scel! Áblinnest!"*

A terrible howl filled the room. Laura dropped the cross and clapped her hands over her ears. Wind rushed out the window in a fierce gale, drawing out snow and wood, loose debris, and glass like an explosive decompression. Laura huddled over Dana, but Shepherd stood there and withstood the squall until the winds died and peace settled upon the room.

Laura uncovered her ears.

Silence.

A lamp lay on its side, spinning near the window. The ticking of the grandfather clock, which had somehow survived, was soothing. The storm outside ebbed to flurries.

Laura sat up. "Now? *Now* is it over?"

Shepherd was silent, his eyes closed. He seemed to be in a trance. "Well?"

His silence was unnerving. She was about to shake him when he opened his eyes with a look of resignation. "No. It's not over. That was just a temporary victory."

"What?" Laura said, alarmed, voice rising. After that horrendous calamity, how was it not over?

"That wasn't Anna Flecher, nor her ghost. It's the house itself." Shepherd scanned the room with an increasing look of anxiety. "I've misinterpreted what's happening here. The house itself is the source of the haunting."

"What? How?"

"When Anna died, I cast a spell binding her spirit to her tomb." He looked old, weary, his shoulders slumped with an air of regret. "I didn't understand the consequences at the time—I didn't realize she had been buried alive, either. Somehow, she bonded with the brickwork to preserve some essence of her being. When your husband opened the tomb, that spirit and the house gradually merged and became one."

Laura looked around the room, the gravity of his words dawning in fearful comprehension.

"I couldn't understand why I never sensed her actual presence in the house." He shook his head with a grimace. "I thought she had cloaked herself. Now I know. I believe Anna and the house are one and the same and have become immensely powerful. We've weakened them but—"

Shepherd stopped, a burgeoning look of horror crossing his face. Laura cringed. "What?"

"There's a second possibility. She may have invoked some spirit or demon to exact her revenge. In that case, the presence of Anna Flecher has been a ruse. If so, we have very little time—"

A harsh crack overhead. Something shifting, breaking.

As they looked up, the broken end of a twelve-by-twelve oak truss swung down, tracking Shepherd as he bolted to evade the pendulous beam. It struck a glancing blow, knocking him to the ground. The gold cross flew and skittered across the floor.

Too stunned to move, she watched helplessly as a second timber fell, crushing his chest. Laura gasped, horrified. Shepherd looked gravely injured, near death. He feebly raised a hand, beckoning her. Laura crawled over on her knees and took his hand. Felt a warm infusion flow up her arm. The same sensation she felt taking Sally's hand. It was a message. He was passing the solution to her.

He mouthed two words, *Finish it!*

Shepherd coughed once. His head lolled to the side. Dead. Eyes open in surprise, a thin rivulet of blood running from his open mouth.

Finish it?

No no no!

I'm not finishing anything. I'm grabbing Leah and Dana and getting the hell out of here!

But his dying thought had lodged in her brain and held her in a trance. Blossomed like a flower. The solution was obvious. She needed to dismember the beast. The necessary tools sat outside, in the Range Rover.

Seventy-Three

Dynamite and gasoline.

Shepherd realized he might need to destroy the house to eradicate Anna Flecher and he was right.

Slowly, Shepherd's plan unfolded in her mind, a series of vivid images. He had come prepared for this contingency. Fifteen sticks of dynamite and ten gallons of gasoline. Those were the tools that would end this. All along, it had been the house. Anna was dead, had been for five hundred years. Somehow, she had transferred her power and rage to the house itself, and the house had become the monster.

But with his last words, he mentioned a spirit or demon. He had to be talking about Anna. What else could he have meant?

No matter. Either way, she needed to destroy the house to end this. Otherwise, they would never be safe.

On the floor, Dana stirred. Sitting up, she looked around the devastated room, a baffled expression on her face. She saw Ashley and screamed. Laura stepped into her line of sight and blocked the view. She had to get Dana out of here. Away from the horrors in the room before she came fully unglued or fainted again.

Laura tugged her arm, pulling Dana to her feet. "Get up! Get up! There's no time to explain! Take Leah and get out of here."

"What about you?" Dana tried to look at Lucas. Laura took her by the shoulders, turned her, and pushed her toward the kitchen.

"I'll follow you. Take Leah and go. You're not safe here."

She snatched the truck keys from the table where she'd left them, one of the few things in the room unscathed by the mayhem that had just visited.

Another timber fell. Laura dodged it but felt the house regrouping, rallying to kill her, too. She muddled her thinking, trying to hide Shepherd's planning under a screen of banal thoughts. This was about more than the house. The outcome would mean life or death for the rest of them. Perhaps she was irrelevant, but Dana and Leah were not. She needed to end this madness to save their lives.

Laura pushed Dana through the library, the sitting room, and finally the kitchen. They dressed Leah together. She pressed against Dana a few times to feel close to her, to draw strength. Helped Dana with her coat to keep her moving. Laura grabbed the silver amulet and tucked it into a pocket in Dana's parka. Pulled the zipper shut.

"Keep that in your pocket. It'll keep you both safe and should protect the truck as well."

"What are you going to do?"

"End this. Now, go slowly and carefully, but go! Go to the White Birch or, better yet, get to Auburn if you can. I'll be minutes behind you."

With final hugs and kisses, she nudged them out the door. The storm had intensified again and flashes of lightning lit the night sky, illuminating the fury of the storm. She watched Dana struggle toward the Silverado, leaning against the wind. Then strapping Leah into her seat. Jumping into the driver's seat.

Looking back one last time, Dana waved.

"I love you!" Laura yelled. "Don't forget the four-wheel drive!"

She heard the engine start. The truck crawled up the drive, turning onto the fire lane. The taillights disappeared into the snow.

Hyperfocused on the task ahead, Laura slipped into her parka and ran to the Range Rover. Popped the hatch and found two five-gallon gas containers and a wooden box with the dynamite. Inside the box, the sticks were wired together, attached to a small device with an antenna. It was all clear. She latched the case shut and grabbed the rope handle on the left side. Lugged it to the front door. It wasn't as heavy as she expected.

The front door wouldn't open. The latch was rigid—frozen. Laura couldn't budge the latch or the door, and in that moment, she understood. The house knew the plan as well and had locked her out. Shepherd's plan was specific. The dynamite and gasoline had to be at or near the center of the house. A blast from the outside would be ineffective. She knew just how sturdy the house was from the explosion that had injured Nate.

A hollow sensation of defeat fell upon her.

She kicked the door and yelled, "Fuck you!"

Her voice sounded small in the wind. She was freezing. Had to get out of the weather to think. There *had* to be a way. She ran back to the Range Rover. Set the case of dynamite next to the gas cans and slammed the hatch. Hopped into the driver's side, pulled the door shut, and pushed the heat to high. An invisible clock was ticking. She was running out of time and the house was winning. Laura noticed an amulet on the dash and sensed its significance. It protected the vehicle.

With a sudden flash of insight, Laura realized this vehicle was her way in. She would it drive right through the wall.

She knew the construction of the house well enough. Remembered Nate and Lucas talking about it and knew the door and porch were too solidly constructed. Too strong to breach. Something about twelve-by-twelve timbers supporting the center mass of the house. In contrast, the sitting room was close enough to center, and smaller timbers in that wall supported the exterior.

Laura moved the Honda to the edge of the drive. She would need it to leave. Climbed into the Range Rover and backed up the drive, aiming the truck to roll down and hit the wall dead center.

The remote detonator sat on the center console. She snatched it and slid it into her pocket. Shifted to drive and jumped out. Laura stood and watched, rubbing her frozen hands together as the Range Rover lurched forward and rolled fifty feet, striking the house directly under the sitting room window.

The wall barely moved. Reluctantly, Laura walked down and climbed in, throwing the vehicle into reverse. She didn't know if the impact with the wall would detonate the dynamite, but it hadn't. Good.

She would need to drive the SUV through the wall.

Laura revved and backed up fifty feet. Hit the accelerator and rolled forward, slamming into the house.

The wall buckled inward.

Another strike or two would do it. Laura was desperate, obsessed with ending this. The safety of her family, of Leah and Dana, depended on it. She backed up and smashed into the wall again.

And again.

On the fourth attempt, she backed to the top of the drive and stared at the wall, willing it to fail. Jammed the accelerator to the floor.

It was an exhilarating ride. The Range Rover bolted down the drive and crashed through the wall, plowing across the sitting room, demolishing chairs and tables before slamming into the fireplace. The airbag blew, knocking her senseless for a moment.

She came to and looked around as the smoke from the airbag cleared.

Jammed against the fireplace, the Range Rover was close to center of the house. She tried pushing on the door, but debris held it shut. Tried to shift sideways, to kick the window out or slip out the back, but an intense wave of pain stopped her cold. Lightning shot up her leg to her spine in a paralyzing jolt of agony. She cried out in pain.

Laura looked down. Her right leg was jammed between the seat and the lower edge of the dash forced down by the impact. She was stuck. Any amount of movement was excruciating. Her leg must be broken. She was further hobbled by her broken arm and couldn't pull herself free. Couldn't move, couldn't reach the gas pedal, but she could touch the brake.

Laura shifted into reverse, hit the cruise control, and began bumping the speed up. The engine revved, the Range Rover shuddered, but it was also stuck. The wheels spun uselessly on the hardwood floor. She was going nowhere.

The house trembled. The floor shook and tilted. Laura recognized the danger. The house was fighting back. It would vomit the Range Rover out like bad shellfish, outside where it would be useless.

Time was running out.

She had only one move left. Laura knew it and didn't fight it. Resigned to the idea there was no other way, she slid her fingers around the remote control detonator in her pocket. She felt calm, or numb, she didn't know which. It was over. Everything finished. Lucas,

Jacob, Ashley, her marriage, and finally, her life. All done. Not how she saw her life ending. She had always imagined herself growing old with Lucas, surrounded by oodles of grandchildren.

She embraced the calm feeling and focused on her breathing, finding a mindful state. Fixed an image in her mind of Leah and Dana, of Lucas and Jacob in a better time. Said a prayer for Dana and Leah. That they find safety. Happiness. And most of all, freedom from this house. She knew Dana would love and care for Leah as well as she had.

Believing the house and Anna Flecher would be destroyed once and for all, Laura closed her eyes.

Took a breath and exhaled.

Pushed the button.

Seventy-Four

Dana pulled the sundress over Leah's head and drew her hair back in a ponytail. Gave her a kiss and said, "You're beautiful, Leah. You look just like your grandma."

It was true, and a constant reminder her mother was gone—not that she needed reminding. Four months had passed and there were few moments that she didn't think about the death of her parents and the violent explosion that destroyed the house that night. Her memories were fractured bits and pieces that returned most often in her nightmares—when she slept at all. Her physician explained she suffered from post-traumatic stress disorder and it might be months before she slept normally. Mostly, she tried to block and forget the things she'd seen and poured her love and attention into Leah.

They were off to visit Uncle Nate. He'd regained consciousness a month ago after nearly seven months in a coma. He was still having difficulty dealing with the death of his wife, his brother, and Laura. Dana knew he needed all the love and support they could muster, so she and Leah went to visit almost every day.

A continuous procession of law enforcement people had come

knocking on her door in the past few months. They had so many unanswered questions.

What transpired between her mother and father?

She didn't know. Nor did she want to.

Did she know Shepherd?

She didn't. Had never met him.

Why was Shepherd at the house?

No clue. While she could guess, she wasn't going there. It was easy to sidestep all the questions, claiming a lack of knowledge, because she didn't live there. Her parents weren't getting along and had been fighting. They were in the throes of a divorce and, beyond that, she knew little. She had left that night before events reached a climax. Her parents were dead. She wanted to be left alone. That was her story and she stuck to it.

The explosion and subsequent fire destroyed the house. After law enforcement released the property, Dana hired an excavating contractor to bury the remaining debris in the crater that was once the basement. They removed the drive and covered the lot with fresh soil. A priest performed a blessing and purification rite. Dana then donated the land to the Kettle Moraine State Forest.

That aspect was closed.

The death of her parents would never be settled. In the end, she wasn't sure what happened. The few bits of the story she did know were too crazy to tell. The explosion and fire had been devastating, and the state crime lab couldn't draw any definitive conclusions about how Shepherd or her parents had died. No one could make any sense of the circumstances. Shepherd's presence, the dynamite, none of it. Death by misadventure was the final ruling. The story briefly made the national news. The sensational destruction of the house and the bizarre circumstances of their deaths made for compelling copy. Writers and producers, who saw the elements of a movie, came next. Dana turned them all away.

Dana never told Nate the entire story. Never would. The nightmare of Ashley's transformation she had buried deeply but imperfectly. The horror of it remained vivid in her dreams. She saw a therapist once a week, and it was helping a little. She didn't tell her the full story either. There was no rational way to describe it, no rational answers. None. Dana gave her the same story. They left before the craziness started.

Pulling up to the Evergreen Rehabilitation Center, she saw Nate sitting outside on a bench in the warm spring sunshine. He waved. He was finally walking again, slowly. Dana thought of Ashley for a microsecond and pushed her away. It was a new day.

"Hey guys." Nate stood and hobbled toward them.

Leah ran to him. "Uncle Nate! Let's go for a walk!"

"Yep, let's do that, pretty girl."

"Uncle Nate?"

"Yes, sweetie?"

"Did you lose your wallet?" Leah had become very articulate in the last few months.

Nate frowned. "Yeah. How'd you know that?"

She twisted girlishly with an angelic smile. "I know where it is."

"You do? Where?"

"Inside your sofa. I had a dream and I saw it there."

Thank you!

Thank you for reading *Shepherd's Warning*. I hope you enjoyed it. As an independently published author, I rely on all of you wonderful readers to spread the word. If you enjoyed *Shepherd's Warning*, please tell your friends and family. I would also sincerely appreciate a brief review on Amazon.

An excerpt from *Quinlan's Secret*, Book 2 in the series follows.

Again, thank you!

Cailyn Lloyd
http://www.cailynlloyd.net

Acknowledgments

Many people had a hand in helping me finish Shepherd's Warning and I am grateful for their advice, criticism, and support.

Nancy Boyle, my late aunt who encouraged and critiqued my first attempts to write this book. Jennie Lloyd, who pushed me to pick this up again and finish it. Lucy Snyder, Michael Garrett, Michaelbrent Collings, and Susanne Lakin who helped edit the manuscript and wrote insightful critiques. Amanda Robinson who copyedited the final draft. Katie Lloyd who proofread the manuscript.

My sincere thanks to all of you.

Books by Cailyn Lloyd

Shepherd's Warning (2019)
The Elders Book 1

Quinlan's Secret (2020)
The Elders Book 2

Hayward's Revenge (2021)
The Elders Book 3

The Mill (2022)

Quinlan's Secret

One

"By the way, it's haunted," the man said, standing by the bar, shuffling paperwork.

"What? Now you tell me?" Josh Abelson looked at the old guy critically for any hint he was joking. Greg Fitzsimmons had been odd from the get-go, quirky and humorless, an aging hippy from another era with long grey hair pulled back into a man-tail, his face a craggy testament to a life lived hard. Fitzsimmons was the former owner of this tavern, a rundown corner bar with battered plank floors, cheap stools, and oak woodwork darkened by age and decades of smoke.

The old guy put a hand on his shoulder. "No big deal. Adds a little character to the place."

"What do you mean, exactly, by haunted?" Josh asked. Why was he asking? He didn't believe in ghosts. It was probably just a legend, a story told over beers and passed down over the years. Why tell him now? They had signed papers, the sale closed. The tavern was his.

Fitzsimmons shrugged. "The usual. Noises and shadowy figures in the basement. The occasional footsteps overhead when no one's up there. The waitresses won't go in the basement. I'm surprised you haven't heard the rumors." The old guy put a finger to his nose like he was going to pick, then snatched it away at the last second. Yuck.

Rumors? *Yeah, right.* Josh stifled a chuckle. "I don't believe in any of that nonsense—"

"Yeah, neither did I. They seem harmless enough though."

"They—?"

"The ghosts." Fitzsimmons said, his stony expression unwavering.

The guy had to be pulling his leg. What did it matter? Josh planned to gut the place and convert it to a stylish brew-pub. The bones of the place were sound, the foundation solid, the location ideal. The neighborhood had run down over the years, but now young affluent couples were buying the old houses in this sleeper community and renovating them or tearing them down and building anew.

He hadn't asked the neighbors about the place because when he reopened, he had no intention of welcoming the old crowd: a bunch of Boomers who, like the owner, sat around bitching about their wives, politics, and the useless Millennial generation. Josh was GenX and thought the younger crowd was just fine.

Fitzsimmons looked around. Oddly, Josh detected no nostalgia in that last glance. "Well, Mr. Abelson, it's all yours. I hope it's everything you ever imagined." He let out a humorless laugh that sounded vaguely creepy and slapped his hand on the bar. He turned and walked toward the front entrance.

"It will be." Josh closed his eyes, listening to the receding footsteps. The door banged shut a moment later.

So long, weird old dude!

The tavern was silent, the late afternoon sun shining through grimy windows. It didn't look like a dream, but it was. After twenty years of legal practice, Josh had exhausted all interest in his profession and longed for a new career, a second life. He probably had enough money to retire now if he wanted, but at forty-eight, he wasn't yet ready for a life centered around yard work, a fishing boat, or golf.

Owning a tavern had become the dream over the years. Instead of being tied to a rigid schedule in a professional office, he would hang out at the bar when he wanted. Let others do the work when he needed a break. Come to know his clientele, hopefully establish a diverse group of regulars. Manage a kitchen—even if he had no clue what he was doing yet. He was a quick study and had a knack for learning new skills. He'd spent weeks driving around, meeting and talking to bar owners, picking their brains, trying to learn any and every detail about the trade, and was already well-schooled in the general specifics of running a business.

Josh surveyed the barroom. Undoubtedly elegant once, the luster was long gone. The oak bar, almost forty feet in length, had been sorely neglected. The back bar, also oak, looked equally shabby, marred by stains, the finish cracked and darkened with age. The floors were maple, the ceiling embossed tin, the walls paneled with some once-popular crap from the '80s. The place looked beyond salvage but Josh had a gift, the ability to envision the woodwork restored, the walls finished in plaster with oak accents, booths, tables, oak bar stools; he could see it all in glorious detail in his head.

The building itself, built in 1854, was brick and had been a bank originally. The tavern, with all the ornate woodwork, came later in that century. Upstairs, over the bar, lay a large apartment that hadn't been lived in for decades, a space Josh intended to renovate as well. He and Kiera, his girlfriend, planned to live in the apartment after the tavern opened when they needed to stay close at hand. They had talked about living together but couldn't decide who would give up their house. Perhaps they would sell both houses and buy a new place. For now, Kiera thought the apartment was a perfect interim solution and they would worry about it after the bar was up and running.

Josh wandered around the room for a few minutes, dreaming, picturing the floor layout, the booths, the tables, the decor. He felt good, a sense of accomplishment. He had focused on a goal and gone for it with his usual vigor, the way he'd built a practice from scratch and turned it into a thriving law office.

A name engraved dead center on the back bar caught his attention:

Thorson Kuenlang

Probably the carpenter. Maybe the original owner. Worth checking out.

Josh eyed himself in the bar mirror. Dark hair, brown eyes with some early age lines. Not bad looking—quite handsome according to his girlfriend. Was he nuts doing this now? He would know soon enough.

He walked down the stairs to the basement—a dingy, poorly lit hole filled with all manner of junk: old taps and kegs, broken stools and tables, a pool table, a couple of slot machines that might be a hundred years old, cases of empty beer and soda bottles—apparently, the old guy didn't believe in chucking anything. It looked like a hoarder's dream and smelled of mildew, oil, stale beer, and neglect. Christ, there could be a ghost lost in there somewhere. The haunting was a quirky story and one he could use for a little added atmosphere. Every old place, it seemed, had a ghost. It was virtually a rule.

Tomorrow, everything would change. A crew would throw this junk into dumpsters and haul it to a landfill. All but the slot machines—those he would restore for period decor in the bar. The paneling upstairs would go as well, along with every stick of furniture in the building. Another crew would gut the second floor to the studs.

Just then, a stack of broken chairs tipped and clattered to the concrete floor.

"Holy shit!" Josh started and then laughed. Must be the ghosts welcoming him to the bar. He hadn't chosen a name yet. Suddenly, *The Haunted Tavern* popped into his head. It had a certain raw appeal. He made a mental note to check to see how common the name was.

The Haunted Tavern?

Maybe.

He couldn't wait to share the story with Kiera.

Printed in Great Britain
· by Amazon

84717521R00224